PRAISE FOR THE NOVELS OF MAYA BANKS

"Takes readers into the black depths of anguish . . . Her characters are a testament to the strength of the human spirit and to the power love has to heal even the deepest wounds."

—Linda Howard, *New York Times* bestselling author

"Incredibly awesome . . . I love Maya Banks and I love her books."

—Jaci Burton, *New York Times* bestselling author

"Really dragged me through the gamut of emotions. From . . . 'Is it hot in here?' to 'Oh my GOD' . . . I'm ready for the next ride now!"   —*USA Today*

"[A] one-two punch of entertainment that will leave readers eager for the next book."   —*Publishers Weekly*

"Any book by Maya Banks is a book well worth reading."

—Once Upon a Twilight

"For those who like it naughty, dirty and do-me-on-the-desk HAWT!"

—Examiner.com

"Hot enough to make even the coolest reader sweat!"   —Fresh Fiction

"Definitely a recommended read."   —Fallen Angel Reviews

"[For] fans of Sylvia Day's *Bared to You*."   —Under the Covers

"Grabbed me from page one and refused to let go until I read the last word."   —Joyfully Reviewed

"An excellent read that I simply did not put down . . . Covers all the emotional range."   —The Road to Romance

"The sex is crazy hot."   ok Reviews

MASTERED

THE ENFORCERS

Maya Banks

BERKLEY BOOKS, NEW YORK

BERKLEY

An imprint of Penguin Random House LLC
375 Hudson Street, New York, New York 10014

This book is an original publication of Penguin Random House LLC.

Library of Congress Cataloging-in-Publication Data

Names: Banks, Maya.
Title: Mastered / Maya Banks.
Description: New York, NY : Berkley Books, 2015. | Series: The enforcers ; 1
Identifiers: LCCN 2015037899 | ISBN 9780425280652 (softcover)
Subjects: LCSH: Man-woman relationships—Fiction. | Sexual dominance and
submission—Fiction. | BISAC: FICTION / Romance / Contemporary. | FICTION /
Romance / General. | GSAFD: Erotic fiction.
Classification: LCC PS3602.A643 M37 2015 | DDC 813/.6—dc23
LC record available at http://lccn.loc.gov/2015037899

PUBLISHING HISTORY
Berkley trade paperback edition / December 2015

PRINTED IN THE UNITED STATES OF AMERICA

10 9 8 7 6 5 4 3 2 1

Cover photo: Black Leather Spikes © Imageman/Shutterstock.
Cover design by Rita Frangie.

Penguin
Random
House

MASTERED

Evangeline stared in the mirror, barely recognizing the wide-eyed woman staring back at her. She didn't react as her friends Lana, Nikki and Steph hovered around her, putting the finishing touches on her makeup and hair, ensuring everything was perfect.

"I can't do this," Evangeline muttered. "This is insane and I can't believe I let you guys talk me into this."

Nikki fixed her with a hard stare in the mirror. "You're going. No backing out now, girlfriend. I'd pay money to see the look on that jackass's face when he sees exactly what he's missing out on."

The jackass in question being Evangeline's ex-boyfriend, Eddie.

"I'd say he didn't miss anything at all," Evangeline said quietly, embarrassment washing over her all over again.

Lana's eyes were fierce and Steph's scowl was intimidating. Any other time, Evangeline would be heartened by their display of loyalty and friendship. But she regretted confiding in them the humiliating details of her breakup with Eddie. She should have just told them they'd decided to go separate ways. Except that Evangeline had already told her friends that she was a virgin and that her last date with Eddie was the night. She was going to give him her virginity, confident that he was the one.

What a hopeless, flaming idiot that made her. His words still rang in her ears. Every single one had been like a knife to the heart, only he hadn't been content to simply plunge the blade. He'd twisted it, drawing out her pain as much as possible.

"Eddie is an asshole," Steph hissed. "Hon, we all knew it. Don't you remember us trying to talk you out of giving it up for him that night—or any night for that matter? You have nothing to be ashamed of. Nothing. He's a dick."

"Amen," Nikki said fervently. "Which is why you're going to march into Impulse like you fucking own the place. You look hot. And I don't say that as your best friend trying to make you feel better about yourself. I say that as another female who is aware that a much hotter female is in her territory and I'd like to scratch her eyes out because I know I don't have a chance in hell of looking as good as she does."

Evangeline's head reared in surprise and her startled gaze found Nikki's in the mirror.

Lana shook her head and sighed. "You don't get it, Vangie. And hell, I think that's half the turn-on for guys. You have no clue how beautiful you are. You're all big eyes, gorgeous hair, a figure to die for and you're good and sweet to your soul. If you had any hint of interest, you'd have men tripping over themselves to get next to you. They'd treat you like the queen you deserve to be treated as, but you honestly have no idea and that just makes them want you even more."

Evangeline shook her head, utterly baffled. "You guys are crazy. I'm a twenty-three-year-old recently ex-virgin who's as gauche as they come. I'm barely off the farm and have a southern drawl that makes New Yorkers roll their eyes and want to pat me on the head and say, 'Well, bless your heart.' I'm a fish out of water here and you all know it. I should have never come here. If it weren't for Mama and Papa, I'd go home and find work there."

Lana threw up her hands. "One day someone is going to make you see you the way everyone else sees you. Eddie is a smug bastard and saw you as a conquest. He knows he's not good enough to lick your shoes and he sucks in bed, but he'd never admit that so he tears you down instead."

Evangeline lifted her head. "Please. Can we not talk about Eddie tonight? It's bad enough I might see him even though he may have changed his mind about going tonight. He could have lied about wanting to take me like he's lied about everything else. I'm not prepared for this. I'm scared to death and I have no wish to be humiliated all over again."

"Sweetie, the point of tonight is to see him. Or rather for him to see you so he can kick himself in the balls for what he could have had," Nikki reminded her.

Steph shoved a VIP pass into Evangeline's hand, making sure she took it and didn't lay it aside.

"I could only score one or one of us would go with you. But the line is long and people wait all night and never get in. With this pass, you walk straight to the front, show the bouncer manning the door the pass and voilà. You're in. And then, girlfriend? You work it. You walk in there, head high, like you don't need a man, and you give every man, including Eddie, a taste of what they could have but can't touch. You have a few drinks. And if Eddie looks your way, you do not cower. You do not lower your head. You stare him directly in the eye and you smile. And then you don't pay him another second of attention, like he doesn't exist. Dance if you want to. Flirt. Get your mojo back. Your confidence. And when you're ready to go home, you call the number on the card I gave you. Wait fifteen minutes and then go outside. Your ride will be there and then you get your ass back here to us and give us the 411 on the entire evening."

Lana touched her shoulder. "And listen. If anything, and I mean anything goes wrong, you call or text us. We can be there in no time flat and we're not doing anything tonight. We'll be here for you when you get home, but if you need us before then, you let us know. I don't care how long that damn line is. I'll kick the bouncer's ass if he tries to keep us from rescuing one of my girls."

A smile hovered on Evangeline's lips and her eyes gleamed with amusement, not because she didn't believe Lana. She absolutely did. Her friends were fiercely protective of her, of each other, and Evangeline had no doubt that Lana would take on a two-hundred-plus-pound bouncer— and win—if she knew Evangeline needed her.

She reached for Lana's hand and squeezed. Hard. Then she glanced up to include Steph and Nikki in her grateful gaze.

"You guys are the best. Y'all have done so much for me. I don't know how I'll ever repay you."

Nikki rolled her eyes and Steph just snorted.

"Like you haven't been there for us every bit as much? You haven't nursed us through our share of broken hearts, held our hair while we puked after getting shit-faced over some asshole guy who isn't good enough for us? Then told us that the douche bag who broke our heart wasn't fit to touch the hem of our shirts much less anything else? Sound familiar?"

Steph's reproach made Evangeline grimace. Because she was right. Everything they were doing now for her, she'd done for them. But she wasn't used to being the recipient. She didn't date much. Hadn't dated at all in the first two years after she'd moved to the city from the small town in the south she'd been born and raised in. She'd been too focused on working, taking extra shifts, saving as much money as possible to send back to her mama.

It wasn't until Eddie had walked into the bar where Evangeline waitressed and then kept coming back night after night until he had worn her down that she'd agreed to go out with him. He'd come on hard and fast, but Evangeline had rebuffed him. Looking back, she could see that she'd been nothing more than a challenge to him. Like waving a red flag in front of a bull's nose. By holding him off and not putting out, she'd only made him that much more determined to get into her pants.

The fact that he was the first to do so just made his victory all the more sweet.

Bastard.

She nearly bared her teeth as anger made her cheeks go hot, but she didn't want to mess up her carefully applied lipstick or makeup. The girls had spent an hour making sure she was made up to perfection. And the entire time they'd hovered, offered their unconditional support—in between muttering threats that didn't bear repeating against Eddie—and boosting her nonexistent confidence.

And it was because of these three women that Evangeline was going to walk into the club that Eddie had been bragging about being a member of, even though the mere thought of it made her want to hide under her bed for a week, and she was going to pull it off. Bold. Beautiful. Confident. Give Eddie a taste of exactly what he could have had.

Her mouth nearly turned down into a moue. He'd *already* had her. And by his accounts, it was nothing special. No, not even that. It—she—had been terrible. How the hell was she going to walk into a club and make a man regret fucking her over when he'd already had what her friends said he'd regret what he could have had?

It was more likely he'd laugh in her face and ask her what man would ever want a frigid bitch like her.

The confidence she'd spent the entire afternoon summoning fled in a heartbeat and she glanced up at her friends in the mirror, her mouth opening to call the whole thing off, when all three of them pinned her with their fiercest glares.

How did they do that? They knew exactly what she was about to say. But then they'd always been able to read her like a book. For that matter, according to Eddie, so could everyone else. He made it sound like a bad quality. Honesty. Not playing games or pretending to be something she wasn't.

She didn't mind it with her girls because it made her feel special. Like they were close enough friends to know what she was thinking at any given time. But it hadn't been remotely comforting to find out that apparently she was transparent to everyone else in the world as well.

How the hell was she ever supposed to protect herself, guard herself and keep from getting hurt if she couldn't disguise her thoughts and feelings?

"Don't even think about it," Lana warned.

Nikki knelt down so she was eye level with Evangeline where she was perched on the vanity stool. Where she'd spent the last hour being fussed over by her friends. Her sisters. Her expression was gentle and understanding.

"Listen to me, honey. You need to do this for yourself. Not for us. Sure as hell not for Eddie. Not for anyone else but you. He took something from you and you need it back. If you let him get into your head and you start believing that shit he fed you, then he wins. And you cannot let him get to you that way. Because what he said is bullshit. It is not true. And I won't have you believing it. So get it out of your head now. You have fifteen minutes until the taxi gets here to take you to the club, so get yourself sorted out. Do whatever you have to do, but do it for you."

Evangeline blinked furiously to keep tears at bay. Her friends would kill her if she ruined her makeup. They'd have to start all over and she'd be way late to the club and it would only give her added incentive to back out. And Nikki was right. This was something she needed to do for herself.

Eddie had taken something from her and not just her virginity, which, by the way, was vastly overrated. *Sex* was overrated. He'd stripped her of her dignity and what little confidence she possessed. He'd left her with nothing but humiliation and no sense of self-worth.

No man was worth that, and it pissed her off that his words still stung. The sex? Completely unmemorable. But the words she'd never forget. They'd burned a hole in her brain and caused a wound she wasn't sure could ever be repaired.

If tonight would give her any part of the spine she so desperately lacked, then it was worth walking into a crowded, popular club alone and riding it out.

Her friends hadn't wanted her to go by herself. Not at all. But Steph had only been able to get her hands on one VIP pass, and VIP passes to Impulse were rare and precious, reserved for beautiful people. Rich people. Important people. Evangeline was none of those, but what would it hurt to pretend for one night that she did fit into that world?

Why couldn't she be Cinderella for one night and maybe get back a little of her own by flaunting in Eddie's face what he'd thrown away? Because Evangeline might not have had the most self-confidence in the world, but she did have confidence in her friends' abilities to make *any* woman look hot.

Tomorrow she could go back to being boring, quiet and mousy Evangeline. Working late nights at a bar where the tips were good and the owner looked out for his girls and she could put Eddie behind her for good. Not to mention swearing off men for good. She wasn't here to find a man, to date, or even to have a sex life. She was here because her family needed her support, and for them she could and would put her life on hold indefinitely.

Sure, she had dreams and goals. Things she wanted out of life that didn't include waitressing in a pub wearing a skirt that barely covered her ass and heels that had her feet screaming for relief at the end of the night. But for now her job provided what she and her family needed. There was plenty of time to pursue her own path. She was only twenty-three. She'd work four, maybe five more years. Stockpile enough money so that her mother didn't have to worry about finances.

She'd made a promise to herself that by the time she turned thirty, she'd do what she wanted. Make a life for herself. Have a life she could be proud of and surround herself with good, solid friends like Steph, Nikki and Lana.

She wanted to go to school. Learn a profession. She wanted to be more than a waitress barely scraping by. Her parents hadn't been able to afford to send her to college. She'd only managed to finish high school by gaining her GED because she'd been forced to get a job as soon as she was old enough to work so she could provide for her family.

She had no regrets. She'd do anything for her mother and father. But that didn't mean she would live this life forever. Someday . . . Someday she'd have better. She wanted a husband and children. A stable relationship. Just not now.

"You ready?" Nikki asked, bringing Evangeline abruptly back to the here and now.

Evangeline huffed in a deep breath, squared her shoulders and looked at herself in the mirror. She did look pretty. She wouldn't go as far as to say *hot* as her friends had described her, but she wasn't ugly. She was even above average, even if she owed it all to her friends' magic touch with cosmetics and doing hair.

"Yeah," she murmured softly. "I'm ready."

Drake Donovan pulled up to the entrance of the employee parking lot situated in the back of Impulse and quickly punched the security code into the console of his car, waiting impatiently for the gate to open so he could pull through. More often than not, his driver squired him everywhere, but when he went to the club he drove himself so he could leave at will without waiting for his driver to collect him.

He pulled into the space marked RESERVED, the closest spot to the entrance. There were many reserved spaces that spanned the front of the lot, all for his partners, but he refrained from ever putting his name—or theirs—not wanting to announce to everyone who exactly parked where.

Collecting his briefcase, he climbed from the car and set a brisk pace to the back entrance, where again he'd have to enter the security code to gain access, but when he was mere steps away, a woman suddenly pushed her way in front of him, forcing him to take a hasty step backward or collide with her, something she evidently had no issue with.

He gave her a cursory once-over and mentally cursed. She was scantily clad, with a lot of makeup and an expensive hairstyle, and there was sultry invitation in her hazel eyes, though the color was hard to make out with all the smoky eye makeup that covered from eyebrows to eyelashes.

"Mr. Donovan," she gushed, reaching to put her hand on his arm.

He flinched away, his stare glacial. "You're trespassing on private property, or did you not see all the signs and the fact that the only way into this parking lot is via a security gate?"

Her heavily painted lips turned down into a pout, but clear invitation still shone brightly in her eyes.

"I was hoping you'd like some company tonight," she said breathlessly. "I can be very accommodating."

Her look informed him that if he told her to drop to her knees right there on the pavement and suck him off, she'd do it with no hesitation and in record time. Jesus. The only way she could have gotten in was to have climbed over the high fence surrounding the employee parking lot. Or . . . someone had let her in. And if that was the case, heads were going to roll and someone was going to get fired. As soon as he got upstairs, he'd review the surveillance footage to determine just how this woman had gotten past his security.

He prided himself on impenetrable security. Even if she had attempted to climb over, she most certainly should have been detected and apprehended and escorted off the premises long before Drake ever arrived.

"Unfortunately for you, I'm not in a very accommodating mood tonight," he said in an icy tone.

He immediately inserted the earpiece that would key him into all the activity going on in the club, his direct link to all his employees, and he barked a quick order.

"I need security to the parking lot now."

The woman's eyes widened in fear. "What are you going to do? I only wanted to please you. You're a very handsome man, Mr. Donovan. I think once you've had a taste of what I can offer you, you won't be disappointed."

"I'm more disappointed that you're making me late for work and you're trespassing where you don't belong."

The door burst open, and two of his bouncers ran toward Drake, tense, alert and ready for action.

"What's up, boss?" Colbin asked.

Drake pointed at the now-furious-looking woman.

"Escort her out immediately, and from now on if anyone, and I mean anyone, gets into this lot who doesn't have clearance, I'll fire every single person in charge of surveillance."

"You have no idea what you're passing up," the woman hissed, her fingers curling into claws.

"Oh, I know damn well what I'm *passing* on," he drawled. "And I couldn't be any less interested in a skank who throws herself at me with promises to please me when the very sight of you displeases me very much."

She launched herself at Drake, her long, painted nails aimed directly at his face.

Matthews stepped between her and Drake immediately, and Colbin curled his arm around her waist, lifting her effortlessly as she let out a shriek of outrage and began kicking and thrashing, trying to lash those nails across his face.

"Fuck," Colbin bit out. "Get yourself together, bitch. You're making a fool of yourself. Mr. Donovan has no interest in you, and furthermore, he does not tolerate invasion of his privacy. If he wants you, he'll contact you. Don't ever come at him like this again, or you'll find yourself sitting inside a jail cell. Consider yourself lucky, he's letting you go with only a warning this time."

"Bastard," she threw out at Drake as Colbin hauled her to the gate.

As he walked, Matthews radioed for a car to pull to the gate immediately to get rid of "an unwanted guest," which only made the woman shriek louder in outrage.

"I'm sorry, boss," Matthews said in a sober voice. "I have no idea how she got in, but I'm going to find out right away and make sure it never happens again."

"You do that," Drake snapped. "And while you're at it, arrange to have barbed wire installed at the top of the fences. A few guard dogs wouldn't be amiss. You'll just have to take the time to acquaint all my employees with the dogs and ensure they don't mistake them as intruders. This is ridiculous."

"I'm on it, boss. I won't fail you."

Drake walked dismissively by Matthews and spoke into his com. "Viper and Thane. Pull surveillance from the employee parking lot for the previous two hours and have it set to play in my office. I want it ready to go as soon as I get to my office. I'm on my way up."

"You got it," Thane replied immediately.

Drake shook his head in disgust. The woman was no different from the women lined up down the block outside the entrance to Impulse, all eagerly awaiting the opportunity to get in. Some would; some wouldn't. There were a few couples, both one-nighters and steady relationships, but mostly women—and men—came here to hook up, be seen, up their status and pretend to be what they weren't.

He strode inside and merely nodded at the greetings from the employees he passed, in a hurry to get to his office, where he had a bird's-eye view of everything that went on in his club. He catered to exactly the clientele that Impulse attracted, but it didn't diminish his disgust or impatience with the type of people who frequented his establishment.

He even indulged when it suited him, but he never kept a woman for more than one night—two at the absolute most—and there were two places he never brought a woman: his office at Impulse or his home. He had very exacting standards when it came to the women he took to his bed, the number one being absolute submission and him being in complete control, just as he was in control of every aspect of his business and personal life.

He'd created his world, his empire, by being ruthless and cutthroat when it was necessary, and he had no regrets, because he was a man who was feared by many and given absolute respect and deference. That fact served him well. He had no weaknesses to exploit. There was no way to penetrate his carefully guarded defenses and his top-of-the-line security. If it made him arrogant to consider himself God, so be it, because he *was* God. At least in *his* world.

Maddox and Silas were waiting in his office, their expressions grim.

"I hear you had a problem in the parking lot," Maddox said.

Silas just stood there, his stare inquiring, but then he wasn't a man of many words. He didn't need words to get his point across. And people weren't exactly lining up to have a conversation with him since a mere look usually scared the piss out of them.

"Apparently," Drake said acidly.

Even as he spoke, he reached for the remote and focused his attention on the screen where the surveillance footage of the parking lot would be displayed. Impatiently, he fast-forwarded until finally he discovered the source of the breach.

"Son of a bitch," Maddox growled.

Drake's expression was grim as he watched one of his newer employees pull in and park at the very back of the lot and get out as though he was merely showing up for work. It wasn't until he was well into the building that the backseat door opened and the woman who'd thrown herself at Drake crept surreptitiously from the vehicle, hunched down so as not to be seen.

"Fire him," Drake snapped in Maddox's direction. "Escort him off the premises and then eliminate his security clearance to all entrances to the club."

Maddox wasted no time departing to do Drake's bidding, leaving Silas alone with Drake. Drake took a seat at his desk and made sure all the monitors that covered every inch of the club were online. Then he turned his attention to Silas, the man who took care of any problems Drake encountered. He also cleaned up any unwanted messes. He did so with unflappable efficiency and never failed.

"I want you to pay Garner a visit and tell him he's behind in his payments and he has precisely forty-eight hours to pay up or he loses my protection. Make it clear I'm not bluffing and if he fails to come through, he's on his own and he's a dead man."

Silas nodded. "I'll leave now."

Drake nodded. "Report back to me as soon as you've spoken to him and let me know the situation. He owes me a lot of money. You can also tell him that if he doesn't pay up, the least of his worries will be Vanucci because I'll come after him myself and I'll make whatever Vanucci will do to him look like child's play."

"Consider it done," Silas said, even as he turned and disappeared into the far corner where the darkness concealed another exit from the office.

Drake clenched his jaw. Just another day at the office, only the desperate woman throwing herself at him pissed him off more than Garner defaulting on past-due payments. If he wanted a woman, he never had to look far. He damn sure didn't need some bitch clinging to him like a burr, expecting him to fall all over himself to take what she so vulgarly offered.

Women didn't call the shots with him. Ever. If he saw something he wanted, he took it. He was in control. Always. No exceptions. Not a woman. Not anyone. And he planned to keep it that way.

Evangeline stepped hesitantly from the cab after paying the fare— money given to her by her girls with a look in their eyes that said *Don't even think about refusing*—and for a moment she stood there like an idiot, nervously surveying the line that extended down the sidewalk and wrapped around the block.

Then realizing how conspicuous—and out of place—she looked standing there gawking like a moron, she started toward the entryway, where a burly, scary-looking bouncer stood in front of a roped-off area that led to the inside, his huge arms crossed over an even huger chest.

She swallowed nervously as he caught sight of her and obviously saw her intention to walk in. His gaze narrowed and flitted up and down her, his lips thinning. Her back went up, as did her chin. She'd had enough of feeling unworthy and she'd be damned if she was judged and found lacking by a freaking bouncer.

A glance down the sidewalk told her why he was looking at her like she was nuts. Beautiful people stood, waiting for their opportunity to get in. Glitzy, glamorous. Women in expensive dresses, heels, jewelry draped from head to toe, hair that probably cost a fortune to have made up at the stylist. And then there were the men. Polished. Preppy. Rich looking. Some alone, no doubt using Impulse as hunting ground for a pickup and an easy lay. Others were there with their date for the evening, an arm wrapped securely around a gorgeous woman.

She was so jealous that for a moment she couldn't breathe. What it must be like to be one of those beautiful people. To be able to take their looks and bodies for granted. To be able to get any man they wanted with a snap of their fingers.

She noticed that she'd caught the attention of those at the front of the line. Women openly sneered at her, mocking glances thrown her way as if to tell her, *As if you'll get in.*

She turned her attention back to the bouncer, who was now just a body space away, and he stepped forward, speaking before she could say or do anything.

"Quota has been filled tonight," he said simply. "Sorry, but you'll have to go elsewhere. Or home," he added after another sweep of her body.

Her cheeks scorched hot at the judgment in his gaze. He hadn't even told her that the line formed at the rear. He hadn't even told her she'd have to wait. He'd dismissed her. Told her she was unwelcome in a place like Impulse, and that just pissed her off.

So she pulled out her trump card, snapping it angrily in front of his face, holding the VIP pass so it was impossible for him not to see.

"I don't think so," she hissed between her teeth.

He looked surprised. And then uneasy. Hesitant even. And this was not a man she'd think was ever indecisive. Then she realized he was actually debating refusing her access even though she had the "golden ticket." A coveted VIP pass that allowed its owner to enter, no questions asked. He would know that someone important in the club had given it to her. He didn't have to know it hadn't been given directly to her. No one in their right mind ever gave away a VIP pass to this club, so his only logical conclusion was that it had been given to her personally and she wasn't about to correct his assumption.

Still, he didn't look happy at all as he reached down to unlatch the velvet rope that was strung between two metal poles just outside the doorway to the club.

"Have a good time, miss," he said formally, as he motioned her by.

She glanced at the line from the corner of her eye, drawing smug satisfaction as she saw more than a few mouths drop open. Some expressions were openly outraged. She even heard someone protest that she had gotten in while they were still standing out on the sidewalk waiting.

"VIP pass," the bouncer rumbled, by way of explanation.

Yep, that pretty much said it all. VIP meant an all-access ticket to everything in the club. Steph had been there before and had brought her up to speed on the club, the layout, so she wouldn't make a complete fool of herself by not knowing what the hell she was doing once inside.

Though Steph had told her about the front bar area, she was still surprised by how pleasantly quiet it was when she made her way into the lavishly decorated social area that was sectioned off from the dance floor and the huge bar in the center of the dance floor.

It was a genius idea to have a quieter area with a bar so people could actually talk and hear one another instead of yelling over the music. It would also give her time to have a drink in a quiet area so she could work up her courage to venture onto the dance floor.

Steph had explained that the dance floor was like a stadium with the bar in the center and the dance floor surrounding it on all sides. Then beyond the dance floor were the public places to sit. These were un-enclosed areas with tables and chairs to rest after dancing and have a drink, although conversation was pretty much out.

Above the public seating were the private boxes. These were enclosed rooms with a waiter or waitress assigned to each, and music could be heard or not heard with the flip of a switch. They were larger and more comfortable sitting areas than the public seating below with couches, plush armchairs and a large table for setting drinks and food on.

The only thing it lacked, Evangeline had dryly remarked on, was a bed for people hooking up to have sex. She'd shut up quickly when Steph had seriously informed her that there were even more private rooms at the top of the club, access strictly monitored, which meant you had to be pretty damn important—or rich—to get in, and *they* were equipped with all the necessary comforts for couples to do as they wanted.

How Steph knew all this, Evangeline didn't know, and she hadn't asked, though she'd seen Nikki and Lana's open curiosity and knew they would certainly ask at first opportunity. Evangeline figured if Steph had wanted them to know, she would have volunteered where she got her info, so she hadn't pursued the matter and had continued asking questions before either Nikki or Lana could pounce on the opportunity to grill their friend.

Evangeline made her way to the bar, pondering how many drinks she could afford and how she should space them accordingly so it didn't look so obvious that she didn't belong. If she bought one, she could nurse it a long time and at least look like she was doing something other than standing around looking and feeling out of place. But then again she needed at least one drink in her to fortify herself before venturing onto the dance floor, where she would likely see Eddie and whoever his latest conquest was.

She glanced down, wondering if she was out of her mind for thinking, even for a moment, that Eddie would look at her and feel any regret for what he'd thrown away so callously. Even a freaking bouncer had found her lacking, so who was she kidding?

She murmured her order to the bartender and he smiled at her, his eyes twinkling. It was the first overt gesture of welcome she'd received since arriving at this place, so she smiled back. A genuine smile. One that said *thank you*. He winked at her and then began making her frou-frou girly drink, as the girls called them. Hey, she couldn't help it that she was a complete lightweight when it came to alcohol. Just because she served the stuff every night didn't mean she partook of it.

Besides, she liked fruity drinks and she especially appreciated that the bartender stuck one of those tropical umbrellas along with a cherry into the drink just before sliding it over the bar to her.

"On the house, babe," he said when she carefully pulled out one of the bills from her precious cache in the tiny clutch she had draped cross-body so she didn't have to worry about dropping it or laying it down and forgetting about it.

She lifted her startled gaze to him. "But you can't do that. You'll get into trouble!"

He winked again and just shook his head before heading down to attend to another customer.

Well. Maybe not everyone found her a miserable failure. And he was pretty cute. No, not cute. There was one thing she was picking up on even though she hadn't ventured far into the club yet. The men who worked here weren't pretty boys. They were guys who were buff and built and looked like they could handle themselves in a fight. And the women were beautiful. Classy looking and elegant. There would be no looking down one's nose at one of the waitresses here because they looked like high-society chicks who just happened to be serving drinks. Apparently being beautiful was not only a requirement of being allowed into the club but also to work here.

She was so out of place it wasn't even funny.

She turned around, bringing the glass to her mouth, noticing several glances thrown her way. She fidgeted uncomfortably. Was it that obvious she didn't belong? One could only take so much judgment even if she had marched in here determined to get some of her own back.

After observing yet another set of eyes flashing in her direction, she decided she'd had enough. This was absurd. What was she trying to prove? And why? She didn't have to prove anything to anyone but herself, and she knew she was better off without Eddie. She hadn't come in here so he'd drop to his knees and beg her to come back. Not that it wasn't an appealing image if for no other reason she could kick him in the balls and tell him, *Over my dead body*.

An ache filtered into her chest. No, she'd simply come because she'd wanted him to know he was wrong. That she wasn't a mousy, passionless woman. She could be beautiful. Even if none of it was real and was, instead, courtesy of her friends' skill with hair and makeup. Not to mention the dress and shoes they'd outfitted her in. The way-too-form-fitting dress that outlined every single curve and dip of her body. A dress she would have never dared to wear before even if her friends forever despaired of her hiding what they called a "hot mama body."

Whatever. They were her friends and they were entitled to be biased. But Evangeline knew the truth. Just as Eddie also knew the truth, and she was a fool to come here and think for a moment he'd change his mind and regret anything.

She was about to turn and place her drink back on the bar and then swiftly take her leave when she saw him from the corner of her eye.

Oh shit, oh shit!

She froze, not wanting to turn quickly to hide in case he'd already seen her, because she would *not* make it obvious that she was trying to hide. Instead she pretended interest in the dance floor through the wide soundproof double doors to her left as though she were just finishing up her drink before opting to make her way out onto it.

Maybe he hadn't seen her. Maybe he was leaving.

Laughter sounded close. Too damn close.

Shit.

All her maybes went right out of the door. Where she wished Eddie had gone.

"What the hell are you doing here, Evangeline?" Eddie asked, amusement thick in his voice.

She slowly turned her cool gaze on him, purposely widening her eyes as if surprised to see him.

"Oh hello, Eddie," she said. She nodded politely at the woman clinging like a burr to his arm. The woman who did not look pleased that Eddie was talking to Evangeline. "I would think it's obvious what I'm doing here. What does anyone do here? They have a few drinks and dance. Which is precisely what I intend to do. If you'll excuse me, I'm heading onto the floor. Good to see you. Hope y'all have a good night."

She started to slip past Eddie, but his hand flew out and cut painfully into her arm. She whirled in shock, staring at him like he'd lost his mind.

"Let go!" she said hoarsely. "Eddie, you're hurting me!"

He laughed cruelly. "What's your game, Evangeline? Come to find me? Beg me to come back to you? Want to go another round with me after I kicked you out of my bed? Come on, sweetheart. No one is that desperate. Sticking my dick in your cunt was like fucking a snowdrift."

Evangeline was shocked by his coarse language and the fact that he was speaking loudly enough for the entire bar to hear. Her cheeks burned in mortification and she staggered as though he'd struck her.

"Let go of me," she hissed.

But his grip only grew tighter, bruising her fair skin. She'd wear his fingerprints for days.

The woman at his side laughed, the sound tinkly and abrasive, like ice cubes dropping into a glass.

"Oh, *this* is the one you were telling me about," she said in a silky voice.

She stared at Evangeline, fake pity in her eyes.

"Too bad you weren't woman enough to keep him," she purred. "But you can bet I'll be woman enough to keep him satisfied."

Evangeline was too shocked, too mortified to respond. She should have responded with cutting remarks of her own. Not showing either of them how much they'd ripped her apart. Her only triumph was that she managed—barely—to keep the tears that burned the edges of her eyes at bay because that was more humiliation than even she could bear. He'd made her cry once. Never again would she allow him to do it.

"What I think," she said, proud of her calm, even tone, "is that you and your little prostitute should skitter on out of here and back to the alley where you belong. And if you don't let go of my arm, I'll press assault charges."

Eddie's eyes narrowed as fury washed over his features. His cheeks grew red and mottled as he advanced, pushing farther into her space until she could feel and smell his hot, fetid breath blasting her face. Menace burned brightly in his eyes, and she knew it was about to get even uglier.

"You little bitch!"

3

Drake Donovan saw her the moment she walked into the club. He was sitting high above the dance floor in his private quarters, several surveillance monitors strategically placed for easy viewing of every inch of the club. He didn't just own the club and assume a hands-off approach. He owned many businesses and he had a tight leash on them all. And he closely monitored the goings-on any time he was here.

He quickly zoomed in on the curvy blonde who warily entered the front bar, her eyes wide as she took in her surroundings. A blistering curse blew from his lips even as he continued to track her every movement.

Someone was going to lose their goddamn job over this.

Drake had a strict policy about who was and wasn't allowed in his club. And innocent, naïve-looking girls like the one who'd just walked hesitantly into his bar without a man at her side to protect her was definitely not someone who should have ever gotten by his bouncer.

Fucking Anthony knew better. What the hell was he thinking, allowing her in? Heads were going to roll. Just as soon as he got her the hell out of his club with the understanding that she was never allowed back.

And yet he hesitated because she fascinated him. There was something about her, and he couldn't put his finger on what. He watched intently as she hesitantly made her way to the bar, where she was treated to a wink and a smile from Drew, his bartender. A man he suddenly had the strongest urge to fire for no other reason than that he was flirting with the blue-eyed enchantress. Drew flirted with all the females. So why was Drake so up in arms over his harmless flirtation with a woman who would never be back in Drake's club, for fuck's sake?

He let out his breath in a long exhale when she turned away from the bar and faced in the direction of the dance floor. He was treated to an up-close, full-frontal view, and it was spectacular.

Everything about her did it for him, and yet she was the complete antithesis of the women he usually fucked. And judging by the many appreciative male gazes and the decidedly unfriendly looks from the women, he wasn't wrong in his assessment of her.

Hell, she'd end up causing a damn riot if he didn't get her the hell out and soon.

A woman looking like her in a club like his? Those big wide eyes, a curvy body in a dress that left nothing to the imagination. A woman who screamed innocence and inspired a man to want to get her into bed as fast as he could so he could teach her how to please him.

Yeah, she was serious trouble with a capital T. But all he could think about was getting her out of the fucking club and into somewhere private before some other guy made a play for her.

He was so absorbed in his perusal of the unknown woman that he didn't notice the guy with a skank practically shrink-wrapped to his side blazing a trail directly toward her.

He saw the woman's head come up and he zoomed in with the push of a button, focusing the camera directly on her. There was surprise in her eyes, but something else too. Something Drake didn't like at all.

Fear.

The man spoke to her, and it was obvious that what he was saying wasn't at all nice or complimentary. The woman's face went white, and she teetered like her legs were about to go out from beneath her. And the man's fingers were wrapped around her arm.

He saw her wince in pain just as he also saw the man tighten his hold on her. Then the man advanced even farther, getting into her space.

Drew, the bartender, was leaping over the bar just as Drake hit the button for Maddox. Goddamn it. Goddamn it!

Maddox was there in three seconds.

Drake pointed at the monitor. "Go get her. *Now*," he barked. "Bring her to me and make damn sure the man accosting her is thrown out, taught a lesson and never allowed back into *any* of my establishments."

Maddox's eyes reflected shock, and Drake knew why. No one but his most trusted men were ever allowed in Drake's private quarters. And certainly no women had ever been here. But it was a testament to Maddox's training and loyalty. He didn't hesitate. Didn't ask questions. He merely nodded and was gone in a flash. On the monitor, Drake saw Drew hold up, a pissed-off look on his face, his brow creased in annoyance. Maddox must have radioed him and told him that the man was his.

All his employees wore earpieces so that he or his men could communicate with them at all times.

Drew looked like he was about to disobey his directive from Maddox and lay out the guy anyway when Maddox appeared on the scene. Drake wouldn't chastise or discipline his employee as he would normally if a direct order was disobeyed. He well understood Drew's rage and why he couldn't stand for the woman to remain in that asshole's grasp another second.

Drake watched, his eyes glittering with satisfaction as Maddox pulled the guy up off the floor by his collar—after landing three lightning-fast punches that left the guy senseless—and tossed him toward a pissed-off Zander, another of Drake's men who'd instantly appeared at Maddox's command. Zander hauled him toward the door, the back door, where Silas and Jax would be waiting. They would all give the little asshole a dose of his own medicine by overcompensating the odds to teach the little bastard a lesson. A little three-on-one was exactly what a man deserved for abusing a defenseless woman, even though even one of Drake's men could have done more than a sufficient job against the fucking pussy.

Evangeline sucked in her breath in fear—and pain—as Eddie got into her face, his expression murderous. His grip on her arm was crushing, and he'd flung off his girl du jour, which freed his other hand.

Her glance skittered to that hand, which was now balled into a fist, and he lifted it. Oh my God! He was going to hit her and there was nothing she could do about it. She tried to lift her knee and ram it into his balls, but her damn dress was so tight she couldn't raise her leg more than a few inches.

She began struggling wildly, her eyes darting around the room, pleading for someone—anyone—to intervene. Were they all just going to stand by while he assaulted her in public?

She managed to get one hand into his face, raking his cheek with her nails, a pitiful defense when she was so much smaller and wasn't nearly as strong. He roared and she knew she'd made a very bad mistake.

She saw his fist coming at her. Tried to duck but knew he'd hit her. Knew he'd probably knock her out, leaving her completely helpless against God only knew whatever else he planned to do.

But then to her complete bewilderment, a hand, a really huge, beefy hand, lashed out and caught Eddie's fist as if it were nothing more than a child's. An enormous man loomed over Eddie, a killing rage flashing over his features. He squeezed Eddie's hand and Evangeline could swear she heard bones snapping.

Eddie let go of her completely and screamed. He actually screamed. She winced because wow, it was pathetic. A grown man screaming like a girl. The man continued his assault, bending Eddie's arm until Eddie went to his knees, whimpering like a kicked puppy.

Evangeline backed hastily away, wanting only to get out as fast as she could. She would have run if her legs hadn't been wobbling so badly.

The man, seemingly unruffled by Eddie on his knees begging piteously, turned and pinned Evangeline with dark green eyes. She swallowed because, whoa. Not only was the man seriously hot, but he was extremely intimidating. In that moment, she didn't know if she was more terrified of Eddie or the guy who'd intervened on her behalf.

"*You*, don't move," he clipped out.

She locked her knees and nodded, wondering why she'd just obeyed this man. But then there *was* the fact that he looked like he could crush her like a bug—hell, he'd just crushed *Eddie* like a bug, and Eddie was a lot bigger than Evangeline—that was the deciding factor in her compliance.

Shit, shit, shit. What the *hell* had she gotten herself into? She knew this had been a bad idea and that she should have never let her girlfriends talk her into this complete debacle. She needed to apologize *fast* and then swear she'd never come back and get the hell out as fast as she could. Go home to her girls and eat a pint—no, a gallon—of ice cream and at least give them the satisfaction of hearing of Eddie's humiliation.

Eddie was on the floor in a fetal position now, and Evangeline just now noticed that the bartender was just to her side, a look of disgust on his face. Had he intended to intervene? For that matter, a quick look around the room told her that everyone thought Eddie was a pathetic excuse for a man. She'd take what little satisfaction she could derive from that. A few bruises on her arm was a small price to pay to see him so humbled. She wasn't so nice and forgiving that she'd expend even a morsel of compassion or pity for Eddie's plight because he deserved every single thing done to him tonight.

Okay, so her arm would hurt like hell for a few days. But still.

The man who'd commanded her to stay, like she was some trained dog, turned his attention back to Eddie and then roughly yanked him up by his collar and tossed—yes, tossed—Eddie like a rag doll to another man who was as big and as intimidating as he was. The new guy, someone she hadn't even noticed until now, simply turned, dragging Eddie behind him, away from the entrance where Evangeline had entered the club, as though he weighed absolutely nothing. How had she not noticed the new guy's arrival? He was every bit as impressive as the guy who'd intervened on her behalf and then ordered her not to move, and certainly not someone she'd ever overlook in any other circumstances. Geez, but suddenly the small front bar was filled with hot, badass-looking guys who had simply materialized in a matter of seconds and prevented Eddie from punching her directly in the face. He could have easily broken her jaw or her nose, and God only knew what other damage he would have inflicted if not for the men who'd effortlessly put a stop to his assault. No matter how badass and intimidating they looked, they hadn't once threatened her or made her feel unsafe. Nervous? Yes. Because she'd been commanded not to so much as move from where she stood, but as naïve as it made her sound, she truly didn't believe these new men would lay a finger on her. Maybe that made her stupid and a complete moron, but given a choice between them and Eddie, who she knew meant her serious harm, she'd take the unknown without a second thought. And that gave her a measure of comfort and reassurance.

How they pulled that off she would never know, because these men were not men who would ever go unnoticed even in a much, much larger crowd. They were big, tall men, with broad shoulders, ripped muscles and faces you could break a stone on. And they all looked . . . pissed. At her? For her? It was hard to tell, although not one of them spared a glance in her direction. No, their anger and disgust was solely focused on Eddie and the pitiful sight he made squirming around on the floor.

Eddie was not a small man, but these guys? They made Eddie look like a scrawny boy.

She swallowed. Hard. And her hand automatically went to her arm as the man who'd intervened on her behalf turned his attention fully on her now that Eddie had been dragged away.

She idly wondered where exactly they were taking him, but then decided she needed to be more worried about how she was going to get out of here. Or if they were taking *her* anywhere. Panic swamped her and she could feel the beginnings of a full-scale mother of all anxiety attacks. Not what she needed tonight. She just wanted to call the number her girlfriends had provided and be picked up and out of there as soon as humanly possible.

"Um, thank you," she stammered out. "I'll just be going now. I shouldn't have come."

The man's expression gentled and he put his hand out to her shoulder. She flinched involuntarily, a natural reaction after being assaulted by another man. He frowned, his eyes narrowing, as though he'd been insulted by her response, intentional or not, but his displeasure wasn't in any way reflected in his touch.

It was exceedingly gentle and he gave her a reassuring squeeze even as his frown disappeared and he regarded her almost tenderly.

Now Maddox understood all too well Drake's reaction and his instant call for Maddox, Zander and Silas to intervene, because this was one mean son of a bitch taking out his rage and humiliation on a beautiful woman half his size.

He also understood Drake's uncharacteristic response to this particular woman because she was a lone sheep in a pack of vicious, bloodletting wolves.

"Are you okay?" he asked quietly in a very gentle tone, not wanting to frighten or intimidate her further. It was obvious to anyone that she was absolutely at her breaking point, and it fired all the protective instincts he'd seen reflected. She needed extremely gentle care or she was going to fall apart at any moment. And fuck it all, but that pissed him off royally.

He wanted to be outside teaching the little bastard a lesson even though the others were more than capable of beating the little bastard, a lesson he wouldn't soon forget. He just wished he could take part. But this woman needed very careful handling, and now he understood Drake's adamancy that Maddox take care of the woman and see her safely to Drake's quarters. If Drake hadn't already staked a claim, she would be coming home with him tonight and never have to worry about the asshole he'd gotten off her ever coming within a mile of her.

"Yes. No. I *will* be. Just as soon as I leave," she muttered.

Clearly Evangeline was losing her mind. Guys like him weren't sweet and caring. He'd probably be horrified if she ever voiced the opinion that his touch was gentle and his expression tender. He'd likely take it as an insult.

He shook his head.

She looked at him in panic. "What does that mean?"

"I'm sorry, but I can't do that," he said softly. "The boss wouldn't like that and he doesn't like to be kept waiting. Mr. Donovan wants to see you. He sent me to get you." Then his lips curled in disgust as he spared one quick glance over his shoulder as if to reassure himself the matter with Eddie was fully resolved. "And to take out the trash." The last rumbled from deep within his chest, and she could tell he was pissed all over again.

Then she really panicked.

"But why? I didn't do anything! I was standing here minding my own business and that . . . that . . . asshole assaulted me," she sputtered.

His gaze darkened as fury crept over his features, and she wished she'd just kept her mouth shut. Then, as if he'd realized he was scaring the crap out of her, his expression went bland, and then the gentleness was back in both touch and expression.

"I truly am sorry," he said, his voice soothing. "But Mr. Donovan wants to see you. He sent me to get you, so that's what I'm going to do. I won't hurt you. I'm Maddox, by the way. And I'll tell you now, Drake is an intimidating son of a bitch, but he will not hurt you. Do you understand what I'm telling you? Don't act afraid. You will tell him what made that asshole act like a douche bag before he got thrown out of the club. Furthermore, that bastard will *never* be allowed back into any of Drake's establishments, but he'll take it one step further. He has contacts all over the city, and that dickhead will not only be banned from any business Drake owns, but he will be blackballed from any similar establishments."

She sent him another startled look. He was introducing himself like this was some social thing when he was, in effect, holding her prisoner. Just not in so many words.

"E-Evangeline," she managed to get out.

He smiled then, and wow. He had a killer smile. Her knees went a little weak and she was suddenly glad his hand was still curled around her shoulder. Otherwise she might have face-planted.

"Very pretty," he murmured. "Now, if you'll come with me, I'll take you to Mr. Donovan."

The panic was back. Fear skittered up her spine and flooded her face.

Maddox had started to propel her in the direction of a set of stairs just outside the doorway leading to the dance floor when he saw her face and immediately stopped, staring directly into her eyes.

"He won't hurt you. *No one* will hurt you. You have my word."

"Then why . . . I don't understand," she said in frustration. She wanted to ask more but he stopped one more time and turned, gently cupping her cheek in a very surprising motion because he didn't look like a man who made affectionate or comforting gestures, and he'd been nothing but extremely gentle and compassionate toward her ever since he'd put a stop to Eddie's assault.

"*You* didn't do anything, Evangeline. Now, please, come with me."

She didn't get to finish her endless questions because once more she found herself moving toward the stairs. She wasn't sure exactly how he managed it. Her feet certainly didn't want to obey. *She* didn't want to obey. And yet in a matter of moments they were at the stairs. But then he bypassed them and entered a dark hall that did little to allay her fears.

He obviously felt her tremble because he gave her shoulder a reassuring squeeze and then suddenly he settled her against him, pulling her into the crook of his arm as he pushed the button to an elevator. An elevator?

"Relax," he murmured. "I swore to you no one would hurt you. And I never break my word."

"Never?"

His eyes flashed with amusement as the elevator door whooshed open. "Never."

"It's got to be a requirement," she muttered, as the elevator closed and then began its assent.

He looked at her in confusion.

"For working here," she said patiently. "It has to be a requirement."

"What is?" he asked, clearly puzzled. "Not breaking my word?"

"Being hot. Everyone's hot here. Even the bouncers. And the waitresses. And whatever you and those other guys are. It should be a crime."

She said it like it was a crime, and well, it was. No one should be this freaking gorgeous. Or nice. They all looked too badass to take the time to reassure a confused woman who was scared out of her mind. The bouncer at the front door. The bartender. Hot guy number one, who'd crushed Eddie like a bug. Hot guy number two, to whom hot guy number one had tossed Eddie. Not to mention the other hot guy who'd appeared, apparently to help hot guy number two escort Eddie out. The waitresses. And then there were the clubgoers themselves.

"And apparently only beautiful people are allowed here," she muttered under her breath but apparently loud enough that Maddox could hear, judging by the laughter brimming in his eyes. "I knew it was a mistake to come. I don't belong here. I should have just stayed home."

At that he immediately sobered, and he had that scary look back. He stared fiercely at her. His eyes narrowed as he studied her, disbelief reflected in his beautiful eyes.

"You don't think you're beautiful?"

Her mouth gaped open. "Duh! I don't *think*. I *know*! You can't change what is."

He didn't look at all happy with her statement, but before he could respond, the elevator opened directly into a darkened, spacious room. She had to blink to adjust to the lower lighting and realized the only light illuminating the room came from video monitors placed on the wall. Surveillance. So that was why someone had ridden to the rescue. Well, thank God for that, because it wasn't as if any of the other customers were going to intervene.

Maddox cursed softly, shaking his head as he propelled Evangeline into the room. He'd opened his mouth as if to speak or respond to her statement but snapped it shut the minute the elevator opened. But he still looked pissed, which she was beginning to think was also a requirement of working here. Hot and perpetually pissed. She had to say, when not directed at her, the hot and pissed-off look was pretty damn hot.

"Her name is Evangeline," Maddox said.

"Leave us," a deep male voice sounded.

She glanced around, trying to find the source of the voice. She turned back to Maddox because suddenly Maddox didn't seem to be so bad. And Maddox had been nice to her. Well, except for the kidnapping and not-allowing-her-to-leave part.

But Maddox had melted away, the elevator door already closing, leaving her alone with whoever the mysterious Mr. Donovan was.

Shit, shit, shit.

Realization struck her that she'd just jumped from the frying pan into the fire and there was no one to save her this time.

4

Evangeline glanced nervously around the room, shivering as a feeling of power surrounded her. She could swear she smelled the man, and it was intoxicating.

"Um, Mr. Donovan?"

Once again she glanced anxiously, trying to pinpoint his location.

And then she saw him. He stepped from the shadows of the far corner of the room, and her eyes widened in surprise and in pure female appreciation. Whoa. Now she got it. She understood the rules and who they were inspired by. If Mr. Donovan ran Impulse, it certainly made sense that someone as beautiful as him would surround himself by equally beautiful people.

She stared in fascination as he regarded her intently, his dark eyes raking over her, making her feel suddenly exposed and extremely vulnerable. She swallowed hard because she could swear she saw a flash of interest in his arresting liquid brown eyes. Maybe Eddie *had* hit her because clearly she was out of her mind. But it was a nice fantasy.

He wore his hair short, and he had a polished, sophisticated look that screamed wealth and power. His features were sharply defined, with a hard set to his jaw. He had a broad, muscled chest and shoulders, and was a lot taller than she was. She'd have to stand on tiptoe just to reach his chin!

Her gaze was drawn to his mouth. Over and over again, she came back. After checking out a different feature, her gaze flitted back to the hard line of his mouth, and she felt all tingly imagining what his mouth would feel like on her skin.

Heat scorched over her body followed swiftly by mortification for even entertaining such ludicrous thoughts. As if a man like him would even give her the time of day.

Then suddenly he strode forward, a determined, pissed-off look on his face, and she braced for the inevitable confrontation.

To her complete shock, he gently grasped the arm that Eddie had bruised, and turned it so he could inspect the extent of her injury. Fury blazed in his eyes, but he didn't let go of her arm, though his hold was infinitely tender.

Chill bumps erupted and raced across the arm he was touching, and a peculiar sensation welled in the pit of her stomach. Her vagina clenched and her nipples tingled, suddenly hypersensitive, and became rigid points. She had the urge to cross her arms over her breasts because she was sure he could see the imprint of the puckered ridges through the thin material of her dress.

What the hell was happening here? Had she entered an alternate reality? This was so not her. She didn't spaz and become a walking hormone around a man—any man. She didn't have time for men, and the one time she'd made the time . . . well, it was obvious what that got her.

And suddenly the beast was unleashed, and she tried to take a hasty step back, but his firm yet gentle grip on her arm prevented her from doing so.

"What the hell were you thinking coming into a place like this?" he demanded, fury lacing his every word.

She immediately dropped her gaze, shame and mortification seizing her in a grip that rivaled Eddie's earlier assault on her arm.

"I know I don't belong," she said in a voice barely above a whisper. "I know I'm not good enough to be in a place like this. Where only beautiful and rich people come."

Her voice grew more resigned and subdued with every word. She could barely speak for the humiliation knotting her throat.

"I'll just go now. I'm sorry I was a bother. I caused a . . . scene. I won't be back. I promise. You won't *ever* have to worry about me showing up here—or anywhere—again."

She tensed in his hold, fully expecting him to let go and let her walk out. When his grasp remained intact, panic kicked in and she looked frantically up at him, blanching at the rage in his eyes.

"Please. Let me go. I swear to you I'll never come back."

His expression was carved in stone, that hard jaw she'd observed earlier much more noticeable now.

"Then why *did* you come?" he asked bluntly, making her cringe at his crassness.

Was he really going to make her spell it out to him? Give him a play-by-play of her lack of worthiness to grace the premises of his club? And damn her propensity for always blurting out the truth, no matter how painful. It was a flaw she would be thrilled to be rid of. But no. Before she was even cognizant of what she was saying, the whole ugly story came pouring out.

"The man who assaulted me is my ex . . . boyfriend. Lover. Whatever. Though I'd hardly consider us lovers," she said bitterly. "I was a challenge to him. *Was* being the key word. He knew I was a virgin, and so he coaxed me and wined and dined me, pretending interest because he wanted to be m-my f-first," she stammered out, heat scorching her entire face.

Drake cursed savagely, startling her with his vehemence, but she plunged ahead, only wanting to be done so that maybe he'd finally let her go.

"As soon as I finally gave in, stupidly thinking that he was someone special, he dumped me on the spot. He said I was a terrible lay. I overheard him complaining to his friends, people. I don't know who they were," she said painfully. "He said that sticking his dick in my c-cunt—" She broke off, mortified over her use of the offensive word. Then she took a deep breath and closed her eyes. "He said it was like fucking a snowdrift. And it definitely wasn't worth the three months he had to wait for me to give it up. He repeated the sentiment tonight to my face."

"So you came tonight to see him?" Drake asked incredulously. "Why the hell would you want to do that? For fuck's sake, did you want him back?"

Her head snapped up, her anger surging hot through her veins. "No," she hissed. "Not now. Not *ever*. My girlfriends talked me into coming. Said I needed to get back some of my own. Steph had a VIP pass, and they spent an hour making me up. Shoes, killer heels, hair, makeup, the works.

"They thought I should let him see what he'd shit on," she said dully. "I told them it was stupid. This place is for beautiful people. Even the people who work here are gorgeous. Everyone is freaking perfect. And then there was me, sticking out like a sore thumb. The people in line outside knew I didn't belong. The people inside knew I didn't belong. And you obviously knew I didn't belong because you sent your goon to get rid of me. So if you'll just let me be on my way, I'd appreciate it. I've already promised I'll never darken the door of your club again. This has been a humiliating enough night as it is, and I can only take so much."

He gave her a look that was a combination of bewilderment and super pissed off.

"You don't think you fucking outshine every bitch out there and that they don't know that?" he clipped out angrily. "You didn't see that the skank with your ex was ready to rip your hair out by the roots because she isn't as gorgeous as you and never will be? There isn't a bottle made that can duplicate the kind of beauty you have. And those bitches in there don't hold a candle to your kind of shine, and they hate you for it."

She looked at him absolutely stunned, her eyes wide with shock.

He swore viciously, causing her to flinch again.

"No, it's obvious you don't see it," he said in a grim voice. "You don't see your own goddamn appeal, and that makes you even more attractive to men."

"You don't have to say that to make me feel better," she said softly. "It's kind of you, but the truth is always better. I prefer to keep it real. I know what I am and what I'm not. I accept that."

Before she could process what the ever-loving hell he was doing, he pulled her roughly into his arms so she landed with a soft thud against his chest. He tilted her chin up, his hand nearly covering half her face it was so large, and then he crushed his mouth to hers, devouring her lips as though he were starving.

It was the equivalent of being struck by lightning. Every nerve ending in her body promptly jolted, and she gasped, opening her mouth to his advancing tongue. He probed delicately, with patience that contradicted his impatient, seemingly angry movements.

She let out a delicious sigh because that *mouth*. Oh God, but she'd been so right about his mouth and lips, but now that she'd experienced his tongue, suddenly her attention wasn't quite as focused on his lips.

He tasted—and smelled—divine. Hot, alpha, badass male. Arrogant. Confident. And so yummy looking she couldn't fathom that she was standing in his office while he was thoroughly kissing her in a way she'd never been kissed before.

And she'd only known him for all of five minutes!

She put her hands up to his chest, her intent to ward him off, but as soon as her palms made contact with the muscled wall, they stopped and simply absorbed his heat as she leaned further into his kiss with a soft sigh of surrender.

. . .

Drake had heard all the not-good-enough, not-beautiful, don't-belong bullshit he was going to put up with for the night. Evangeline, Angel. Yes, her name suited her to perfection. She was the most beautiful woman in the entire goddamn club, and here she stood spouting shit that she truly believed. And in no way was he going to be able to change her mind with just a few words, so he did what he'd been dying to do ever since he'd seen her walk through the door of the front bar.

He hauled her against his body so she landed against his chest, the plush softness of her breasts searing his flesh even through two layers of clothing—his and hers. Then he crashed his mouth down on hers and feasted like a man long deprived of such beauty.

His lips lightened and he licked delicately over the full plump bottom lip, nipping lightly with his teeth, a request for her to open her sweet mouth so he could get inside where it was even sweeter.

With a stuttered gasp, she complied, though he wasn't sure if she'd actually made the cognizant decision to allow his tongue access or whether she was merely starving for air, since she hadn't taken a single breath since his mouth had crashed down on hers. But he wasn't waiting around to find out.

He thrust his tongue inward, nearly groaning aloud as she tentatively met his thrust with just the tip of her tongue. A brush so soft, it was like a butterfly's wings.

God, if her mouth tasted this sweet, he could only imagine how sweet her pussy would taste. And he had a sudden urgency to find out.

He wrapped his arms around her, hauling her body into his until there was *no* space between them, until her softness melted into his much harder frame and molded to his. He could feel her breasts, even the turgid points of her nipples through what had to be a sheer, lacy bra for all the protection it offered. For that matter, she likely wasn't wearing one since the dress didn't allow much in the way of the inner trappings.

Just the thought of there being nothing between him and those beautiful breasts, those nipples thrusting against his chest, except the sheer dress she wore had his dick roaring to life and surging against his pants like a randy teenager making it with his girlfriend for the first time.

Mindful of his desire to taste her feminine nectar, he reached down and swept her into his arms, ignoring her sudden cry of alarm. She didn't fight him. If she had, he would have offered her reassurance that he damn sure wasn't going to hurt her. She merely lay rigid in his arms, her breaths coming in sporadic bursts, her cheeks a delectable shade of pink.

She was flush with arousal and he enjoyed savage satisfaction over the fact that she wanted him. Fucking a snowdrift? Her ex had to be out of his fucking mind. Drake didn't need to be balls deep inside her to know she'd have him going up in flames. He was about to come in his pants and he hadn't even gotten her on his desk or her dress up to her waist.

He set her ass on the edge of his desk and with an impatient gesture, he swept the surface of his work area clean, knocking the contents to the floor. Shit scattered in all directions and her eyes widened, her pupils dilated so that only a thin ring of blue circled the black orbs as she stared warily at him.

Not giving her any time to think, much less gather her scattered emotions, he eased her down until she lay flat on her back on the desk and her legs dangled over the side of his desk. It made him a complete bastard because he was absolutely taking advantage of a woman who was still reeling from the events of the night. But at the moment, he didn't give a fuck because he was consumed by the need to taste her. To give her a taste of what her shithead ex hadn't bothered, or was unable, to give her.

She would leave here satisfied completely and then she'd return to him. Oh yes, she would be his. She just didn't know that. Yet.

He gently slipped her shoes off, hesitating just a second because the idea of him being between her legs with only those shoes had his dick already leaking pre-cum. That was for later. He'd fuck her in those shoes and nothing else.

He dropped the heels onto the floor and then shoved her dress up her legs and over her hips to gather around her belly. She was clad in lacy, sheer panties that covered golden curls at the V of her thighs. He tugged the thin band, sliding the sheer material down her thighs to her heels and let them drop to the floor.

Impatiently, he nudged her thighs apart and groaned when he got an unimpeded view of her glistening arousal. The pink lips of her pussy beckoned him and he lowered his head, running his tongue between her lips from her slick entrance to her quivering clit.

She cried out and arched violently upward, her legs shaking spasmodically. Clamping his hands on her hips, he held her firmly in place as he began sucking and licking in long strokes. Moisture surged onto his tongue and to his satisfaction he'd been right. She tasted every bit as delicious as he'd imagined.

He could die a happy man between her legs, his tongue lightly fucking her, tasting her from the inside out. With light laps, he worked his way up to her clit and circled the taut bud until she let out a keening wail. Then he rimmed her entrance with the blunt tip of one fingertip, slipping only the slightest way in.

As she got wetter around his finger, he grew bolder with both his hand and his tongue. He stroked her velvety walls, reaching deeper to the slightly rougher area of her G-spot. As soon as he exerted light pressure and suckled gently at her pulsing clitoris, she went wild, bucking, her breaths loud and forceful.

"Oh my God," she said in awe, wonder in her voice. "I had no idea it could be this way, that it could feel so good. So . . . *perfect*."

Her words slid over his ears like the finest silk and he experienced an ego boost like no other he'd ever felt. This woman deserved a man who could satisfy and please her in bed, and he had every intention of being that man. He was claiming her, putting his stamp on her, even if he didn't fully possess her tonight.

Knowing he would have her fully, completely, gave him a surge of sheer male satisfaction.

He gently sucked her pulsing clit between his lips as he added a second finger, stroking in and out.

"Oh. Oh!" she gasped. "I don't want it to end. It's too perfect. Oh my God. What do I do? I feel like I'm coming apart!"

"Let it happen, Angel," he murmured. "Let yourself feel the pleasure and forget all about the past. This is how it should feel when a man takes care of his woman and isn't a selfish bastard out to please only himself."

He stretched her more with his fingers and then began to stroke in and out, enjoying the silky walls of her pussy. He licked and sucked at her clit until her entire body was rigid, her bottom lifted entirely off the desk as if desperate for his mouth.

He felt the ripple of her pussy around his fingers and cursed the fact that it wasn't his cock. He was so hard that it hurt and his straining erection felt as though it were about to split apart. He'd never wanted a woman so badly in his life and he'd damn sure never been this aroused—and unselfish.

"Give it to me," he demanded. "Come in my mouth, Angel. Let me taste you."

He withdrew his fingers and then moved his mouth down to her opening and slid his fingers up to her clit to caress as he licked and sucked her sweet juices.

Her cry splintered the quiet and she went wild, bucking and writh-ing as she exploded into his mouth, on his tongue, bathing his chin with her creamy nectar. He gentled his ministrations, knowing how hyper-sensitive she would be as she came down from her orgasm, but he con-tinued to tongue her, lapping up every drop of her essence.

And then she went utterly limp and when he raised his head, he saw her dazed expression and the hazy, dreamy look in her eyes. She was the most beautiful sight he'd ever seen.

Her gaze found his and uncertainty, shame and embarrassment replaced the look of euphoria that had been present. She looked away, her cheeks flushing.

Drake gently lifted her to a sitting position and then slipped her underwear back on, then eased her from his desk and straightened her dress before bending to slide her heels back on her feet.

He cupped her cheek, softly caressing her jaw with his thumb.

"Maddox will take you home now, but he'll be back to pick you up at seven sharp tomorrow night to bring you back to me."

She nodded numbly, obviously dazed and confused, bewilderment bright in her eyes. She didn't even register Drake summoning Maddox back to his office and didn't react when Drake cupped her face with both hands and kissed her lingeringly.

"Tomorrow, Angel. Until then, dream of me."

5

Evangeline sat in the back of the luxurious car, utterly still with shock. She should be shaking like a leaf and completely freaking out. Okay, so she *was* freaking out, but she wasn't broadcasting that to the big silent man who'd been charged with "seeing her home." The same man who'd intervened and prevented Eddie from hitting her.

Did he know what had happened in Drake's office, or whatever the heck he called it? It seemed more his lair and he was some brooding dark beast. A beast who had the most wicked mouth and certainly knew how to use it to pleasure a woman.

Mortification swept over her, nearly destroying her carefully constructed composure. She'd allowed herself to be escorted from Drake's office as if they'd simply had a conversation and he was thoughtful enough to ensure she got home safely. But on the inside she was a hot, writhing mess, still shaking from the aftermath of the most mind-blowing orgasm she could imagine.

Not that she had anything to compare it to, but surely all orgasms weren't *that* earth shattering. If they were, then all everyone would ever *do* is have sex. The world would revolve around down-and-dirty sex.

If she had a man like Drake, it would certainly be all she ever wanted to do. If he was that talented with his mouth, then what about the other parts of his body? Imagining his cock deep inside her nearly made her orgasm all over again, and she glanced furtively at Maddox, praying she hadn't just given herself away with the betraying quiver that stole over her body and set all her girly parts to tingling all over again.

She was still hypersensitive. The exquisite, sumptuous leather she sat on vibrated erotically over her swollen, throbbing clit as the car navigated through Brooklyn. It was the worst sort of torture because it was a good distance from Impulse to the apartment she shared with her three roommates in Queens.

She didn't chance staring at Maddox too long. She didn't want him aware of her scrutiny. That, and she was positive he'd take one look at her face and see her every thought reflected, and that would truly send her over the edge on a night where her nerves were already frazzled and frayed to mere threads. And she was barely hanging on to those fragile threads as it was.

He was utterly unaware of her anyway, his gaze fixed ahead at a point over the driver's shoulder as if studying the streets, alert at all times. Was he expecting them to be carjacked or something?

She almost laughed but knew that too would give away her mounting hysteria.

Surely escorting errant women from his boss's club wasn't in his usual list of duties. If she hadn't had the night from hell—and heaven, God, the last part had been pure bliss—she could almost summon sympathy for him and his job of babysitting her all the way to Queens.

They continued the drive in silence and when they were but minutes from her apartment, she breathed a sigh of relief. But then Maddox shocked her by turning his attention to her, the first time he'd even acknowledged her on the ride home.

"Are you all right?" he asked gently. Then he shook his head, evidently irritated with his own question. "Of course you aren't all right. But *will* you be?"

Her mouth fell open because she'd gotten the distinct impression that she was a tedious job, an unwanted one at that, but now genuine concern, and worse, *sympathy* was reflected in his eyes, making her wince.

She didn't want this man's pity. Or Drake's for that matter. The evening had been a disaster. Well, except for the bone-melting, oh-my-GOD orgasm Drake had given her, because it had been *painfully* obvious to everyone at that damn club that she didn't belong, no matter that Drake had tried to dissuade her of that notion.

"I'm fine," she said quietly.

He cast a doubtful look in her direction. One that told her he saw right past her obvious lie, but then she'd never been able to deceive anyone. She was everyone's version of Miss Goody Two-Shoes, which was why Eddie had seen her as a challenge and wanted to be the one to shame and humiliate her. To conquer the ice queen and be smug over his victory. Some victory. He'd been *terrible* in bed, and it had only taken Drake's mouth and nothing else to reveal that much to her.

"Okay," she muttered. "I *will* be fine. Happy? I'll get over it. I always do."

He frowned at that, his eyes glittering with sudden anger, but he clamped his lips shut, thank God. She had no desire to bare her soul a second time to a complete stranger as she'd done with Drake within five minutes in his presence. Her and her annoying, ridiculous habit of blurting out the truth, no matter how humiliating. She'd mentally kicked herself at least a dozen times for not telling him it wasn't any of his business. But then there was the fact that Drake didn't appear to her to be a man to ever be told to mind his business. She'd convinced herself that he scared the holy hell out of her, but then he'd been extraordinarily tender—and sweet—to her, and she hadn't been able to summon fear when he was making her mindless with his mouth. But after? When she'd partially regained her senses? He definitely terrified her.

The driver rolled to a stop in front of the aging seven-story apartment building that was far older than she was. She and her girls lived on the top floor and the elevator had stopped working a year ago, something the cheap asshole landlord hadn't ever seen fit to fix. It made carrying groceries, or even worse, walking up those six flights of stairs unbearable after a long night at work with aching, swollen feet.

Evangeline didn't wait for the driver or Maddox to get out. She quickly opened her door and stepped onto the curb, hoping neither man would bother to get out and would be on their way, more than happy to be rid of her.

No such luck, but then nothing about this night had gone right, so why would now be any different?

Maddox climbed out on his side after checking for traffic, which wasn't much given the lateness of the night and the fact that for all practical purposes it was a one-way street since vehicles were curbside parked on both sides, making it a tight squeeze for two cars to pass in opposite directions.

He came around to stand beside Evangeline and stared up at her dilapidated building, a scowl forming on his face.

"You live here?"

She stiffened at the implied criticism and snobbery, and she fixed him with an icy glare of her own.

"It's all I can afford and I share it with three other roommates. We do fine. It has all we need."

He shook his head and reached for her elbow, but she evaded his grasp.

"Thank you for the ride home," she said, politely distant.

He ignored the obvious dismissal and his hand closed around her elbow as he herded her toward the entryway.

"I'm walking you up to your apartment."

There was a stubborn glint in his eyes that told her no amount of arguing was going to sway him on the matter. She sighed and threw up her free hand.

"Whatever. Let's just get it over with. I've had a long night and I'm ready to face-plant on my bed."

His mouth twitched ever so slightly. She could swear he was battling a smile, but then none of the men who worked for Drake that she'd seen tonight looked like they smiled. Ever.

When he headed for the elevator, she pulled up and shook her head, directing him toward the stairs.

"The elevator doesn't work. We'll have to take the stairs."

He frowned. "What floor do you live on?"

"Top," she said, already bracing herself for his reaction.

"Jesus," he muttered.

Then he simply bent down, gripping one of her hands and anchoring it on his shoulder.

"Hold on to me."

She had no time to question and it was a good thing she was too befuddled and rattled to disobey his order because he lifted one foot, causing her to teeter, and slipped one of her heels off. After her bare foot was solidly back on the floor, he repeated the action with her other shoe before easing her hand back down to her waist.

Her shoes dangled from his fingertips and with his free hand, he pressed his palm to her back and ushered her to the stairs.

"What on earth are you doing?" she asked in a strangled tone, finally managing to find her voice.

"You'll break your damn neck climbing six flights of stairs in those toothpicks you call shoes," he growled.

She rolled her eyes as they began their climb. "I'm very used to wearing heels like these."

He cocked a mocking eyebrow at her. "Can't say I'm convinced after tonight's fiasco. You damn near killed yourself."

She uttered a growl of her own and pinned him with her most ferocious frown. "Well gee, excuse me all to heck. I was a little more concerned with getting out of the way of a fist trying to make contact with my face than I was about staying upright in my shoes."

It was the wrong thing to remind him of. His expression went utterly glacial and a murderous look entered his eyes.

"He won't fuck with you again."

The conviction in his voice made her uneasy. She used sarcasm to avoid thinking too hard about the certainty with which he'd made that particular statement.

She lifted one eyebrow. "So you have a magic ball? You can see into the future and you know he'll never come at me again?"

"Trust me. He will never come within a mile of you."

Her stomach quivered and she swallowed the fear quickly forming a knot in her throat. He wasn't joking and she did not want to know how he knew this and why he was convinced that Eddie would never be a problem for her again. Some things were just left better unsaid. Ignorance was bliss, and it was a motto she'd adhered to her entire life. No reason to make any drastic changes now. If it ain't broke, don't fix it, her mama always said.

"This is it," she said in a hushed voice when they reached the end of the hallway. Her apartment number was 716, but the six was turned sideways and the seven dangled precariously upside down. It would fall any time and she'd been meaning to fix it herself since her landlord was a useless piece of crap who never bothered to grace the building with his presence unless someone was late on rent. Then he was Johnny-on-the-spot and pounding on their door, threatening immediate eviction, even though it wasn't legal.

"Jesus," Maddox muttered again.

Knowing that if he walked into her apartment with his badass protective routine, her roommates would never let her go to sleep until they pried out the entire soap opera that had been her night, she unlocked the door and opened it just enough so she could slide through. Then she turned back, putting her entire weight against the flimsy door, as if he'd have any problem pushing past her. For that matter, he could kick it down without breaking a sweat.

"Seven. Tomorrow," Maddox said crisply, suddenly all business. "Don't come down. I don't want you waiting on the street. Stay inside until I come up for you."

She barely managed to control her flinch. Barely. Even so, she was certain she'd gone completely pale.

After giving her the best sexual experience of her life, Drake had calmly told her that his driver would be at her apartment the next night at seven and she was going to spend the evening with him. Just like that. He didn't ask. He planned without consulting her about … anything … and she was supposed to just meet his driver and go God only knew where with a scary-as-hell man who also happened to have a positively sinful mouth and an equally sinful body.

She'd been too shattered by her orgasm to do anything but nod dumbly when he'd given her his crisp instructions, and then she'd been herded out of the club and into the car that drove her home.

"Seven," she answered, nodding to reinforce the lie.

And then she shut the door, thanking God the girls weren't all waiting in the tiny living room for all the gory details of her evening. She leaned back against it, closing her eyes, her control finally breaking, and she began shaking from head to toe. Even her teeth chattered as she relived every sinfully decadent moment of being sprawled across Drake's desk as he went down on her like a starving man.

There was no way in hell she would be here at seven tomorrow. She had work, rent to pay and money to send home to her mother. And nothing, not even a very scary, *very* sexy man who made her tingle in places she'd never tingled in before was going to prevent her from taking care of her responsibilities.

She hadn't moved so far away from her tiny southern town to a city with a bigger population than her home state to be a party girl or even to have fun. She'd come to the city because her family needed her, and she wasn't going to let them down.

It was the height of cowardice, and Evangeline made no excuses, nor did she even attempt to offer any when she left her apartment well in advance of seven o'clock the next evening.

Though she'd been granted a temporary reprieve when she'd gotten home and her girlfriends weren't waiting up—much to Evangeline's utter astonishment—to make her spill all the gory details of her evening out at Impulse, they had awakened her the next morning by all piling onto one of the twin beds in the room she shared with Steph and literally pounced on her.

Evangeline had grumbled and whined about them waking her up when she had to work a late shift that night, but they'd ignored her and informed her she had time for a nap. *After* she gave them every single detail, word for word, of the ultimate payback they'd cajoled her into. As if she had a prayer of going back to sleep after recounting it.

She hesitated for a long time, biting her bottom lip until her friends grew concerned, and Evangeline knew she would have to spill or they'd assume far worse than what had actually happened, and they would absolutely have no compunction about paying Eddie an unexpected visit and beating the ever-loving hell out of him.

And one wimpy guy against her three ferocious, positively evil—their best quality, in Evangeline's opinion—friends? Wouldn't have a chance in hell. Then Evangeline would have spent the rest of her day figuring out how to afford to bail all three out of jail, when raising the funds to bail just one would have been impossible.

Her friends were loyal and protective, and their friendship was unconditional. Evangeline wouldn't trade them for anything in the world, which was why, despite her humiliation over the events of the night before, not to mention the OH-MY-GOD ending and her leaving like a mute automaton, programmed to obey without question, she poured out the entire story.

The first part involving Eddie was actually enjoyable, and now that she had distance and wasn't *existing* in that moment, she could actually find amusement in what a complete spineless wuss he was and what a complete moron she'd been to have ever allowed him to have sex with her. Especially allowing him to be her first. Despite the amusement she was able to summon, the humiliation was still ever present in her mind, because how stupid and naïve could she have been? She wasn't a stranger to hard life lessons, but this was one she would have been more than happy to take a pass on.

Her friends found it vastly amusing as well, once they got over their rage at the way Eddie had humiliated her and had actually assaulted her in public! But Evangeline had assured them that he had *thoroughly* received his comeuppance and he had ended up being far more humiliated than Evangeline.

It was then Evangeline had paused in the retelling, and Steph, ever the astute bulldog who never let anything go, narrowed her eyes suspiciously as she stared Evangeline down. She had the uncanny ability to make Evangeline feel like a guilty schoolgirl caught cheating on a test.

"Okay, all of that went down within minutes of you getting there. I mean, you had only just arrived and gotten a drink when Eddie came up to you with his little tramp clinging to his arm. What he had to say couldn't have lasted more than a few minutes at most before the bouncer dude got involved and tossed Eddie and his floozy out, but you were gone a hell of a lot longer than that. So what else happened?"

At that, Nikki and Lana both clued in to what Steph was getting at, and Nikki pinned Evangeline with a piercing stare that was almost as squirmworthy as the ones Steph was so famous for.

"You're holding out on us," Nikki accused.

"Yeah, no kidding," Lana muttered. "Spill, girlfriend. We mean everything. And don't leave a single detail out or swear to God, me, Nikki and Steph will all make a trip to Impulse, find this bouncer who took care of Eddie and find out *exactly* what happened afterward."

Evangeline groaned, because they absolutely would. The men who worked with or for Drake—she hadn't exactly been able to figure out the dynamics of that situation in the short time she'd been there—were *all* badasses. She hadn't *needed* more than a few seconds in their company to figure *that* much out. Anyone with eyes and any modicum of common sense could tell these were not men to fuck with. Ever.

She nearly laughed at the mental image of Maddox being confronted with three petite but very stubborn, determined women who were like pit bulls latched on to a prime steak when it came to something they wanted. They wouldn't be intimidated or put off by Maddox—or any of the other badasses who worked at Impulse. The poor guy—or guys— would never know what hit them.

Well, except for Drake. She very nearly shivered at the memory of him simply looking at her. Like he was peeling her, layer by layer, and seeing every single thought, reaction or emotion she so carefully *tried* to hide from the rest of the world. For all the good that did her.

No, her girls wouldn't have a chance with him. And though her friends weren't intimidated by much, one look from Drake would likely send them scurrying in the opposite direction. Which was what Evangeline should have done, and she still questioned why she hadn't done just that. But she'd been in shock and utterly overwhelmed by the entire sequence of events. Nothing had gone according to her friends' carefully laid-out plan. But then Evangeline had never really truly believed it would, but foolishly, she'd allowed herself to be talked into the whole sordid mess. And what a mess it was.

She bit into her bottom lip, a sure sign of agitation. Her "tell," as her friends often told her—in an attempt to get her to quit it. Not that it did any good. Because if she did relate what all happened after Maddox took care of Eddie . . . well, they would get it into their heads to go confront Drake, and that was the *last* thing she wanted. For a variety of reasons, the foremost being their safety. A close second was, well, it was humiliating enough already. To have her friends march down to Impulse and make a scene with Drake over it?

She shuddered at the thought. She'd already come across as a complete wimp incapable of taking care of herself, and having her friends go to bat for her would only further solidify that fact.

Steph's narrowed eyes and deep frown softened, and a look of concern creased her pretty features and she asked in a gentle voice, "Vangie, what *happened*?"

Evangeline swept them all with a glance. Not a look she gave her friends often, because she was too wimpy to cause conflict and she was the peacemaker of the group. She was a perpetual pleaser, much to her friends' dismay. They wanted to toughen her up. Make her more of a bitch on wheels—what they considered themselves, and they were *so* not. They were the very best friends any woman could have. But Evangeline just wanted peace. She didn't want a chaotic existence. She liked her quiet life, her small group of friends and her job at a local pub that wasn't even in the same stratosphere as a place like Impulse, but it was frequented by locals—except for Eddie, of course, who'd only been at the pub to seduce her. Policemen, firemen and EMS personnel in particular, which made her *feel* safe. More evidence of her naïveté, no doubt. The patrons were friendly and remembered her by name, and the tips were good, thanks to her gorgeous legs, fuck-me shoes and sweeter-than-sunshine smile—according to her friends. Because she sure as hell didn't remotely regard herself in that manner. Their description of her made her hysterical with laughter, but she loved them dearly for their unconditional love and support and for the effort they put into trying to convince her they knew her better than she did herself. The endless hours they spent bolstering her self-confidence, and the absolute conviction she saw in their eyes and heard in their voices, warmed her inside and out.

Evangeline had merely rolled her eyes and informed them that any waitress who made the effort to remember their names and their preference in drink and to make them feel welcome after a long shift would receive the same.

Steph had snorted and then pointed out that if that were the case, they'd all be making as much in tips as Evangeline did.

With a sigh, Evangeline plunged ahead, because she was in a no-win situation. If she didn't tell them everything, they'd haul themselves down to Impulse, interrogate Maddox and then God only knew who else and likely end up in Drake's office.

And if she did confess *every* single thing? Who was to say the outcome would be any different? Only in this case, they might well skip Maddox and the other minions and go straight to *Drake*.

So she did something she never did with them because she trusted them absolutely. Never questioned them or their loyalty. But she also knew once they gave her their word, that even if it killed them—and it would in this case—they'd keep it. She set conditions.

"I'll tell you the rest but only if you *swear* to me that one, it *never* leaves this room and remains between the four of us. And two, you're to leave it alone. I mean completely alone, as in you forget it as soon as I tell you and there will be no confronting anyone, no questioning anyone, no investigating anyone or being nosy. You have to swear it," Evangeline repeated emphatically. "Or my lips are sealed."

The three looked shocked but each nodded in turn, though Steph didn't look at all happy at having to promise something before she even knew what Evangeline was going to reveal. Her lips twisted into a mutinous line, but Evangeline stared her down, never once averting her gaze, until finally Steph threw up her hands in surrender.

"Okay, okay," she said in exasperation. "I promise." She glanced at Lana and Nikki and then added, "We *all* promise. Now will you just get on with it? We're dying of curiosity here!"

Satisfied that she had their consent, and knowing that they'd never go back on their word, Evangeline falteringly related everything that happened after Eddie had been tossed from the club. She left nothing out. No words that Drake had said to her. They were burned into her brain, so it wasn't as though she would ever forget them.

By the time she finished, her cheeks were on fire and no doubt so red that she looked like she was sunburned. The room felt way too hot and she desperately needed a cold shower, or even better, a bathtub full of ice she could submerge herself in until her flushed and aroused, traitorous body rid itself of the lingering aftereffects of Drake's mouth, lips, tongue. His touch. God, just his touch had sent her up in flames. She didn't dare imagine if things had gone further and they'd had full-on sex complete with penetration of *more* than just his tongue. She could feel yet another wave of heat invade her body, and every single one of her girly parts tingling in wild anticipation. She had to stop this!

How on earth, *hours later*, could just remembering all the things he'd done turn her into a complete hormonal mess? She didn't even have the courage to hold her friends' gazes anymore and had long since fixed her stare at a distant point so she *couldn't* see their reactions.

When she finally dared to sneak a glance at her friends' expressions from underneath her eyelashes, their mouths were agape and their eyes wide with complete shock. And for once in their lives, particularly Steph's, who never had a shortage of anything to say, they were utterly speechless.

Nikki's mouth popped open and shut several times in a row while Steph just stared in stupefaction. Surprisingly, it was Lana, the quietest of the three, who finally managed to squeak out, "*What?* For real? Are you *serious?*"

And it *was* a squeak. Barely audible due to the obvious disbelief cracking her words.

Seemingly Lana's breaking the stunned silence began a barrage of questions from all directions until Evangeline covered her ears and groaned, sinking back onto her pillow and closing her eyes. She reached for the second pillow and would have pulled it over her head to shut them all out, but it was promptly snatched from her grasp and Evangeline found herself staring up into Steph's outraged features.

"Oh hell no," Steph huffed, her eyes flashing as her head hovered directly over Evangeline's face. "You are not getting out of this." Then she stopped, clearly at a loss for words for a second time in mere moments— twice in a matter of seconds? Her hand flew above her shoulder, palm up and fingers splayed wide in a universal gesture that screamed *what?* Her expression said everything else her gesture didn't cover... Like *why?* And *how?* And holy crap! *Really?*

If it weren't for the fact that the events were all too real and they had happened to *Evangeline*, she would have found her friends' reactions comical and would even now be holding her sides and laughing hysterically as if she'd managed to successfully pull off the mother of all pranks, something she wasn't remotely capable of because her girlfriends informed her she was too guileless and wouldn't even begin to know how to deceive someone.

They made it sound like a crime, or at the very least a cardinal sin.

Did people pride themselves on being deceitful or worse, being convincing and successful at it?

Evangeline sighed because yes, she was indeed everything her friends accused her of, though *accused* was too strong a word. They despaired of her naïveté and her inability to be catty and bitchy to those who deserved a good setdown. They were forever telling her she was too sweet, too innocent, too forgiving and trusting for her own good.

They loved her dearly for the very things they considered shortcomings, but they worried that those characteristics would end up being her ultimate downfall. Maybe they were right, but Evangeline couldn't change who she was any more than she could change who she *wasn't*. Hadn't last night solidly proved that beyond a shadow of a doubt?

And well, she didn't *want* to change. She liked herself just fine the way she was, shortcomings and all. No one was perfect. It just so happened she had more imperfections than most. So what? There was nothing she could do about it, so why waste time and energy she didn't have trying to be someone that not only could she never *possibly* be, but also that she had no *desire* to become?

Put like that, last night hadn't been the disaster Evangeline had immediately labeled it, and peace settled over her, pushing away some of the still-vivid and all-too-fresh humiliation cloaking her, even as her friends continued to stare her down looking like they were ready to rip her hair out by the roots if she didn't *further* explain the shocking revelation she'd dropped on them as though it had been a live explosive.

"He actually went down on you in his office? On his *desk*?" Nikki asked in a hushed whisper, evidently having reached the breaking point of her patience and deciding Evangeline was going to have to be interrogated since she still wasn't forthcoming with all the juicy details her friends craved.

"God, you make it sound so . . . sordid," Evangeline said with a soft groan. "I feel like I should be in church right now, or at least at confession."

"Hon, I think one has to be Catholic to go to confession," Lana said dryly.

"Stop distracting her!" Steph said in a near shriek, her agitation making her even more agitated. "And Vangie, I hate to break it to you, but it *was* sordid. In a really delicious, oh-my-God, goose-bump-inducing kind of way. I need to sign up for that kind of sordid, because nothing I've ever done has even come close to that kind of hedonistic delight."

Evangeline lifted one eyebrow in surprise. She'd expected . . . She frowned, giving her head a light shake to clear the confusion. She wasn't entirely sure what she'd expected. Maybe condemnation? Disappointment? Judgment?

But that wasn't at all what she saw reflected in her friends' gazes. There was a myriad of responses, almost too many to sort through, but nowhere did she see anything that made her feel ashamed or even sorry for what she'd done. But then she hadn't *done* anything. She'd just been a clueless—a completely clueless—participant, if she could actually call her response actual participation. She'd merely allowed *him* to happen. To take over and control every aspect of the shattering, life-altering sequence of events that had begun as simple, petty payback. There was no blaming shock, being overwhelmed, or even the fact that her senses had been so scattered that she wasn't even cognizant of what was happening. She knew who was to blame, and it wasn't Drake. It was her own damn fault for not having the fortitude and daring to put a stop to the entire farce. She didn't have a brave bone in her body, and last night had only proved that beyond a shadow of a doubt.

Worse, she'd *known* exactly what he was doing—what he was *going* to do—and she'd quivered to her bones, shaking violently with suppressed need and longing. He'd awakened a fire that had long lay dormant within her, and God help her, she'd *wanted* it, *craved* it *and him*—with every breath in her body. With wild desperation that still bewildered her, because the wanton woman she hadn't even known existed had responded with complete abandon to a man she'd known for all of a few minutes. For once in her life she'd given in to spontaneity. Done something completely out of character. Grabbed onto the moment and reveled in every single second of unimaginable pleasure. Like in her most erotic fantasies she'd never shared with anyone. Not even her friends. Because they shamed her, and more than that, they frightened her, because in no way, in any of her wildest fantasies, was she in control of any aspect. She belonged to a man who cherished her, protected her, spoiled her endlessly, but in return he was demanding, ruthless even, with an edge of danger and mystery that clung to him like a second skin, one he wore with the comfort and ease of someone well acquainted with such a lifestyle.

What kind of messed-up person did that make her? She closed her eyes again, refusing to dwell on things better left in the past. If she had her way, she'd never see him again because she sure as hell would never venture into places like Impulse where even the hired help were seen in a more superior, deserving light than she was.

It might make her the biggest coward on earth, but even if she wasn't scheduled for work that night, there was no way she would be here at seven that evening waiting to be collected like a "possession" and expected to do unimaginable things—even if the thought of those things sent her body up in flames.

She gave a small sigh, ignoring the looks of growing impatience and irritation on her friends' faces. One taste was all she'd ever allow herself and it would have to be enough. Because Drake Donovan was not a man to be trifled with. He demanded and expected unquestioning obedience. That much was obvious in his demeanor.

She had to work tonight until closing, and no matter that her girls had told her she could always take a nap after giving them the scoop, Evangeline knew she didn't have a prayer of going back to sleep. Not with the vivid details from the night before still playing over and over in real time in her memory.

No, she'd simply leave early and go on. Get caught up on some of the things that had piled up over the last few weeks and had been largely ignored by the other workers.

But first, she'd give her friends what they wanted—what they deserved—because they'd never held back from her, nor would they ever.

Then she'd worry about what to do about Drake Donovan. Just as soon as she looked up every piece of information she could find about just who this man was and what he could possibly want with someone as insignificant as her.

7

Evangeline was exhausted when she stumbled out of the pub an hour after the official closing time. Her feet were killing her, swollen from the many busy hours rushing drinks to customers in very uncomfortable heels. She was sorely tempted to take them off and just walk barefooted home. She'd been so frazzled by all that had occurred the night before and the exhausting interrogation from her roommates that she'd forgotten the pair of comfortable flats she brought to work to walk home in. Now she was stuck walking ten blocks in the wee hours of the morning in shoes she wanted to toss into the nearest trash can. At least she had an even larger amount than her already generous nightly tips stuffed into her pocket, so her misery was a little more bearable given that she could send more than usual back home to her mother.

She was so dead on her feet and already dreaming of at least twelve hours of sleep that she didn't even see the man outside the pub until she nearly bumped into him. Her adrenaline spiked and her heart nearly pounded right out of her chest as she stumbled back, assuming a defensive position.

A scream lodged in her throat as she frantically assessed the potential threat. Then she recognized the man, but realizing she knew him only ratcheted up her fear, and her first instinct was to run for her life.

Maddox, Drake's minion, stood nonchalantly in front of her, effectively blocking her escape, his stance deceptively casual. She nearly allowed hysterical laughter to escape her mouth at the idea of having time to pry her too-tight heels from her feet and run for her life because this man would have her before she got the first shoe off.

"My apologies for frightening you, Evangeline," he said in the same gentle tone he'd used at Impulse when he'd rescued her.

"*Why* are you here?" she stammered out. "How did you even know where to find me? What do you want?"

She sounded desperate and frightened, but she didn't even bother trying to disguise that fact. What woman wouldn't be terrified in her situation? She was surprised she'd even been able to articulate the questions for him that had come out more of a squeak than any sort of actual coherent speech.

Maddox's expression was bland but there was a hint of warning in his eyes. "It's not a good idea to keep Drake waiting. You were to be at your place at seven o'clock sharp and I had strict instructions to take you straight to him. And he is a man who expects—demands—obedience and compliance. In *all* matters."

Her unease was fast paralyzing her as the last of his words sank in. *All* matters? He demanded obedience in all matters? Who did he think he was? God? What the hell had she gotten herself into by allowing herself to be coerced into going to that damn club? Damn it, but she should have just listened to herself and refused to set foot in that place. Where was her spine? Oh yeah, she didn't have one.

He made a deliberate show of checking his watch before his gaze returned to hers, warning still clearly visible.

"It's now four in the morning, which makes you nine hours late, and Drake doesn't wait nine hours for anyone."

Evangeline bared her teeth. "Good! But if that's the case, then why are you here? By your own admission Drake waits for no one and it's been nine hours. If he's not waiting for me, then why are you here scaring the crap out of me?"

Amusement flashed in Maddox's eyes. "It would appear he's making an exception for you. My advice is not to make him wait any longer by standing here arguing at four in the morning."

Evangeline's mouth dropped open. "Are you serious? What gives him the right to order me around or expect me to comply with his *demands*, like I'm some minion or one of his employees?" She shook her head, because this had gone way beyond creepy. Even more so than the bizarre events at the club and in particular in Drake's office. "You're *all* crazy! Certifiable. Besides, I had to *work*. You know, that thing called a *job*, in return for which you receive a paycheck? Some of us don't have the luxury of taking off on a whim. I have bills to pay and a family to support. I *need* this job, and I'm sure as hell not blowing off work just because the almighty Drake Donovan decided he wants my presence for God only knows what reason. That would make me as insane as the rest of you!"

Once again, amusement flickered in Maddox's eyes, but there was also a gleam that looked suspiciously like . . . respect at her defiance and bluntness. She was not a rude person, but nothing in her responses could possibly be construed as anything but rude. Not to mention dismissive, and although her association with Drake and his watchdogs had been brief, she knew they were not men who were *ever* dismissed and certainly not by a meek, timid woman.

When he didn't immediately respond, frustration made Evangeline lash out again.

"What could he possibly want with me? We exist in completely different stratospheres. I'm nothing. I'm average at best. Nothing to look at. The stereotypical plain Jane who wouldn't even draw notice in a small group, much less a crowd!"

At that, Maddox's expression went from amused to pissed and mean in the blink of an eye, his gaze glittering dangerously.

"Bullshit," he snapped, not expounding further.

Instead he gently cupped her elbow, anchored his arm around her waist and began walking her toward a parked car just a few feet away. The same car he'd taken her home in the night before. He ignored her sputtered protests and her attempts to break his hold on her and merely tightened his grip, slowing his pace to ensure she didn't trip or stumble in the ridiculous heels she wore. How could such a badass, scary guy use such extreme care to ensure her safety when he was kidnapping her? It just didn't make sense and her brain was already fried from the night at Impulse and then an extra-long shift she'd spent entirely on her feet.

When they got to the car and Maddox opened the back door, panic kicked in and she immediately backed away only to collide with a very large, muscled man who didn't so much as budge as she squirmed and began to fight.

Instead he very gently eased her back and began to solicitously seat her.

"You can't just kidnap me!" she exclaimed, true fright nearly making the words she intended to scream come out more as a croak because her throat was rapidly closing in.

"And yet you didn't protest overly much when I very gentlemanly handed you into the car," Maddox said dryly.

"Define 'overly much,'" she snapped. "Because from my viewpoint I certainly did not go meekly like a lamb to its slaughter. I'm sure it appeared that way to you because you could snap me in half with your fingers, but it doesn't mean I'm not here under protest."

But then she looked down to see that she was indeed seated quite comfortably on the soft, expensive leather, wondering how on earth he'd managed to get her into the car with such minimal effort. Despite her bravado about fighting and not being led meekly to slaughter.

Self-disgust filled her because yes, to a man like *him*, it most assuredly would look like she did his bidding without a single objection.

"I was afraid you'd shoot me," she muttered under her breath.

But Maddox heard and his lips twitched suspiciously, though she suspected he rarely if ever smiled. That too seemed to be a requirement to work in Drake's establishments. Gorgeous, badass, well built, intimidating, *scary* and no smiling. Ever.

He shut the door and started the walk around the back of the vehicle to get in on the other side. Evangeline immediately yanked at the handle, fully intending to be out and running as fast as her shoes allowed before he got in.

But nothing happened. She tore at the handle, cursing under her breath, words that would have her mama washing her mouth out with soap because no true lady ever even thought the words Evangeline was spitting out in rapid succession.

Then a warm, comforting hand closed over the one not frantically grasping at the door handle. He squeezed, halting her futile attempts to open what amounted to a child lock that prevented opening the door from the inside. So now she was nothing more than a recalcitrant child, a nuisance Maddox had been sent on an errand to retrieve because she'd stepped out of line. A line she had no knowledge or understanding of. Things just didn't happen like this in her sheltered existence. She felt as though the night she'd been bullied into going to Impulse she had crossed into an alternative reality that had an entirely different set of rules and she had no idea what the hell they were!

"Evangeline."

Though not forceful or intimidating sounding, there was still a command for her attention. For her to look at him. One she felt compelled to obey despite the fact that she had no wish to face this man. She chastened herself for even contemplating obeying the order and yet, to her dismay, she found herself complying. How screwed up was that? If she couldn't even stand up to one of Drake's underlings, then how on earth was she going to have a chance against Drake himself? She was beyond fright and panic at this point. She was fast entering meltdown stage and wondered if somehow she could stealthily retrieve her cell phone from her bag and call 911. But she had no idea where Maddox was taking her and no actual crime had been committed. Yet.

Reluctantly, but unable to defy his command, she turned her head, her gaze lowered, eyes downcast as defeat settled over her. She sagged against the seat, exhausted both mentally and physically, tears burning the corners of her eyes. She inhaled sharply, calling on all her flagging reserves to pull herself together. This man would not see her cry, nor would he see her as a weak, helpless woman who'd accepted defeat.

"Evangeline, look at me," Maddox said softly.

His hand still gripped hers but his thumb rubbed softly over her delicate skin as though to comfort her. And the really stupid, screwed-up thing about it was that it did give her a small measure of comfort. Surely if he planned to murder her, he wouldn't be trying to offer her reassurance. She nearly groaned aloud, because again, her extreme naïveté was taking over her brain. Serial killers were often normal, average men who gained the trust of their victims before viciously ending their lives.

Knowing she was being a coward—and, well, she *was* a coward—she slowly lifted her eyes to meet Maddox's intense gaze. She hated conflict and any sort of confrontation and yet here she was, on her way to the mother of all confrontations. She wanted to dig a very deep hole and bury herself in it.

"You will not come to any harm," he said in a tone that couldn't possibly be misunderstood as a lie. "Drake will not hurt you in any way. Nor would he ever allow anyone else to hurt you. I know you have no reason to trust me, or Drake for that matter, but I swear to you on my life that you will be safe at all times. I will escort you personally to Drake and once you are with him, no one, and I mean *no* one, will be able to get within a mile of you. And while he is most certainly capable of handling himself in any situation, he is surrounded at all times by a security team and they are the absolute best at what they do. They are highly trained and there isn't a single one of us who wouldn't give our life for Drake, and now, by proxy, you."

She stared at him in utter bewilderment, trying to take in everything he'd just said. There were so many insane responses swirling in her head that she was dizzy from it.

"You'll forgive my skepticism," she said, trying to keep the tremble from her voice that betrayed her fear. No, *fear* was too tame a word. She *feared* spiders and bugs. Drake *terrified* her. "But he sent you to kidnap me. No amount of pretty words or explanations changes the fact that I was taken against my will. You wouldn't take no for an answer. My absence at the seven o'clock pickup time he commanded of me should have been signal enough that I had no desire to accept his dictate. And for that matter, he never *asked* me to meet him. He didn't offer me a *choice*. He told me to be at my apartment at seven and that someone would be there to pick me up and bring me to him. And I was so freaked out and just wanted to get as far away from that place as possible that all I did was nod, because if I told him no then, how was I supposed to know if he would have even let me leave? Now *you* tell *me*. What sane person wouldn't be scared out of her mind? And what sane person would blithely accept the assurances of a man who looks like he could break me in half with nothing more than a *look* that I won't be harmed and I'll be safe? What about this entire freaky four-in-the-morning stalkfest would convince *any* woman that she's safe or that the man who gave the order for her to be kidnapped doesn't plan to hurt her?"

Maddox's face softened, remorse reflected in his eyes, surprising her with how much it transformed his appearance from a man not to be fucked with ever to someone who actually possessed a conscience. He seemed to truly regret that he'd frightened and intimidated her, as if that had never been his intention and he was appalled that she'd perceived his actions that way.

Not to say that he was still not an extremely alpha badass man who could probably mow down an entire crowd of men without suffering a single injury. But then all the men at Impulse, even the freaking bartender, looked like they were former special forces. Or navy SEALs or some equally ferocious military unit she'd never heard of. Where on earth had Drake found a veritable army of men who were built like concrete buildings? She'd be willing to bet that bullets bounced right off them and that even a grenade wouldn't slow them down. Much.

She reined in her crazy, hysterical thoughts before she got *too* carried away and forced herself back to the matter at hand.

"I am sorry that you were frightened," he said gently. "That was never mine or Drake's intention. Drake . . ." He paused a moment as if to say exactly the words that wouldn't further petrify her. "Drake is a law unto himself and he is well used to compliance. He built an entire empire and amassed his fortune by hard work and never backing down. No one gave him anything. He was on his own at a very young age and learned the hard way that life is what you make it, and if you stand around waiting for a handout or for someone to give you anything, then you'll never get anywhere."

He paused, grimacing, as if what he was telling her was top secret, classified military information and that if Drake knew all he was telling her, Drake would probably have his balls.

"He is a very private man," he continued, confirming Evangeline's suspicion that Maddox divulging anything remotely personal was a cardinal sin. "He didn't get to where he is by being soft or tolerating insubordination."

Evangeline's eyes narrowed and she held up a hand to stop Maddox, something he was likely unused to judging by his narrowed eyes, but at the moment, she didn't care.

"That's all well and fine when it comes to his business and his employees," she said acidly. "How he conducts his business is of no concern of mine, and if his employees are willing to tolerate working for a dictator, that is their business. But I am not his employee. I do not work for him. I am nothing to him, and as such, I find his actions—his arrogant assumption that I have to fall in line and obey him or acquiesce to his demands—quite frankly absurd. It's the height of arrogance. He can play God in his little corner of the universe all he wants, but I am not part of that universe and he is completely crossing the line with his actions."

Maddox sighed and looked like he wanted nothing more than to stop the car and toss her out. No doubt any number of women Drake had sent him to "summon" had flattened Maddox to get to Drake as fast as they could. But she'd also learned, in their very brief acquaintance, that Drake's employees were obviously very well trained and loyal to a fault, so no matter how much of a pain in the ass Evangeline was for Maddox, he wasn't going to show up and face his boss empty-handed. Which meant she had to resign herself to her fate and hope to hell Maddox was telling the truth when he said no one would harm her.

8

Evangeline made a turtle look like a speed demon as she navigated the hallway to the now-closed club where her apparent meeting with Drake was
to take place. Maddox simmered with impatience, but he reined it in and
walked with her, one hand at the small of her back, the other stretched
across his midsection to grasp her trembling arm. He likely thought if he
didn't have a firm grasp on her, she'd face-plant, and, well, he wasn't wrong.

When they'd pulled into a reserved parking space at the rear of the
club she'd sat rigid in her seat like a statue, her jaw clenched tight to prevent her teeth from clattering. The club? Really? At this hour? Had he
been waiting for her here all night only growing more annoyed when
she didn't make an appearance? Or did he simply work late and tend to
business matters while his employees announced last call and cleared
the place so cleanup could commence?

Maddox had walked around to her side and opened the door and
then stood there several long minutes before sighing and looking very
much like he wanted to throttle her. Finally, he'd taken matters into his
own hands and simply reached in, slid one arm beneath her thighs and
the other around her back and plucked her from the seat and up against
his chest as effortlessly as if she were an infant.

That had put a stop to her stillness and refusal to move. She smacked and shoved at his chest, demanding he put her down. She'd be damned if he had to carry her into the club like an unwilling captive. Even if that was precisely what she was.

Only when they'd gotten just inside the doorway had Maddox relinquished his hold on her and carefully set her back on her feet, both hands grasping her shoulders until she was steady enough to walk.

More than once during the interminable walk to the elevator she heard him mutter something about "damn shoes" and "you're going to break your damn neck."

By the time they were in the elevator and it began its ascent to Drake's office, Evangeline's chest was so tight she couldn't breathe. When she unsuccessfully tried to gasp and suck air into her starving lungs, panic completely took over and she began to shake violently.

Beside her, Maddox swore viciously and then firmly grasped her shoulders, turning her to face him. He lowered his head until their eyes met, and his gaze was fierce.

"Breathe, damn it. Don't you dare pass out on me. Pull it together. You've stood up to your asshole ex, me *and* Drake and didn't back down despite your repeated claims that we could snap you like a twig, so don't go soft on me now, for fuck's sake. You have far too much pride to walk into Drake's office like this."

Then he broke off, shaking his head.

"Forget that. You have too much pride for me to have to *carry* you into Drake's office, which is precisely what's going to happen if you don't snap out of it and calm down."

His voice was whiplike and had the same effect as if someone had cracked one over her skin. Suddenly heat bloomed in her cold cheeks and her throat relaxed, air rushing into and filling her lungs.

She was weak with relief and fast approaching her wall after being carried this far by fear-induced adrenaline. Her knees wobbled and threatened to buckle, but she shoved off Maddox's attempts to steady her, opting instead to distance herself from him and prop herself up against the far side of the elevator.

How freaking long did it take for the damn thing to rise what couldn't be more than a few floors? But then her meltdown and Maddox's sharp reprimand had lasted mere seconds, though it felt like an eternity.

She was feeling so claustrophobic and humiliated by her ridiculous display of cowardice that she sighed in relief when the elevator halted and the doors swooshed open. And then she realized that she would now be facing a man far more scary and intimidating than Maddox, and after what little Maddox had divulged about his boss, Evangeline knew that Drake would not be pleased to have been kept waiting for over nine hours now.

Maddox had herded her from her position in the back of the elevator, but when she reached the threshold of Drake's office, she halted abruptly and tried to take a step back, only to collide with Maddox's massive chest. It took every ounce of pride and discipline she possessed not to groan out loud or do something even more humiliating like burst into tears or have another epic meltdown and pass out at Maddox's feet.

She took a steadying breath and then steeled herself, her spine going rigid. Her chin thrust upward in defiance and she searched angrily for Drake's location, determined not to be cowed when their gazes eventually found each other.

She reached back instinctively, before she could stop herself, seeking the reassurance of Maddox's body with her hand and found . . . air. Damn it! The man was a veritable escape artist. This was the second time he'd "escorted" her up to Drake's lair and then disappeared into thin air. She hadn't even registered the elevator doors closing. And now she was trapped with a man Maddox had flat-out told her did not like to be kept waiting and expected absolute compliance with his every order.

Well, hell. She closed her eyes, giving up on the idea of boldly seeking out Drake—wherever he was lurking—and refusing to back down from his stare.

"You're late," Drake said, allowing his displeasure to sound in his statement.

But even as he issued the admonishment, he took in her appearance and the fact that she was obviously exhausted and dead on her feet. She could barely remain upright in those ridiculous heels and looked like she'd take a header at any second.

He knew well why she hadn't been at her apartment at seven as he'd instructed. She'd gone to work in a damn pub and been on her feet for hours in shoes that amounted to an accident waiting to happen. She was pale, and fatigue was etched in every facet of her face.

With a muttered curse, he stalked to her, gently took her arm and then promptly guided her to the couch. He planted both hands on her shoulders and pushed her downward so she had no choice but to sit.

"Lie back and relax," he said tersely.

Then he went to one bended knee and removed her shoes, swearing again when he saw how swollen her feet were. She looked utterly bewildered, her eyes wide as though this were the last thing she'd expected. But then he hadn't exactly done much to convince her he wasn't a heartless, cold bastard, some kind of monster who'd pounce on her at the first opportunity.

Without a word, he began to massage one foot, taking care not to hurt her or cause her discomfort.

She emitted a soft moan and for a moment, her eyes closed and she sagged, some of the tension evaporating from her body. He worked on the first foot, covering every inch and paying special attention to her tender arches. Then he turned his focus to the other, giving it equal care.

He watched her intently, absorbing every reaction and the sheer pleasure reflected on her face. She was so fucking responsive. Absolutely honest, no faking. She was genuine to her toes and so damn beautiful his balls ached.

Last night had given him a hard-on he'd carried the entire night, making sleep impossible because every time he closed his eyes, he tasted her, smelled her, could hear her soft cries of ecstasy, and he replayed having her spread out before him on his desk like a goddess being offered up as the most priceless of treasures. Certainly nothing money could buy and nothing a man with his power could produce on command, and that was something rare and precious indeed. Something worth a thing he wasn't used to demonstrating. Patience.

It had taken every ounce of his restraint not to tear his pants down and plunge so deeply into her that she would feel him to her soul. He still wondered why he hadn't. Only the nagging warning in the back of his mind telling him he had to tread carefully with her and not push her too hard, too fast, had kept him from slaking his hunger without regard for whether he scared the holy hell out of her. She'd been freaked out enough by him going down on her. It was equally obvious that her only lover—her dickhead ex—hadn't given her anything. He'd just taken. Her ex had let go of something most men would kill for, but Drake didn't spare an ounce of pity for the idiot. His loss was Drake's gain, and he intended to move in, take over and make damn sure that from now on she was in his bed, under his command. And by God, she'd never go without anything in his power to provide her.

He let his hands slide leisurely from her foot and she murmured a light sound of protest.

"Why the hell are you working yourself to death in that shithole bar every night?" he asked bluntly.

She made a huffing noise and glared at him.

"You could at least continue the fabulous foot massage if you're going to interrogate me," she said in a disgruntled voice.

He nearly laughed before he caught himself. He didn't laugh often, and when he did, it wasn't usually out of amusement. People tended to get nervous when he laughed. Nor did he smile. But he was amused by her show of bravado. She was intimidated, and uncertainty was evident in her body language, but she was damned if she was going to show it. Good. The last thing he wanted was a meek doormat. Yes, he demanded obedience and submission, but that didn't equate to his woman being a mindless robot, programmed to do his bidding with no thoughts or opinions of her own. He liked her fire. And her pride. He liked that most of all because it was a trait he was intimately familiar with and respected.

He closed his palms around the other foot and resumed his gentle ministrations.

"You going to answer my question now?" he asked in a deceptively mild tone.

Sudden alarm replaced the look of languid pleasure and her body went rigid when just moments earlier, as soon as he'd begun massaging her feet, she'd melted bonelessly against the back of the sofa. She bolted upright, her feet dropping from his hands to the floor with a thud.

He cursed, his already fraying patience threatening to completely unravel along with his anger.

"What the hell is wrong now?" he demanded, his narrowed gaze aimed at her.

If he thought the not-so-subtle reprimand would make her back down, he was wrong. She stared up at him with wide eyes that were laced with worry and he was seized by the need to allay any fear she had. Goddamn it, he didn't want her to be afraid with him, but she wasn't exactly making it very easy for him. .

"My girlfriends," she stammered out. "Oh my God. They're probably out of their minds with worry. They may have even already called the police! I was already late getting off work and then I was dragged into a car by your henchman and brought here. What time is it, anyway?"

Drake sighed and managed to rein in his simmering temper. Barely. He didn't give a rat's ass what her roommates thought, but he did care that Evangeline was in obvious distress, and he did care that the police could already be involved. If questioned, Evangeline would no doubt have any cop convinced that Drake *had* abducted her and was even now holding her against her will.

Something he planned to rectify immediately. She would stay. There was no doubt about that. But it would certainly not be against her will. He was never going to get to that point, however, because of the incessant interruptions. He not only despised interruptions and inconveniences, he simply didn't tolerate either. So why the hell was he suddenly doing just that when it came to one infuriating, exasperating, stubborn woman?

Because you want her as you've never wanted another woman.

There was that. Even though the admission didn't sit well with him at all. Evangeline was a complication he didn't need. But damn if he didn't want her. Complications, frustration, inconveniences and all. He almost shook his head. Hell of a thing to find himself in this predicament over an unwilling woman. His men—those closest to him, men he called brothers in every sense of the word—would laugh themselves silly if they even had a hint of the turmoil one small, fragile, infuriating female was causing him.

"Can't you text them?" he asked mildly, even as he registered that she was frantically digging for her cell in her purse.

Her gaze lifted and she bit into her lip. "Yeah, I'm going to text them right now. I should have texted them the second your goon made me get into the car with him, but I wasn't exactly thinking straight at the moment. And to be honest, if I tell them where I am and why, me texting them isn't going to do any good. They'll definitely call the police and haul ass down here themselves."

As she spoke, she was typing away on a very small, hopelessly outdated cell phone, murmuring each of the recipients' names as she added them to the group text.

Drake shrugged. "So tell them you're somewhere else. You don't owe them an explanation, nor do you answer to them for your actions."

She huffed impatiently. "Look, Drake. They know all about what happened here last night. They also know I am not the type of person to be 'somewhere else' at almost five o'clock in the morning after working a long shift and being dead on my feet. I'm not a party girl nor do I have men lining up to take me out on dates, so no matter what I tell them, they're going to smell a rat, and they're smart. They'll put two and two together, and here will be the very first place they'll look for me. Whether I text them or not. Whether I tell them I'm perfectly okay and not to worry. Because that's what friends do. They have each other's backs and they worry about each other, and they're especially protective of me because they know I'm a naïve twit who's incapable of recognizing a predator when I see one."

She glanced down at her phone, worry furrowing her brow.

"They haven't responded. I should call Steph. They're probably freaking out."

Drake sighed, not even attempting to hide his irritation and displeasure as she called and evidently didn't reach this supposedly worried-out-of-her-mind friend, because Evangeline rattled off a message saying she wouldn't be home and that she was sorry for not contacting them sooner.

Her girlfriends seemed like gigantic pains in the ass, and she'd probably be much better off without them, because it sounded a hell of a lot like they smothered her, judged her, kept her in line and expected her to gain their permission to so much as take a piss.

He mentally winced because he was every bit as controlling, but his method of control and dominance was not even close to what her girlfriends apparently considered their way of managing her life, or rather micromanaging her life. He would always have her best interests at heart. He was almost certain he couldn't say the same about her girls.

Damn it all. If all Evangeline had said was true, and he had no reason not to believe her, then she was right. A text wasn't going to head off a potentially ugly confrontation and the cops showing up at his club and him having to answer to kidnapping and coercion charges. Since Evangeline hadn't received a response, and her phone call had gone unanswered, he was going to have to throw one of his men under the bus and have him take care of the matter personally.

"Maddox," he snapped, knowing his man would hear at his station outside Drake's door, the exit on the opposite end of the elevator that not many knew of, and judging by Evangeline's sudden look of wariness and her quick glance at the elevator as if expecting him to appear from it, she hadn't noticed the other door in the far corner. She likely thought he was a paranoid, psychotic bastard, and, well, she'd have at least part of it right. He hadn't survived in his world this long without a healthy degree of paranoia and common sense not to offer his trust freely.

Maddox entered in an instant, his expression wary as he sent a scowl in Evangeline's direction.

"Go assure Evangeline's roommates that she is perfectly all right, but she won't be coming home tonight, or any other night for that matter. Inform them that she's moving in with me and will be in contact with them in the next day or two and will explain everything to them then."

"What?" Evangeline's shriek made Maddox wince. She didn't look frightened as one might expect. No, she looked outraged and indignant.

Satisfied she wasn't about to become hysterical with fear, Drake ignored her reaction, instead picking her feet back up and resuming his ministrations, which forced her to recline back onto the couch. Because while she might not dissolve into hysteria, she might well punch him right in the face, so distraction was necessary immediately and she'd definitely enjoyed the foot rub he'd already given her.

Maddox clearly had no liking for the task Drake had assigned him. It was evident in his disgruntled expression.

"What the hell did I do to deserve to be put on difficult and recalcitrant women duty?" Maddox muttered. "Surely you can come up with more creative ways of punishing me, Drake. Defuse a bomb? Stop an assassination attempt? Be a substitute day-care worker for a week?"

Evangeline sent Maddox a saccharine-sweet smile at his acid sarcasm.

"I certainly didn't ask to be dragged from my workplace at four in the morning to face a man who is clearly out of his mind or has mistaken me for someone else entirely. And if I hadn't been dragged here, I would be home, and therefore my roommates wouldn't be out of *their* minds with worry and you wouldn't have to deal with difficult, recalcitrant women. Though I'd pay money to see you in a day care with mini spawns of Satan nagging you and pulling you in forty different directions."

Her smile was mockingly sweet, a definite smirk lurking on her lips, but her words were tart with a distinct edge that amused Drake. Evidently Maddox was as well.

Maddox gave her a quirk of a smile, amusement glimmering in his eyes, and then, just before he turned to exit, he gave her a two-finger salute as if to say, *Touché.*

As soon as Maddox departed, Evangeline aimed a ferocious albeit cute glare in Drake's direction and opened her mouth, no doubt to blast him with both barrels, so Drake did the one thing guaranteed to silence her.

He fused his mouth to hers in a hot, breathless kiss, though he wasn't sure who was the more breathless, him or her. A savage groan worked its way from his chest and into his throat, escaping into the sweetness of her mouth. He swallowed her gasp of surprise and dropped her feet, leaning forcefully into her, grasping her hands when they went to his chest to shove him away.

Instead, he clasped them there over his chest, letting her feel the rapid beat of his heart, allowing her to *feel* her effect on him. Not something he would normally ever allow to happen, but damn it, he was treading in unfamiliar waters here. He'd never had to deal with a reluctant female when it came to his advances. He was well used to women tripping over themselves in their haste to get to him, to gain his attention. Not try to run as fast and as hard in the other direction as possible.

Reluctantly, he eased his lips from hers, noting the swollen, delectable bow of her mouth and that delicious little funny quirk in the corner. He couldn't help himself. He flicked his tongue out and licked at it, coaxing another tremble from her already quivering body.

"Now, I'd like an answer to my question," he said in a deceptively lazy manner. One that might fool someone else into thinking he was merely asking a simple question, one that could either be answered or not.

Her eyes narrowed, telling him without words that she definitely hadn't missed the hint of command in his tone.

"Why are you working in that place night after night, running yourself into the ground, to complete exhaustion? Where men touch you, put their hands on you and God only knows what else," he growled.

He was becoming more pissed by the minute, and he was seething as he stared at her. The idea of those bastards putting their hands on what he'd already claimed, fondling her, disrespecting her, had his teeth on edge, and his temper, already bad enough, was fast becoming overwhelmingly foul.

"It's not that bad," she said, immediately becoming defensive.

"Bullshit," he barked, startling her with his vehemence. "I had men in the bar all night. They saw exactly the kind of shit you endure on a nightly basis. Remember the asshole who wouldn't take no for an answer when you oh-so-politely told him to get fucked?"

She blushed. "I didn't say any such thing."

"No, but you should have. Remember the man who intervened when it could have gotten ugly? And, Angel, it *would* have gotten ugly very fast were it not for my man. The one who gave you a hundred-dollar tip? He was one of mine. Now think about it for a minute. Did anyone else there offer to help you? What if my men hadn't been there?"

Humiliation flashed in her eyes and she turned her head sideways in an attempt to hide her reaction from him. But he caught the flash of tears and it nearly ripped his insides out.

"I'll give it back," she whispered. "I had no idea it was a setup. I didn't earn that. I refuse to take pity money."

He flinched at the look in her eyes, the evident blow to her pride, the one thing she held fast to when it appeared she had nothing else. Damn it. That was *not* what he wanted.

She dug into her pocket, several twenties and smaller bills falling out as she yanked. She retrieved the folded hundred-dollar bill and thrust it at him as if she couldn't bear to touch it a second longer.

"I don't want it. I *won't* take it," she said, revulsion twisting her lips until he wanted to kiss them back to the sweet, luscious state they had been in mere seconds before.

Drake swore, making her wince. Then he collected all of the scattered bills, folded them carefully and stuffed them back into her pocket.

"My men were there at my order to check the place out as a potential investment. It's for sale, or did you not know that?"

Her eyes widened in surprise. "No. I had no idea. What does that mean? Am I going to lose my job? Oh my God, Drake, what am I going to do? I know it doesn't look like much, but the tips are good, and I make more money working there than I did working two jobs back home."

The fear in her eyes was very nearly his undoing. The thought of her working two jobs made him want to smash something. He was sure her tips were very good. Far more than the average waitress working there. Hell, on a good night, she probably pulled in as much as his girls did in his club. With that inherent innocence and bone-deep sweetness? A smile that lit up a city block? The fact that she was so fucking . . . nice? And that wasn't even taking into account her looks. Those big blue eyes, the long silken mass of hair that made a man itch to run his hands through it, and that ass. God, that ass. Delectable. Plump. Just enough jiggle when she walked to make a man lose his mind. And her tits. Fuck, he could recite all her good qualities all night and never get to the end. She was the total package, and when men looked at her, they did a double take, especially after talking to her for just a few minutes, because they were all wondering how the hell such a perfect woman existed. And then they set their sights on how to get next to her. In her bed, between her legs, and how to stay there, because who the fuck—other than her dumb-ass ex-boyfriend—would be stupid enough to ever let her go once he'd had a taste of all she offered?

Jesus, he had to stop because she was staring at him oddly, obviously waiting for him to say whatever he had been about to say next, and he was too busy extolling her virtues and mentally covering her with NO TRESPASSING signs because he was staking his claim and he'd kill the man who tried to take what was his.

"You're missing my point," he said as patiently as he was able when he wanted to smash something, dispense with the niceties and drag her home and keep her there under lock and key. "Only Maddox knew about you, and he remained outside so you wouldn't see him and bolt. Whatever tip my man gave you was because he wanted to and felt you earned it. He had no idea you belong to me."

"What?"

"I'll ask you a third time, and Evangeline, I am not used to having to ask more than once. Ever. Why the hell are you working yourself to death in a place like that? Subjecting yourself to that kind of treatment from men who have no respect for you and treat you like an object. Who harass you, put their hands on you and disrespect you on a nightly basis."

She sighed, closing her eyes, but not before a single tear slipped down one pale cheek.

"I have to have that job," she choked out. "I'm not from here, the city I mean. As I'm sure you can tell. I come from a small town in the south. I've had to work my entire life. I had to drop out of high school and get my GED so I could work. College wasn't an option."

"Why?" he asked softly.

She went on as if she hadn't heard.

"My father worked in a local factory and was injured and disabled as a result. Workman's comp refused to pay, citing some ridiculous, trumped-up loophole that I still don't understand. But he couldn't work as a result. My mother also has health issues. My father was our only means of support. I could have gone to college," she said wistfully. "I was a good student. I qualified for an academic scholarship to a state university, before I had to drop out. But Mama and Papa needed me."

Drake's lips tightened as some of the pieces fell into place. It was suddenly making a lot more sense than it had a few minutes earlier.

"I was working two jobs at home and they were barely making it," she said, shame shadowing her gaze.

Most notably absent from her statement was how *she* had made it, because he already knew enough about her present circumstances to know that she would have given every penny to her parents, only keeping enough for her bare necessities. And they were very bare.

"Steph, one of my current roommates—she and my other roommates, we all went to high school together and we stayed in touch. They moved to the city. They wanted out of our small town. Wanted bigger and better. I don't blame them. But I had a responsibility," she said, her chin notching upward, fire entering her eyes. "My family is my only responsibility—my priority before all else. I will not fail them.

"Anyway, she called me and said they were a roommate short and they could get me a job making better money, good tips, and they had a small apartment that wouldn't break the bank with my share of the rent. So I moved up here and I send money back to my parents every week. I pay my portion of the rent, utilities and groceries, but every spare penny goes to my mother so she can care for my father."

Drake was growing angrier by the minute. His entire jaw ached because it was clamped shut against the tirade that was just waiting to be unleashed. He wanted to end this farce immediately and take over, but he needed to know what he was up against. Every single detail.

"When I can, I take extra shifts," she explained. "If I'm lucky, during the holidays, I can get seasonal part-time work, which enables me to send all of that extra to my mom."

"And in the meantime you work yourself to the bone. You go without. You put yourself in unimaginable danger, not to mention work a demeaning job where men assume your body is theirs to do with as they please."

Her gaze flew upward at the whiplike anger in his tone, and genuine puzzlement shone in her beautiful eyes.

"This shit is over," he bit out. "You need a keeper. Someone to take care of *you* for once in your life. You're moving in with me. You're finished working yourself to death in a place where men put their hands on you, maul you, say shit to you no man should *ever* say to another woman. Furthermore, your parents will have no financial worries any longer. And neither will you."

Her mouth gaped open and her gaze turned incredulous as she stared back at him as if to determine whether he was serious. He returned her gaze unflinchingly, telling her without words that he was serious as a heart attack.

"Are you crazy?" she shouted. "You can't just tell me I'm moving in with you like it's a foregone conclusion."

"It is," he said calmly.

"The hell it is! You're . . . you're out of your mind!" she sputtered, throwing her hands up like she wanted to yank her hair out with frustration. Then she shook her head adamantly. "You can't just keep me prisoner!"

He smiled and responded in a lazy drawl. "Can't I? But, Angel, I can assure you, as far as prisoners go? There will never exist a more pampered, spoiled and indulged captive. And I can guarantee you won't be trying to escape after you've had a taste of all I can give you. And just a warning, Angel. I give a lot. Everything. But I take every bit as much as I give."

"This is crazy," she whispered. "What exactly do I tell my friends? My girls? My family? I can't just disappear off the face of the earth. They'll go crazy. And I can't leave my roommates hanging. They can't afford the apartment without my share of the rent. I don't make much, but neither do they and it's a stretch to afford a two-bedroom even between four people."

"Your girls will be taken care of. Their rent will be paid so your absence won't cause them any hardship."

Her lips drew into a mutinous line. "No. I won't let you do that. You can't buy me. Or my friends. You aren't paying me for sex. God, that would make me a whore! A prostitute. How could I look at myself in the mirror every morning knowing I'm some man's plaything. A *paid* plaything."

He was getting pissed, and he made no effort to hide that from her. "I'm not paying for sex. I don't *ever* have to pay for sex. What I give to you, whatever I choose to give to you, are gifts. Gifts I expect you to accept and think of creative ways of expressing your gratitude. You're mine for as long as our arrangement lasts, and that puts your girls in a bind. And I'm responsible for that bind because I'm a selfish bastard who takes what he wants and won't accept no for an answer. So I'll cover their rent because me being selfish puts them in a bind, and I won't be responsible for three women losing their home because of my demands."

"Oh," she said softly. Then she shook her head. "This is insane. This sort of thing doesn't *happen*."

"In my world it does," he said, amusement in his voice.

"There is only one world," she snapped. "And we all live in the same world."

"And that is where I intend to prove you wrong, Angel. My world, my rules. I answer to no one, and no one fucks with me or what's mine."

"And is that what I am? Yours?"

"For the time being? Yes."

She looked instantly uneasy, her eyes worried and apprehensive.

"And what happens to me when you figure out I'm not all that and you don't want me anymore?" she asked quietly.

"You will always be taken care of, Angel. I'm not a complete bastard. If the day comes that we no longer are compatible, then you will be taken care of for the rest of your life. You needn't have any concerns that I'll cast you off and leave you to fend for yourself. That will never happen. You have my word on it."

Drake reached up to take one of her hands and gently pulled it down until it was completely encircled in his.

"You're a beautiful woman who deserves far more than what you're getting out of life, and I'm going to make you see that, no matter how long it takes. You're a woman any man would be on his knees to have. And you're as attracted to me as I'm attracted to you. I didn't imagine you coming all over my mouth last night."

Her face went beet red and she hastily averted her gaze, but he reached with his free hand to cup her chin, gently forcing her to face him once more.

"You were so fucking beautiful and so wild, and I want to be the man who gently brings you to heel. I want to be the man who takes care of you, the man you ultimately answer to, the man who controls you."

"Controls?" she asked incredulously. "Do you even know how obscene that sounds? No one controls me!"

"I do—I will. But you'll blossom under my care. Have no doubt there. There will not be a more spoiled, adored woman on this earth, because what is mine I take care of in all ways, and your happiness, your protection, your life comes before all else."

She looked at him in utter bewilderment. "Why would you do this for a woman like me? You could have any woman you wanted."

She broke off, blushing furiously, her eyes dropping in shame and God only knew what else. Fury rose inside him, and he was forced to loosen his grip on her hand or risk hurting her.

"Explain what you mean by a woman like you. And be careful how you word it, Angel, and how you say it, or I'm not going to be very happy with you."

She swept her hand down the length of her as if that explained it all. Then she sent him a helpless look that suggested she had no idea how to explain what in her mind was a very obvious fact.

"You have no reason to be ashamed or embarrassed," he said through clenched teeth. "And you will be neither with me, because that will not please me. Who you are, what you are, is what I *want*. Not your fucked-up idea of who and what I want. I know when I see something whether I want it or not, and I wanted you the minute you walked into my club. Your not believing me or thinking otherwise is bullshit. But you'll figure that out in your own time."

"There's no way I can ever pay you back," she said desperately. "I'll never be your equal. I'll never be able to pay back the kind of money you're talking about."

"That's where you're wrong," he said in a soft voice that made her shiver.

In that moment, she looked very much like prey being stalked, and he was the predator closing in on his prey. Hunted. He could deny none of those things when that was well what he was doing.

"Nothing is ever free," he continued, taking advantage of her momentary silence as she grappled with the things he had said and was saying. "The price is you. All of you. I'll own you. Every inch of you. I'm a man who is always in control of everything in my world. My world, my rules. And you have to play by my rules. I especially demand control when it comes to the women in my bed. Do you understand what I'm telling you?"

"N-no," she stammered out, clearly not understanding.

He swore softly. "Such a fucking innocent."

For a moment he simply trailed a finger down the line of her cheek and then brushed the pad of his thumb over the full curve of her lips. He could feel the sudden exhalation of her breaths as they sped up and the trembling increased. But it wasn't fear. She was aroused.

"Dominance, Angel. And your submission. Your complete and utter submission. In all things, but especially in my bed. You don't deny me anything. What I want, I take. What I choose to give, I give. You don't have a choice, and you don't get to tell me no. Ever."

"You're talking about rape!" she said in a horrified voice. "About taking my choices completely away from me!"

Drake scowled, allowing her to see how angry her response made him.

"Now you're just pissing me off. You'll be willing. I guarantee you'll love every single thing I choose to do to you. You'll beg me for more. You won't even think about saying no. When you step into my world, I own you. I possess you. There isn't a single inch of your beautiful skin that will go untouched, unworshipped. No part of you I won't fuck. You went up in flames on my desk, all laid out like a gift, and never once did you say no. You lit up the minute I touched you. You were wild, uninhibited, and you held nothing back."

Her eyes became dull, shame and embarrassment crowding into their depths.

"Goddamn it, Angel. You will not be ashamed of anything that occurred between you and me. Ever. You will not take something that fucking beautiful and twist it into something shameful and ugly.

"That motherfucker who did a number on you and made you feel like you were nothing was a fucking idiot. He had something that men would kill for and he pissed it away. He's an inept bastard who wouldn't know what to do with a woman. He's the inferior fuckwad and he knows it, so he lashes out to make himself more than the fucking coward he is. He gets off on belittling others so he can feel better about himself. He knows he's a piece of shit and the only way he can deal with that knowledge is to knock down everyone around him, especially women. It's a high to him because it's the only time he feels like anything other than the worthless piece of shit he and the rest of the world knows he is."

Evangeline's look turned to one of absolute wonder, her eyes filling with something that made Drake uncomfortable. She looked at him like he was some fucking hero, and that made him wince. He wasn't a hero. He wasn't a good man. He was a selfish bastard willing to go to any lengths to make this woman his.

"I don't know what to say," she whispered.

Drake inhaled, realizing he was about to do something he *never* did. *Ask.*

"Give me a chance, Angel," he murmured. "Give me the chance to prove to you all I've said. To do all I've said I will do. Will you at least agree to give me a chance?"

She studied him for a long moment, clear indecision warring with hope, fear and . . . curiosity. Finally, she closed her eyes, but when they reopened, resolve shone like a beacon.

"Yes," she replied softly. "I think I must be crazy, but yes. I'll give you a chance."

"Us," he corrected. "You're giving *us* a chance."

But there was still an air of hesitancy about her, as if she regretted her impulsive response, and Drake knew he had to get her out of here and to his apartment fast.

Before she came to her senses and ran like hell.

9

Drake was no fool, nor did he feel an ounce of remorse for hustling Evangeline out of Impulse and into his waiting car before she had time to second-guess her hesitant acquiescence. He had also issued a sharp command to his driver to get them to his apartment building with no delay, an order Brady immediately complied with, and to Drake's immense satisfaction, the car pulled to the front of the skyscraper housing his penthouse apartment in record time.

Evangeline had sat beside him, motionless and quiet, seemingly frozen in place. Her eyes were wide, almost as if she were struggling to take it all in. Or perhaps she was just coming to grips with the enormity of her decision. Not that he'd given her much in the way of an option. His request was hardly worded as one.

But again, he hadn't become successful in business—or in personal matters—by hesitating when an opportunity presented itself. When— not if—Evangeline gathered her shaken senses, he wanted it to be on his turf. Where she couldn't run from him. No escape. He couldn't very well pull out every weapon of persuasion in his arsenal if he was persuading thin air. Which was where she would have vanished if he hadn't taken swift advantage of her shock and momentary loss of her wits.

If that made him a bastard . . . Well, he'd certainly been called—and for that matter, was—a hell of a lot worse. In the end, what mattered was that he got what he wanted.

Evangeline. Angel. His angel.

In his apartment. His bed. Under his firm hand and protection. For as long as he wished her to be there.

For the first time, he hadn't already put a finite time on a liaison. Hell, he wasn't even considering this anything so casual. The days of one-night stands, or even the occasional weekend when he kept the same woman and sated his desires until Monday morning when his work-week began, and the rare weekend he took off, were over.

All he knew was that she was here. With him. About to enter his home. A place he never took a woman—any woman—and he had no intention of letting her go any time soon.

He frowned, uncertain of what to make of that particular revelation. For the time being, he shoved it firmly away and compartmentalized it in his mind to reflect on later. Much later. After Evangeline was taken care of and the matter of their relationship settled.

He opened the door, reaching for Evangeline's hand, even knowing she couldn't open the opposing door into the street. She didn't resist when he stepped onto the sidewalk, carefully pulling her with him. He anchored his arm around her waist as she too stepped from the car, and he ushered her quickly to the entrance and into the lobby where the elevator doors had already been opened by the doorman who worked the night shift.

The doorman courteously extended his arm toward the inside of the elevator and murmured a respectful, "Good night, Mr. Donovan." But Drake didn't miss the quick lift of one eyebrow as the doorman's gaze swept over Evangeline huddled against Drake.

Drake sent him an icy look that had the man retreating as Drake inserted his key card for his floor. He was well aware of the doorman's surprise, given that Drake never brought women to his home, but the man should have had more discipline than to allow his thoughts to be broadcast through his body language.

As the elevator began its ascent, Evangeline wobbled slightly against him, and he silently cursed those damn shoes he'd been forced to put back on her swollen feet. Then he simply bent and wrapped his fingers around one delicate ankle, ignoring her gasp of surprise as he lifted first one foot to remove the offending heel and then the other. She was forced to hold on to his arm to maintain her balance.

When she reached to take them, he simply shoved them underneath his other arm before once more curling his free arm around her waist, solidly anchoring her back to him.

"You won't be working in these again," he said bluntly. "You won't be working at all. The only time you'll be wearing heels is if you're out with me or I want to fuck you in them."

She stiffened and her eyes sparked when she tilted her head up so their gazes met. She opened her mouth but the elevator stopped, the doors opening immediately, and Drake took advantage by pulling her forward and into his foyer.

They had walked only a few steps when Evangeline abruptly halted. He glanced down, bracing for the inevitable protest, the regaining of her senses, or perhaps she'd finally figured out exactly what she wanted to say but had been too overwhelmed to do so before. But she merely stared wide-eyed, not at him. She wasn't paying him the slightest bit of attention.

Her gaze swept the sprawling, spacious open-concept apartment, a dazed expression on her face. And then she finally swung it up to meet his, puzzlement and awe swirling in her eyes.

"This is your apartment?" she barely managed to whisper. "I didn't think they made apartments this large in New York."

He wanted to kick himself in the head. His wanting to get her to his apartment as quickly as possible was because he didn't want her too overwhelmed. If anything, seeing and being in his apartment had tipped her the rest of the way off the ledge.

Not knowing what else to do or say at just that moment, he started to pull her into the shelter of his arms to offer her comfort, but just as his fingertips brushed over her arms to take hold, his intercom buzzed.

Evangeline jumped and turned as though she expected someone to be behind her. Drake, however, was pissed.

He strode the few steps to the wall where the speaker was mounted and slammed his thumb over the button.

"What?" he barked.

There was a slight hesitation, and then Thane's voice bled into the room.

"Uh, Drake? You might want to come down here. We have a situation."

"What situation?" Drake asked in an icy tone. "I distinctly left orders with all my men that under no circumstances was I to be disturbed."

Thane sighed loudly. "This woman showed up at the club right after you left and demanded to see you. She then said that if I didn't produce you immediately, she was calling the cops. I brought her here so whatever burr she has up her ass can be removed and we don't incur unnecessary trouble."

There was another slight pause as Drake mentally ran through every curse word in his dictionary. And then some.

"And Drake, it might be a good idea to bring Evangeline with you."

Before Drake could respond to that absurdity, a screech blasted through the intercom that made him wince.

"Damn right Evangeline better be with him so I can see for myself she's okay, or swear to God, I'll call the cops and report Drake Donovan for kidnapping and I'll tear this whole damn building apart to find her if I have to."

Evangeline let out a sound of dismay, and Drake turned to see her stricken, mortified expression. She closed her eyes but bristled with humiliation, which made Drake want to put his fist through the wall. This was not how things were supposed to have gone, and this wasn't going to do anything to settle Evangeline's fears.

When Evangeline opened her eyes, Drake lifted one eyebrow in question. She promptly sagged like a deflating balloon. She covered her face with both hands as if wishing to be anywhere but where she was. Drake could already feel Evangeline slipping from his grasp, and something akin to panic skated up his spine. He never panicked. Nor did he fear. What would be, would be. And yet he found himself holding his breath in dread.

"It's Steph," she said quietly as she let her hands slide slowly from her eyes. "She's one of my roommates. And Drake, she's serious. You don't know her. She will absolutely call the police and God only knows who else. I have to go down there."

"Not without me," Drake said, his tone carrying a bite he hadn't intended.

He shoved the button on the intercom.

"Sit on her, Thane. I'm coming down with Evangeline and by God, *Steph* better be there when we arrive."

He turned to Evangeline and extended his hand, waiting for her to slide her much smaller hand over his. He experienced a fierce sense of satisfaction when her flesh met his, but as his grip tightened in preparation to take her into the elevator, he could feel her trembling.

Doing his best not to frown and scare her to death, he instead pulled her close to him and slid his knuckle under her chin, gently nudging it upward.

"You aren't alone, Angel," he murmured. "I'll be with you the entire time. You just have to inform your friend of your choice."

Left unsaid was that he too would have to be informed of her choice because he was no longer certain she would choose him. Her friend might very well coax Evangeline away. His jaw tightened just thinking about the possibility. Under no circumstances would he let her go. She was worth fighting for.

With that in mind, he sent her a questioning look. She correctly interpreted the silent question as to whether she was ready, and she nodded. Drake pulled her to his side, tucking her beneath his shoulder as they entered the elevator.

The ride down was silent, and Evangeline's gaze remained fixed on the floor the entire time.

Damn it! He just needed time. A few days. So he could show Evangeline the world she was entering. Instead, as soon as they'd walked inside his home, her friend had arrived, effectively dragging Evangeline crashing back to earth.

As soon as they exited the elevator, Drake saw a very determined-looking redhead stalk forward, Thane behind her looking pissed. Well, that made two of them.

"Evangeline, thank God," Steph said as she barreled toward them.

To Drake's surprise, Evangeline nestled closer to his body as if seeking comfort or support.

"To what do we owe this interruption at this hour?" Drake demanded.

Steph's eyes narrowed. "I had to make sure Evangeline was okay. When she didn't come home, we thought something horrible had happened."

"Well, as you can see, she's just fine," he drawled. "Now if you'll excuse us, it's been a long day."

Steph's frown deepened and her eyes shot daggers at him.

"Evangeline is perfectly capable of speaking for herself," she said acidly. "I'd like to know what she wants. Preferably from her."

Drake felt Evangeline stiffen, her features drawn in mortification. Shame dulled her eyes, no hint of the vibrancy that made staring at her so entrancing. He swore viciously under his breath and started to put an end to this shit right now, but Evangeline drew in a deep breath and stepped from the protective refuge of his body.

His pulse ratcheted up and he had to fight to maintain an air of indifference. He'd never allow anyone to see his pain if she left with her friend.

"As you can see, I'm fine, Steph," Evangeline said in a soft voice. "I'm sorry to have worried you, but I did call you and left a voice mail saying I wouldn't be home tonight. I texted you, Nikki and Lana, as well. And then Drake sent Maddox over to personally reassure you that I was okay."

"Yeah, a hired goon who looks like he just got out of Rikers," Steph said, anger still seething in her voice.

Evangeline's earlier look of shame and defeat evaporated and her spine went rigid. She stared back at Steph, her gaze unflinching as her face flushed. But not in embarrassment. No, his angel was pissed.

He fought to hide his reaction—his surprise—and forced himself to remain a bystander and allow Evangeline to fight her own battle unless it became apparent she was backing down. She further surprised him by walking up to Steph and getting right in her face so there was no possibility of misunderstanding. She pointed her finger directly into Steph's chest, eliciting a look of complete shock on her friend's face as if Evangeline had never stood up to her—or any of her so-called friends.

"You will *not* talk about Maddox that way," Evangeline snapped. "He has been nothing but kind and patient with me. He intervened at Impulse when Eddie would have likely put me in the hospital. He was kind, respectful and gentle. He took me home, made certain the apartment was safe and told me he would be there the next night at seven because Drake wanted to see me. But I had to work and so Maddox waited for me at the pub until I got off and drove me to Impulse to meet Drake, where we agreed on a personal matter that will *remain* personal. You have no right to judge Maddox or Drake or Thane, for that matter, who went out of his way to let you know I was okay, when you know nothing about them. And furthermore, you are clearly questioning my judgment. My wants and my needs, which I remind you, are my concern. Not yours. I don't tell you how to run your life, Steph, and I expect that same respect in return."

Her hand swept toward Thane, who was wearing a look of shock mixed with approval. Pride even. Thane lifted his gaze to Drake as if to say, *You picked a good one.* Drake merely nodded his agreement.

"And Steph. You showed up at Impulse after being told I was fine and what my plans were for the night and threatened Thane unless he brought you to wherever Drake and I were. Has he hurt you? Has he threatened you in any way? Because the way I see it, he has treated you with far more respect than you've afforded him. I expected more from you, Steph. I expected your faith and trust in me to make my own decisions. I don't need your, Lana's or Nikki's approval or permission to do anything. I don't interfere in your personal lives, and yet you interfere with mine at every turn. And just to remind you, I never wanted to go to Impulse. It was the last place I wanted to go, but the three of you railroaded me into going, and the result was a night of humiliation I'll never be able to forget."

She shuddered and clasped her hands over her upper arms as if she were suddenly cold. Drake could contain himself no longer. He stepped forward and wrapped her securely in his arm, replacing her hand on the arm facing away from his body and rubbed up and down both for warmth and comfort. And to let her know he had her back.

Thane looked completely bewildered and discomfited by Evangeline's defense of him and Maddox. There was a different look to his eyes when he gazed at Evangeline now. One that held a glimmer of respect, and Thane didn't respect many people.

Drake's admiration grew even more because he'd been right, or rather his gut instinct about his angel had been dead-on. Her sweet, soft, delicate feminine appearance, in fact, disguised a woman with an iron will and determination that wouldn't allow anyone, even himself, to run over her. No matter that she thought the opposite. She clearly thought she was timid and weak and hated conflict, and she likely did. But it didn't mean she couldn't hold her own and stand up for what she thought was right. His arm tightened around her, giving her a gentle squeeze of approval as pride settled over him. As did peace. He'd chosen well. He hadn't been wrong about her at all.

Steph looked taken aback, her mouth falling open at Evangeline's outburst. She glanced between Thane and Drake like she was sizing up two serial killers. Then her gaze drifted back to Evangeline, clear disbelief reflected on her face. Before she had time to respond to Evangeline's blunt, impassioned statement, Evangeline pressed while she had the advantage.

"I'm fine, Steph. You were told I wouldn't be home tonight or today or whatever it is. There was no reason for you to come here and cause a scene. I'll call you, Lana and Nikki in the next day or two and explain everything. Until then, I would appreciate privacy and no more embarrassing scenes at this hour of the morning."

Steph pinned Evangeline with a ferocious stare, one Drake imagined worked to intimidate Evangeline most of the time. Only this time, his angel didn't seem in the least fazed.

"You better do just that," Steph snapped. "Because if I don't hear from you personally in the next *twenty-four* hours, I'm coming back with the police."

Then she shifted her furious stare at Drake, who merely looked at her as though she were a nuisance.

"There isn't a place in this damn city you can hide from me, and so help me God, if you hurt Evangeline in any way, I'll cut off your balls and make you eat them."

"Since that's not ever going to happen, your threat is completely hollow," Drake said in a dismissive tone. One that said it was time for her to leave. Now.

He lifted his gaze to Thane and sent him a silent look of apology. Thane mouthed his words but Drake could clearly see what he'd said and only barely managed to hold back his laughter.

Thane had said *Fuck me*.

"Thane will see you home now," Drake said in a formal voice, remaining cold and aloof toward the woman who'd nearly ruined the entire evening. For that matter, she might well have for all he knew, because he had no idea what was going on in Evangeline's mind.

Not waiting for any more drama or theatrics, Drake drew Evangeline to his side and guided her back to the elevator. Her eyes were closed the entire way up, her features still frozen with mortification.

He gently escorted her into his apartment, this time giving her no time to ponder the size and elegance of it. He ushered her into the bedroom and she immediately began to tremble against him.

Something went soft inside his heart. It was an alien, uncomfortable feeling. One he was not used to at all.

But she looked exhausted, lost and so confused that all he could do was pull her into his arms as he'd wanted to do before they were interrupted by her roommate. At first she was tense against him, but as he did nothing more than hold her against him and stroke a hand through her hair in a soothing motion, her own arms crept around his waist and she relaxed.

She laid her cheek against his chest and he felt her soft sigh all the way to his bones. It was a sound that would make a man do anything to make this woman happy.

"Get ready for bed, Angel," he said gruffly. "You're tired, your feet hurt and you've had a very long couple of days. The thing you need most right now is sleep. However, you sleep with me, in my bed. Every night. No exception."

Slowly she nodded, her cheek rubbing up and down his chest.

"Don't get me wrong, Angel," he murmured. "There's nothing I'd love more than to make love to you all night so that when you wake up you'll know exactly who you belong to. But you're dead on your feet, and for now, just having you in my bed, in my arms, is more than I could have dreamed of."

When Evangeline awoke, two things immediately registered. One, Drake was no longer in bed with her and two, it was well into the morning. Likely approaching noon and yet exhaustion still weighed her down and all she wanted to do was snuggle deeper into the covers and go back to sleep.

As she shifted to a more comfortable spot, turning to where Drake had slept, her hand instinctively reaching for any lingering warmth or evidence that it hadn't been a dream, her gaze lit on a folded piece of paper with her name scrawled across it.

Forcing herself to a sitting position, she crossed her legs and reached for the note, hesitantly opening it, unsure of what it would say. Then her brow furrowed as she took in the contents.

Your things are in the living room to put wherever you like. But just so you are aware, only your personal keepsakes and mementos were brought over. Your clothing, shoes and accessories were thrown out. One of my men will be there waiting to take you shopping for anything you require, and I expect you to buy everything you need. My man will have a list of the necessary accoutrements, and the salespeople at the shops you will be escorted to have already been given my instructions as well as your

measurements and will have appropriate selections for your viewing
when you arrive.

Her measurements? And for that matter what was wrong with her clothes? Why would he just throw them out without even consulting her? How wasteful was that? The clothes certainly weren't expensive by his standards, but she'd had to save to buy each and every item and she'd never been able to go and buy an entire wardrobe or anything. She bought a pair of jeans or a T-shirt or a pair of shoes. When she had the means to do so. Sending money to her parents was her first priority. Her comfort was a far second on her list. It stung that he'd so thoughtlessly discarded clothing that she'd worked damn hard for. So what if they were bought in a thrift shop or on the clearance rack of a bargain shopping center? She'd paid for every single thing with her own money. No one had given her anything and she took pride in that. Never once did one of her roommates have to cover her share of the rent, because she made sure that after sending money to her family, she had enough to cover her part of their living arrangement and pitch in on groceries. She also did most of the cooking so they didn't spend money eating out, which meant she saved more money for the necessities. Drake was obviously ashamed of her, and that ate at her. She had her pride. She knew she wasn't anything to look at, and she still couldn't fathom what she was doing here in his apartment with instructions to go shopping for an entire new wardrobe where one outfit would likely cost more than all the things Drake had so blithely tossed out.

She felt . . . humiliated.

She jumped, her pulse accelerating when a phone rang next to her on the bed. She glanced warily, looking for the source, to see an expensive high-tech cell phone that would take her a year to save for and was definitely a frivolous expenditure. She glanced back at the note to read further and saw that Drake had informed her the phone was hers and that he would be calling her later in the morning.

She tentatively picked up the phone, hoping she was hitting the right button, and murmured a hesitant hello. His answer was crisp, businesslike.

"Justice is on his way. He may already be there. He's taking you shopping."

She felt an unexpected sense of disappointment that it wasn't Maddox. He had been the nicest to her and wasn't quite as intimidating as some of the other men Drake worked with. And then she shook her head because she was crazy. They were all dangerous and complete strangers to her, and yet she was to trust them because Drake instructed her to.

She hesitated and bit into her bottom lip, bothered that she was even required to go on a shopping trip. If she wasn't good enough for him as she was, then she sure as hell wasn't going to change everything about her just so she met his standards. Whatever the hell they were since he hadn't exactly been forthcoming on those yet.

He seemed to pick up on her sudden silence, and she wondered if she should add mind reading to his growing list of accomplishments, though it appeared as though there was nothing he couldn't do or accomplish. But then money, or rather having money, lots of money, seemed to come with a completely different set of rules and parameters that favored the "haves" over the "have-nots."

"What's wrong, Angel?" he asked in a soft voice that suggested he would not be pleased nor would he believe her if she simply said nothing or pretended that he was imagining things. It would be an insult to his superior intelligence.

She flinched, not wanting to get into what was bothering her.

In a subdued, quiet voice she responded. "Why did you throw away all my clothing, even my underwear and my shoes? If I'm not good enough for you the way I am, then why would you want to change me into something I'm not? It wouldn't be real. Unless that's what you want and any woman would do. A woman you play dress-up with like a doll and make her 'good enough' to be seen with you. I'm proud of who and what I am," she said fiercely. "I paid for every single item of clothing you thoughtlessly threw away. I liked them. More importantly, nobody bought them for me or gave them to me. I worked for everything I have and by throwing practically everything I own away you sent the message loud and clear that I'm not good enough, and you're sending one of your minions shopping with me so I don't embarrass you in front of others."

The line went silent, and she tensed because she could practically feel his seething anger through the phone. She swallowed nervously and closed her eyes, thinking that maybe he would be just pissed off enough to wash his hands of her now and let her go back home.

Instead, he sighed, and she imagined him running an agitated hand through his hair, his lips set into that firm grimace that made him look so intimidating.

"Angel, the clothes you have are shit. Now don't get me wrong. You being you and as beautiful as you are, you rock that look. But other women would never be able to pull off your kind of shine in shit clothing. This has nothing to do with you embarrassing me, and it sure as fuck has nothing to do with you not being good enough for me. It has everything to do with the fact that you're mine now and I take care of what belongs to me. Which means that what you wear, the shoes, the jeans or dresses, and especially the underwear, I pay for. I wanted to do something nice for you and you need nicer clothing, not shit you had to walk into a fucking charity shop to buy. My woman will never wear anything that's been worn by another woman. Period. So get that fucked-up shit about you not being good enough or you embarrassing me out of your head right now or you're just going to piss me off. Because it's complete bullshit and I won't have you thinking it every time you put on something I bought for you."

Evangeline was stunned into silence and sat on the edge of the bed, mouth gaping open. This time, however, he didn't take her silence as her being upset or angry, as he'd picked up on her earlier silence. How the hell could the man tell when he needed to address something when he wasn't even within a mile of her, much less able to see her or gauge her body language or facial expressions?

"I've got to go now. I have an important meeting. Justice should be there soon if he's not already, so you might want to make yourself presentable because I'll be damned if another man sees what's mine and mine alone to see. He's going to take you to eat and then shopping. I don't want you hungry."

And she thought she couldn't get more flustered than she already was.

"I need to know you get me," Drake said impatiently. "The words, Angel. Give me your acceptance."

"All right," she finally said in a near whisper.

"Good." And she could hear the satisfaction in his voice. "Now get a move on and get dressed so Justice doesn't see what he shouldn't and then I have to beat his ass."

She thought he'd already hung up when his last statement came through.

"And, Angel, just so you know, I will not be pleased if you refuse to accept any of the items I have arranged for you."

Slowly she ended the call and let the phone fall to the bed, then glanced back at the note that she still hadn't finished reading. She started at the beginning again, quickly skimming to the parts she hadn't yet read. At the very bottom, in Drake's distinctive scrawl, was written:

And call your girls and give them your new number so I don't have to have my men haul one or all their asses out of my apartment again at five in the morning.

She laughed and then drew her knees up, hugging them to her body as she looked around in wonder. Was this really happening to her? How on earth had she fallen down the proverbial rabbit hole into an alternate reality?

She shook off the overwhelming sensation that she was fast spinning out of control and called Steph first, because the last thing Evangeline wanted was for the police to burst into Drake's apartment determined to rescue a kidnapped woman. To her relief, all three girls were at the apartment together, so they put her on speakerphone, which meant she wouldn't have to tell the same crazy story three times.

In as level a tone as she could manage, she outlined the events ending with her coming back to Drake's apartment with him. Their reactions were explosive.

"Have you lost your mind?" Nikki squeaked. "Vangie, what do you even know about this guy? What if you go missing and we never hear from you again?"

Evangeline sighed. "Is it too much to ask for a little trust from my best friends?"

"We just think you should give this a little more time, preferably away from him where you're not overwhelmed," Lana said diplomatically. "You have to admit, this is awfully sudden and completely out of character for you."

"Yeah well, so was going to Impulse, but y'all didn't mind coercing me into that," Evangeline snapped.

Until now Steph had been silent, and that should have told Evangeline the worst was to come.

"And how long do you think it'll take this Drake guy to get tired of you and scrape you off? What the hell are you going to do then, Vangie? You can't let yourself be solely dependent on any man, and especially not one with his kind of power."

Hurt splintered through Evangeline's heart, and her sudden intake of breath had to have been heard over the phone, judging by the ensuing silence. But what bothered Evangeline even more was that Steph had scored a direct hit and nipped at an already blooming insecurity over just how long this thing with Drake would last.

"That was uncalled for, Steph," Lana said angrily. "You're acting like a jealous bitch and it's not very attractive on you. Leave Vangie alone. As long as we've known her she's never done a single thing for herself. Maybe it's high time she did, and lived a little."

"I need to go," Evangeline said quietly. "I have to be dressed and ready to go in ten minutes."

"Wait, Vangie, before you go," Nikki said in a rushed tone. "The landlord came by this morning to give us a receipt and a rent-controlled contract. The rent has been paid in advance for two years, with a contract guaranteeing no increase in rent for the next ten. How insane is that?"

"Drake didn't want my leaving to cause you financial problems," Evangeline said quietly. "Lucky for y'all, after he shakes me off, you'll still have a rent-free place to live and a guarantee of no increase for a long time."

Then she quickly ended the call, still bothered by Steph's comment.

Evangeline was so out of her element that she wanted to crawl into the nearest hole and die. She was hopelessly gauche and while Justice, her babysitter du jour, seemed rough around the edges, he certainly knew his way around upscale shops, either choosing or discarding appropriate items with ease.

After the first time Evangeline had reached out to touch a shimmering dress right out of Cinderella's ball and felt the sumptuous material between her fingertips, she'd been in love. Until she looked at the price tag and yanked her hand away as if it had burned her. Oh good God. Was everything in this place so exorbitantly expensive? One dress cost more than she made in a year!

She turned away, her bottom lip between her teeth in consternation. She didn't belong here. This wasn't her world. She didn't fit and she was fooling herself if for a minute she thought she could become a part of it, if only for a little while.

Justice, however, saw her reaction to the dress and made eye contact with the saleslady, who was only too happy to wrap it and add it to the growing pile of purchases Justice was arranging for Evangeline.

At first he'd wondered just what in the hell he'd done to piss Drake off that he had drawn women's shopping duty with a woman who didn't seem to want or need anything. Hell, it wasn't as if he hadn't been wrangled into shopping with and for one of Drake's women in the past, but all he'd had to do was stand back and watch the woman march through the store pointing indiscriminately, leaving Justice to pay the bill, and it was all over in a matter of minutes.

But Evangeline? She seemed absolutely mortified and horrified, especially after she'd looked at the price tag of the dress she'd looked at so longingly, caressing the silk material. For God's sake, it wasn't even one of the more expensive dresses in the shop, which was why he was glad Drake had called ahead with a detailed list of what he wanted the salesperson to have already out and ready for purchase. Evangeline would likely have a stroke if she caught sight of the prices of *those* dresses.

He sighed because this had the look of being one long-ass day, and shopping for women's clothing was like a trip to hell. The things he did for the man he called partner and brother. But he couldn't quite summon irritation at Evangeline because there was something different about her. Never before had Drake taken a woman like this, nor had he acted so forbiddingly possessive from the very first moment he'd laid eyes on her.

And in a way, Justice could see why. There was something about Evangeline, and it took him a while to put his finger on it, but when it hit he realized it immediately. This was no calculating, mercenary woman out to fleece Drake for all she could get in the short time he'd keep her around.

Evangeline was innocent, naïve, sweet to her bones and as genuine as they came. She had a gentle disposition and from all he'd heard from Thane, she was loyal and ferocious in her defense of others, even those she didn't know. She'd dressed her friend down over her disdain of Maddox and Thane, which upped his respect for her tenfold. Women like her did not defend men like him. Especially to their best friends.

But according to Thane, she'd acted like a lioness protecting her cubs and had been furious at the judgment levied against Maddox and Thane by her friend, and she'd taken her down several notches and let her know in no uncertain terms what she thought of her opinion.

It was hard not to respect a sweet, gentle woman who looked like she could be easily intimidated and yet breathed fire when defending people she felt were being unfairly judged.

Justice hadn't been impressed with the women Drake associated with in the past but had never concerned himself over the matter because he never kept a woman more than a few days at most, but Evangeline seemed to be, from all appearances, someone Drake intended to keep around for far longer. Never had he outfitted one of his women from head to toe. He normally gave them an expensive gift—usually jewelry—and then sent them on their way. Justice felt an unfamiliar protective instinct arising in his chest, tightening to the point of discomfort at the idea of Drake callously discarding her when he tired of her. If the man couldn't tell the difference between Evangeline and the bitches he'd hooked up with in the past, then he was a stupid bastard, and if Drake tossed her, the thought crossed Justice's mind that he would be more than willing to step in and give her the respect and care she deserved.

He'd taken her to one of his favorite restaurants before embarking on the shopping trip, and she'd seemed as uncomfortable in the expensive eatery as she did in the upscale designer shops. She'd studied the menu for several long minutes, concentrating so hard he thought her head might burst. When he realized she'd chosen the most inexpensive item on the menu, he'd ignored her request and ordered her a Wagyu steak. She'd immediately squeaked in horror and whispered that it cost two hundred dollars! For a steak! He'd merely smiled and told the waiter to serve him the same and then asked Evangeline how she liked her steak cooked. She looked so befuddled and appalled at the price that he'd gone the middle road and ordered medium for her and medium rare for himself.

When the meals arrived, she'd stared at the small steak, shaking her head in disbelief.

"Just try it," Justice coaxed. "It melts in your mouth. Best steak you'll ever taste. Guaranteed."

"Two hundred dollars good?" she asked skeptically. "Two hundred dollars more than feeds me and my roommates for an entire month."

He'd just grinned at her and cut into his own steak, silently observing her as she gingerly cut a small piece almost reverently as if she hated the idea of consuming something that was exorbitant—to her—in price. But when she'd delicately chewed that first bite, her eyes closed and a low moan escaped her lips that had him clenching his jaw, his own steak forgotten as he watched the sheer enjoyment on her face.

"Oh my God," she said with a groan. "This is amazing."

"Told you," he said smugly.

"It's still not two hundred dollars amazing," she muttered.

He merely grinned and resumed eating his steak, barely tasting it, which was a crime in itself because he was too absorbed in watching Evangeline's first experience with the decadent beef.

After they'd finished, he'd announced they were going shopping, something that would delight most women. Certainly all of Drake's previous women. Evangeline, however, had looked as if she'd just been told she had to clean toilets.

Now, they were nearly done. Only one more destination.

He nearly grinned when she realized their next stop was a lingerie store. And not just any lingerie store. One that dealt with decadent, sexy, alluring garments meant to drive men insane with lust.

Her cheeks flamed bright red and she turned pleading eyes to Justice, and he had to rub his chest to alleviate the discomfort over her obvious embarrassment.

"You can wait outside," she whispered. "It's not necessary that you be here. Drake has arranged an assortment of stuff in every other store we've visited, so I doubt this will be any different."

And then she promptly blushed, likely realizing that Drake had called and given the saleslady what he wanted in exacting detail, and Evangeline would have to face the woman knowing that Drake had been explicit in his wishes.

He smiled gently at her and palmed her shoulders. "Sweetheart, there's no reason to be embarrassed. You're right in that there is a pile of stuff waiting at the counter, and I tell you what. I'll go to the counter and wait while you look around and see if there's anything that catches your eye. Bring whatever you pick out to the checkout and I promise not to give it a single glance. I'll pay for it and then turn my back. But I can't leave you in the store alone. Drake would have my balls for leaving you unprotected for one moment. He wants me with you at all times."

Her flush deepened to the roots of her hair, and his heart softened when he thought he was incapable of such a feat. He briefly touched her cheek.

"You don't have to be ashamed with me, Evangeline. You have nothing to be ashamed of. I'd like to consider us friends."

He nearly choked on the words. *Friends?* Now he was *certain* he was losing his goddamn mind. He had no friends, save the men he called brothers, and he damn sure didn't consider women of any kind friends. He either wrote them off as grasping bitches, or he took them to bed and made damn sure they both had a good time. And now he was spouting bullshit about platonic friendship with a woman most men would have had in their bed before she could blink. Drake owed him. Big.

"Now go do your shopping while I have the saleslady package what Drake has already arranged, and as I promised, when you are finished, I'll give the saleslady the credit card and turn my back. All I will do is carry the bags to the car. No peeking. I promise!"

She gifted him with a smile that momentarily robbed him of breath, and suddenly he could see even more why Drake was so fascinated with this woman. She was the real deal. A rarity in the circles they traveled. Not a fake bone in her body. He was stunned by that revelation and not at all sure what to do about it. An unfamiliar emotion—jealousy—tightened his chest, and he swore violently to himself. Damn Drake and his luck to have found this one before any of the other men who ran Impulse with him.

He watched as she hesitantly browsed the racks, watching closely for the items that she paid extra attention to only to hastily drop when she looked at the price tag. He sent the saleslady a pointed look, and when Evangeline went to the next area, the saleslady promptly collected the items Evangeline had favored but had not chosen because of the price.

To the saleslady's credit, she bagged the things Evangeline had hastily put back so she didn't know they'd been purchased and then rang up the total, sliding the ticket in Justice's direction. Once finished, Justice collected all the bags and escorted Evangeline out to the waiting car.

"Are we finished?" she asked in a wary tone.

He smiled. "Yeah, sweetheart. I'm taking you home now."

He ushered her into the car and then walked around to the street side and slid into the backseat next to her. As they glided into traffic, she aimed her gaze out the window, seemingly fascinated with the city, almost as though she'd never been to New York. Her reaction seemed odd for someone who lived and worked here.

As if sensing his scrutiny, she glanced his way self-consciously and gave him a small smile.

"I never get used to it," she confessed, her hand fluttering toward the window. "I'm not sure I ever will."

"What?" Justice asked curiously.

"All the hustle and bustle. The people. The skyscrapers. All the businesses and cars, the buildings stacked on top of one another. It reminds me of the anthills we had back home when they get stirred up and all the ants run everywhere."

He laughed, noting the southern drawl he found charming.

"Where are you from, Evangeline?"

"Mississippi," she said in a wistful tone.

"And what brought you to the city?"

Pain flashed in her eyes, making him instantly regret having asked a seemingly benign question. She turned her gaze back to the passing scenery as honks and the sounds of traffic blared in the background.

"I needed to make more money to help my parents," she said simply.

The way she said it indicated the subject wasn't open to further discussion, so he didn't press, though now he was curious as to why she would have moved to New York because her parents needed money.

From what he knew of her, she worked late shifts in a bar in Queens. Surely there were better jobs to be had in Mississippi. And the way she'd spoken of the city in comparison to her home, she sounded very much like she was homesick and unhappy here.

He frowned, wanting to query Drake about her situation, but Drake wouldn't take well to that at all. Not that Drake would ever think one of his brothers would poach on his territory, but what was Drake's was Drake's and he kept what was his to himself. Hell, they were all like that. Maybe it was why the group of men who worked with and for Drake had such a strong bond. They had too much in common and understood one another's needs. Privacy being uppermost. And not being questioned and especially not answering to anyone except one another. It was an arrangement that worked well and was extremely profitable.

A sudden thought occurred to him. If Evangeline knew everything about Drake's "business matters," she'd likely bolt like a bat out of hell. His previous women didn't give a shit as long as they got what they wanted out of the arrangement. Evangeline, on the other hand, didn't appear to him to be a woman who could be bought. She was too honest and he couldn't imagine her looking the other way on any unlawful activity.

The very qualities that put her miles above any other woman Drake had ever taken could well be what made him lose her. But then, Drake's track record suggested Evangeline wouldn't be around that long. Longer than the others, Justice was confident of that. But likely not long enough to ever have a clue about the things Drake—and the rest of them—dealt in. And she certainly wouldn't condone their brand of justice. Hell, if she knew her ex-boyfriend was even now recovering from a well-deserved ass kicking, she'd be horrified, no matter how much she hated the bastard.

Justice sighed. Drake had stepped in it this time. Evangeline just wasn't like the other women, and that was going to cause Drake a lot of trouble. Provided he kept her long enough for it to become an issue.

Evangeline kept casting furtive looks in Justice's direction. He didn't turn to face her, not wanting to cause awkwardness. Instead he continued to study her from his periphery. Several times, she inhaled and opened her mouth only to promptly shut it and turn back to the window.

She obviously wanted to ask or say something but was too shy to do so. Why he found that so charming, he had no idea, but at the same time, the thought of her being afraid of him didn't sit well at all. And that thought was even more ludicrous because he, like his brothers, cultivated healthy fear and respect from others. But the idea of Drake's woman being afraid to say something to him? It turned his stomach.

"Evangeline?"

She whirled her head around guiltily and met his gaze a split second before lowering her lashes and nervously fixing her stare on the space between them on the seat.

Impulsively, he reached over and covered her hand with his, feeling her jump beneath his touch. Controlling his frown, he squeezed comfortingly.

"Look at me, Evangeline."

Though it was a command, his voice was soft and encouraging.

Cautiously she raised her chin so that her deep blue eyes fringed in dark eyelashes met his.

"There something you want to ask me? I don't bite. Well, unless you ask me politely," he finished with a grin.

She blinked, startled by the teasing remark, and then to his surprise she burst out laughing.

Dear God, in that moment he was so fucking envious of Drake that he was tempted to instruct the driver to take them to his place, and he'd do his best to make her forget all about Drake Donovan. He'd just tell Drake that the lady changed her mind. He mentally smacked himself on the head and shut down that train of thought. Drake was his brother, as were all the men closest to him. But . . . If Drake stayed true to form and this was a short-lived affair, then Justice would be waiting. Although something told him Evangeline was going to be a game changer for Drake. Whether he knew it or not.

"Evangeline?" he prompted when she remained quiet, though her eyes still sparkled with mirth.

"Uh, Mr. . . ."

She looked to him in sudden confusion.

"Justice," he said gently. "My name is Justice. No Mister. I imagine we'll be seeing one another frequently, so there's no need for formality."

She seemed to ponder his statement, the laughter fading from her eyes, replaced by unease and confusion. This was a woman who had no idea of her place in Drake's life. Drake had better rectify that soon or she'd be gone in a flash.

"Um, Justice, then, what time will Mr. Donovan, I mean Drake, be home, I mean back to his apartment?"

Her uncertainty was killing him. Damn, but he wanted to hug her just to comfort and reassure her, but if he did that, there was no guarantee she'd ever get to Drake's apartment and then Drake would kill him. Or try.

He'd always adhered to the creed of a woman never coming between brothers, but at the moment he considered that some women might just be worth it. He mentally shook his head at the rueful thought and promptly stopped dwelling on what would never happen.

"Drake will be home at six and he doesn't want you to worry about dressing for dinner. He plans for the two of you to eat in tonight."

Panic flared in her eyes and she yanked her hand from him, putting it with her other one, squeezing in agitation. She bit into her bottom lip, her mind obviously going a mile a minute.

"I need to stop at the nearest market," she blurted. "Please?"

He stared at her, perplexed by the unexpected request and the fact that she was obviously upset about something. He shrugged. His orders had been to make Evangeline happy and allow her what she wanted as long as it was safe and Justice never left her side. He pressed the button to the intercom and instructed the driver to stop at the nearest grocery, and took in Evangeline's relief from the corner of his eye. Who knew what had set her off.

A few minutes later, they pulled to the front of a gourmet grocery store that was popular for its selection of the finest products and a wide variety of ethnic foods. Evangeline immediately popped out of the car before Justice could get out and go around to open her door, and she hurried toward the entrance, leaving Justice striding to catch up with her.

He caught her at the door and she regarded him with a frown.

"It's not necessary for you to go in with me. I'll only be a few minutes. You can wait in the car. I'm sure you've had your fill of shopping for the day."

Justice frowned back at her, his jaw set in a stubborn line.

"It's necessary."

She rolled her eyes, clearly disgruntled.

"Whatever," she muttered as she proceeded inside the market.

She grabbed one of the small baskets to put her groceries in, which he promptly confiscated, eliciting another frown from her. Then, muttering to herself, she hurriedly made her way down each of the aisles, her face a study in intense concentration.

He wondered what the hell had prompted this unexpected grocery shopping expedition, but a quick look at her told him she was about to melt down, and the last thing he wanted on his hands was a hysterical female. So he kept quiet and followed her down the aisles, taking the things she picked and putting them into the basket he carried.

To his surprise, she didn't opt for the less expensive items. She chose the most expensive brand names, comparing them meticulously before making her final selection. At the meat counter, she stared at the offerings, and he could almost see the wheels turning in her head as she pensively chewed her bottom lip.

Finally she opted for fresh fish and after handing him the wrapped fillets, she immediately turned and hurried to the section where wine was sold.

It was here she took the longest, staring and studying, muttering under her breath. Maybe the morning's shopping trip had been too much, because clearly she'd lost her mind.

In the end, she chose two bottles. One, an expensive red wine, the other an equally expensive and excellent-quality white.

After that, he thought she might well have lost her mind because she spent another fifteen minutes in the baking aisle, although he couldn't help peeking at the assortment of ingredients she put into the basket, his mouth watering at the possibilities of the delectable desserts that could be made with the things she'd purchased.

"I'm done," she said, though a frown creased her brow as she stared at the items in the basket. Almost as if she were trying to think of anything she'd missed.

After a moment she strode toward the checkout, where Justice plopped the basket down. After the clerk rang up the purchases, Justice saw Evangeline's visible wince, and then she reached into her pocket and pulled out a wad of carefully folded twenties. She looked anxiously at the total reflected on the cashier machine and back at the cash in her hand as if worried she wouldn't have enough to cover it. She slowly counted it out and heaved a sigh of relief when she reached the correct amount with one twenty to spare.

He frowned and caught her wrist just before she handed the clerk the cash. He sent her a look of reprimand and then swiped Drake's credit card to complete the purchase.

Evangeline didn't look happy with him, but hell if he was going to be the one to tell Drake that his woman had tried to pay for several hundred dollars' worth of groceries when she was, or rather had been, living in a shit apartment, working a shit job, struggling to make ends meet. He understood pride. All his brothers did. He—and they—respected it. But Drake would be one mean, pissed-off son of a bitch if he knew Evangeline had forked out money she so obviously needed to buy Drake food.

He grabbed the bags, refusing Evangeline's offer to help carry them, and headed to the entrance.

"Hardheaded too," she muttered. "All these damn rules."

At the car the driver was there to take the bags from Justice, and Justice turned to her, looking at her in obvious question.

"What are you talking about?"

She blushed as if she'd been caught out. Evidently she hadn't intended him to hear what she'd said.

"I was just adding another requirement to work at Impulse," she said.

One eyebrow went up. "Oh? What requirements are you referring to?"

"Obviously you have to be hot and a badass to work at Impulse. I mean, there's not a single person working there who isn't beautiful or a total badass. And just now I realized that there's obviously one more requirement. Hardheadedness."

Justice threw back his head and laughed. He was still chuckling when he escorted Evangeline around the car so she could get in. He was shaking his head as he slid in next to her.

"Well, there went one of the so-called rules," she muttered.

"Do I even want to know?" he asked.

"I left out never smiling as a requirement along with being a hot, hardheaded badass, but you just blew that rule, so I guess it's okay to smile occasionally."

He chuckled and shook his head.

"Now can we go back to the apartment?" he asked in exasperation.

She sent him a disgruntled look. "If I had time, I'd make you shop for another few hours. Just to watch you suffer."

He tried to choke back his laughter, but it escaped. He liked this woman, and he respected the hell out of her for remaining cool under pressure. It hadn't escaped him that the day had been an exercise in hell for her. Nor the fact that she was mortified that someone else was paying for her things.

"You'll do, Evangeline," he said affectionately. "You'll do."

"Well, thank God for that," she grumbled. "I'd hate to get on the bad side of a hardheaded hot badass."

He chuckled again and directed the driver to take them to Drake's apartment. As soon as he issued the order, the lighthearted mood was over and Evangeline became quiet and brooding. And rigid as hell. The entire ride to Drake's apartment, she looked like someone going to her execution.

12

Drake's car pulled into the alleyway of his apartment building, adjacent to the side entrance, and he quickly got out and strode inside. As he rode the elevator up, he loosened the neck of his buttoned-up shirt and divested himself of his suit coat, throwing it over one arm.

He realized he was restless. He'd been that way all day since leaving Evangeline in his bed this morning. There was an edginess to him that defied explanation. An urge to cement his relationship with Evangeline and outline his expectations so there would be no question of his intentions.

Tonight he would have her. But first, they'd have the discussion that had been brewing in his mind all day, followed by a casual, relaxed dinner, which would give her time to digest all he would say to her. And then he would take her, possess her. He would show her to whom she belonged now.

Fierce satisfaction gripped him, and he realized he hadn't anticipated the company of a woman so much in his life. For that matter, for the first time ever, he wasn't already deciding how long his affair would last. He never began an affair without knowing when it would end, and yet he hadn't even considered anything beyond securing Evangeline and making sure she didn't go anywhere for a damn long time.

Hell, was he contemplating an actual relationship as opposed to a quick fuck or a fling? Maybe he was losing his goddamn mind. He was certain his men thought so. And maybe he was, because his world had tilted on its axis the moment he'd seen Evangeline walk into his club, and nothing had been the same since.

When the elevator opened, he stepped into his apartment and immediately swung his head toward the kitchen, frowning. A delicious aroma wafted through his nostrils. He checked his watch, certain he wasn't mistaken on the time. He'd left his office so he would arrive sharply at six, as he'd informed Justice. Surely the delivery service wouldn't have made such a mistake and delivered the food before the requested time.

He had the entire evening meticulously planned, and he didn't like interruptions or unexpected twists.

He tossed his suit coat over the coat hanger by the elevator and walked into the kitchen only to pull up abruptly when he saw Evangeline at his stove manning four different skillets. He was a blunt man and not prone to putting much thought into how things were worded. Not when his words were sufficient to get results.

"What the hell are you doing?" he demanded.

Evangeline jumped, nearly dropping the spatula she held. She turned her head in his direction, her eyes huge in her face as she gazed anxiously at him. Clear confusion was reflected in her vivid blue eyes, and then she cast him a puzzled look that suggested he was in error for asking what she was doing.

"Justice told me you would be here at six, for me not to dress, and that we were having dinner in. I assumed that meant you wanted me to cook. He did say we were eating in," she repeated, as though reassuring herself she hadn't misunderstood what Justice had told her.

There was a tremble to her voice and Drake sighed, realizing how it could well have been misconstrued on her part. The edge of fear and uncertainty in her eyes made his response instinctively gentle. He didn't want to start the evening out on a bad note. Not when so much was riding on it.

"I have no intention of turning you into a domestic slave, nor do I expect you to cook for me. I have a delivery service that brings in the finest meals when I want to eat in. They come in, set the table, and quietly make an exit. I had a delivery scheduled for seven. I had planned for us to talk before we ate."

"Oh," Evangeline murmured.

She looked down at the meal she was preparing, color rising in her cheeks, embarrassment dulling her usually brilliant blue eyes. It was like a physical blow to his stomach and made him feel like the worst sort of ass for being so blunt and making his statement sound like a reprimand. As though she had done something wrong. When actually, the fact that she had prepared a home-cooked meal for him touched him absurdly. His own mother, what he could remember of the bitch, certainly hadn't ever cooked him anything.

"I'm sorry," she said in a hushed whisper. "I can throw it out. I misunderstood. I'm sorry," she said again.

He felt like he'd just kicked a puppy, and it wasn't a pleasant experience. He in no way wanted to hurt her feelings when she'd obviously gone to great effort to prepare what appeared to be a sumptuous dinner.

"Absolutely not," he said firmly. "It smells delicious, and good food should never go to waste. I'll just call the delivery service and cancel our order. How long before dinner will be ready?"

She still wouldn't meet his gaze, and she picked up a large spoon and stirred the ingredients in one of the pans.

"It's ready now. I was just keeping it warm so I could serve it as soon as you got here," she said softly.

He realized their talk was going to have to wait until after dinner, but he wasn't about to start out by hurting Evangeline's feelings and give her reason to erect a wall between them. No matter if it tasted like shit, he'd eat it and compliment her on it because he wouldn't humiliate her in any way.

And he reminded himself again that she'd cooked for *him*. It was a simple thing, but no woman had ever offered to cook for him, much less made the effort to have dinner ready as soon as he walked in the door from work.

He walked over to where she stood and slid his arms around her body, molding her back to his chest. He leaned down and brushed his lips over the bare expanse of her neck, smiling when he elicited a shiver from her.

"If it tastes even half as good as it smells, then it will be excellent."

She relaxed against him, the tension escaping her body.

"Why don't you go change into something more comfortable and I'll get dinner on the table," she said in a shy voice.

He kissed her neck one more time, this time nibbling at the silky skin before disengaging himself from her and heading to his bedroom. Okay, so the talk would have to come after dinner, but the fact that she'd cooked for him said something. She wasn't fighting, and apparently she hadn't had a change of heart.

He'd fully expected Justice to call him and bitch and moan about playing babysitter today, but to his surprise, all Justice had said after he'd dropped Evangeline back at Drake's apartment was, "You've got a good one, Drake. Don't fuck it up."

He frowned. He'd already seen Maddox's reaction to her, as well as Thane's. And now Justice had evidently fallen victim to her charm as well. He wasn't at all certain he liked the impact she was having on his men. She'd have them all eating out of her hand, and he had a suspicion that if Evangeline did get cold feet and bail, one or all three of the men would make a play for her.

Like *hell* that was going to happen.

After changing into a pair of comfortable jeans and a T-shirt, he returned to the kitchen to find Evangeline arranging the plates on the dining room table. When she heard him, she turned, a grimace on her lips.

"I wasn't certain of your preference in wine, so I bought red and white."

"I like both, so I'll have whatever you're having," he said.

She opened a bottle and poured two glasses, then stood nervously, watching him as if unsure what to do next.

"Sit," he said. "We don't want the food to get cold."

He pulled back the chair for her and she slid into it, and then he took the one across from her so he could watch her and see into her eyes. He hadn't even paid attention to what she'd been cooking, but now that he examined the artfully arranged plate before him, he realized she'd blackened a fish fillet with a sauce drizzled over it. There was a baked potato and two side dishes he didn't recognize. But it looked—and smelled—good.

The presentation was worthy of any restaurant he frequented. He was accustomed to fine dining, an indulgence he didn't deny himself now that he had the means to do so. Growing up dirt-poor and always hungry had a way of carving a man's soul. He'd made a vow on his mother's grave when he was eleven years old that her life would not be his. That he would do and have more. And above all, he'd sworn he'd never be hungry again.

While he was miserly with his fortune when it came to business matters, causing his partners to poke fun at his tight purse strings, he had no qualms about indulging in personal luxuries, fine dining being uppermost. So he knew a professional presentation when he saw one. And Evangeline's dish looked every bit as skillful and masterful as those served in his favorite and most exclusive restaurants. It remained to be seen whether the taste matched the appearance, but so far he was impressed. His angel was full of surprises, it would seem. Suddenly he was eager to ferret out her secrets, what made her tick, what lay beneath the veil of sweet innocence and a shine that was impossible to go unnoticed by any living, breathing person within a hundred yards of her.

She fiddled with her fork, peeking up at him from underneath her eyelashes. He dug into the fish and took a bite and then halted. He chewed and then quickly took another bite, not believing what he'd just experienced.

Now motivated to taste the other offerings, he forked into the two unknown sides and then leaned back with a groan. She looked apprehensive, and he noticed she hadn't taken a single bite of her own meal.

"This is amazing, Evangeline. It tastes magnificent. *You* cooked this? Are you sure you haven't pulled one over on me and ordered in?" he teased.

Her face colored but her eyes shone with delight at his compliment, and she ducked her head self-consciously, then nodded.

"I love to cook," she said softly. Then she lifted her head so their gazes met and her cheeks went pink all over again. "I'm pretty good at it, actually. I did all the cooking when I lived back home, and I cook for my roommates to save money so we don't eat out all the time. When I was young, I would go to the library and check out cookbooks and copy the recipes. We couldn't afford cable or satellite television, so I couldn't watch cooking channels, so I learned by trial and error. It's amazing the wonderful-tasting meals you can make with inexpensive ingredients. The secret is in the seasoning. Eating out was a luxury we couldn't afford. Not even fast food, and, well, when I got better at cooking, to be honest, I much preferred my own cooking over greasy takeout food."

He barely managed to stifle the frown forming. When had Evangeline ever had time to live her own life? To have a life of her own, for that matter? From the bits and pieces he'd been able to put together, she'd sacrificed everything for her family, even leaving home so she could make more money, but lived in squalor in order to support her parents. And he still had no idea why her parents couldn't do for themselves. She'd told him her father had been injured on the job and workman's comp found a way out of paying, but what was the mother's story? It made him angry that a beautiful young girl on the cusp of womanhood had put everything on hold to work herself to the bone, setting aside her own wants and desires for others. But then it also made her special. Head and shoulders above others for her sheer generosity and selflessness.

"How old were you when you started teaching yourself to cook?" he asked, already knowing he wasn't going to like the answer.

"Nine," she said, as if it were the most normal thing in the world. "Mom helped as much as she could, but it was more important for her to be with Dad, so I took over the kitchen, and they pretended not to notice when smoke filled the kitchen and I ran through the house opening all the doors and windows," she finished with a laugh.

But Drake wasn't laughing. He was furious. *Nine.* She'd been nine years old when she'd assumed the role of primary caregiver for her adult parents. He had to put his hands down below the table so she didn't see the tight fists that formed. And her attitude said it all. She didn't see anything abnormal about a mere child being forced into adulthood and taking on a mountain of responsibility. Never having a childhood. Much like himself, though their circumstances were vastly different. She, at least, had food to eat and she hadn't voiced a single complaint about the way her parents treated her. In fact, every time she spoke of her family, her face softened and her eyes went warm with love.

But it didn't change the fact that she'd been cheated of things most children took for granted. Did she ever plan to live her own life? To do something solely for herself?

Hell yes. He would see to that. He couldn't change the past for either of them, but he could damn sure change Evangeline's future, and her days of putting her own needs aside for the people she loved were over. He couldn't make her many promises, but he could at least make her that one. Never again would she be in servitude, willingly or not, to others.

They continued to eat in silence as he pondered the puzzle that was Evangeline Hawthorn. And more and more, he came to the realization that she was unlike any other woman he'd ever known, and he wasn't sure what to do with that. Or with her. He was finding himself in a predicament he'd never before experienced.

He handled all the women he'd taken up with, no matter how short of a time it was, with practiced ease. Never missing a step. He performed by rote and his efforts were greatly appreciated and met with delight.

For the first time in his life, he felt doubt over how to handle a woman. The irony wasn't lost on him. It was obvious that he couldn't employ the usual strategy with Evangeline because she wasn't like any of his past women. It might have annoyed another man, but it filled Drake with an eagerness he hadn't ever felt.

She was perhaps going to be his greatest challenge, and he thrived on challenges. He would have to figure out just how to handle her. What pleased her. Because the last thing he wanted to do was insult her or damage her pride. And pride was something she had in abundance. He admired and respected that because he understood pride all too well.

His thoughts drifted to his earlier acknowledgment that he hadn't already set a time limit on his relationship—yes, *relationship*, a word he'd never before used when referring to time he spent with a woman—with Evangeline. Because one thing he knew for sure. It would take more than a few days, weeks or even months to fully learn everything there was to know about his angel. And he looked forward to every moment.

Realizing his plate was completely cleaned, he leaned back in his chair and settled his gaze on what was his.

"That was wonderful, Evangeline. You were wrong when you said you were pretty good at cooking, though."

Her eyes widened, but before she could draw the wrong conclusion, he continued.

"You're an *amazing* cook. I've eaten in more five-star restaurants than I can count, and that was the best meal I've ever eaten. And the fact that you made it for me only makes it more special. Thank you."

She blushed furiously, but her eyes shone with happiness at his compliment. Her entire face lit up and he was momentarily robbed of breath at how radiant she looked. Good God, how had the woman gotten to the age of twenty-three before losing her virginity to an asshole? Men had to have been trying to get into her pants since she was a teenager.

But then he already had his answer to that question. Men hadn't figured into Evangeline's plans or goals. She'd been too busy taking care of her family and working all hours of the day to entertain thoughts of a relationship.

He frowned to himself as he also remembered one very important reason Evangeline wasn't experienced. She had no clue how beautiful she was. She thought she was nothing and nobody.

If it was the last thing he did, he was going to damn well make her see herself the way he—and the rest of the world—did.

"There's dessert too," she said. "No good meal ends without dessert. I only had time to whip up something simple given time constraints, but you have your choice of homemade chocolate mousse with whipped cream topping or cupcakes."

"Both," he said without a single moment of hesitation, prompting her to laugh.

"Somehow I didn't see you as a cupcake person," she said with amusement.

"If it's got sugar, I like it."

"Wait until you try my caramel Heath Bar pie," she said in a dreamy voice. "It's sinful."

"I can't wait," he said in a husky voice that suggested there were other things he couldn't wait for as well.

She smiled and hurried away, returning with an elegant sterling silver tray bearing two cupcakes and two artfully prepared crystal serving dishes of the chocolate mousse. He eyed both, knowing that if dessert lived up to dinner, he was going to be groaning afterward.

He was not disappointed.

"You're already spoiling me," he said as he slid the dishes away and took his dinner napkin to dab at the crumbs that were no doubt clinging to his mouth.

"Certainly not as much as you are me," she said pointedly.

"Good."

Evangeline rose, a smile still shining on her lips, and began collecting the empty plates. Drake frowned and then wrapped his fingers around her wrist, effectively halting her.

"Leave them," he said. "The cleaning lady will be in tomorrow morning. That's what I pay her to do. You and I have things to discuss."

Her instant look of uncertainty made his chest tighten to the point of discomfort. He purposely dropped her wrist and then rose and held out his hand to hers, waiting for her to make the choice of whether to take his hand. He was shocked over his actions. He never allowed others to dictate matters. Or allowed someone else to take the initiative. He was a take-charge man. Ruthless even. And yet here he waited for one small woman to trust him enough to decide to take his hand.

But when her silky soft fingers slid trustingly into his, he was suddenly glad he had waited and not taken the choice from her. Somehow it meant so much more that she'd come to him willingly, no longer any hint of apprehension in her eyes.

He guided her into the living room and settled her on the couch. Suddenly remembering the small box in his pants pocket, he reached for it, still holding on to her hand with his other. He held it out to her wordlessly. He wasn't a mushy, sentimental guy by any stretch and he always let the gifts do their own talking. It had always worked for him in the past.

But she stared at the wrapped package in stupefaction and then lifted her surprised gaze to his.

"Drake, what is this?"

The corners of his mouth quirked into a half smile.

"Open it and find out. Isn't that what one usually does?"

Instead of tearing into it, as most women of his acquaintance tended to do, she stared at it in awe, touching the ribbon and the colored paper reverently. Jesus, had no one ever given her a gift before? No, he didn't want to know the answer to that. It would only piss him off more.

"I'm afraid to ruin it," she said huskily. "It's too pretty."

She was threatening to turn him into knots and he hadn't even cemented that she was his and his alone yet. What this said about the future, he wasn't sure, but he wasn't entirely certain he liked it.

But he smiled indulgently, feeling something remarkably like relaxation settling into his chest. His cell was turned off—something he never did. And all his men had strict instructions, under threat of dismemberment this time, that he was not to be disturbed as he'd been last night. By God, he'd have things between him and Evangeline settled tonight come hell or high water.

Tentatively she began to unwrap it, careful not to make a single tear in the paper. She slid her fingernail under the tape and lifted until she was able to free the box with the paper completely intact. She fingered the ribbon a moment as if savoring the satiny texture, much as he had savored the same satiny feel of her skin.

With the box now sitting on her lap, she stared at it as if she had no idea what to do next. He could see her sudden inhale and the fact that she didn't immediately exhale.

"Open it, Angel," he said in a husky voice he didn't recognize.

Her fingers trembling, she slipped the lid off and bit her lip in consternation when she found yet another box, this one a velvet jeweler's box inside the other. She turned it over and gently shook until the velvet box fell into her palm, and then she turned it over, her thumb clumsily opening the front.

"Oh, Drake," she whispered.

Tears sparkled in her eyes as she looked up at him, and there was clear distress. What the hell?

"You shouldn't have. It's too expensive," she said in a panicked tone.

And yet her finger trailed over the delicate angel pendant on the gold necklace nestled in the box.

"Do you like it?" he asked pointedly.

"I love it," she said without hesitation. "It's the most beautiful thing anyone has ever given me."

The ache in her voice gave him an answering ache in his chest.

"Then it wasn't too expensive."

"But Drake, you barely know me," she protested. "You didn't need to buy me a gift."

"And you didn't need to cook me dinner," he challenged. "And yet you did."

She looked flustered as if she had no idea what to say to that.

He knew if he waited for her to take the necklace out and put it on, they'd be there all night, so he took the box from her lap, removed the necklace from the trappings, and then instructed her to turn around.

She shifted immediately and once again, he was assailed by satisfaction that she heeded his commands without thought. This wasn't a woman who could or would be just anyone's submissive, and that made her all the more desirable to him. No, she was *his* submissive. He didn't fool himself into thinking she was a natural submissive and would react this way with just any man. That she had chosen him, whether she consciously realized it yet or not, was something he would not take for granted, and he would most certainly cherish it for the precious gift it was.

When she turned back around, her gaze and her fingers lowered to the necklace that rested in the hollow of her breasts. He'd nearly laughed when she'd shockingly said it was too expensive. This was the least expensive gift he'd ever given a woman, and yet it was so appropriate that he couldn't pass it up. And there was also the fact that he knew he had to tread carefully with Evangeline. She wasn't a woman to be draped with gaudy jewelry and clothing from head to toe. She wasn't a woman who *needed* those accessories to shine or enhance her beauty. Her beauty needed no such embellishments or distractions.

He slid his hand into hers and picked it up, shifting himself until they were closer, their thighs touching, their hands resting on his leg.

"There are several things we need to discuss tonight, my angel, but first, I want to know what upset you this morning."

Her eyes flew up, startled as she stared at him in obvious confusion.

"Something was bothering you when you left to go shopping," he said patiently. "And it had nothing to do with our phone conversation. I'd like to know what it was."

Her eyes dropped and she fidgeted, her shoulders slumping as he watched her lips turn down into an unhappy frown. Justice had been right, and Drake suspected he knew precisely the source of her unhappiness.

"Did the call to your girls have anything to do with your quietness and the lack of sparkle in your eyes this morning? Because, baby, you shine. You just being you, you shine. Unless something is bothering you or has upset you."

He cursed beneath his breath when Evangeline flushed and her lips trembled. She turned her head to try to hide her reaction—as if such a thing were possible. She was a woman with no artifice. One only had to look at her to know what she was thinking or feeling. It was a good thing she was inherently honest, because she'd make a terrible liar.

He gently cupped her chin and turned her back to look at him, feeling like someone had punched him in the stomach when he saw the tears welling in her beautiful blue eyes.

"Tell me," he said.

"They think I've lost my mind," she said in a weary voice. "They're worried. I don't blame them for that."

"And?" Drake prompted, knowing there was far more to it than just this.

"Steph told me I was a fool to depend on a man so much and asked me how long I thought it would take for you to get tired of me and scrape me off and then where would I be?"

There was an edge of bitterness in her voice that suggested her friend's caustic words had hit an already ingrained source of insecurity within Evangeline. If he could get his hands around Steph's neck right now, he'd wring it. Damn woman had already caused enough trouble the night before. And she called herself Evangeline's friend? Hell, with friends like her, who the hell needed enemies?

"I shouldn't be so sensitive," she hurriedly said, her worried eyes tracking back to Drake's as if she thought he would assume she was fishing for assurances or guarantees. "It was more the way she said it that bothered me, I guess. She sounded . . . angry. Sarcastic. I don't know. Maybe even bitter. Like I betrayed them somehow by just up and leaving. And . . ."

She trailed off, dropping her gaze, color once again flooding her face. She bit into her lip, and it was obvious she hadn't intended to say so much. But he already knew how open Evangeline was and that she was honest to a fault.

"And what?" he gently prompted.

She sighed. "The night I went to the club, she, Lana and Nikki were all about how gorgeous I was and what a fool Eddie was and how he didn't know a good thing when he saw it, blah blah. They told me I don't see that I'm gorgeous. So if Steph really believed all of that, then why would she automatically assume that a man like you wouldn't want a woman like me and would scrape me off at the first opportunity?"

Drake had to breathe deeply to compose himself and control the blistering curse words that burned to spill out. Instead he reached out and framed Evangeline's tear-streaked face in his palms and looked directly into those gorgeous, innocent eyes.

"I imagine there were a lot of things behind that statement, Angel. I'm sure they were all taken off guard and weren't prepared for you to suddenly move out when you've always been their constant source of emotional support. I'm right, aren't I? It's likely you they seek out when they get their hearts broken or someone's pissed them off or they just had a bad day."

Her expression said it all. There was no need for her to respond, so he continued on.

"And I'm sure she is worried about you, but baby, listen to me and listen closely, because you won't like what I'm about to tell you, but it doesn't make it any less true."

Her eyes locked with his, clear question reflected.

"She's a jealous bitch."

Evangeline gasped and would have responded, no doubt denying any such thing, but Drake slid one hand over so his thumb pressed against her lips, silencing any outburst.

"She wasn't lying when she told you how beautiful you are and that you have no clue how beautiful you are. But you aren't a threat when you don't know that fact and don't act on that fact. Don't think for a minute that she isn't eaten up with envy that you're where you are right now and she's where she is right now, and she's jealous as hell that it's you and not her, and I'd bet my last dollar that she wishes she'd never given you that VIP pass to Impulse."

Evangeline looked stricken, but he also saw that his words made an impact. He could see her turning what he'd said over and over in her mind, replaying the conversation and coming to the same conclusion he had.

Then she closed her eyes as more tears silently leaked down her cheeks, colliding with his hands. He leaned forward and, starting from the bottom up, kissed the lines away, first one cheek and then the other.

"It doesn't mean she hates you," he said softly. "I imagine she already regrets her outburst and you'll probably get an apology from her, and you, being you, will accept it and put it behind you and you'll remain friends. Everyone is guilty of jealousy at some point or another. And everyone is guilty of saying things they don't mean or lashing out at someone they love, but it doesn't mean she doesn't love you."

"Thank you," she whispered.

He stroked her cheeks with his fingers, enjoying the simple act of touching her. The conversation wasn't over by far, because despite Steph's intent, she had planted a seed of doubt in Evangeline's mind. One he needed to get rid of before it festered and ruined something beautiful.

"Now, there's something else about that conversation I want to address, and I need you to listen to me," he said, making sure she knew how serious he was being. "You will never go without. You will always be taken care of. If it makes you feel more secure, I'll see to it right away so you aren't without means even when we're together. I'll buy you an apartment if you want to stay in the city, or if you prefer to live outside the city, I'll buy you a house. Either will be in your name, of course. In addition, tomorrow I'll start a bank account for you, unless you already have one of your own, and I'll deposit two million dollars. However, when you're with me, you aren't to spend a fucking penny of your money. What you wear, what you eat, what you drink and anything else will be bought and paid for by me. Understand?"

Evangeline looked utterly appalled. Her expression was so horrified that she looked as if he'd just threatened her with murder. She clapped her hands over her ears.

"Stop! Oh God, just stop! I don't want an apartment or a house and especially not your money. Are you just trying to make me feel worse?"

A shudder of revulsion rolled over her body and she looked as though she would burst into tears all over again.

"That sounds so cheap and tawdry," she choked out. "Like I'm some paid *prostitute*. I'm here because I *wanted* to be here, Drake. Not because of what I could extort from you. Or because you have money. I only wanted . . . *you*. That you would think that . . ."

She broke off and covered her face with her hands, her shoulders shaking with silent sobs.

Drake cursed Steph, himself and this entire fucked-up situation. He knew Evangeline wasn't like the other women he'd had and yet he'd just treated her like them. His attempt to assure her that she would never be put in a desperate situation if they were no longer together had gone horribly awry. He wasn't used to women like Evangeline and he had no idea how to act.

He pulled her into his arms and held her tightly against his chest, deeply shaken at her impassioned outburst. *I only wanted . . . you.* When had anyone ever wanted him the man? For himself and not what came with him? He was so stunned that he didn't even know how to react.

"I'm sorry, Angel," he said gruffly. "That's not how I intended that to sound. All I want you to know is that you're safe with me. And that you will never go without. I swear that I meant no offense. It was a shitty thing to say, especially when I know damn well you aren't a gold digger out to fleece me. I just didn't think before I put it out there. I only want you to know—to believe—that I will always ensure you are taken care of. Do you trust me enough to accept my word on that?"

Slowly, she pulled away from his chest, her eyes glossy with tears, but she stared him in the eye as if studying his sincerity or intent. He'd never felt so scrutinized in his life. Nor had he ever felt himself so lacking. There wasn't a person in the world who could stare Drake Donovan down and make him feel an ounce of remorse or compassion. Except, apparently, a small beautiful angel who he knew was a far better person than him, but he wasn't a good enough man to let her go.

"You explained what me being with you would mean. That I would be submissive to you. That you control me. All of me. And that I don't get a choice and I don't get to say no. And that scares me, Drake. I won't lie. I've never depended on anyone else. Only myself. It's safer that way. I don't get hurt when I don't give power over me to someone else. Please don't take this as me not trusting you, though God knows it wouldn't be unreasonable not to, considering we've known each other less than forty-eight hours. I wouldn't be here if I didn't trust you at least on an instinctual level. And maybe that makes me the naïve fool everyone is forever telling me I am. I just need to know more. You want me to submit. To give you ultimate power over me. How does that work exactly? I mean, what will you demand of me? I have to know everything or I'll just scare myself silly imagining the worst-case scenario."

"I never want you to be afraid of me, Angel," he said quietly. "Never that. I will not hurt you. I have exacting standards and expectations. They may seem extreme, but in my world they are necessary evils."

Her expression was faintly puzzled.

"I never want you to feel caged, but I also realize life with me will be an extreme change for you and you'll need time to adjust. Any time, and I mean every time you leave this apartment or go anywhere at all without me, you'll have a man on you. And only one of my most trusted. You will be protected at all times."

Her eyes widened in alarm, but he plunged ahead before she freaked herself out more than she was already.

"I'll want you available to me at all times. There will be times when I want you with me when I have to go out. When I'm home, you'll be here with me. When you aren't with me, I'll want to know where you are and who you're with at all times. I will not be pleased if you forget to inform me of your plans."

She swallowed nervously.

"I've already informed your employer that you'll no longer be working there."

He broke off when she gasped and shot her a warning look that silenced the protest forming on her lips.

"Your girls are taken care of. Their rent has been paid for the next two years and I secured a written guarantee from their landlord of no increase in rent for the next ten years. And tomorrow, I need you to get your parents' bank account number as well as the routing number so I can wire the necessary funds so that they will no longer have any financial worry, and neither will you continue to work yourself to the bone to provide for them."

Evangeline's jaw was clenched tight and she trembled from head to toe, whether in anger or just emotion he wasn't sure. But knowing how much pride she had, he doubted it was the latter and most definitely the former.

"You stepped into my world willingly, Angel," he said softly. "And therefore, you agreed to my rules, my way. I promised you would be taken care of and never want for anything, and that extends to the people who matter to you."

Tears glittered brightly, hanging on her dark lashes, such a contrast to her honey blond hair and mesmerizing blue eyes.

"It's easy to see what I get out of this arrangement," she said in a strangled tone. "But what do *you* get, Drake? Because from where I'm sitting, you aren't getting the better end of the bargain by a long shot. In fact, I don't see that you're getting anything at all. So *why* would you do all of this?"

"You, Angel. I get *you*. *All* of you. And believe me, you're damn wrong about you getting the better end of the bargain. The way I see it, I'll be forever trying to catch up, because having you is worth more than all the money in the world."

He saw her look of shock and the instant eruption of chill bumps on her arms.

"All you need to do is be you, babe, and from what I already know, that isn't going to be a problem, because you don't have a fake bone in your body. And by being you, you're going to be mine, and I protect and take care of what is mine. Give me your body, your submission, your obedience, your trust and *you*, and everything will be all right. I promise you that."

"I don't know what to say," she said helplessly.

"You've already said enough. You told me yes. You've given me your trust. And to be honest, enough has been said tonight already. Right now, I'm going to take you into the bedroom and make you mine."

13

Drake stood and then simply slid his arms underneath her body and lifted her effortlessly into his hold and strode toward the bedroom. He laid her down on the bed with reverence that brought a knot to her throat. He followed her down, molding his mouth to hers in a hot, breathless kiss that was all consuming.

He broke away only to rain a trail of kisses down her jaw to just below her ear and nibble lightly at the sensitive skin, eliciting a cascade of chill bumps down her body. Then he licked at her lobe before sucking it gently between his teeth, nipping with just enough force to send shivers of desire down her spine.

He leaned up again and his face hovered directly over hers so their eyes met and she could see the burning intensity in his dark gaze.

"You are beautiful, Angel. And before tonight is over you'll not only know how beautiful you are, you'll feel it too."

Oh my God. This man was lethal.

Slowly, as if she were the most precious thing in the world, he undressed her, piece by piece. Each time another item was divested, he would dip his mouth and explore the newly exposed region. She was gasping and arching into his touch and she still wasn't fully unclothed.

When her bra loosened, she experienced a brief moment of panic. Her breasts were just . . . average. Not firm and they wouldn't be "perky" without the aid of a push-up bra. She'd purchased one only because in her line of work, displaying what few assets she had was to her advantage. They weren't saggy. They were just there and a little squishy. Ugh.

"What the hell is going through your head right now?" Drake murmured as he stared into her eyes.

"You don't want to know," she muttered.

"Stop thinking," he ordered in a commanding tone that had her quivering to her core.

His eyes glittered and she got her first true glimpse of the dominant man she'd given herself to.

"Just feel," he said, his voice softening from the dominant alpha male to what could only be described as a purr.

"Okay," she whispered.

His head lowered and she sucked in her breath, waiting, aching, dying for the moment when his mouth closed over her nipple. She let out a wail of both pleasure and frustration when instead, he flicked his tongue over the already rigid peak, tonguing it to further rigidity. Then he turned and gave the other nipple equal attention, his movements practiced and unhurried.

God, they'd been making love all of two minutes and he was already a million times better than Eddie, whose idea of foreplay had been biting—painfully—into each nipple, fingering her roughly and then spreading her legs and thrusting when she was in no way ready for him.

She knew that if Drake spread her thighs and thrust into her right this moment, she would be wet and more than ready.

Finally she got her wish and his mouth closed around her nipple, sucking gently at first and then harder with rhythmic pulls until her vision went blurry.

"Oh God, Drake, you have to stop. Please don't stop."

She knew she wasn't making a bit of sense, but she was nearly delirious with ecstasy and all he'd done was kiss her lips, her neck and her breasts.

He chuckled, his warm breath vibrating against her nipple, making it stiffen even more.

"Which is it, my angel? Stop or don't stop?"

"I don't know," she wailed. "I don't know what to do, Drake. Help me, please."

He lifted his head and looked deep into her eyes, his expression somber and so very sincere. "Trust me, baby. I'll always have you. I'll always guide you. I'll always show you exactly what to do. You just have to let yourself go and trust me to get you there."

She palmed his face in her hands and lifted her head to kiss him, her first act of aggression. "I do, Drake. God help me, but I do. I feel safe with you. I've never felt so safe in my life."

A savage fire blazed in his eyes and she knew her words pleased him, that it was exactly the right thing to do and say.

"Lie back, Angel, and let me love you. We have all night and I plan to take my sweet time pleasuring my lady."

She closed her eyes against the sudden wash of emotion. In that moment she felt wanted. Cherished. Like she mattered. That she wasn't average and a nobody. Drake made her feel so very special, and she didn't have the words to describe how very precious he made her feel. No man had ever looked at her like he did. No man had ever stood up for her, stood by her side and had her back. It was more than she could take in. She was completely and utterly overwhelmed.

"Are you with me, baby?" he whispered. "I want you with me all the way."

"Oh yes, Drake. I'm with you. I wouldn't want to be anywhere else but right here and right now."

He shuddered against her and then lifted himself off her just enough to divest himself of his clothing, and she stared with unabashed wonder at the beauty of this man. Her gaze traveled from the top of his body, over the broad expanse of his chest and finally to his taut abdomen that sported a delicious six-pack. But when her eyes drifted lower still to the whorl of hair at his groin and the enormous, turgid erection, they went wide with shock.

Eddie wasn't a small man, and it had hurt when he penetrated her. But Drake? He made Eddie look like a prepubescent teenager, and she swallowed nervously as she contemplated the fact that if Eddie had hurt her—a *lot*—and Drake was much larger, how on earth would she be able to take him?

His cock was swollen and rigid, straining upward toward his navel, almost lying flat against his abdomen. At her best guess, he had to be at least eight inches in length, and she couldn't even fathom how thick he was. Surely this wasn't possible.

And yet she was fascinated by the sheer maleness of him. His muscled, broad chest. His thickly roped thighs and bulging biceps. He towered over her, well over six feet, making her feel delicate and so much smaller. He could squash her like a bug without even intending to.

Maybe this wasn't such a good idea. Her initiation into sex had been a disaster, and the man about to make love to her was *much* larger than her first lover.

"Angel, look at me," he said in a gentle tone that held none of the dominance of before. "I will never hurt you. Please don't fear me. You've only had the bad, and now I'm going to give you the sweet. You said you trusted me. So trust me to make this good for you—for both of us."

His words fell like a cleansing rain, soothing her fears and apprehension.

"Sorry," she said, attempting to replace her grimace with a smile. "I'm not exactly an expert at this, but even I know you're bigger than the average male."

She hesitated for a moment, holding her breath deciding whether she wanted to risk ruining such a poignant moment. But he needed to know what she was thinking. He deserved to know. He'd been nothing but understanding and patient. She owed him her honesty.

"The first time hurt. A lot. And he was a fraction of the size of you. It's not that I don't trust you. I just worry that I won't be able to *physically* accommodate you without it hurting even more. I want you with my every breath, more than I want to breathe, more than I've wanted anything in my life, but I'd be lying if I said I wasn't a little afraid. Because I want it to be perfect with you, Drake. Because you are so *very* perfect."

His entire gaze softened and she let out a sigh of relief that she hadn't angered him by bringing up her first lover while in Drake's bed. His kiss was warm and full of everything Eddie's had lacked. For several long seconds, he leisurely explored her mouth, lapping gently at her lips, paying particular attention to one corner.

When he drew slightly away, his eyes were serious but full of warmth and sincerity.

"It's not the size that matters, Angel. What matters is that the man ensures his woman is ready and prepared, and yes, able to take him. And I promise you I will make sure you are all of those things before I ever take that final step. And if at any time I do something that hurts you, then it ends. Immediately. And I expect you to tell me you're hurting because I will be very pissed off if you think you have to endure pain to please me. Understand?"

She smiled so broadly that her cheeks ached and tears burned her eyelids.

"Now can we get back to the really, really good parts?"

"I thought you'd never ask," he said huskily.

He pressed his lips to hers again, making love to her mouth, kissing her long and leisurely, tasting every part of her tongue, absorbing her essence, breathing her air, giving her his. Then he slowly traveled down her body, lavishing kisses, nips, suckling her nipples until she was mindless, her desperation growing by the second.

When he tracked lower still and put one firm hand between her thighs to part them, she sighed long and hard, remembering the night in his office, when he'd given her the mother of all orgasms using only his tongue.

Using his fingers, he traced a line down the seam of her folds and then gently parted them, baring her clit and pussy to his sight—and his seeking tongue.

She moaned deep in her throat. That first time had been urgent, overwhelming, like a bomb going off. This time he lapped, licked, suckled and teased, drawing out and prolonging her pleasure for what seemed an eternity.

He slid a finger inside her vagina, softly stroking the walls, reaching deeper to press gently on her G-spot, something she thought was a myth. Sudden wetness soaked his finger and he issued a growl of satisfaction that vibrated over her clit that he was laving with his tongue.

She was going to orgasm and she wanted him inside her, whether he fit or not. She twisted restlessly, silently begging him to possess her. To sink so far inside her that they were no longer two people. Just one.

"Just a little longer, my angel," he murmured against her clit. "I want to make damn sure I don't hurt you."

She nearly screamed, *Hurt me! I don't care! Just make this ache go away.*

He carefully inserted a second finger, stretching her and stroking back and forth until she became even wetter. And then he withdrew his fingers and lowered his mouth to her opening and tongued her entrance, nearly causing her to orgasm on the spot.

He circled the opening, licking and lightly sucking, and then he slid his tongue inward, tasting her from the inside out. She was panting, her entire body tightening in anticipation of something truly extraordinary.

Then his mouth left her and her keen of disappointment was sharp in the room.

His hand calmed her. "Just a moment, Angel. I have to protect you."

A moment later, he spread her thighs even further and positioned himself on his knees between them, grasping his enormous erection with one hand while he continued to stroke her until he was satisfied she was ready.

"Nice and easy," he soothed. "There's no hurry. If you need me to stop, say so, but I'm going to go slow and give you time to adjust."

She felt the blunt head of his penis press against her entrance and she instinctively arched upward, wanting to take more of him, but he held her hips firmly against the mattress to prevent her from doing so.

But he paused and gazed down at her, fierce possession etched in every facet of his face.

"*This* is your first time, Angel. This is what counts. It's your first time with me, and you're going to get respect and reverence and your gift will be cherished as it should have been. I want you to forget everything that came before me. And as this is your first time with me, it's also my first time with you. Don't think that doesn't mean anything. It means *everything*."

Something shifted deeply inside her, her heart going tight and then softening, allowing an opening that had never been there before. That she'd never allowed anyone access to. Emotion overwhelmed her and she was incapable of responding, even if she wanted to. But what could she possibly say on the heels of something as special as what he had just given her?

Himself. Absolution from what she considered the worst mistake of her life. Forgotten. It no longer existed here in his arms. He was right. This was her first time to *make love*.

He pressed forward slowly. Agonizingly slow. But as he gained more depth, she now understood why he'd gone to such lengths to prepare her. Even as wet as she was, she had no idea how he was going to get all the way in. Several times he paused and remained still and used his thumb to caress her clit, causing her to spasm around his cock.

She wasn't sure who was groaning, him or her. But his face was a wreath of strain, eyes closed, head thrown back as if he were experiencing the sweetest of pleasures or the most piercing pain. Maybe both. It gave her an immeasurable amount of satisfaction that she, Evangeline Hawthorn, average and nothing special, could bring this beautiful man who could have any woman in the world such exquisite pleasure.

"Hold on to me, Angel," he said in a strained voice. "Wrap your legs around my waist and tilt your sweet little ass up so I have a better angle."

Eager to comply with his wishes, she quickly did as he instructed and he pushed forward another inch, eliciting a gasp from both of them.

"Do it, Drake," she whispered. "You won't hurt me. You'll never hurt me. Take me. Make me yours. Please. I *need* you. So much. I need you. I need *this*."

He groaned and seemed to wage an inner war with himself, but her "please," or maybe that she'd said she'd needed him, seemed to push him over the edge and he surged forward in a forceful lunge that seated him to the balls deep inside her.

Her eyes flew open as she was bombarded with a hundred different overwhelming sensations. And not one of them was pain. She tightened her legs around him. She dug her nails into his shoulders. And she arched upward to take as much of him as she could.

Still, he thrust back and forth in a slow rhythm, sinking as deep as he could before withdrawing until the tip on his head barely breached her opening, and then he would languidly glide back to his fullest depth.

Evangeline had never felt anything more beautiful in her life. And she never would. She knew that as surely as she knew the sun rose every morning. Her orgasm was blooming like a flower unfurling under a ray of sunshine, and she felt Drake tense above her and knew he was as close as she was. The night he'd brought her to orgasm in his office had been a fast climb to an overwhelming explosion that had left her shattered. This was something so much sweeter, yet no less intense or shattering to her senses. This wasn't merely physical, as it had been then. Her heart was already fast becoming involved, and she was helpless to stop it.

"Together," she whispered. "I'm so close, Drake. I can't—won't—last much longer."

"Then let go. We'll go together," he whispered in her ear.

The world blurred around her but the one thing that remained sharply in focus was Drake's face above hers, him kissing her with breathless passion and tenderness shining in his eyes. Finally it was too much and she latched on to Drake, wrapping every part of her body around him as she began to shatter into a million pieces, like stars scattered haphazardly across a clear night.

He emitted a hoarse shout and then carefully lowered himself onto her body, his hips still gently pumping into her body until finally they stilled and they lay quiet and breathless in the aftermath of something Evangeline had no words for. For something that defied explanation.

Now she knew what it was supposed to be like, and her only regret was that Drake *hadn't* been her first. But no. He'd told her this *was* the first—*he* was the first. Eddie was forgotten, never to be remembered again. Now there was only Drake.

"Be right back, my angel," he whispered. "Need to get rid of the condom, but you don't move."

As if she could. She was utterly boneless and couldn't move if she tried. A few seconds later, Drake crawled into the bed with her and turned them on their sides so they faced each other.

He cupped her cheek and caressed softly. "It won't always be like this. But you needed it this way this time. The way it should have been your first time instead of that asshole hurting you, taking his pleasure and giving none in return. You should have been handled with care and cherished and made love to as tenderly as a woman ever was. I meant what I said. I want you to consider *this* your first time and forget the other dickhead ever existed."

Oh but the man had a way of slipping right past her barriers and setting her world to rights, as crazy as that sounded, considering he'd done nothing but upend her world ever since entering it.

She snuggled into his arms, warm and sated, and couldn't resist running her hands over the muscled walls of his chest and abdomen. Over his shoulders and well-defined arms that bespoke a strict training regimen. This was no man who spent all his time behind a desk, eating good food without care for his body.

He stroked his hand through her long tresses, pausing every once in a while to press a kiss to her temple, her forehead, her lips and even her eyelids.

As some of the hazy euphoria subsided, his earlier words floated back to her and she cocked her head back so she could look at him in the dim light cast only by one lamp in the room.

"Drake?"

"Yes, Angel?"

"What did you mean?"

He kissed her softly before pulling away. "About what?"

"When you said it wouldn't always be like this. What did that mean?"

He cupped her jaw, his eyes suddenly serious. "You know what I am, what I want and what I expect."

She nodded.

"I only meant that our lovemaking won't always be as it was tonight. I enjoy a variety of methods of sex. Rough, soft, hard, sweet. Bondage, spanking, you at my complete mercy, me in control at all times. I enjoy kink. I like the idea of my woman being available to me at all times. And after tonight, there will be no condoms. When I come, it'll be inside you, not a damn rubber. I'll provide you my most recent lab results, and I'll set up an appointment immediately so you have birth control."

Her eyes lowered a moment, but he caught her chin and tipped it back upward, question hovering in his gaze.

"What if I disappoint you, Drake?" she asked hesitantly. "You know I'm not experienced. And that I have no experience in your . . . world. Or with your expectations."

He smiled and kissed her again. "First, I'm going to delight in teaching you everything you need to know to please me, just as I'll learn what pleases you. And second, as long as you give me what you gave me tonight—your surrender, your sweetness, your complete and utter submission—you will never disappoint me, Angel. You shine, baby, from the inside out, and it's the most beautiful fucking thing I've ever seen in my life. You won't disappoint me. It simply isn't possible. I, on the other hand, will likely disappoint you, frustrate you and anger you on a regular basis. I'm a demanding bastard and my demands will, at times, be extreme. But if you stick with me, Angel, if you stay with me and tough it out, and if you don't take back the trust you've granted me, I guarantee you're going to enjoy the ride."

14

Once again Evangeline awoke, snuggled warmly in Drake's bed. Only to find it empty. As she'd done the morning before, she reached over to feel any lingering warmth from his body only to find the sheets chilled, though the indention of his body was still present.

She sighed, wondering if the man ever slept. He obviously kept unusual hours, although he had been home at six the previous evening. Was that an exception for her? Or was his being at his club at four in the morning the exception because she'd kept him waiting?

Who knew? But after last night and her agreeing to ... well, she wasn't entirely certain what she'd embarked on. Oh, he'd been clear enough on his expectations and the kind of relationship they'd have, but there were still a million questions circling her mind. What sane person wouldn't be questioning such a circumstance? But then a sane person wouldn't be in a man's bed for the second morning in a row barely even knowing the man in question, much less have agreed to submit to him in *all* things.

Her hand brushed over something hard against the softness of the sumptuous sheets and she frowned, sitting up. She pulled the covers up to cover her breasts and then laughed. Who was she hiding herself from? There was no one here.

She eyed the box with trepidation, recognizing it as being almost identical in shape and size to the gift he'd presented her with the night before. Her hand went automatically to the necklace he'd given her that still hung around her neck.

Her heart sank. Was this another outrageously expensive gift?

There was a note beside it, but she couldn't bring herself to read it before opening the box that sat there as if taunting her. She made quick work of it this time and opened the jeweler's box to reveal a stunning pair of diamond solitaire earrings.

Oh. My. God.

All she could do was stare in absolute befuddlement. They were huge. She had no idea what constituted a carat, but these had to be in the multiple-carat class of diamond earrings. She hadn't seen *rings* with diamonds this big. And she was supposed to wear them? What if one fell off? What if she lost one?

She could probably buy a house back home with what these earrings cost. It made her faintly ill to be holding something so valuable in her hands, and she hastily set them away and picked up the note.

Jax will come by the apartment at one o'clock to pick you up and bring you to the club. Dress casual, but bring something dressy and sexy to change into later. You'll spend the day with me and come home with me from the club late tonight. I hope you like the earrings. You outshine them any day of the week, but I want my angel to sparkle. Plan to have lunch and dinner with me.

She sagged. Was he purposely keeping her off balance by throwing a new man at her at every turn, or was he simply introducing her to each of the men he insisted would accompany her any time he wasn't with her?

She stared at the glittering diamonds and knew now she'd have to wear them or risk angering him by rejecting his gift. She would just pray one didn't fall off or she didn't misplace them when she took them off at the end of the evening.

Then when she checked the time, she panicked. Drake had told her Jax, whoever he was, would be there at one. It was ten past one now! She *never* slept this late. Even after a long shift, she was always up before the others. There were too many things to do, too many responsibilities to take care of.

Unbidden, something Drake had said the previous evening came to mind. He'd wanted her parents' account number and routing number. She had them, of course, but how was she to explain the sudden influx of money into their account? Never once had she lied to her mother, but she was sorely tempted to tell her something outlandish like she'd won the lottery or something equally absurd.

She was well on her way to a full-scale panic attack when she heard a voice in the distance.

"Yo, Evangeline. Jax here. Drake wanted me to pick you up at one. You need to get a move on. The boss doesn't like to be kept waiting."

She jumped and nearly shrieked but clamped a hand over her mouth to prevent sound from escaping. Her heart was racing from the unexpected fright. And then she got pissed. She was really tired of hearing that Drake didn't like to be kept waiting.

"You tell Drake that he'll just have to get over it," Evangeline yelled crossly. "I'll be ready when I'm ready and not before."

A deep male chuckle was her only response.

Despite her bravado, she scrambled out of bed, turning in circles as she tried to figure out what to do first. Shower. Right. Then she'd figure out what to wear. She would have to figure out how to tackle the issue of her parents when she got to the club because she didn't have time for that kind of a phone call right now.

She was in and out in five minutes, hastily combing through her wet hair and towel-drying the strands as much as possible. Then she headed for the closet where all her things had been put.

Casual. Okay, she could do casual. Casual she was well acquainted with. It was the dressy part that she was clueless about. What exactly did Drake consider dressy?

She chose a pair of outrageously expensive but oh-so-very-comfortable jeans that made her sigh when she pulled them on. Then she grabbed one of the lacy push-up bras she'd chosen and turned her attention to what top she should wear.

The last couple of days had been cooler, though summer hadn't quite given way to fall yet, and she remembered that Drake's office felt like a meat locker, so she picked a short-sleeved cashmere sweater with a plunging neckline with folds that discreetly covered everything it should.

As for the shoes, she went straight for the sparkly pair of flats that she simply hadn't been able to resist.

And then remembering his directive, she hurried into the bedroom and gingerly unfastened the earrings from the holder in the box and slid them into her ears. Nervously, she went to the mirror to check her appearance and stood staring back at a woman she didn't recognize. Her hair was disheveled and her lips were still faintly swollen from Drake's passionate kisses. Most notably, there was a glow to her cheeks and to her eyes that suggested a well-satisfied woman. She looked almost . . . *pretty*. Then she chastised herself for already getting caught up in this make-believe world she'd been transported to and reminded herself that she was still the same average Evangeline. More expensive clothing and jewelry didn't miraculously transform her into something she wasn't, and it was dangerous to get caught up in the fantasy, even if for the barest of moments. It was thoughts like these that would set her up for a horrendous reality check and a fall right back into the world she *really* belonged in.

Knowing she had limited time, she only applied the bare minimum makeup and a sheer lip gloss and then finished with a few swipes of mascara to highlight what she admitted was her one redeeming quality. Her eyes.

But then dread took hold, because she still had to figure out what to bring to change into later. The last thing she wanted was to make a fool of herself or worse, embarrass Drake. Short of calling him and asking him exactly what he wanted her to wear, her only other option was . . . Jax.

She groaned but what the heck. It wasn't as if she hadn't already made a fool of herself in front of every other one of his men. No reason for Jax to be excluded. He'd probably already heard about her anyway and was cursing the fact he'd drawn the short straw today. Or maybe he'd volunteered, wanting to see the train wreck in person.

Nervously she walked out of the bedroom, peeking toward the living room to see a large man sprawled across Drake's couch, remote in hand, a drink in the other.

"Um, Mr. Jax?" she asked cautiously.

Then he turned and she took an instinctive step back. Yes, all of Drake's men were hot badasses who didn't smile and were hardheaded, but this guy was huge! He had tattoo sleeves covering the length of both arms, and the design continued up around his neck, making her wonder if his entire upper torso was one giant work of art. He wore at least three earrings in each ear and his hair was long and unruly in a total "I don't give a fuck" kind of way.

But his eyes. Whoa. His hair was black as a raven's wing, but his eyes were crystalline blue. All she could do was stare mutely as he stared back, obviously waiting to hear what she was going to ask. For that matter, what *had* she been going to ask?

Then he smiled, and as with the others, that smile transformed him from a man not to be fucked with to a man who would stop traffic with only that smile. He stood and walked slowly toward her, almost as if he sensed she might run back into the bedroom and shut the door.

"Just Jax. And you must be Evangeline, unless Drake has two gorgeous blue-eyed blondes holed up in his apartment," he said with a flirtatious grin. "Was there a problem? Do you need something?"

His voice had softened and he stopped several feet away from her, whether by coincidence or out of deference to her obvious nervousness.

"Um, yes. I mean no." She groaned and smacked her forehead.

Jax laughed. "Which is it?"

"Yes, I'm Evangeline, and no, he doesn't have two women in this apartment. At least he better not." She muttered the last under her breath but knew he'd heard when Jax's lips twitched and his eyes gleamed with amusement.

"They weren't wrong about you," Jax said, cocking his head sideways, as though studying her.

Her gaze narrowed. "Who? What are you talking about?" Damn it, she knew she'd been set up as today's amusement for the new guy.

He just grinned. "What can I do for you, Miss Evangeline?"

Then she remembered the whole reason she'd come in search of Jax and wanted to die of embarrassment. She closed her eyes, her face on fire. How did she stand a chance of surviving a single day in Drake's world much less a significant length of time?

Jax softened at the sight of the gorgeous, sweet woman staring at him in obvious distress. Damn, but the others had been right. Her agitation made him want to do whatever had to be done to correct the matter. He'd laughed at Thane, Maddox and Justice when they'd extolled her virtues and told him the impossible. That she was the real deal. Too sweet and innocent for her own good but a tigress when it came to defending people she felt were wronged.

"Evangeline, what's wrong?" he asked gently. "What can I do to help?"

Oh shit. She looked like she was about to burst into tears. If there was one thing he couldn't handle, it was a crying woman.

Instead of responding, she thrust a piece of paper at him. Puzzled, he opened it and read Drake's distinctive scrawl and then looked back up at Evangeline, who was growing more anxious by the minute.

What on earth in Drake's note could cause her this much upset? It was straightforward. Typical Drake. He didn't see anything that should have caused Evangeline to react with such panic.

"What does he mean by dressy and sexy?" she asked, her voice rising with each word. "I'm *not* sexy and I have no idea what his definition of dressy is because believe me, my definition and his are miles apart. And as I'm obviously not sexy, how the hell would I know how to dress the part?"

Jax's mouth fell open. Not sexy? Was she crazy?

"I don't want to embarrass him," Evangeline whispered, tears filling her eyes.

It was all he could do not to pull her into his arms and hug her. For God's sake. He was contemplating hugging someone? He should have known he was being set up when it was suggested that he be the one to collect Evangeline. Since she needed to meet all of Drake's men, Maddox had smugly pointed out.

Jax's lips made a firm line, and then he reached out and took Evangeline's hand, tugging her behind him as he headed toward the closet. He was no fashionista, but he sure as hell knew what looked good on a woman. Especially a woman like Evangeline. Hell, she'd look good in a sackcloth. What the hell was wrong with Drake that his woman didn't think she was sexy? Because if Evangeline belonged to Jax, not a single day would go by that she wouldn't know exactly how desirable she was.

"*You*, stand there," he directed, planting Evangeline in the middle of the huge walk-in closet. "Now, what you have on now is perfect for casual. You totally rock that look. I expect Drake will be in a foul mood whenever another man has to come into his office."

She looked at him like she had no clue what he was talking about.

Jax nearly shook his head. Hell, the others hadn't been fucking with him about Drake's woman. They'd been telling him the honest truth.

"Dressy and sexy for a night at the club means something a little more glittery, fun, even daring." Though he wondered if he should have included that last part. It might get his ass kicked by Drake if his woman showed up in something too revealing and Jax and the others had to spend the entire evening beating other men's asses for ogling *Evangeline's* sweet ass.

"You mean something like this?" she asked softly, reaching toward one of the hangers.

Her fingers glided over the silver-and-white silk material, and he could see the longing in her eyes. At that moment, it wouldn't have mattered if it was the wrong thing for her to wear. There was no way he was going to tell her no.

"Absolutely," he said with a firm nod. "You got shoes to go with that or do we need to make a stop and pick up a pair? Drake will understand."

Her eyes widened in alarm. "Oh no. I have shoes. Besides, I'm already late and as everyone is constantly reminding me, Drake doesn't like to be kept waiting so he's probably already angry."

Jax frowned. "Now wait a minute, sugar. It's true that Drake is an impatient son of a bitch and he doesn't like to be kept waiting, but he will not be angry with you and he damn sure won't hurt you. Besides, I'll simply tell him I got held up and was late getting here to pick you up."

She smiled and for a moment he forgot to breathe. Holy hell, but this woman was death on men and didn't even have a fucking clue.

"That's sweet of you, Jax, but I would never allow you to take the blame for me oversleeping and then having a meltdown because I'm too gauche to know what I'm supposed to wear or how to act. If Drake is going to get mad at anyone, it will be me and not anyone else."

Her jaw was set in a stubborn line that told him she meant business.

"I have the shoes over here," she said, bending over and rummaging through several boxes before producing a pair of iridescent high heels that would look killer on her already gorgeous legs.

Then she frowned. "I should probably bring makeup and toiletries. Do we have time for me to pack a quick bag?"

"Sugar, you take all the time you need. I'll just wait in the living room."

He was almost to the door when she called out to him.

"Oh! Jax, I almost forgot. Can you do something for me, please?"

Hell, she could ask him for damn near anything and he'd do it or die trying.

"Sure thing. Just name it."

"There's a box of cupcakes on the bar in the kitchen. Can you get it for me? I was going to just keep them here for Drake, but since we're going to the club and there are plenty to go around, I thought I'd bring them for the guys."

He was at a momentary loss of words. Cupcakes? She was bringing the guys at Impulse *cupcakes*? Drake might never live this one down, so it was with glee that he cheerfully agreed to collect the box and wait for her in the kitchen.

Evangeline carefully put the dress into one of Drake's garment holders, grabbed an overnight bag and stuffed the shoes and all her toiletries and makeup inside and then hurried into the kitchen to see Jax stuffing what was left of a cupcake into his mouth.

When he heard her, he looked up, ignoring her accusing look and the hand on her hip. "Holy shit, these are fucking awesome. Where did you buy them?"

She fidgeted uncomfortably. "I made them."

His eyes bugged out. "*You* made them?"

She ducked her head but nodded. "I like to cook. And bake."

"Oh my God, I'm in love," he groaned. "Any chance you can forget that you were bringing the box for all the guys and let me take it home with me?"

She grinned. "No. But I'll pretend you didn't already have one so you can have another when we get to the club."

"Good. I'm starving. Haven't had a chance to eat yet."

Evangeline frowned and put her stuff down on the counter and then shoved a startled Jax around to the other side of the bar and made him sit.

"What are you doing?" he asked, clearly baffled.

"Feeding you. I have leftovers from the dinner I made Drake last night. It won't take but a few minutes to warm up and as you said, we're already late, so what's a few more minutes, right? Traffic was so terrible."

Jax laughed. "I like you already."

"It won't be as good as it was last night," she said in an apologetic tone. "But it won't be bad. Promise."

"You actually cooked dinner for Drake?"

"Yeah. I thought I screwed up and pissed him off. He had placed an order with a delivery service for seven, but I misunderstood when he said he'd be home at six and that we were eating in. I assumed he wanted me to cook, so it was kind of awkward. Until he tasted my cooking," she added with a grin.

A few minutes later, she set a plate of leftover fish and the sides, minus a baked potato, in front of Jax and blinked as he literally inhaled it.

"Jesus, Mary and Joseph," Jax muttered. "You're a goddess. If that was supposed to be not as good as last night, then it's a wonder Drake survived and is alive and working today. Because that was heaven in my mouth.

Is there anything you can't do? A beautiful, sweet, compassionate woman *and* she can cook? Why do I never find them first," he said mournfully.

Evangeline flushed with pleasure over the obvious sincere compliment, but then she swiftly took the plate and set it in the sink.

"Okay, we better get going or Drake is going to strangle both of us," she said, only half joking.

On cue, Jax's phone rang and he groaned. "That's the boss wondering where the hell his lady is."

"Yeah, you need to tell him about the horrible traffic jam we're in," she said with a perfectly straight face.

Jax laughed and then said the strangest thing. "Oh man, Drake is going to supply the guys with the most amusement we've encountered in a damn long time."

15

Drake stifled the urge to look at his watch again, knowing that Silas and Hatcher would pick up on the fact that he wasn't focused on what he should be focused on, which was the current handling of an issue that needed to be acted upon quickly. And Maddox, damn the man's hide, who perpetually lurked in the shadows, a mere raised voice away, would know exactly where Drake's mind was and it wasn't on one Eddie Ryker. For that matter, Justice *and* Thane were currently sitting on Drake's sofa for reasons unknown to Drake, leaning back as if they had nothing better to do than be on permanent break. He'd address their purpose for being here as soon as he dealt with the most pressing issue.

"So what do you want done, Drake?" Silas asked in his quiet, unruffled tone.

Silas was an enigma, one that Drake would never admit to not having ever figured out. He knew enough about the man he considered one of his most trusted and valued partners to not worry that his loyalty would ever lie elsewhere, and he knew, only from what he'd been able to dig up as public record, that Silas's childhood had been the worst kind of hell, but he didn't know much *else*.

If it were anyone but Silas, that wouldn't sit well with Drake at all. He didn't hire men who wore shadows like others wore clothing. But in Silas he saw a kindred soul, and he also saw a man who placed great value on a man's word, particularly his own. In all the years they'd worked together, he'd never known Silas to break his word once given. Regardless of circumstance. And Drake would know otherwise. He made it his business to know everything about the men he trusted. Except, he thought ruefully, he'd made an exception with Silas since no one knew anything about the man other than what he chose for them to know.

Drake glanced at Hatcher, whose expression was bland and unruffled, though his fists were clenched at his sides, a sure sign of his irritation. Drake frowned at the tell. Men who broadcast their mood, thoughts or intentions were the ones most likely to get themselves killed.

"You will handle this, Silas," Drake said, making a sudden reverse decision when before he'd fully intended to give the assignment to Hatcher. Though he had implicit trust in Silas when it came to taking care of problems that arose, this task was beneath his abilities. Any of his men could do what needed to be done, and though he suffered no conscience over using any of the men he partnered with and had made very wealthy men, he had to admit that every once in a while he grew concerned with the considerable burden that Silas, for the most part, bore alone as Drake's clean-up-and-take-out-the-trash man. Silas was too valuable, too integral to Drake's many less-than-aboveboard assignments.

If Silas knew that it had even crossed Drake's mind to shield his muscleman, it would be a betrayal; Silas placed much emphasis on loyalty and carrying out any task Drake put to him, regardless of how dirty his hands got in the process. But then the entire reason Drake chose Silas for that particular role was that he could simply turn it off, do the job impersonally and without emotion or suffering a fit of conscience, two things Drake demanded of all his men, but especially Silas.

Silas wouldn't question Drake's decision or his motives, but if he had, he would have simply been honest about the fact that of all his men,

Hatcher had been with him the shortest period of time, which meant he still had to prove his mettle not only with Drake but with his partners and brothers.

He shot Hatcher another quick glance, satisfied that at least he showed no outward reaction to Drake's decision. But then he could hardly blame the man for his anger toward Eddie when Drake wanted nothing more than to hunt the little bastard down and kill him himself.

But this wasn't about Eddie, directly. Eddie had already received a message very loud and clear, courtesy of Silas, Jax and Justice, to give Evangeline Hawthorn a wide berth in the future. One he was still no doubt recovering from. *Except* he'd shown up in Steven Cavendar's nightclub the night before. And not only had he been allowed entrance, but he'd also availed himself of his VIP status and all the perks that accompanied VIP treatment.

Drake had done his homework on Eddie and had only grown more disgusted, if such a thing were possible. He didn't have money, or a job for that matter, or the ambition to do anything more than to live off his parents' largesse and toss around money without a second thought in his bid to impress women and men alike. He wanted something he had no hope of ever receiving. Respect. He was a parasitic leech and there was no doubt in Eddie's mind that once he'd set his sights on Evangeline, it was a fait accompli and she'd fall into his lap like a ripe plum just ready to be bitten into.

He'd certainly picked the wrong woman when he chose Evangeline and was barking up the wrong tree entirely. Evangeline wanted, needed, craved a forceful, dominant man, and he doubted she'd even realized it yet. Eddie, even if he had been satisfactory in bed, would have failed her on every other level that it was possible to fail a woman. He was weak, spineless and unapologetic about his lifestyle and what his parents' fortune gave him by proxy. As an only child, he'd been shamelessly spoiled, and he knew nothing about the real world or where Drake and his men and Evangeline had come from, what they had made them-selves into. He was a whiny petulant prick who expected nothing more than to crook his finger at a woman and have her clinging to him like a lifeline.

Until Evangeline. And she had not only stung his pride by making him put on all his charm to seduce her, but she'd made a fool of him and worse, he knew it, though he'd never admit to such a thing. He'd been on a mission to take Evangeline's virginity and to toss her the day after, never to be thought of again.

"Just how big a lesson did you teach our good friend Eddie?" Drake asked Silas, in a swift shift in thought. "Because I'm thinking if he was out partying at Cavendar's all night, he didn't get half of what he deserved."

His statement ended in a snarl that suddenly had Maddox material-izing in the far corner of the room where the nearly hidden doorway stood. He watched the goings-on through narrowed eyes as if deciding whether he needed to intervene.

"I'm surprised he was walking," Silas said in his characteristic de-tached, unemotional tone.

Drake scowled. "Are you saying he has magical healing powers, then?"

His sarcasm lay heavy over the now-quiet room.

Hatcher merely shrugged. "A man will do a lot when his pride is involved. After the first several doors were shut in his face, he probably got desperate. And we all know Cavendar is a greedy whore who'd sell his mother for the right price. How Eddie got in and whether he was ambulatory wouldn't be of consequence to him. Only that he was seen and not shunned. And just as Cavendar can be bought, I doubt the women who Eddie usually keeps company with give a fuck that he looks like he was hit by a semitruck just as long as he keeps them happy. And gives them carte blanche with his parents' money."

"Which is precisely why I want you to go have a chat with Cavendar," Drake said pointedly to Silas.

Silas nodded.

"Report back to me . . ." Fuck. He almost forgot himself and the fact that he would be with Evangeline for the rest of the day—and night. "I'll touch base with you tomorrow," he amended. "I expect the matter to be resolved by then."

Again Silas only nodded.

"Should have just dumped the asshole in the Hudson," Maddox said darkly, speaking up for the first time.

A gasp from the elevator made all four men swivel in that direction. Evangeline stood next to Jax, who was shaking his head as if to say they were all stupid fucks for forgetting themselves.

Hell. Just how much of their conversation had she heard? But Evangeline never once looked in Drake's direction. She focused only on Maddox, clear indecision in her eyes, but to Maddox's credit, he didn't skip a beat. He strode toward her, took the things she was holding in her hands, and promptly dumped them into Silas's bewildered arms—something Silas had no liking for because it drew attention to him when he would have silently slipped away, as he did around all newcomers—and then Maddox hugged Evangeline and smacked her noisily on the cheek.

"How's my favorite kidnappee?" he teased.

Drake had to rein in his temper over Maddox's spontaneous display of overdone affection. He knew well why he'd done it. If Drake hadn't allowed himself to be distracted, something he found himself guilty of with increasing frequency ever since Evangeline had walked into his club that first night, then he would have damn well known she and Jax were on their way up in the elevator. Hell, he would have known the moment they hit the entrance to the club.

When Evangeline continued to regard Maddox warily, he sent her a look of indulgence and laughed.

"Don't go getting all timid on me now, sweetheart. You've already shown me your claws. Don't worry. I didn't really dump anyone into the

Hudson. It was merely wishful thinking on my part. One has that kind of reaction when their accountant informs them, after filing an extension and paying estimated taxes due because all my K-1s from my investments don't come in until well after April fifteenth, that I owe substantially more than he first estimated."

Even Silas blinked in reaction to how convincing Maddox sounded. Not lost on Drake was the fact that Maddox had purposely used terms Evangeline wouldn't possibly be familiar with given her economic status, and well, rich or poor, no one loved the IRS.

Evangeline laughed, the melodious sound easing the tension in the room.

"You poor baby. I have something to make you feel all better," she teased, just as he'd teased her.

Drake's teeth were now baring themselves. Evangeline was here. Over an hour late, and he didn't buy Jax's trumped-up excuse about a fucking traffic jam, but she was here, which meant that everyone else should *not* be here. And yet here they all stood. He realized then just how *much* of a distracted idiot he was. His men knew Evangeline was coming in to the club today. Those who hadn't met her were no doubt dying of curiosity, and those who had just wanted an excuse to see her again. Suddenly Maddox's threat of dumping someone in the Hudson sounded very appealing, only in this case it was going to be a *lot* of someones.

Evangeline reached for the box Jax was holding, and he adopted a wounded puppy-dog look that had Drake wanting to beat his head on the desk. Were his men turning into complete pussies? For fuck's sake.

"Hand it over or you don't get one," Evangeline said, her attempt at sounding menacing making Thane and Justice chuckle.

Jax sighed and made an elaborate show of reluctantly handing over the box—or was it a covered *plastic food container*?

Evangeline cracked the lid, reached inside and, to Drake's eternal surprise, drew out one of the cupcakes she'd given him for dessert last night. She held it temptingly under Maddox's nose.

"All better now?"

He narrowed his eyes. "That depends on whether you poisoned them or not."

"If I did, it's nothing more than you deserve. I'm sure your accountant would thank me."

Another round of laughter sounded and Drake leaned back in his chair, any effort to disguise his irritation now gone. Not that anyone paid him any attention.

"Are those *cupcakes*?" Justice asked incredulously.

He and Thane were both eyeing Maddox and Evangeline as if they'd sprouted a third head. Drake supposed he *could* see the humor in the fact that a woman bearing cupcakes had walked into Drake's inner sanctum where no woman had ever been before. Much less bearing fucking cupcakes.

Evangeline turned in Thane and Justice's direction, but Jax cleared his throat. Evangeline rolled her eyes and then handed him one of the baked treats. Drake had a bad feeling that his angel was going to have his men trained like dogs by handing out puppy treats whenever she came near.

Then she walked over to where Thane and Justice were lounging on the leather couch and dutifully handed over a cupcake.

What she did next astounded Drake.

She first walked over to Hatcher, who glanced nervously between her and Drake as if gauging Drake's reaction or perhaps determining whether he should even be speaking to Drake's woman.

"Hi," she said in a shy voice as she held out a cupcake. "I'm Evangeline."

Hatcher took the cupcake and smiled at her. "Hello, Evangeline. I'm Hatcher."

But when she then turned her attention to Silas, who had since melted into the farthest corner, one that was so dimly lighted that Drake was surprised she'd located him with such ease, it seemed the entire room held their breath.

She walked right up to the big man, who stood as still and silent as a statue, and issued a shaky smile. Drake realized then that for all her false bravado, she was, in fact, terrified. All of his earlier irritation fled as pride surged in his veins. Evangeline was doing just as he'd asked her. To walk into his world and accept it—and him. And she'd obviously sensed that by accepting him, she was accepting his men as an extension of himself.

His jealousy evaporated because she was doing this—all of it— for *him*.

He sat back, a small smile on his lips as he watched Evangeline tilt her head to look up at Silas's much taller frame.

Then she simply reached into the container, pulled out a cupcake and held it out for Silas to take.

"Hi," she said, repeating her earlier introduction to Hatcher. "I'm Evangeline. I promise I didn't poison *your* cupcake. Just Maddox's. And"—she leaned forward, whispering conspiratorially—"I made sure *his* had sprinkles and pink frosting."

Laughter sounded behind her, but she kept her solemn attention on Silas as he slowly reached out, his palm up. She gently set the cupcake down in his hand and he stood there in bewilderment, a perplexed look in his eyes as if he had no idea what to do with Evangeline.

That makes two of us, brother.

"We're having fucking *cupcake* parties now?"

Zander's voice boomed over the quiet room with the effect of a gunshot. Evangeline jumped, knocking the cupcake from Silas's hand. As it fell to the floor, it landed on his pants, leaving a glob of frosting.

"Oh my God, I'm *so* sorry," Evangeline said in a stricken voice even as she hurried to scrape the frosting from Silas's knee. "I hope I didn't ruin your pants. That was so clumsy of me."

Mortified tears sprang to Evangeline's eyes, and her embarrassed flush extended from her cheeks all the way down her neck. She no longer looked at any of the men in the room. Instead her gaze was solidly focused downward as she scrubbed ineffectually at the mess on Silas's pants.

Drake cursed, wanting to murder Zander on the spot for the damage he'd inadvertently done. For a few brief moments, Evangeline had overcome her shyness and uncertainty and had begun to relax around Drake and his men. Now she looked as though she'd like nothing more than for the floor to open beneath her and swallow her whole.

Silas sent Zander a killing stare and then to everyone's eternal shock, he leaned down and carefully took hold of Evangeline's hand that was still brushing frantically at his pants.

"Evangeline," he said quietly. "It's all right. It wasn't your fault. If Zander had anything resembling manners, he wouldn't have barged in here and scared you half to death. You can be sure I'll send him the dry-cleaning bill."

Drake sent Zander his own murderous glare, one that promised retribution. Zander's look of puzzlement only served to enrage Drake further because the stupid fuck had no idea what he'd just destroyed in three seconds' time.

Evangeline's expression remained worried, tears still glistening in her eyes, and she nearly dropped the container she held in her other hand because she was trembling so much. Silas rescued it and set it aside before reclaiming her hand so that he held both in his.

Now that Silas's grip ceased the shaking in her hands, the quiver of her chin was more pronounced. It looked as if it was taking every bit of her control for her not to burst into tears and flee the room as fast as she could.

Drake couldn't bear her obvious despair and opened his mouth to bark a command that would clear the room in seconds, but before he could speak, Silas tightened his grasp on Evangeline's hands and stared down directly into her eyes, sincerity radiating from him.

"If there's another left, I'd love to have one," Silas said, as if she were offering him the moon.

Drake watched as every single one of his men's mouths dropped open as Silas effectively soothed Evangeline's fear and embarrassment with a few simple words and a comforting touch.

Evangeline's smile would have lit up an entire city block as she reached for another cupcake and delivered it into Silas's waiting hand. Then Silas sent Zander a withering glare over her head.

"You owe the lady an apology," Silas said, his voice like ice. "*Drake's lady.*"

"Ah hell," Zander swore. "I guess I just ruined my chances for a cupcake."

Drake saw Evangeline sneak a glance into the container and for a moment, he thought she was going to give Zander one, but instead she picked up the cupcake and turned the container upside down, signaling that there were no more.

"Sorry," she said quietly. "But this one is for Drake."

The others snickered and Maddox looked at Zander with a somber expression.

"Trust me, dude. You do not want to get on the bad side of this one."

Drake ignored the goings-on as Evangeline hesitantly entered his space, walking behind his desk to stand in front of his chair that he'd pivoted around to watch her exchange with Silas.

"I'm sorry I was late," she whispered. "We weren't really in a traffic jam. I overslept."

Drake fought his smile but then gave up, not giving a fuck who saw his reaction to the angel standing in front of him holding a cupcake.

"I know," he whispered back, absurdly pleased that she wasn't even capable of such a small deception.

A small smile curved her lips, one quirking upward a little higher than the other. "If I give you the last cupcake, am I forgiven?"

He drew her in between his splayed knees, the cupcake still in her upturned palm.

"That depends on whether you'll lick the icing off my lips when I'm done."

A blush scorched her cheeks, but she needn't have worried. His men had disappeared the moment Evangeline had approached his desk. They might be irreverent fools for the most part, and they'd certainly stretched the limits of Drake's patience by occupying his office when they knew Evangeline was coming in, but they knew full well when to make their exit.

When Evangeline hastily looked around and realized what Drake had already known, she relaxed and a devilish glint entered her eyes. She swiped one finger over the top of the cupcake, leaving a dollop of frosting on the tip. Then she reached over before he realized what she was up to and smeared the frosting right across his mouth.

He blinked in surprise and then yanked her forward until she tumbled into his lap, the cupcake completely forgotten. She stared up at his lips and whispered, "Yum."

She *almost* pulled off the naughty vixen act. But then she promptly ruined it by blushing to the roots of her hair, causing Drake to throw back his head and laugh. As afternoons went, this was by far the most disordered, chaotic and as far from the usual boring ritual one he'd had in a very long time. All thanks to an impish, golden-haired, blue-eyed angel and a Tupperware container of cupcakes.

16

Evangeline hesitated, knowing she'd impulsively thrown down the gauntlet, and she couldn't very well take a napkin and wipe the frosting from his mouth. She was faintly horrified at what she'd done, but it had been a compulsion she couldn't ignore. His teasing had instantly given her the image of kissing and licking every bit of the delicious frosting from that hard mouth and, before she could think better of baiting the lion, she acted.

Who was this woman she'd never thought existed? She was acting like a sultry temptress and while one part of her was a little mortified, the other part of her was applauding the initiative she'd taken.

The look in Drake's eyes had told her that she hadn't made a mistake and now he was waiting, an air of expectancy surrounding him, for her to finish what she'd started.

Tentatively she cupped the hard line of his jaw and then leaned in, her tongue darting to the corner of his mouth where more of the icing had collected in a blob. She flicked, removing the sweet-tasting substance, and Drake groaned, giving her courage to continue.

She pressed her mouth to his, smearing the icing on her lips even as her tongue came out, licking delicately over the male flesh. Then she slid her tongue inward, so he could taste the frosting they now shared.

She sucked in his quick exhale, savoring it before continuing with her slow, sensual removal of the frosting. She covered every inch of his mouth, licking and sucking until there was nothing left but their lips fused solidly together. With one last, leisurely lick, she broke away, breathless, her gaze seeking his in anticipation of his reaction.

His eyes glittered dangerously and she shivered, wondering just what she had provoked. That look made her feel deliciously hunted, like she was prey and he was a predator poised to pounce.

He hoisted her up until she was on her feet and then stood, pushing her back a short distance. Facing her, he wordlessly reached down and unfastened his slacks, shoving them down his hips. Then he reached into his boxers and pulled out his straining cock.

All she could do was stare at his enormous erection, her breath held in anticipation. Excitement, nervousness and a host of other sensations scuttled around in her belly until she felt light-headed.

"Take your fingers and coat every inch in the frosting," he said.

Shocked, all she could do was stare incredulously at him, not at all sure what she'd gotten herself into. She was frozen and incapable of moving. All it appeared she was capable of was standing there with her mouth gaping open.

His eyes narrowed and she knew she'd displeased him, which left her with an odd sense of failure that she didn't at all like.

"Are you questioning me?" he asked in a dangerously quiet tone.

"N-no," she stammered out. "But . . . but what if someone walks in?" she asked in a desperate, hushed tone, as if the walls had ears, and from what she'd observed so far, they did indeed seem to have just that.

He frowned, his look of displeasure intensifying along with the sinking sensation in her chest.

"First, no one would dare intrude when I'm alone with my woman, and furthermore, if I tell you to suck my cock and someone *does* walk in, I expect you to keep doing exactly as I've instructed. Do you understand?"

She bit into her bottom lip to quell the instant protest on her lips. Instead she slowly nodded her acceptance.

"Who do you belong to, Angel?" he asked in a harsh tone.

"Y-you," she whispered.

"Who owns you? Who are you to always obey *without question?*"

Oh God. What had she done? And was this truly what she wanted? The sane part of her screamed no, that she was crazy for even contemplating it. The impulsive part of her reminded her that she had signed on for this fully aware of Drake's demanding, dominant nature. It wasn't as though he hadn't been clear enough in his expectations. He couldn't have been more blunt.

"You, Drake," she said, relieved that she sounded stronger and steadier than before.

He reached out to cup her chin firmly in his hand.

"Then you need to get on your knees and put your mouth where I told you."

Dutifully, she sank to her knees and then shakily reached for the cupcake, swiping a goodly amount onto her fingers. Her touch was tentative as she smeared the sticky substance down the length of his extended cock. Satisfied that she'd done as he'd asked, she tossed the cupcake into the wastepaper basket near Drake's desk and then turned back, eyeing his erection with new appreciation.

She knew he was big. Her body had protested his intrusion when he'd made love to her, but she'd been too mindless with pleasure to really pay attention to his size. But now, she wasn't so sure she was going to be able to pull this off.

He had to know she'd never done this. Surely he did.

"Evangeline," he said, his voice not as terse as it had been before.

She glanced up at him, swallowing nervously.

"I'll guide you. If I wanted a woman who was an expert at giving head, there are any number of women I could have. But your innocence is a turn-on like none I've ever experienced. I like that I'm the only man who has felt your sweet mouth around his cock. Relax. I promise that my being inside your mouth will be nothing short of perfection."

Buoyed by his words and absurdly happy that he wanted her, that he liked her inexperience, she leaned forward, placing her hands on his thighs only for him to gently pry them away and lower them to her own thighs.

"Keep your hands down. I'll direct your movements. All you have to do is relax and trust me."

She realized in that moment, misgivings and all, that she did trust him and she couldn't even say why. God only knew the rocky, tumultuous start of their...whatever this was between them...didn't lend itself to blind trust, but she felt safe with him and some part of her knew he wouldn't hurt her.

After ensuring her hands were in their proper place, she leaned up on her knees and tentatively swirled her tongue around the bulbous head of his cock, licking it clean. Then she opened her mouth wider and began to slide him further into her mouth, working her tongue around his girth so that no spot was left untouched.

To her dismay, he was only halfway in when she felt the tip brush against the back of her throat. She'd been right. There was no way she could take all of him. Not without making an embarrassing spectacle of herself and gagging. How humiliating would that be? She had no knowledge of deep-throating, something she'd only heard of by listening in on her friends' more bawdy conversations. According to them, men liked women who could deep-throat very much. But then Drake had contradicted that claim by saying if he wanted a woman who was an expert at giving head, as he'd described it, there were no shortage of women he could call on. He'd told her he wanted *her*. That had to mean something, right?

"Relax, Angel," Drake said gently. "I like it long and slow. Getting off quickly in such a sweet mouth would be a crime. Take a deep breath. I'll guide you. Breathe through your nose. I won't overwhelm you."

His words had a calming effect and she instantly relaxed. His fingers tangled into her hair and he palmed her head with his hands, holding her firmly as he took over.

He thrust forward, his instructions replaying in Evangeline's mind. He paused a moment and she peeked up at him from underneath her lashes to see his face creased in ecstasy. He withdrew and then pushed in again, deepening his thrust.

She felt a moment of fleeting panic and forced herself to breathe out through her nose and relax.

For several long minutes, he leisurely thrust in and out, each time gaining more depth as he allowed her to become accustomed to the experience and his considerable size.

She sensed the change in him immediately and knew he was nearing his breaking point. His grip on her head tightened and his movements became less gentle. He was hot and silky and so very hard in her mouth, sliding over her tongue again and again.

"I'm going to fuck your mouth, Angel. And I'm going to fuck it hard."

Before she had time to react to the statement, he began thrusting harder, fucking her mouth just like he'd fuck her pussy. She didn't have time to react or overthink or even panic. She was too focused on staying as relaxed as possible and remembering to breathe. It took every ounce of her strength not to choke or gag, but she was determined not to disappoint him.

A tiny burst of liquid escaped on her tongue, surprising her. And she knew he was very close.

"Swallow it, Angel. Do not let one drop escape the mouth I'm about to come in."

She shuddered at his words, her entire body tingling, her nipples and clit swollen and aroused. So much so that a single touch would catapult her into orgasm.

She'd never performed oral sex on a man, much less swallowed his ejaculate. And he'd given her strict orders not to allow a single drop to escape her lips. She closed her eyes, giving in to Drake's urgent demands and simply giving herself into his care, knowing she wouldn't fail as long as he was in control.

He thrust hard, at one point his balls bumping her chin. His entire body was rigid and his hands were making a tangled mess of her hair. He couldn't seem to remain still, his fingers and hands constantly stroking and caressing her head as he murmured words of encouragement and praise.

And then he thrust hard. Harder than any of his previous thrusts. And she felt an explosion of hot liquid hit the back of her throat and quickly fill her mouth. Remembering his strict order, she hastily swallowed and then swallowed again as more replaced what was already gone.

He continued to thrust, though his movements had slowed and lacked his earlier urgency. Semen bathed her tongue, the insides of her cheeks and the very back of her throat, filling her with the very essence of him. And she swallowed it all, ensuring that nothing escaped.

When he finally began to pull from her mouth, she lovingly bathed him with her tongue, wiping it clean of his release just as she'd licked every bit of frosting from it before.

Then he reached down and carefully pulled her to her feet. She was shaking, her senses shattered by what had just occurred. She'd never really had any interest in going down on a man. It just seemed too messy, too much work and well, not very pleasant. But Drake had changed her opinion on that matter in only a few minutes.

She loved that she could bring him so much pleasure, that in fact, in her own way, she had a measure of power over him.

"Go get cleaned up," he said in a husky voice. "The bathroom is through there." He pointed in the direction of a door. "You won't be disturbed. Go ahead and change into the clothes you brought for tonight and I'll have food brought up so we can eat when we get hungry."

17

Evangeline felt like a fairy princess as she surveyed herself in the mirror, critically going over her makeup, how the dress fit, her hair that she'd pulled atop her head and had fashioned loose curls to fall gently down her neck.

Try as she might, she couldn't find fault with her appearance. God only knew she'd spent enough time fussing over every single aspect of it.

Time to face the music. Memories of the last time she'd come into this club still had the power to shame her. Nothing had changed *except* her status as Drake's woman. Did that suddenly make her above average? As the saying went back home, you can put lipstick on a pig, but you still end up with a pig.

Certainly the dress was to die for and cost more than the dress she'd chosen that night, but it wasn't as though Evangeline had tried to walk into the club in a designer knockoff. She tried to look for any discernible difference that made her suddenly more worthy of being at Impulse, but she was at a loss.

But at least she didn't have to worry about being thrown out, getting assaulted or Eddie showing up to ruin the evening. She'd already figured out that Drake hadn't lied when he said he protected what was his.

A light shiver skittered over her body as Maddox's words filtered through her mind. He'd been very serious when he'd told Evangeline that Eddie would never harm her or come within a mile of her. The look in Maddox's eyes had been menacing and she absolutely believed him, but she didn't want to dwell on the *how* he was so certain and to what lengths he'd gone to ensure such confidence when he'd assured her that Eddie would no longer pose a problem for her.

Drake owned a club, but she'd gleaned from words dropped here and there that Drake had multiple business interests. She wasn't altogether certain she *wanted* to know what all he dealt in that he required the security detail he utilized and hired men who looked like they could snap a man's neck with a mere look.

No, she didn't want to know. Some things were better left unsaid, unknown. Maybe that made her a bad person. Unethical. Not to mention stupid and naïve. But all she wanted to focus on was whatever this thing between her and Drake was and seeing where it took them.

He'd been angry. No, *angry* was too harsh a word. *Annoyed* was perhaps a better description when she'd hesitated and appeared to question his authority after agreeing to obey his dictates and submit to him. And yet she'd been *aroused* by the authority so evident in his voice. Did it make her crazy? Had he managed to uncover a part of herself she hadn't known existed—would've likely *never* have known if not for him? She simply couldn't imagine responding to another man the way she'd come to life at his touch. Every single one of his men was incredibly hot in his own unique way, and yet she felt nothing more than appreciation for their sheer masculine beauty. *They* didn't cause her to have extremely erotic fantasies.

Knowing she'd taken far too much time changing and arranging her hair and applying makeup and that Drake was probably annoyed—again—she gave herself one last once-over and smoothed her dress before taking a deep breath and slipping her heels on.

Her hand hovered over the doorknob as she gathered her courage to walk back into Drake's office, praying he approved and would be pleased with her appearance.

Swallowing back a gulp and straightening her spine, thrusting her chin up so she at least gave the impression of poise and confidence, she opened the door and walked as calmly as she could toward Drake. But inside she was a seething mass of nerves.

As soon as the door opened and Drake came into view, his gaze locked on her and fire burned in his eyes. He was silent, but his look said it all. He took in every aspect of her appearance, his gaze making a slow perusal from head to toe that had her cheeks burning every bit as much as his eyes.

"You look magnificent," he said in a low, husky, sexy-as-hell voice that made all her girly parts tighten and tingle. "My angel has transformed into quite the temptress. I'm tempted to change my plans for you for the evening and keep you here all to myself. I don't like the idea of sharing such an enchantress with anyone. I'd much prefer to have you in my lap so I could lick and taste and touch you the entire night."

She flushed with pleasure and delight at the sincerity in his voice and the ... possessiveness. She'd never considered herself a woman who would be attracted to a man so *forbiddingly* possessive, but the idea that he considered her *his* and was *over*possessive of what he now considered *his* called to a part of her previously undiscovered. She liked it. A *lot*. What woman wouldn't like belonging to a man like Drake Donovan and being pampered, spoiled and cherished to such an extreme?

"The dress suits you. It was made for you, and those heels ... I'm going to fuck you in nothing but those heels later. But babe, no dress, makeup or shoes can make a woman like you *more* beautiful than you already are. You shine, no matter what you have on, and *especially* when you have nothing on at all. There's not a woman who exists who'd look as good as you do in that dress and those heels. It's all you. Don't ever forget that."

There was no hint of anything but complete conviction in his words and in his expression. And God, the ownership she saw so clearly in his eyes made her knees wobble. The image of him fucking her in just her heels made her clit swell and pulse to the point of discomfort.

This was a man who could have any woman in the world, and yet he'd chosen her. She didn't understand it. Couldn't even fathom it. But at the moment she was caught up in a fairy tale and had no desire to question the fact that this gorgeous man thought she was beautiful and that he wanted *her*. Not another woman. Her. Evangeline Hawthorn. Just an ordinary girl. Nothing special about her and yet he made her feel wanted *and* special.

She closed the distance between them and leaned down so their lips hovered a mere breath away.

"I'm glad you approve," she whispered.

And then she kissed him, uncaring of the fact that she'd have to re-apply her lip gloss. Right now she *had* to kiss him. Had to show him what his words had meant to her.

She fed hungrily at his mouth, sucking at the tip of his tongue when his lips parted and then delving deeper so she could taste him, consume him.

A low growl rumbled from his throat, vibrating over her tongue, sending shivers dancing down her spine.

She slowly drew away, and he frowned as if he was in no way finished with her yet, but she wanted to drown in his gaze again and bask in the desire and approval in his dark eyes.

"*Approve* is hardly an apt description, Angel. I'm not sure whether you're an angel or a demon in an angel's guise. I've never been so affected by a mere kiss."

"Me either," she whispered.

He smiled then. "Tell me, Angel. Just how many men have you kissed?"

She flushed and looked away in embarrassment. He cupped her jaw and gently guided her gaze back to his.

"I didn't ask to shame you. I'm hoping to hell that you're going to tell me that you've only kissed one other man, because he sure as hell doesn't count, which would make me the first. The first that *means* anything. Because the thought of that pleases me a hell of a lot and I don't give a damn about your inexperience. I want to be the man to teach you pleasure and eroticism. I want, in time, for you to forget all about Eddie Ryker and believe that I was your first in all aspects of lovemaking."

Her heart did funny things, momentarily robbing her of breath. Then she smiled, not knowing how devastating that smile was on the male population.

"Eddie who?" she asked lightly.

He growled and became the aggressor, kissing her until she was panting for breath.

"Now *that* is what I want to hear," he said as he stroked his thumb over her swollen mouth.

"And for the record, Drake, you *were* the first," she said softly. "What Eddie did could hardly constitute anything but a quick lay where he took his pleasure and gave me none. You are the only man to have ever given that to me."

He looked extremely satisfied with her response. He loosened his hold on her and allowed her to step back, his gaze still drifting appreciatively over her body, giving her a decadent thrill. He really did like what he saw. There was no faking his response to her and it was such a heady sensation. Like she was having the most wonderful dream, one she never wanted to awaken from.

"Go and get comfortable," he said. "The food will be up shortly and then afterward I'll have two of my men escort you down. I want you to enjoy your night as you should have the first time you came to my club."

She turned quickly before he could see the dismay on her face. She remembered all too well the reactions of the other patrons. Just because she was Drake's woman now didn't change who and what she was, and she would still be judged and deemed unworthy, no matter how *Drake* saw her.

"Evangeline."

His voice halted her just as she was about to sink into one of the comfortable-looking armchairs that sat at an angle to his desk. She turned, her expression inquiring.

"It will be okay," he said softly.

She briefly closed her eyes, determined not to ruin her makeup by allowing herself to get upset over that night all over again.

"You have no idea how horrible that night was for me, Drake. *Before* Eddie even made his appearance."

Drake's eyes narrowed. "Explain what you mean."

She sighed, wishing she'd just kept her thoughts to herself, and she damned her compulsion to blurt out the truth no matter how awkward or embarrassing. Nobody wanted to hear her train of thought, and yet she forever just vomited out the unvarnished truth.

"Evangeline?" he prompted.

Damn it, but he wasn't going to drop it. She was already acquainted with the particular tone he'd just used when saying only one word. Her name. It wasn't a request. It was an order and one she felt compelled to obey, despite her overt discomfort over rehashing the events of that night.

She let out another resigned sigh and reached deep within for strength and composure.

"As soon as I stepped out of the cab, people were judging me. The people in line. Even the damn bouncer dude, or whatever his title is. The guy who mans the door and either lets people in or tells them to get in line. But he didn't even tell me to get in line. He told me to leave. And every single person in that long-ass line was smirking and looking at me like I was a moron for even trying to get into a place like Impulse. Then when I showed the guy who told me to leave my VIP pass, he looked like he'd just swallowed a lemon, and the people in line weren't subtle about their outrage that someone like me was being allowed in while they were standing on the sidewalk waiting. They looked at me like I was some sort of bug. Others just outright laughed."

She paused to take a break, surprised at the anger that still simmered over that whole humiliating experience.

"Once I got inside, it wasn't any better. Everyone was staring at me like I was some alien who'd arrived in a UFO. They were smug, amused, snotty, and I felt like I was under a microscope. The only person who was nice to me was the bartender. *He* was sweet. And *nice*. He treated me like a normal person, like I was every bit as good and welcome as the others, while the rest of the people in the front bar treated me like I'd crashed a party I wasn't invited to. It was horrible. I'd already decided to just leave. I was stupid for allowing my girlfriends to talk me into ever going, but then Eddie made his appearance with a woman Velcroed to his side whose look very clearly told me, *I'm prettier than you, classier than you, better than you and I can satisfy my man, unlike you, who were a disaster in bed.* And my stupid pride wouldn't allow me to walk out because I didn't want him to think I was ashamed or embarrassed to run into him. So I stood there, hoping he wouldn't notice me. No such luck," she muttered.

"There is no possible way for a man *not* to notice you, Angel. Unless he's dead," Drake said dryly. "You sell yourself far too short, but I'm going to work on that."

She shuddered and continued on as if he hadn't spoken. "It was horrible. The entire night was just...*horrible*. And now I'm supposed to walk out there and endure it all over again? Pretend that night didn't happen and everyone around me isn't judging me, laughing at me and wondering how I even got past the gatekeeper in the first place?"

If she hadn't been so raw from reliving that night all over again, the look on Drake's face would have terrified her. He was coldly furious, his eyes flat and his jaw clenched so tight that it had to be painful.

"None of that will happen tonight," he said in a soft voice that held a hint of menace. "All of my employees know your status and that you are to be given whatever you request and that you are to be treated with the utmost respect. My men will be close at all times, and rest assured, if anyone disrespects you in any way, they will be dealt with and it won't be pretty. Furthermore, if anyone crosses the line with you or so much as looks at you wrong, I want to know about it immediately. I want your word, Evangeline. You will tell one of my men so they can notify me and the issue will be resolved swiftly. I will not tolerate any disrespect directed at you."

"Okay," she said in a shaky voice, having learned that Drake wanted words, not gestures or nods.

His voice gentled, as did his expression and his eyes. "I want you to have a good time tonight, Angel. I'm not such an asshole that I would set you up for embarrassment, nor would I ever put you in a position where you would be uncomfortable or awkward. I have a surprise planned for you and I think it's one you will like and as such, I think you'll forget all about the first time you came to Impulse."

She sank into the sumptuous leather chair as she processed his cryptic statement and cast a curious glance his way.

He smiled. "I want you to have fun tonight, Angel. From all I've gathered you've not had much fun in your life. You've been too busy working and providing for others."

Her heart skipped a beat and she couldn't help the smile or the warmth that suddenly invaded her chest at the sweet gesture.

"And speaking of which, I still need the name of your parents' bank and their account number as well as the routing number. I'll have my assistant call and get wiring instructions tomorrow morning. But first,

I thought you'd like to call them and apprise them of the situation so the deposit doesn't come as a surprise."

Panic immediately replaced the euphoria she'd just experienced.

"Oh my God, Drake. What do I tell them? How do I suddenly explain a wire transfer that obviously didn't come from me? What will they think? It will look suspicious, not to mention it will put all kinds of questions into their minds about me and what I'm doing or what I've done to warrant such a sudden influx of money."

She could feel the heat invading her cheeks. Shame. How to explain Drake and her relationship with a man she'd known for just a few days?

"What if they think I'm a drug dealer or a prostitute?" she asked in horror.

In her tiny hometown, if someone suddenly came into money under mysterious circumstances, the gossip mill would be in full force, and that was the last thing she wanted for her parents. If it were only she who would suffer, she wouldn't care. But she *did* care about how her parents were treated and what was said about them. And she did care what her parents thought of her.

"What am I exactly?" Evangeline whispered as she continued to stare at Drake in complete meltdown. "Your mistress? A paid companion?"

Then she stopped and buried her face in her hands, uncaring of the fact that she'd have to do a serious retouch of her makeup.

"This is not me," she choked out. "This is not the person I am, letting someone else, let alone someone I barely know, step in and take care of my problems for me. I could take hating myself or even being ashamed, because there is nothing I wouldn't do for my mother and father, but I do care if they are disappointed or ashamed of me, because they would never want me to do anything that goes against the way I was brought up in order to help them."

She expected anger, even fury etched into Drake's features and sparking in his eyes when she finally summoned the courage to remove her hands from her face. But she saw none of those things. In that moment, an inexplicable bond formed between them. One of understanding. And pride.

Neither spoke, both aware of the connection, not on a physical level, but on an emotional level. They might live in completely different worlds, but things like pride and a sense of self-worth were universal, and in that area they were on common ground. Just two people with something in common. No financial or social divide. People. Just people. Experiencing and respecting things that had no barriers.

"Would you prefer I call them and explain, Angel?" he asked softly.

It was tempting. God, it was so tempting. She hated conflict, avoided it at all costs because it ate at her for days, even weeks, after the conflict had subsided. But she had to retain control over *some* part of her life, having lost every other aspect of it in her brief acquaintance with Drake. And she was many things, self-admittedly a coward and one who kept her head solidly buried in the sand, but she'd be forever shamed if she was too afraid to face the two most important people in her life.

"N-no. No," she said more firmly the second time. She sucked in a deep breath. "This is something I have to do. I owe them an explanation, and it should come from me, not from a man who is a complete stranger to them. That is not who or what they raised me to be. Above all else, they taught me to take responsibility for my actions and never to hide behind others. I may hide from myself, but I will never be accused of hiding behind another person."

Again there was a deep flare of respect in his eyes, making them appear deeper and darker than normal. And in that moment, she realized that Drake's approval—his respect—meant a hell of a lot more than it should given the fact she barely knew the man.

"Did you remember to bring your new cell phone or do you need to use mine?" he asked mildly, as though she weren't about to make a call that had the potential to send her into an epic meltdown.

"I brought it," she said, even as she glanced hurriedly around the room, her befuddled mind trying to remember where she'd put her purse.

"If you're looking for your handbag, you took it into the bathroom with you."

She flashed him a grateful look and then surged upward before she lost her courage and all but ran into the bathroom, where her bag rested on the counter next to the sink. She fumbled for the phone, realizing she hadn't entered her contacts into the new one. Not that she had many. In her present state, she would be doing well to punch in her parents' number by memory.

She was sliding her fingers over the glossy surface of the touchscreen, frowning in concentration, when she walked back into Drake's office. Returning to the chair she'd just abandoned, she sank into it as she lifted the phone to her ear.

Her gaze lifted and met Drake's, and she felt a drowning sensation. Like they were magnetized and she was being pulled toward him and absorbed. Without thinking or rationale, she slipped the phone away from her ear and hit the button for the speakerphone option and then she got up, moving toward Drake. She set the phone faceup on his desk and would have stood beside it while she conversed with her parents, but just as her mother's familiar voice came over the speaker, Drake caught her wrist and tugged her around the corner and into his lap. He then reached for the phone, sliding it so it was closer to Evangeline.

Suddenly she didn't feel as nervous. Calm pervaded her frazzled nerves and she soaked in Drake's strength and his show of support.

"Hi, Mama," Evangeline said in a cheerful voice.

"Evangeline? Is that you? Did you lose your phone? I almost didn't answer. I get so many of those annoying telemarketers and scams claiming I owe the IRS some obscene amount of money. It's ridiculous, I tell you. When a person can't even answer her own phone without being harassed by someone who can't even pronounce the word *penalty* or *taxes owed.* But then I remembered it was your area code and well, what if something had happened to you and someone was trying to notify me? I'd feel awful if I ignored that call."

Drake's lips twitched in amusement and his eyes gleamed with mirth.

"I'm fine, Mama," Evangeline said, hastening to reassure her mother before her imagination ran wild and she conjured all sorts of horrific things that had happened to her daughter.

Her mom had been convinced that Evangeline would be mugged, raped or murdered within the first week in such a sinful city. She and Evangeline's father had pleaded with her not to move to New York, and they hadn't wanted her so far away from them. To say they were extremely overprotective of Evangeline was an understatement.

She bit into her bottom lip, knowing that when she explained her situation her mother—and her father—would freak out and beg her to come home. Drake gave her a comforting squeeze and a nod of encouragement that was badly needed. In that moment she wanted to bury herself in his broad chest and just hold on tight.

"I have a new phone. The old one . . . uh, well, it crashed on me and I can't be without means of communication."

She winced at the white lie, because she never lied, and she didn't like the feeling of dishonesty. Guilt swelled in her gut and she prayed for forgiveness for this one fib.

"Oh, of course. I'm glad you did the sensible thing and bought a new one right away," her mother said. "It wouldn't do at all for you to live in that big city and not have a way of calling for help. What if you got hurt? Or someone attacked you. Why, just the other day I read a news article about two women who were accosted in New York City. You can't be too safe these days."

Evangeline flinched, closing her eyes as the lie swelled and grew, because she hadn't bought the phone. Drake had. So far Drake had bought everything. She sat in Drake's lap and listened as her mother extolled the dangers of living in a city where one's neighbors couldn't be counted on and people would walk right by someone in need.

She had tried to explain to her mother the stereotype of New York and that in fact it was quite safe, even if Evangeline lived in a sketchy area. Or rather she used to. Yet one more thing she had to tell her mother. But her mother refused to believe that a city as large as New York could possibly be safe and had told Evangeline that she was a sweet and trusting soul and cautioned her on a regular basis not to let herself be misguided. Oh how misguided her mother would think she was presently, throwing caution to the wind and handing her life over to a man she'd known mere days.

Drake shook against her and she glanced sharply at him, wondering what was wrong, but she saw him silently laughing, amusement clearly showing on his features.

"Um, Mama, is Daddy close to you? Can you put him on too? I have some things to tell y'all."

"Of course."

There was a long pause as her mother seemed to digest Evangeline's request, which wasn't unusual, so Evangeline could only think there was something in her voice that her mother had picked up on.

"Honey, is everything all right?" her mother asked anxiously.

"Evangeline, how are you, baby?"

Her father's raspy voice washed warmly over Evangeline's ears, making her momentarily so homesick that she couldn't breathe. Drake squeezed her and she sighed. Whether in person or over the telephone, she telegraphed her emotions like the freaking Jumbotron in Times Square.

"I'm fine, Daddy," she said lightly. "The question is, how are you? How have you been feeling lately?"

"I get by just fine," he said gruffly. "You're worrying your mother, so you need to spit out whatever it is you want to tell us so she doesn't get her feathers all in a ruffle."

She couldn't help but soften all over and smile. God, she missed them. More than anything she wanted to go home and see them, but the cost of an airline ticket was money she wouldn't be able to give her parents and right now, they needed financial support more than they needed her to visit.

But then Drake was changing all of that. Maybe . . . She shook herself from that train of thought. Her parents might be taken care of, a fact she was grateful for, but Evangeline had no job now and no means of raising the amount of money needed to visit her family. She was truly dependent on Drake for everything, and her heart sank at the ramifications of that fact.

"I'm no longer waitressing at the pub," Evangeline said, deciding to start with the more minor announcements and work her way up to the more shocking ones.

"Praise God," her mother said fervently.

"Good," her father said in a firm tone. "I never did like you in a place like that. A bar is no place for a good girl like you. I hated that you had to do it because I can't provide for my own family anymore."

Her heart ached at the pain in her dad's voice. Didn't he know that she'd do anything, anything at all, to give back all they'd given her when she was growing up?

Drake's hand rubbed up and down her arm, pausing at her shoulder before resuming the idle motion. He was solidly absorbed in the conversation now, a thoughtful expression on his face.

"I've also met someone," Evangeline said softly.

As she spoke, she glanced up at Drake, pleading silently for him to understand the fabrication she was about to create. Her mother and father simply wouldn't understand. The nature of Evangeline's relationship with Drake would baffle them, and she had no doubt the both of them would be on the next flight . . . Wait, no, her father would make her mother drive all the way to New York because he'd be carrying his shotgun and he'd pepper Drake's ass with buckshot for "dishonoring" his little girl.

"I work for him now," she hedged. "It's a good job. Fantastic salary. And benefits," she added hastily for Drake's hearing.

His eyes gleamed and his white teeth flashed. He looked so incredibly hot that she could feel her body jump-start and come to life. Her nipples puckered and strained outward and she wiggled uncomfortably on his lap in an effort to alleviate the sensitivity between her legs.

"Why, that's wonderful, dear!" her mother gushed. "When do we get to meet him?"

Evangeline panicked, avoiding Drake's gaze, because she wasn't going to be presumptuous. Not when he, as he'd bluntly told her, called all the shots.

"Soon," Evangeline said vaguely. "But there's more. He didn't like me working at the pub."

Before she could continue, her father interrupted.

"Good. Sounds like a man with a good head on his shoulders and like someone who'll look after my little girl. I'm glad he talked some sense into your head."

Drake chuckled, covering the sound with his hand while Evangeline glared at him.

"When he insisted on knowing why I worked such long and late hours there, I told him that I was working to help my family."

Her mother emitted a sound of distress and Evangeline closed her eyes, knowing how important her pride was to her. Something she and Evangeline's father had passed on to her.

"He wants to help," Evangeline continued, trying to cover the awkward moment. "He's adamant that I no longer work there, and so he's going to wire money into your account tomorrow. I wanted to call to let you know so you didn't think it was a mistake or draw the wrong conclusion."

Her mother gasped in surprise but recovered quickly. "Just how well do you know this man, Evangeline? Does he treat you well? You can always come home. You know that. We'll get by. We always have."

It was then that Drake surprised her and picked up the phone, turning off the speaker as he put the phone to his ear. Before she could demand he give the phone back to her, he began speaking to her mother.

"Mrs. Hawthorn, my name is Drake Donovan and I care a great deal for your daughter, and where she was working is a dangerous place."

Evangeline launched a protest only to be immediately silenced by a firm squeeze from the arm surrounding her body.

"Not only that, the apartment building she lived in is not in a good neighborhood and is not well maintained. She lived on the seventh floor and the elevators haven't worked in at least a year. Her locks were so flimsy a child could break in. I was not going to idly stand by and allow her to continue endangering herself when I am in a position to help in any way I can, and I intend to do just that. My first priority is Evangeline, and as you are her first priority, then you are important to me as well because I want her to be happy, but most of all I want her to be safe. She was working herself to the bone, exposed to men who would think nothing of hurting her, and *that* I will *not* allow under any circumstances. I understand your concerns. I share them. But rest assured, Evangeline will be perfectly safe under my protection and care, and I think we can all agree that if you are provided for financially, that will be one less burden she has to bear."

There was a prolonged silence on Drake's end as he intently listened to whatever her parents were saying, and she was squirming with frustration and impatience at being left out of a very important conversation concerning her! The longer she sat there, trapped by Drake's hold, the angrier she grew until she was seething with it.

"She will be under my constant protection, and she will be residing with me from now on. She will be safe at all times and her happiness is of utmost importance to me, something I think the three of us share. I would not be much of a man if I did not do everything possible to alleviate Evangeline's worry and stress, and part of that is ensuring that the people she loves most are provided for. In the past, she took on that task single-handedly. That's going to change starting now. Now she has me. I will gladly provide you with all my contact numbers as well as the phone number of our residence, and you should have Evangeline's new number now that she has called you. You are welcome to call at any time; however, if you should have any concerns and especially if you have need of anything, I would prefer you go through me, just so Evangeline is caused no unnecessary worry."

Evangeline gave Drake a stricken look. Was he cutting off her communication with her parents? Was he restricting her access to them?

He hugged her to him and brushed a kiss across her brow as he listened to her parents' response.

"Good," he finally responded. "It would appear we are all in agreement in this matter."

Evangeline felt the burn of helpless tears. *Everyone but me.* But the words remained unspoken, only echoing in her mind.

"Yes, sir, I completely understand, and in your position I would feel exactly the same, and I make you a promise. Evangeline will *always* be safe with me, and I'll move heaven and earth to make her happy and not regret her decision to give me her trust."

But she was already regretting it, no matter that it appeared her parents, in particular her father, had given their blessing on the whole messed-up situation. Because she felt the ends holding her together, her life, loosening and starting to unravel faster and faster and her control evaporating under Drake's dominance. She wondered how she could possibly remain intact under someone as powerful and demanding as

Drake, without becoming someone altogether different from who she was. Evangeline.

She might not have much, but she'd always known who she was and where she stood. Now Drake threatened everything. She was so shaken by what had just transpired, and perhaps she'd been too caught up in the whole Cinderella fairy tale that she hadn't truly comprehended the magnitude of what she'd agreed to.

Or perhaps she'd known exactly what she was getting into and that secret part of herself that had reveled in Drake's authority had asserted itself and reached out for something she'd been missing, an essential part of herself that would have been denied. She could resist and risk being unfulfilled, thus returning to her ordinary, predictable life. Or she could embrace the unknown but tantalizing life Drake was offering her and perhaps discover who she truly was and what the *real* Evangeline wanted.

18

Drake knew Evangeline was upset and off balance when she hastily scrambled from his lap when his phone call to her parents had ended and she'd muttered some excuse about needing to touch up her makeup.

He wasn't going to call her out on it or remind her that she'd promised to relinquish control to him and that she'd given him her trust. He didn't want to ruin the night he had planned for her. And it was understandable the way she'd reacted. The more he got to know her and peeled back the delicate layers that made up the woman he now called his, he liked who and what he saw. He was *fiercely* proud of her. He was asshole enough to admit that rarely had he truly felt respect and admiration for, much less pride in any of the women he associated with, but his angel was on a completely different plane. She was a challenge he simply could not resist, even if he wanted to, and he definitely wanted her, the entire package, and he was anticipating every step in their relationship. He just hoped like hell that she could manage to handle all that he dished out, because he planned to return in equal measure everything she gave to *him*.

She was a woman deceptively fragile and naïve looking but with an inner core of steel. And after listening in on her conversation with her parents and then speaking to them himself, he also realized that he'd come to some errant conclusions where her parents were concerned.

He'd been angry. No, not angry. He'd been *furious* at what he'd considered a case where two people who should have been protecting Evangeline were in fact taking horrible advantage of her. Now, after hearing the obvious love and affection the three of them held for one another, he knew that her parents didn't like Evangeline giving up so much for them any more than Drake did. It was *Evangeline* who was determined that she would do everything in her power to provide for the people who'd loved and raised her. Not many young women would put their life on hold indefinitely in order to do the right thing.

Only he had heard the relief in both her mother's and her father's voices when Drake had told them she would never work in the pub again and that he would ensure her safety at all times. In retrospect, he was glad he'd muted the phone before interrupting the conversation, because hearing what her parents had said would only hurt her and make her feel the worst sort of failure.

They didn't want financial help at the cost of their daughter. Yes, they most certainly needed the money she sent them on a regular basis, but they'd rather have Evangeline in school and happy, leading her own life, than tying her future up in her parents, always putting their needs before theirs. They were obviously both guilt ridden and wanted more and better for the daughter they clearly adored. Drake intended to make that happen for Evangeline and by proxy her parents.

Her father was especially concerned because he'd informed Drake, in a tone that could not be mistaken for anything but the warning it was, that Evangeline hadn't had boyfriends in high school, though plenty of boys came sniffing around. As a result she had little experience and was entirely too trusting. It worried him that she lacked the sophistication of the urbanites in New York City and would be taken advantage of. Yet another thing that Drake and Evangeline's father wholeheartedly agreed upon.

But it was the last thing her father had said that had rattled Drake's usually unshakable composure. He'd told Drake that Evangeline kept mainly to herself, shunning relationships, never seeing or recognizing her own appeal. But when Evangeline loved, she loved with her entire heart and soul, and never would a woman be more loyal or true to the man she loved. And that if Drake ended up being that man, he would be the most fortunate man in the world.

He nearly cursed as he waited for Evangeline to make her appearance. He wanted her to smile, to be happy and to shine. To light up the entire room when she made her appearance in the private box he'd arranged for her. Her every whim would be catered to, and no expense would be spared when it came to her enjoyment of her surprise.

He was saved any further introspection when Evangeline re-appeared, her makeup refreshed, but there was a dullness in her eyes he didn't like at all. Something was clearly bothering her and he wanted her to be happy and enjoy her night, not be miles away in her head.

He sighed and held out his hand, gratified when she complied and walked to where he still sat behind his desk. He pulled her once more into his lap, but this time she didn't relax in his hold and melt into his body as she'd done before.

"Angel, we have an agreement. If something is bothering you, no matter how big or small, you are to confide in me, and it's obvious you have something on your mind. I want nothing to ruin this night for you, so until you tell me what's going on in that head of yours, you stay here with me."

She looked . . . sad. Damn it. He didn't like his reaction to her obvious unhappiness. Or that it mattered so much to him.

Then she turned to look at him, fear and trepidation reflected in her eyes.

"You told my parents to call *you*, not me, that you didn't want me to worry unnecessarily. Are you cutting off my access to them? Will the only information I get about them come from you now? Will I even be allowed to speak to them?"

He cursed softly, realizing how she could have misconstrued the one-sided conversation she'd heard.

"That is not at all my intention. They are free to contact you and you are free to contact them. However, if they have a need, I expect them to come to me and not you because I won't have you worrying over something I have the power to fix."

Slowly she nodded, her body sagging with relief. Then she cast a sorrowful look at him.

"I'm sorry. I'm failing you already. I promised to trust you and yet I question you at the first opportunity."

In ordinary circumstances, yes, Drake would be impatient and pissed. He would already have cut a woman loose for Evangeline's transgressions. But Evangeline's were understandable, and he couldn't bring himself to admonish her when her worries centered on others and not herself.

He pressed a kiss to her forehead. "You haven't failed me, Angel. I imagine we will both make mistakes in our relationship's infancy. You be patient with me and I'll be patient with you."

She smiled, the sparkle back in her eyes. "Now what's this about my surprise?"

He touched the bare expanse of her back, unable to stifle the urge to simply touch her silken skin.

"I believe I said that first we would eat. You must be starving. Besides, it's not time yet for your surprise."

Her mouth turned down into a cute pout, though he doubted it was intentional or that she even realized she was pouting. Then she frowned and glanced downward at her dress in disgust.

"I probably should have eaten before changing. I'll probably make a mess of my dress and I'll have to do my makeup all over again."

"No, you won't," Drake said calmly. "Because every bite you eat will come from my hand."

She turned, her eyes widening in surprise.

"Yes, my angel. You're going to sit right here in my lap while I feed you and I'm going to enjoy every minute of it, and if there is any mess on your mouth, I'll be more than happy to clean it up for you."

Her look was puzzled. "Why would you want to feed me? Isn't that something I should do for you as your submissive?"

It was the first time she'd overtly acknowledged and said aloud what she was, and it pleased him that it came naturally with no thought or hesitation.

He gave her a squeeze, letting her know he was pleased with her question and the acceptance in her voice.

"I too have responsibilities as your dominant," he said. "Yes, you obey me, answer only to me, but it is also my job to take care of you and see to your every need. The act of feeding my woman is very intimate and it's something I enjoy; therefore you are pleasing me."

"Oh," she said softly, a thoughtful look creasing her brow as she processed his explanation.

A knock sounded, heralding the arrival of the food Drake had ordered to be sent up. Evangeline tensed, but he kept his arm around her so she didn't bolt from his lap, and he gave her a warning squeeze that had her immediately relaxing against him once more.

"Come," Drake said.

The door opened and one of the kitchen staff pushed a cart from the elevator and hurriedly began carrying over the plates to Drake's desk, arranging the entrées and utensils, and poured wine for both Drake and Evangeline. Mere seconds later, he and Evangeline were alone once again.

He tightened his hold on her, pulling her closer to him so she rested against his chest and so he could reach around her to still be able to use the arm holding her as he cut the succulent steak into bite-size pieces.

Then he speared a piece and gently held it to her lips, waiting for her to open her mouth and accept his offering.

Her tongue ran nervously over her lips, making him almost groan, before she parted them and allowed the fork to slide sensuously into her mouth. She made a small hmming noise as she chewed.

"Good?" he asked.

"Very," she said in a husky voice.

As he continued feeding her, pausing from time to time to take a bite himself, she relaxed more and more until she was completely molded to his body. He could feel the motions of her chewing and swallowing, how her body moved against his, and he was seized by contentment that had eluded him for far too long.

He noticed that every time he ate a bite and then forked a bite into her mouth, she took her time, holding on to the fork and allowing it to slide over her tongue as if she were absorbing every part of his tongue that had just touched what was now in her mouth. It was completely innocent. He doubted she was cognizant of what she was doing, but it was arousing as hell and his erection was no doubt making a permanent imprint on her ass.

Discomfort be damned. He wasn't moving even an inch to alleviate the ache in his groin because he liked her exactly where she was. She was his. She belonged to him. He could have her any time, any way he wanted, and he savored that knowledge. Never had he taken things with a woman this slowly, but Evangeline wasn't just any woman, and for her, the waiting made things all the sweeter.

But tonight . . . Later, when he took her home. He would show her his dominance and demand her submission. Physically. His angel was tough. Her looks were deceiving, as was her naïveté. She possessed more inner strength than most men he knew, and yet she had the softest, sweetest spirit that captivated others on sight.

He had no doubt that what he had planned was nothing she wasn't ready for and couldn't take. He just wished that the night were over so he could take her home and sate the erotic fantasies that had taken over his entire being since the moment he'd first laid eyes on her.

Finally Evangeline leaned all the way back into Drake's embrace, tucking her head beneath his chin, and let out a contented sigh.

"I can't eat another bite. I *want* to, but I'm about to die I'm so full," she said ruefully.

He pushed the plate away and enfolded her in both arms, enjoying the feel of so much feminine softness in his arms. There wasn't a better feeling than holding a contented woman against him. Contentment he was responsible for. It was a huge ego boost and he could readily admit that.

He nuzzled his face into her hair, being careful not to mess up the elegant knot she'd arranged or else she'd flee to the bathroom and redo it all over again, and he much preferred her to stay right where she was for the time being.

"You were right," she said softly, her breath softly whispering over his skin.

Curiosity overcame him because he was fast learning that Evangeline spoke whatever was on her mind, and he was positive that he would never be able to predict exactly what was on her mind at any given time.

"What was I right about, Angel?"

"It is very intimate to have someone feed you," she confessed. "I would have thought it silly before. But it was . . . It . . . aroused me."

He smiled at her inherent honesty, applauding his decision to make a blond-haired, blue-eyed angel his.

"It aroused me as well," he said huskily.

"Too bad you made other plans for me," she said in a mischievous voice.

He chuckled. "Oh, don't worry, Angel. I have more planned for tonight than just your surprise. In fact, I have a lot planned for when we get home."

She squirmed on his lap, obviously turned on by his insinuation, and he nearly groaned out loud, because her squirming was not helping his dick and the fact that he wanted nothing more than to bury his dick as deep inside her as possible.

She sighed. "You're such a tease, Drake. How am I supposed to enjoy my surprise now when I know what happens after?"

He cupped her breast through the thin layer of the dress she wore and thumbed at her nipple until it was hard and jutting outward. And then he captured her gasp with his mouth as he kissed her long and hard until both of them were struggling to catch their breath.

"You have a good time and then we both will have a good time together."

The ride home was unnervingly silent, but at least Evangeline sat nestled against Drake's hard body, curled underneath his arm, her cheek resting against his broad chest. His hold was possessive, which she'd decided at some point over the past few days, she liked. She liked it a lot. She felt as though for the first time she belonged. That she fit in, though the idea of her fitting into his glittering, excessive lifestyle was absurd. And yet there it was. She had her first real sense of belonging since she'd left her parents' home to move to the city.

Who would have ever thought that she would have had so much fun in the very club she'd endured such humiliation in just a short time ago? Short in literal time, and yet it seemed a lifetime ago. So much had happened since that fateful night. In a twisted, really screwed-up way, her decision to agree to her girlfriends' plan—and the subsequent disaster that ensued—was responsible for where she was now and more importantly *whom* she was with now.

As her mother always said, fate worked in mysterious ways and trying to predict the future was like trying to prevent water from sliding through your fingers. She sighed and snuggled a little closer into Drake's side.

Drake's head turned in her direction, his chin rubbing over the top of her head.

"What was the sigh about?" he asked.

She made a shrugging motion and pushed her face into his chest. For once she didn't blurt out the truth. How could she explain what she didn't even fully understand herself? Not to mention that while her experience with men was limited, she was pretty sure uttering words like *fate* this early in a relationship would cause most men to hit the brakes hard. She was getting ahead of herself and needed to remember, for the first time in her life, not to focus on next year, next month, next week. Live in the moment. Today. Take each day as it came and enjoy the ride.

Surprisingly Drake didn't question her further. Perhaps he sensed her sudden introspection. They rode the rest of the way in silence, his warmth surrounding her like a cocoon.

When they arrived at Drake's apartment, he pulled her from the car in his gentle grasp and wrapped a protective arm around her body as he hurried her toward the entrance. Then he dismissed the two men who had accompanied him, men she hadn't even noticed until then, and they promptly melted into the shadows, leaving her to wonder if she'd imagined their presence.

When they exited the elevator, Drake took off his suit jacket and tossed it, as he did every other time he arrived in his apartment, over the coatrack just inside the door, and he began unbuttoning his sleeves, rolling them carelessly upward as he sought to make himself more comfortable.

"Did my angel enjoy her night in the club?" Drake asked. "Although you rather reminded me of a princess holding court among your many admirers. You were quite the hit on and off the dance floor."

He smiled indulgently at her as she flushed with sudden self-consciousness. Initially she'd been nearly as excited about a night out at Impulse as one might be over a funeral, but she had to admit she'd actually had fun once she loosened up and let herself go with it.

Being a VIP was pretty cool, but being Princess VIP, as Maddox had quickly dubbed her, was unlike anything she'd ever imagined. She'd compared everything that had happened so far to a fairy tale on more than one occasion, but tonight? It was like a high-tech, futuristic, absolutely rocking fantasy that put the traditional tellings of fairy tales to shame.

She'd smiled, she'd laughed, complete strangers had been nice to her, and even as badass as Drake was, there was no possible way he could have arranged on such short notice for an entire club full of people to all play roles and pretend to suffer her existence. So the only possible conclusion to be had was that . . . magic had happened.

Somewhere out there, she had an invisible fairy godmother who'd waved her magic wand and altered Evangeline's entire reality. And the best part? It was well past midnight, and her prince was standing right in front of her with an absolutely delicious look on his face.

She threw herself into his arms, hugging him fiercely. "Thank you. It was the best evening *ever*. But my favorite part was the time we spent together alone in your office when you fed me."

She promptly blushed, discomfited that she'd just put it out there like that. She made herself sound like a satisfied cat purring because her master had given her a treat.

He cupped her chin and lifted it so their gazes met. "I'm very glad you enjoyed being fed by my hand because it's something I plan to do often. I am very serious about taking care of you, Evangeline. In all ways. And tonight, I'm going to show you a side of me and yourself that until now you haven't seen or experienced. Are you ready for that?"

She swallowed nervously, but trust burned tightly in her chest, and excitement scuttled through her belly, suddenly making her jittery with anticipation. Her mouth went dry, and she ran her tongue over her bottom lip. He reacted visibly to her innocent action, his gaze burning a heated trail over her mouth and then lower . . . and lower still.

"Go into the bedroom and undress," he said softly. "I want your hair down. But leave the stockings and the shoes on. I want you positioned hands and knees on the bed with your knees as far to the edge as you can comfortably support yourself without falling off. I'll give you a moment to prepare while I make a few calls."

Though Drake's tone had been unhurried, the last thing Evangeline wanted was to not be prepared when he made his appearance, so she hurriedly went into the bedroom and undressed, ignoring the natural modesty that screamed in mortification at the explicit set of instructions Drake had given her.

She removed everything, carefully putting all the gifts Drake had given her into one of the small jewelry boxes that had accompanied one of the presents. She tossed her dress into the closet along with the shoes and quickly shed her undergarments and then remembered he'd wanted her stockings and heels to remain on.

Cursing, she slipped her heels back on and then took her bra and panties off, not daring to check her appearance in the mirror as she hastily unpinned her hair. She didn't want to know what she looked like or what Drake would see when he entered the room.

When she returned to the bed, she eyed it nervously, mentally going over the directions Drake had given her and wondering just how to position herself accordingly. Finally she crawled onto the bed, planting her palms firmly into the mattress and inching her knees back until they were on the edge of the mattress, her legs and heels dangling from the bed.

She felt intensely vulnerable, knowing she wouldn't be able to see Drake when he entered the room since she was faced away from the doorway, and she wondered if he'd purposely instructed her so that he would have the element of surprise. She already knew he wanted—demanded—the upper hand in everything.

Then she wondered if she'd hurried too much and how long she would have to wait there in this position because Drake hadn't been specific about how many phone calls he had to make or how long they'd take. Again, something he likely had done to draw out her anticipation.

Her entire body was on fire, tingling, as she imagined what he would do, how he would touch her, how rough and demanding he would be. She remembered his warning after he'd made love to her that first night. That she'd needed it like it should have been her first time but it wouldn't always be like that with him.

She shivered, far from being afraid. She found herself eager to feel the moment when he unleashed his power on her. She should be afraid and yet she couldn't summon true fear of him. She feared the unknown, not knowing exactly what he planned, but she didn't fear *him*.

It had taken months for Eddie to coax her into his bed, and even then, despite thinking that he was "the one," she hadn't truly wanted to take that step with him. Now, she realized she hadn't completely trusted him, and rightly so. And yet after mere hours in Drake's presence, he'd given her a mind-blowing orgasm and then he'd made such exquisite love to her that Eddie, or rather her experience with Eddie, was nothing more than a distant and fast-fading memory. An unwanted one at that.

She closed her eyes, giving herself over to the euphoria slowly creeping over her body, leaving her in a lethargic, passion-induced fog. So immersed was she in that warm, hazy cloud that she didn't immediately register Drake's presence in the room. Not until he wrapped his hand in her hair, bunching the strands together in his grasp and pulling slightly so her head came up was she fully aware of the fact that he was standing right behind her.

Then he pushed forward, forcing her face to the mattress, instructing her to turn so her cheek was pressed against the bed and she could breathe. Then to her utter astonishment, he pulled both her hands behind her to rest in the small of her back and began looping rope around both wrists, tightly restraining her.

A protest lodged in her throat and she swallowed it away, refusing to show any resistance to the first display of Drake's dominance. Sexually. The forceful way he had her do his bidding excited her. That she had absolutely no control over the situation only heightened her anticipation. Already her breaths were coming in small pants. Every muscle in her body was rigid. Her nipples were so rigid that any pressure against them was sheer torture, and a pulse had begun between her legs that had her twisting restlessly in an effort to relieve the ache.

"Do not move," Drake said harshly, causing her to jump and refocus.

He reinforced his dictate with a sharp smack to her bottom. At first it stunned her as fire spread over the cheek he'd not so delicately spanked, but almost as soon as the burn and the pain began, pleasure immediately took over, sending a warm glow over her skin. She was dizzy, balancing on the razor's edge between pain and pleasure, and Drake was apparently an expert in knowing a woman's limits.

She closed her eyes at that thought or it would ruin her entire night. She didn't want to know how many women had come before her or would come after. She only wanted to experience all the pleasure Drake could give her, no matter how long their relationship lasted.

His palms massaged the globes of her bottom and then his fingers dipped low, one sliding inside her vagina, and he delicately fingered the walls as they desperately clenched around him, wanting more, wanting him. Not just his fingers. She wanted all of him.

Now that she knew she could accommodate his size, she was eager to enjoy his possession of her as often as she could. Because she knew deep in her heart that there would never be another man who would pleasure her as Drake would. There would never be another man so in tune with her who would go to such great lengths to give her what she wanted and needed.

"Tonight is for me," he murmured. "There will not be a single part of your body that will not bear the mark or feel of my possession. I'm going to brand you so there is no question as to whom you belong to, body and soul."

She sighed, closing her eyes as she languidly allowed the forceful words to wash over her like a gentle mist. She needed this. Wanted it. The realization was swift and shocking. But after being the caretaker for so long, always the one to take over and make decisions and to accomplish whatever needed to be done, for once someone was doing those things for *her*. Taking away the necessity of her making all the decisions and bearing the responsibility. With Drake she could simply let go and enjoy being under *his* control.

"My angel can take a lot," he said. "You look like and *are* such a fucking innocent. A rarity because of the treasure you are, beautiful on the inside and out. But you mask an inner strength most men don't possess, so I have no doubt you can take whatever I dish out tonight and that you'll enjoy every bit."

She shivered and a soft moan escaped her parted lips, and Drake squeezed her ass with one hand while probing even deeper into her pussy with his other hand. She'd already grown to know when he was pleased by his body language and the way he touched her, and she knew he liked her response, her simple moan of acceptance and of arousal.

Something Drake had said in the very beginning floated across her mind. *You don't get to tell me no. Ever.* It should have alarmed her because she was at his complete mercy, and he could do whatever he chose in this moment and there was nothing she could do to stop him. But she didn't want him to, and she realized she trusted him as much on a physical level as on the emotional level she'd already acknowledged. This man would not hurt her. Even though he'd said tonight was about him, she had no doubt that she would derive every bit as much pleasure from it as he would.

He delivered another stinging smack to her other cheek, and this time she didn't jump and the pain didn't even register because she knew that pleasure would instantly override any initial discomfort.

Another low moan escaped her breathlessly and he swore softly as he eased his fingers from inside her.

"You like that," he said, his satisfaction evident in his words. "You went so fucking wet around my fingers when I spanked that sweet ass. And I'm going to fuck that ass, Angel. But I'm going to work you up before I do. I'm going to make you so mindless that you'll beg me to fuck your ass."

Her eyes widened with shock because she'd never even contemplated anal sex. It was definitely at the top of her list of "hell no" things she never wanted to experiment with. But with Drake? Not that he'd give her any choice, but she found herself not so unwilling to try—and accept— whatever he chose to do to her.

"I won't hurt you, Angel," he said softly. "I'll push you. I'll test your limits. And while you'll ride the edge between pleasure and pain, you'll feel far more pleasure and you'll also learn that when a man knows what he's doing, pain is pleasure. The mixture can be heady and unlike any- thing you've ever experienced before. But it's my job not to take you too far and to make sure the pleasure far outweighs any pain you feel."

The sincerity in his voice made her melt, and she suddenly felt eager for him to begin. She wanted to experience every single thing he'd promised. She twisted and squirmed restlessly, her body already going up in flames at mere words. How much more intoxicating would it be when he put into action those things he'd promised her?

It earned her another smack on her plump ass, something he didn't seem to mind at all. In fact, he'd acted nothing but approving of her body, imperfect as it was. She had a smaller waist, but it was far from flat and it was squishy in places, much like her breasts. But her hips flared, giving a rounded shape that seemed almost out of proportion to her waist and even her breasts. And her backside was plump, too plump for Evangeline's liking, which was why she rarely wore form-fitting clothing.

The only problem was that since Drake had prearranged most of the clothing she had purchased, it had nearly all been form-fitting and what he considered sexy on her.

Nothing he'd said, either verbally or in his body language, suggested he found anything wrong with her "plumpness." Evangeline's girlfriends rolled their eyes and reprimanded her every time she used the word *plump* when describing herself, but what was the use in lying to herself? She had a mirror and she could see she was not what society viewed as the perfect woman. And Drake, who could have much more desirable women with the flick of his fingers, had chosen her and grew angry when she downplayed her assets or lack thereof, and he very bluntly told her it was bullshit.

And then she remembered that night when he'd said in a very straightforward manner that in no way appeared to be him saying stuff to placate her, that the other women had treated her as they did because they weren't as beautiful as Evangeline, and that hers was a natural beauty that most women spent hundreds of thousands of dollars chasing but could never achieve what Evangeline had been gifted with naturally.

How on earth was she supposed to react to that?

She knew she wasn't ugly, but neither was she anything earth-shattering. She was simply average. In between. And yet Drake saw her differently. It was there in his eyes when he watched her, unaware that she studied him covertly. For whatever reason, he was attracted to her, and furthermore, she had a hard time believing he did all the things he'd done for her in their very short acquaintance that he regularly did with his other women.

He'd ensured that her friends and family were taken care of because he hadn't wanted her to have that worry any longer. He wanted her to relinquish all control and cede ultimate power to him. God, she liked—no, *loved*—the thought of that way more than she should as an independent woman well used to providing for herself and her family with no help from anyone.

Drake's voice broke into her contemplation, a bite to his voice.

"Are you here with me, Evangeline? Because if there's something else you have to be doing, by all means don't let me keep you."

She blinked and turned as much as she could so she could look at him, and she nearly flinched at the undisguised anger in his voice.

Shit. She'd checked out on him, and she doubted anyone ever made that mistake.

"I was thinking," she said softly, honestly. She knew no other way to be, even to her detriment.

"About?" he prompted in an icy tone. "Because when I'm fucking you, I better be the only goddamn thing on your mind or we have a serious problem here."

"I was thinking about how beautiful you make me feel," she said, her voice so sincere he couldn't possibly think she was being deceitful. "I've never felt beautiful before. Not until you. It's an unnerving sensation and yet it's the most wonderful feeling in the world. And . . ."

She paused, but Drake was still looking at her, though his expression had lost the iciness and anger.

"And," he said, more gently than before.

"That while I already acknowledged to myself that I trust you, on an emotional level, I realized here and now when you could do anything to me you wanted, that I'm utterly powerless and helpless tied up, in your bed, and that I'm no match for you physically, that I know you won't hurt me. I *know* that, Drake."

He looked bemused, as though he didn't know how to respond to her impassioned statement.

"I'm sorry if it appeared I wasn't paying attention to you," she said quietly. "*All* I was thinking about was you and the anticipation of what you will do to me. I don't want you to hold back, Drake. You were right. I am stronger than I appear and I won't run screaming from your apartment because you show me everything you've told me will eventually happen. I want the real you and everything you can offer me both physically and emotionally."

She was very careful to keep the word *financially* out of her statement, and she knew he recognized the omission as well. She never wanted him to think she was with him for what he could provide financially. It would only cheapen what they had, and she wanted nothing to tarnish the beauty or progression of their relationship.

His entire expression softened and there was no longer any hint of anger or annoyance reflected in his eyes or his tone when he spoke to her again.

"Do you have any idea how rare it is to find someone as refreshingly honest as you are?" he asked in a husky voice.

She closed her eyes self-consciously, heat scorching over her face at the way he looked at her. As though he could see so much more than others could about her. Even her friends. What her girlfriends thought was a fault and something that would only bring pain and embarrassment for Evangeline, Drake clearly saw differently.

She sensed that this was a man who'd endured a lot of dishonesty in his life, which very likely explained why he was a very blunt, straightforward man. He didn't sugarcoat things or try to appease others.

And she supposed it made sense that if he hadn't had many people in his life who were honest, and he was a man who told the unvarnished truth, that he would appreciate those same qualities in Evangeline, whereas she saw it as simply being herself and deceit not being part of her nature.

It hadn't gone unnoticed by her that his men, those he trusted most and who seemed to be more than the average, run-of-the-mill employees, shared all of the traits Drake possessed. Blunt, straightforward, no tolerance for bullshit, and like Drake, they absolutely commanded obedience and respect from those around them.

"Look at me, Angel," Drake said in a firm command that had her eyes flying open so she could once more meet his gaze. "Never are you to feel shame because you're an honest, genuine person. They're rare and unfortunately they are also the people who tend to get taken advantage of the most. I never want you to think that's what I'm doing here. I want you. I intend to have you. But in no way will I ever take advantage of you."

"Sometimes I'm too honest," she whispered. "Not everyone wants to hear the truth, and not everyone wants to know what I'm thinking at any given moment."

His hand slid over the curve of her backside and then to her inner thigh, rimming her entrance with one finger.

"I always want to hear the truth," he said in a very serious tone. "Especially when it comes to you and what you're thinking or feeling. I never want you to feel as though you have to lie to me about anything. If I don't have that from you, then it means two things. That I'm not doing my job right, and it also means I have failed to maintain your trust. Neither of those is an acceptable scenario."

She breathed out a sigh of relief. For so long she'd had to guard her words so carefully, not ever wanting to inadvertently hurt anyone's feelings. It was hard to go against something so solidly ingrained in her by her parents. But she also refused to outright lie, so more often than not, she merely said nothing at all.

"It means more than you'll ever know that I can be myself with you, Drake," she said, staring deeply into his mesmerizing eyes.

He added another finger, stretching her, making her moan. Her eyelashes fluttered closed as pleasure raced through her body, leaving a fiery trail as though she'd been burned by his mere touch.

"Open your eyes. I want to see you when you come," Drake said, all vestiges of gentleness and tenderness erased from his tone and features.

She shivered because once more he'd slipped so easily back into the role of the ultimate dominant male demonstrating his power and control over his woman.

She obeyed instantly and knew he approved of her obedience. Maybe to others his body language didn't broadcast much at all. Or the nearly imperceptible change in his eyes. But she had already learned what each expression meant, or at least the ones she'd been subjected to so far.

And then a thought occurred to her and she frowned, searching out his gaze as he continued to lazily finger her.

"I thought you said tonight was for you," she said in a husky, sexy-sounding voice she didn't even recognize.

His eyes glittered and his smile was almost cruel looking against the harsh lines of his face. The man was one sexy beast of an alpha male. There was not one thing about him that didn't do it for her. She hadn't imagined men like Drake even existed except in fiction.

He was a man feared by others, recognized for his power and predatory nature. As a rule, she'd always avoided men like Drake, so she had no explanation for why she'd been so inexorably drawn to him and his dominant nature. Even now she should be terrified. Not anticipating every single one of the things he'd promised to do to her.

"Angel, if you don't think me getting you off when you're on your knees, ass thrust in the air and you soaking my hand when I make you come isn't for me, then you are very wrong. Yes, tonight is about me. It's about what I want and what I want to do to you. And watching you go off at my touch, my tongue and my dick? Yeah, that's all for me. What man's world wouldn't light up when a woman who looks like you is all tied up in his bed like the innocent angel you are?"

Her chest tightened to the point of pain because damn . . . What could she possibly say in response to that?

And then she could say nothing more at all because Drake began pushing her harder, using one hand to explore her most tender and sensitive flesh while using the other to alternate lightly flicking her nipples, stroking her breasts and belly and then sliding his hand down her spine before administering another swat to her bare behind.

She was panting, knowing she wouldn't hold out much longer but God, she didn't want it to end, no matter that he'd promised her that this was only the beginning.

She began to tremble violently, leaning further down into the mattress because her arms wouldn't support her weight. Her orgasm was building into an enormous, overwhelming entity and she wondered whether she'd even remain conscious through it. She was too mindless, completely out of control, and had no semblance or cognizance of anything but Drake and his touch, the sound of his voice.

She couldn't think. She could only feel as she spun wildly out of control, inching closer to the yawning abyss and into the moment when she flew over into free fall with only Drake to catch her, to protect her, as he'd promised he'd always do.

"That's it, Angel," Drake said, his voice rough and laced with arousal. "Let go, but do not look away from me at any time. When you come, I want to see those gorgeous blue eyes grow hazy and watch the pleasure that I'm giving you and know that no other man will see what I will be seeing. No other man will have what you are giving to me or be able to give what I give to you. You are mine, and before this night ends, you'll know who owns your body and soul."

It was hard not to completely surrender to the moment and close her eyes as her entire world shifted after Drake's impassioned statement of truth. His truth. His rules. She was his to own, to possess, and never would she have thought such simple words could forge a direct route to the very heart of her. Was this—Drake, his dominance—what she'd been missing in her life? The answer formed instantly and insidiously snaked its way through every cell in her body.

But she focused on Drake, as he'd commanded, her gaze locking with his, and it was the electric spark forming an instant connection with him that went far deeper than the physical pleasure she was feeling that finally hurtled her over the edge and into sweet oblivion.

It felt as though she fragmented and then shattered into a million tiny pieces, but now that her eyes were locked with Drake's, she couldn't break away for anything in the world. Seeing her pleasure reflected in his gaze was the most erotic, powerful thing she'd ever experienced in her life.

And in this moment, she felt completely safe, as if nothing could ever hurt her again. As long as she was in Drake's arms, nothing could touch her. The outside world ceased to exist. Her former life, her way of life, faded, evaporating until there was only here and now and the world she'd willingly walked into. Drake's world. Maybe it made her crazy for being so impulsive, so out of character for her. But she wasn't crazy about one thing. Whatever this was between her and Drake was all too real. So real that it frightened her, but at the same time she was also gripped by a sense of true belonging, something she hadn't felt since the day she'd left her parents' home to move to New York and work.

And now that she had that, had Drake, she wanted him and everything he had to offer more than she wanted her next breath. In time her natural fears and concerns would work their way out. She had to believe that, because she wanted this too badly to consider even for a moment what her life would be like after tasting something so beautiful and all-consuming.

How could she ever go back to her old life after experiencing the world where Drake made all the rules and answered only to himself, and others around him answered strictly to him? He'd introduced her to an exciting, colorful world, not one steeped in gray and the monotony of her day-to-day routine, performing her tasks and taking care of her responsibilities by rote.

She purposely shoved away all thoughts of a world where Drake didn't exist, not wanting anything to ruin this moment when Drake claimed her, exerted his dominance physically, the only part of their relationship that was as yet uncemented.

She was only partly aware of him stripping off his clothing as her breaths came erratic and heavy in the aftermath. Before she could even process the explosive effects of her orgasm, and the fact that she was still quivering from head to toe and the throb between her legs was already crying out for his touch once more, he roughly cupped the globes of her ass and pushed up and outward.

The huge head of his erection prodded at her opening and he thrust hard, shock rippling through her body as her swollen tissue fought his forceful invasion. He had such a tight grip on her ass that she knew she'd wear his marks for days to come, and she loved the fact that whenever she sat for the next few days, she'd feel that reminder of his possession of her, and that she'd wear the signs of his ownership and dominance.

He withdrew until she could feel his cock barely rimming her entrance, and then he thrust into her more powerfully than before, a gasp escaping when she realized she'd taken him to the hilt and that she could take no more of him.

This was nothing like the first time, when he'd been so exquisitely tender and gentle, taking her slowly, with reverence that had brought tears to her eyes. And then his words, about how she needed the first time with him to be the way her first time with any man should have been.

His warning that it wouldn't always be like that hovered in her mind, because now she was getting a taste of what was to come and what being with him would entail, and it excited her, aroused her, so much that she could already feel the welcoming edge that signaled the slow climb to another orgasm.

She felt impossibly stretched, felt the burn deep inside her that blurred the nearly indecipherable line between pain and pleasure, melding the two seamlessly together until all she knew was sheer ecstasy.

"Going to ride you hard and long, Angel. And then I'm going to have that sweet mouth and then that even sweeter ass. And then I'm going to come all over you and mark you, so that you'll know precisely who you belong to."

She shuddered violently, mere words sending her closer and closer to another explosive orgasm. She loved the descriptive and explicit way he talked. Low and dirty but so very sexy. His words were as provocative and arousing as his touch.

He began driving into her, ruthlessly opening her to meet his powerful forward surges. His hands slid to her hips, his fingers digging deep as he held her firmly in place and then yanked her back to meet his next thrust.

Then one hand covered her bound hands while the other went to tangle in her hair, pulling hard, so that her head was lifted from the bed and she could see him, legs apart, hunched over her behind as he penetrated her deep and then remained there as he stared at her.

For a long moment, they simply shared, without words, the power of the magnetic pull between them. As if both were helpless to end it. She didn't want it to end and judging by the brooding, determined look on his face, he felt the same as she did.

Then he closed his eyes, his big body shuddering against hers as he slowly withdrew from her aching body.

He walked around to the side of the bed and then lifted her so she was on her knees, her hands still tied behind her back. Then he got onto the bed, positioning himself so she was between his splayed thighs and his back rested against the headboard.

He pulled her down, framing her face with his hands, and positioned her mouth over his engorged erection.

"Open," he said roughly. "But don't move. Don't do anything but remain how I've positioned you while I fuck your mouth as hard as I can."

Bent over as she was, hands tied behind her back and Drake grasping her head, directing her movements, she had no choice but to follow his dictates.

He lowered her head once her lips parted and pushed in hard and deep, stopping at the back of her throat with a guttural groan that vibrated through his penis and into her mouth. His hands tangled in her hair, lifting it up and away from her face so he could have an unimpeded view of her sucking him off.

She wished *she* could see the erotic scene. Just the fact that she was giving this man so much pleasure had already reduced her to a quivering glob, her senses so heightened that she was precariously close to orgasming from the sheer act of pleasuring him.

She hummed around his enormous erection and was rewarded by another inarticulate, strangled noise erupting from his throat. She smiled around his cock and relaxed so he could have complete, unfettered access to her body and whatever he chose to do.

He swore violently, his hands and movements suddenly stilling. Alarm made her pulse ratchet up. Had she done something wrong? Had she hurt him?

As though sensing her sudden tension, he stroked a hand through her hair and tilted her chin upward enough that his cock slid most of the way out and she was able to see his expression.

"I'm close," he admitted. "Too damn close and I'm not ready for it to be over with."

She smiled even as her tongue performed a delicate dance around the head of his penis.

"I want that ass, Angel, but it's going to take time to prepare you for that. I'm going to untie you because I want you to use your hands to pleasure yourself while I ready you and then especially when I get inside you so that you feel no pain."

She flushed at the idea of essentially masturbating in front of him, and as if sensing just what she was thinking, he hoisted her up so she was kneeling between his knees facing him. He smiled and thumbed her swollen lips.

"Trust me, babe. It won't be the easiest to take me unless you pleasure yourself, especially when I first get inside you. The point is to have you so far gone and desperate for release that you'll be begging me to go hard and fast so you can get off, and just so you know, you don't come until I tell you. Because if it's all over for you and I'm only just getting started, it isn't going to feel as good, and I plan to fuck your sweet ass for a long time."

Her entire body became heated and she fidgeted between his thighs, already impatient to experience Drake's complete possession. He freed her hands and gently rubbed her wrists to ensure she had experienced no discomfort. Then he tossed the rope to the floor and cupped her chin, looking directly into her eyes.

"Position yourself like you were before, knees to the edge of the bed. Put your head down and rest your chest on the mattress so you can reach yourself and be able to rub your clit however it makes you feel good. I'm going to get some lube from the bathroom. In the meantime, I want you like I told you to be and I want to see you touching yourself and getting yourself worked up when I get back."

There was a distinct edge in his voice, one that told her not to even think of disobeying him.

She slid from beneath his thighs and then got onto her hands and knees and inched her way back until she was on the edge of the bed. Then she leaned down, letting her face and chest rest against the mattress, and wiggled experimentally as she positioned her hand on her pelvis. She let her fingers slide slowly lower until she stroked her already throbbing clitoris and gave a soft sigh of contentment as streaks of pleasure wafted through her veins.

Drake was gone and back before she even registered his departure. She was so absorbed in the decadent sensations she was experiencing that she didn't realize he'd come back until his hand slid over her ass, startling her and yanking her out of the cloud she'd become immersed in.

"If you start to come, stop touching yourself," Drake said. "When I tell you to come, then get there, because it means I'm about to come and I want you with me."

"I'm with you, Drake," she whispered softly, smiling in a way she knew he found pleasing because of the sudden fire that blazed in his eyes.

He rubbed his thumb over the seam of her ass, the lubricant a cool contrast to his much warmer hands. Then he slid the blunt tip of a single finger just inside her puckered opening and she sucked in deeply, her eyes widening in surprise at just how big his finger seemed.

"Touch yourself," Drake bit out. "I haven't told you to stop. I'm going to fuck your ass whether you prepare yourself or not. The choice is yours."

If she was so resistant to just his finger, she had no idea how his enormous erection was ever going to make it. She needed no second reminder and she didn't want to displease Drake by defying him, so she began to gently rotate her finger around her clit until she found the right angle, the right amount of pressure and the speed she needed in order to distract herself from the gentle, yet persistent probing as Drake ensured she was well lubricated enough to take him.

Remembering not to stop touching herself when he fit his cock to her opening, she closed her eyes and concentrated only on the pleasurable sensations her fingers gave her. But then the overwhelming pressure and the burn that accompanied his initial breach of her tiny entrance became something else entirely.

She was edgy, *on* edge. Wanting him to stop and yet at the same time wanting him to thrust in as hard as he could and put an end to both their misery.

She whimpered low in her throat, a sound that made him stop immediately.

"Too much?" Drake whispered, even as he pressed forward more.

"No. I want more, Drake. Please, I need more. I'm so close and I want you so deep inside me. The pain is no longer pain. The pain is pleasure."

And then suddenly he plunged deep inside her and she yelled hoarsely, her fingers leaving her or she would have orgasmed instantly. She panted, her body heaving as Drake remained buried to his balls in her ass.

Oh God, it was the most incredible sensation she'd ever imagined. Never would she have thought she would find pleasure in this act. The idea of it seemed repugnant. But now, in this moment, it was symbolic of Drake's complete possession and his exerting his complete dominance over her.

She needed this. Needed him.

He pulled slowly out, retreating inch by inch until she clutched only the head of his penis. He paused a moment and then powered into her again, wringing another cry from her.

"Oh God, Drake. It's too much. I won't last," she said helplessly. "What do I do?"

"Shhh, Angel. I'm not finished yet. Put your hands forward, palms down on the bed, and keep them there until I'm ready."

Reluctantly she did as he commanded and then closed her eyes in preparation for what came next.

He wasn't as rough as he'd been in her pussy and with her mouth, but he was also firm and unyielding, gaining depth with every thrust. But he set a slow, almost leisurely pace, stroking in and out until her world went completely hazy around her.

After what seemed an eternity, he twisted one hand in her hair while keeping a firm hold on her hip with his other hand, and he pulled upward, forcing her neck back.

"Touch yourself now, Angel. I'm close, so you need to catch up."

Eagerly, she slid her hand between herself and the bed once more and found her sweet spot, groaning instantly when the first thrill washed over her.

"I don't need to catch up," she said breathlessly. "Just do it, Drake. I'm so close. I want it hard. Rough. However you want me. I want to be that for you. Only for you."

He released his hold on her hair and then grasped both hips, tilting her up even more, and then he began to thrust long, hard and as deeply as he could. She felt a spurt of moisture from herself as the first waves of her orgasm broke and rushed over her like a tidal wave consuming everything in its path.

She screamed and went wild beneath him until finally he pressed her forward, trapping her firmly between the bed and his body as he continued to drive over and over into her.

And then suddenly his weight lifted and he yanked free from her ass just as she felt the hot spray of his release splash onto her back and behind. Then he thrust back into her, holding himself deep as he twitched and convulsed, emptying the last of his semen deep within her body.

"Never a more beautiful sight," he said gruffly. "You're mine, Angel. All of you. Have no doubt now that you belong only to me and another man will never touch or take what is mine."

20

Predictably, the next morning Evangeline woke alone in bed, Drake no doubt having vacated it long before. She had no idea how he managed to keep the hours he kept and even how he had the time to work her into that busy schedule.

She closed her eyes in dismay when she saw that this morning's offering was the same as it had been all the mornings since she'd officially moved in with Drake. She dreaded seeing what outrageously expensive gift he'd chosen for her this time.

With a resigned sigh, she opened the gift first, avoiding for now the note Drake had left her.

It was a dazzling and no doubt priceless tennis bracelet with huge diamonds that encircled the entire piece of jewelry. It matched the diamond earrings he'd given her, and now she worried he'd soon be giving her a matching necklace as well.

The only gift she never took off was the necklace Drake had given her because it was symbolic to her. It represented his pet name for her, a name only he used, and it had been the first gift he'd given her. But at the time, she hadn't realized this would become a daily ritual of him buying her expensive pieces of jewelry that made her feel guilty because of how extravagant and unnecessary it was.

She was uncomfortable over the thought behind the gifts. If he was trying to buy her when all she wanted was him. She felt guilty wearing such priceless jewelry when her parents and friends lived day to day, paycheck to paycheck.

Yes, Drake had seen to her friends and family, but it still bothered Evangeline to be living in such luxury and being showered by gifts that the cost of one piece alone would cover her parents' expenses for an entire year.

With another sigh, she carefully put the bracelet back into its box and got out of bed to go place it next to the others before returning to see what Drake had to say this morning.

Going to be a long day in the office. I have several matters to take care of and several meetings to attend. I'd like you to cook something that will keep or be able to be warmed over, since I won't know an exact time I'll be there. I'll call you on my way so you can warm it up again for my arrival. Zander will be by this afternoon to get a grocery list from you and run out for whatever you need for tonight. Enjoy your day in and rest. I was hard on my angel last night.

Evangeline's lips tightened. She couldn't even go to the market to get the few things necessary to cook a meal? Was she a prisoner after all, no matter what Drake assured her of? She knew one thing. She wasn't staying cooped up in his apartment all day while Zander played errand boy. It was a beautiful day and the forecast had been for cooler, more fall-like temperatures today and the rest of the week. She had no intention of not getting out and staying shut in every day.

Since she didn't know what time Zander would arrive—and what was up with Zander being her babysitter du jour anyway? Hadn't he been in the doghouse last night? Or was she to be tossed between Drake's men one by one until she reached the last of the pack and started over from the beginning?

She shrugged. Oh well, she didn't know what time he was due to arrive, and there was a market within easy walking distance. If he wasn't here by the time she'd showered and dressed, she'd run down to the market herself and get the necessary items for dinner.

While she showered, she mentally went over the possibilities, wanting something more elegant than she typically served her girlfriends, when making every dollar stretch as far as possible was also a necessity.

Then she remembered the steak—Wagyu steak?—that Justice had taken her to eat and how expensive it had been. The question was, what kind of market would even sell such expensive meat, or could one even get it outside the fine restaurants that served it?

She had a recipe for a simple, delicate butter sauce because meat that tasted that good needed nothing heavy to mask the natural flavor, and well, butter made everything better, or so her mother always said. Green beans would be a perfect complement, as would a mouthwatering gourmet homemade mac and cheese recipe she had, and she could add lobster to jazz it up. Which only left potatoes because steak without potatoes was an unpardonable sin in her book.

Scalloped potatoes or simply baked potatoes with Drake's choice of toppings?

She had completed her menu by the time she dressed in a comfortable pair of jeans and lace-up tennis shoes. She chose an oversized sweater with a comfortable neckline that layered over her breasts, only giving a hint of her cleavage, which was displayed much better thanks to the new bras she'd purchased.

She eyed the ever-growing selection of jewelry Drake had given her but opted not to wear anything but the angel necklace. It was simple and not too ostentatious. It suited her when the other stuff was just not her.

After applying light makeup and brushing out her long hair, she chose to leave it down so it would dry faster. Then she went into the living room to find her purse so she could be on her way.

She was so preoccupied with her thoughts that she didn't notice Zander until he cleared his throat and she jumped, emitting a startled yelp. She backed warily away, cursing Drake's men's propensity for appearing out of nowhere. Did Drake give them free run of his apartment? Or did they just not believe in knocking, for God's sake?

"Sorry for frightening you once again," Zander said. "Drake told me you would know I would be here."

"He said you were coming by, not that you would be here when I got up," Evangeline muttered. "Apparently the idea of knocking or buzzing up to let someone know you're here is something that escapes all of you."

Zander grinned. "I'll get out of your hair as soon as you give me the list of stuff you need from the market."

Evangeline frowned. "Actually, I'm going shopping. What you do with your afternoon is up to you."

Zander's smile faded, and he looked uneasily at her. "Uh, that wasn't my understanding."

"It is now," she said firmly. "I'm going shopping. Whether you come is entirely up to you."

Then she turned to walk toward the open elevator doors.

"Shit. Drake's not going to like this," Zander muttered behind her.

She punched the close door button and watched in amusement as Zander's expression turned murderous just as the doors shut in his face, preventing him from getting on with her.

She rode down and walked by the surprised doorman before he could open the door for her, and she stepped into the brisk air and blinked against the sudden wash of sunshine. She'd been right. It was truly a spectacular day. She inhaled deeply, feeling as though she were seeing the outside world for the first time since she'd entered Drake's world.

Not taking too much time to savor the feel of freedom, she started down the street toward the market that was just a few blocks away, her list memorized. Zander caught up to her at the corner as she was waiting for the crosswalk light to turn green.

He grabbed her elbow and whirled her around, his eyes glittering with fury.

"What the hell do you think you're doing, woman?" he all but roared at her. "Are you just trying to piss Drake off?"

"The more appropriate question is whether he's trying to piss *me* off," she returned sweetly. "I just love how my shopping trip, which wasn't supposed to include me by the way, was planned and arranged when no one but me knows what I'll be cooking and what I'll need, including brands, spices, ingredients, et cetera."

"That's what a list is for," he growled.

Her cell phone rang and she fumbled for it, and then seeing Drake's name as the incoming caller, she looked accusingly up at Zander.

He shrugged. "You dug your own grave."

"Hello?" she said warily.

"What the fuck do you think you're doing?" Drake clipped out.

"I'm going shopping so I can cook dinner, like you instructed," she said defensively, not liking at all that Zander was standing a mere foot away and could likely hear every word Drake said even with the sounds of traffic all around them.

"Maybe you don't remember the conversation you and I had where I was very specific in that I was to know where you are at all times and that if you were going out you were to inform me of your plans and that I would not be pleased if you forgot."

His tone was icy and he was obviously furious. Not just angry. He was, as Zander had said, *pissed*.

"I wasn't given that choice," she said in an icy tone to match his. "I was told to give him a list and I was told he was going and that I was not. I prefer to do my own shopping, especially when it comes to a menu I've meticulously planned. He refused and intended for me to remain in the apartment the entire day when it is an absolutely gorgeous day outside and I wanted to shop for my own groceries. Therefore my only choice was to go myself."

"All you had to do at any time was pick up the phone and call me," Drake said, anger still vibrating in his voice. "You could have told me what you wanted and then I would have been aware of your whereabouts instead of receiving a call from the man I assigned to protect you telling me that you gave him the slip and were even now God only knew where in the city."

She went silent, her mouth dropping open. He made it seem so simple, and yet nothing about Drake's words suggested she had any choice or say in the matter.

"If you make such a mistake in the future, I will not be as forgiving or understanding," Drake said in a cool, slightly more calm voice. "Now do your shopping and don't make Zander's job any harder than it is. His job is your safety, and he can't do that job if you're not with him."

"Okay," she whispered, embarrassed by the sudden sting of tears at her eyelids.

He ended the call and she stared a long moment down at the now-blank screen, and then she slipped it back into her purse, refusing to meet Zander's gaze.

He sighed beside her and then reached out a tentative hand to squeeze her shoulder.

"We haven't started out on the best foot, have we, Evangeline?" he asked ruefully.

"Tattletale," she muttered.

He chuckled, some of the tension easing. And then his voice became somber once more.

"He's right about one thing. You shouldn't be going out alone. It's dangerous. You could be hurt. Your safety is my job, so let me do it and then both our lives will be a hell of a lot easier."

Then he let out an exaggerated sigh. "I assume this means we're walking and you'll expect me to carry everything back?"

She gave him a small smile that seemed to delight him, and, well, she had been a bitch to him. It wasn't his fault. He was only following orders.

She sighed back. "I'm sorry for making your job difficult. It isn't your fault."

He seemed perplexed and uncomfortable with her apology.

They walked the rest of the way, Zander providing a shield around her so that no one so much as brushed her on their way by.

After spending nearly a frustrating hour perusing the beef counter and even going to a local butcher, Evangeline was beginning to wonder if Wagyu beef even existed outside the restaurant Justice had taken her to. Maybe it was specially imported. Cooking excellent meals with what she made do with was something she was good at. Fine foods, *expensive* gourmet foods, however, were beyond her realm of knowledge.

"What the hell are you looking for and not finding, Evangeline?" Zander asked in a frustrated tone. "Maybe if I knew, I could help."

Her eyes lit up and she grumbled to herself for not having thought of it earlier.

"Do you have Justice's phone number? Is he busy?" she asked anxiously.

Zander couldn't hide his perplexed expression as he stared wordlessly back at her.

"Do you or don't you?" she asked in exasperation. "Do you want me to be shopping all afternoon, or will you call Justice for me?"

The answer to that question was obvious when he immediately dug out his phone, punched a button, and then handed the phone to her.

"Yo man, how's angel duty going. Any disasters befallen you yet?" Justice asked cheerfully.

"That depends on what you consider a disaster," Evangeline said sweetly. "I would say inserting one's foot into one's mouth might be considered somewhat of a disaster."

"Oh shit," Justice said with a groan. "Hello, Evangeline. Everything okay? Why you calling me from Zander's phone? You should have my number and all the guys' numbers programmed into your cell."

"Oh," she said. "I didn't look. I mean, I asked Zander to call you. I didn't know I had your number. I barely know how to work the damn thing."

"Is there something you need?" His voice took on a more serious tone. "Are you in trouble?"

"No, no, well, nothing serious. You remember the restaurant you took me to and ordered that ridiculously expensive steak?"

"Yeah," he said in obvious puzzlement.

"I can't find that steak anywhere," she said in frustration. "Drake wants me to cook tonight and he likes steak, so I thought I'd buy some Wagyu steak and grill it. But I can't find it anywhere."

Justice chuckled. "No, of course not. But tell you what. I'll make a phone call right quick. Have Zander take you back to that restaurant and ask for the chef. He'll know you're coming and he'll hook you up."

"Really?" Evangeline whispered, in awe of the obvious connections not only Drake had, but his men as well. Was it really that simple and had she wasted an entire hour when a simple phone call would have provided her with instant results?

"Yeah, really. Let me go so I can make that call. By the time you get there, the chef will be expecting you."

She ended the call and handed the phone back to Zander. "Um, he says to tell you to take me to the restaurant where he took me to eat Wagyu steak the other day."

"Fuck me. You're making Drake Wagyu steak tonight and I'm not invited?" Zander asked in a cute, sulky tone.

"No, but if you're nice to me the rest of the day, I'll save you some leftover dessert. It's even better than my cupcakes. Promise."

Zander groaned. "Drake's a lucky bastard. I hope he knows that."

"I hope so too," Evangeline murmured, low enough for Zander not to hear.

Judging by the arched brow and curious look sent her way, she hadn't been that fortunate.

"Oh, he knows," Zander said softly. "Don't ever think otherwise, Evangeline. If you think he's this way with other women, you're wrong. You're special to him, even if you haven't realized it yet."

She wasn't at all sure what to make of that statement, so she let it go as they began the short walk to the restaurant.

As Justice had told her, when Evangeline and Zander arrived at the restaurant, though it wasn't yet open for lunch hours, they were immediately let in and led back to the kitchen, where they were met by a middle-aged man she assumed was the chef.

He smiled when he saw her and enfolded her hand between both of his.

"Justice tells me you enjoyed my steak the other day."

"It was the most wonderful steak I've ever had," Evangeline said honestly. "I wanted to cook it for dinner tonight but haven't been able to find it anywhere."

The chef went over to the counter where a butcher-wrapped package lay out, and then he wrapped it in plastic wrap so it wouldn't leak and handed it to Evangeline.

"The secret is in not undercooking it," he explained. "These steaks are heavily marbled, so if a person normally eats their steak rare, I would suggest cooking them medium rare. But don't overcook them either. You want the fat to dissolve just enough and to be warm all the way through. If they aren't cooked enough, you end up with jellylike consistency from the marbling instead of the juicy succulence you should experience. Overcook it and, well, you have a burned mess that has none of the wonderful taste that it should."

"Thank you so much," Evangeline said, smiling radiantly at the kind older man. "I have no doubt dinner will be a wonderful success thanks to your generosity and expert advice. How much do I owe you for the meat?"

The chef blinked and immediately looked discomfited. Zander smoothly inserted himself and said, "Drake has an account with the restaurant. He'll be billed. You don't need to worry about it."

People had accounts with restaurants? For that matter they had relationships with the chefs that made it possible to get what was no doubt proprietary meat from the chef to cook at home?

The more she saw into Drake's world, the more aware she was of just how clueless she was when it came to having money and connections. It all sounded like something out of a ridiculous movie. Not real life and definitely not *her* life.

Then she surprised the already bewildered chef by impulsively hugging him.

"Thank you for doing this for me. I have no doubt dinner will be superb tonight, thanks to you, and rest assured you'll get the credit for providing such an amazing meal."

The older man flushed. "It was my pleasure, Miss Hawthorn, though from what I hear of your culinary expertise, I'd take you on and put you to work in my kitchen any day of the week, although I'd probably fast be out of a job."

It was her turn to blush, and she wondered how on earth this man knew anything about her cooking.

"I won't keep you any longer," Evangeline said. "I need to get home so none of what I've purchased is spoiled. Thank you again."

Zander herded her from the kitchen and out of the restaurant, where once more she blinked and squinted at the bright autumn sun.

"You need a pair of damn sunglasses," Zander muttered.

She shot him a strange look and then shook her head. But as they headed down the sidewalk, Zander stopped at a name-brand boutique and dragged her inside, where he proceeded to make her pick out a pair of outrageously expensive designer sunglasses that horrified her once she saw the price tag.

She mutinously shook her head, refusing to even consider buying such an extravagance. He merely ignored her and since she wouldn't make a choice, he chose the two he thought looked the best on her and just gave her a look she was becoming well acquainted with since it was one Drake and all his men wore like a second skin. The one that said, *You won't change my mind.*

After he paid for them, he plucked a pair and slid them on Evangeline's nose, adjusting them to his liking before they stepped from the shop. He seemed rather pleased with himself and Evangeline didn't have the heart to put a damper on his mood, so she kept her thoughts of the ridiculousness of paying hundreds of dollars for a pair of sunglasses to herself. A five-dollar pair from a grocery store or pharmacy would have certainly sufficed.

But what she wore was a reflection on Drake, and she doubted he would be pleased to see her wearing anything but what he considered the best.

And it was because of her exasperation and her inattention to her surroundings that she tripped as they headed down the sidewalk and went sprawling before Zander could catch her. The impact of hitting the concrete took her breath away as Zander's colorful curses filled the air.

"Jesus Christ, Evangeline, are you all right?"

His concerned face filled her vision as he gently turned her to look at her. She reached up, worried she'd broken her sunglasses and when, in fact, they came away in two pieces, she nearly burst into tears.

"I broke them," she said tearfully.

"Fuck the sunglasses," he said, fury lacing his words. "I'm more concerned whether you broke anything on you. Can you get up? Do you hurt anywhere?"

She let him help her up, wincing when she stretched her leg to its full length.

"Just my knee," she said. "I think I just scraped it. God, I'm so sorry. I'm so clumsy."

Zander bent right there in the middle of the sidewalk, forcing her to hold on to his shoulder for support as he examined the tear in her jeans and moved the material right and left so he could assess the damage.

"You're bleeding," he said grimly. "I can't fucking see well enough to know how deep the laceration is or if you'll need stitches. I need to call Drake."

"No!" she burst out. "For God's sake, Zander. I scraped my knee. The world isn't ending. Drake does not need to be disturbed at work because I'm an idiot who fell and scraped her knee. He has a very busy day and said he had several meetings and that he'd be late arriving home. I don't want to disrupt his schedule over something so insignificant."

Zander frowned, having no liking for her response. He knew Drake well enough to know that if Evangeline was involved and especially if she was hurt, he wouldn't give a fuck about some goddamn meeting. But she looked like she was on the verge of a complete meltdown, and given that she'd already been on the receiving end of a pissed-off Drake this morning, he could well imagine why she wouldn't want to risk provoking his anger again even though Zander knew damn well Drake would be anything but pissed.

"Zander, please," she begged. "This is embarrassing enough without involving Drake."

His expression softened and then he shook his head before picking his phone up. To Evangeline's dismay, he seemed to have not been moved by her entreaty.

"Yeah, Zander here. I need you to come get me and Evangeline and have Drake's doctor on standby. I'm taking her to get checked out."

There was a long pause.

"No. She doesn't want Drake to know. She just took a fall. Her knee hurts but I can't exactly examine it in the middle of a fucking public sidewalk. Just get here."

After Zander gave whoever he was talking to his and Evangeline's location, Zander ended the call and then gathered the bags he'd dropped when Evangeline fell. Then he curled his huge tattooed arm around her waist.

"Lean on me and try not to put much weight on your hurt leg," he said. "We need to get somewhere you don't get knocked over by some asshole pedestrian in a hurry. Preferably somewhere you can sit so you aren't putting any strain on that knee."

He all but carried her and the bags a short distance away under the awning of a restaurant and settled her into a bench intended for waiting customers. When the woman manning the door would have protested them sitting, Zander sent her a ferocious glare that promptly had her shutting her mouth and retreating hastily to her post.

"Who did you call?" Evangeline asked.

"Justice. He's not far or he would have called someone who was closer than he was to come get you."

"Is a visit to the doctor really necessary?" Evangeline asked with a frown. "We should just go home. I can doctor it myself. It's not serious. It doesn't even hurt that much anymore."

"We *are* going home," Zander said calmly. "Drake's personal physician has a clinic on the second level of Drake's building. He has a practice, but his primary job is to see to Drake and Drake's employees' needs. And believe me, we're a full-time job," he added with a grin.

But Evangeline didn't return his smile. Her brow furrowed in thought over what Zander had told her. Drake required a personal physician?

As in one who looked after the needs of him and his men? Were their jobs that dangerous? For that matter, she had yet to figure out precisely what Drake and his men did for a living. Surely owning a nightclub didn't command the kind of wealth Drake and his men possessed and certainly wouldn't be cause to have a personal doctor to patch someone up on a regular basis.

She felt faintly ill, wondering just what she had gotten herself into and if she was already in way over her head.

"How bad are you hurting?" Zander asked bluntly.

She looked up at him, squinting when her gaze met the sun beyond Zander's broad shoulders. He frowned and dug out the other pair of sunglasses and promptly perched them atop Evangeline's nose.

"It just stings a bit. You're completely overreacting," she muttered. "One would think I got shot."

Zander wasn't amused, and it was the fact that his expression became as grim as it did that made her wonder if being shot was a possibility. Was her coming to harm why Drake was so overzealous when it came to her having protection any time she left the apartment?

If she thought for a minute she'd actually get an answer, she'd ask Zander just that question, but she knew he'd bite off his tongue before ever telling her anything. So she sighed and resigned herself to a visit to the doctor.

She was surprised when only five minutes later, a sleek car she didn't recognize the insignia for pulled up, and to her further surprise, not only did Justice step from the car but so did Silas.

And it would appear Silas's presence came as a surprise to Zander as well, judging by his reaction.

Justice shrugged as they neared where Evangeline still sat on the bench.

"Silas was with me and when he heard what went down, he said he was coming."

Unspoken was that no one ever likely refused Silas anything.

"I just hope to hell he doesn't scare the shit out of her," Zander muttered so only Justice could hear.

Evangeline immediately bristled and shot upward, wincing as her knee protested the sudden and unexpected movement. She pointed her finger at Zander. "To date, you are the only one who has frightened me. Not to mention how rude you were. And you dare to suggest that a man who has impeccable manners and who made considerable effort to ease my embarrassment after I dumped a cupcake all over his pants—which was *your* fault, by the way—would somehow frighten me? Quite frankly, I'm better off with him."

Silas stood staring at Evangeline as though she were an alien, surprise written clearly on his features. And then he simply walked to where she was shakily standing and put one arm around her.

"How much does it pain you?" he asked quietly.

"Enough," Evangeline muttered. "I just want to go home. It's not that bad and it certainly doesn't warrant a visit to Drake's doctor who also conveniently has a practice in Drake's building. Hell, Drake probably owns the entire building."

"He does," Silas said in his somber voice.

Evangeline closed her eyes. She shouldn't have gone there. It was her own fault for opening herself up for that.

Silas squeezed her, giving her silent reassurance. She wasn't so sure why the others seemed to have a healthy fear of and respect for this man. Well, the respect he had no doubt earned, and it was owed. But the fear she didn't understand, nor did she understand why they would think she would be afraid of him when he'd been nothing but gentle, kind and compassionate with her.

And because she was thinking those things and because whatever she thought always seemed to make its way out of her mouth, she put it out there before she could think better of it.

"W-would you go with me to the doctor?" she whispered so the others wouldn't hear. "Zander seems to think you frighten me, but truthfully *he* scares me more than any of the others, and I would feel more comfortable, if I *must* go see this doctor, if you were with me instead of him."

Silas went completely rigid, and she realized she'd just made a huge mistake. Damn her and her propensity for saying what was on her mind. She needed a gag stuffed into her mouth on a permanent basis.

"I'm sorry," she said sincerely. "I've already interrupted your day with what is not anything remotely resembling a serious accident. I really should just go back to Drake's apartment and clean it up. Band-Aids are miracle cures, you know."

"It would make me very unhappy to ever know that a woman like you ever feared me," Silas said, as sincerely as she had spoken. "The fact that you don't fear me and in fact defend me to the others raises you in my esteem considerably. If having me with you makes you more comfortable, then I'll go. No further explanations are warranted or necessary. Now, I'm going to help you to the car. Zander can get back to the apartment with your bags on his own dime while Justice and I take you to the clinic."

"You aren't a bad person, Silas," she whispered. "In fact, I think you are a perfect gentleman. You'll never persuade me otherwise."

A shadow fell over his eyes before he blinked it away, but in that shadow she saw past pain, memories, things that had shaped the man he was now. And then just because it seemed like the right thing to do, she hugged him, trapping his much larger frame against her smaller one, and squeezed hard.

"Thank you for coming so quickly. I'd rather Drake not know about this, but if we don't get moving, the dinner I'm supposed to prepare won't get done on time and I don't want Drake to be even more unhappy with me than he already is."

Silas frowned. "I'm sure he will be more than understanding if you don't cook dinner at all, considering you injured your knee and who knows what else in your fall."

Evangeline shook her head. "I don't even want him to know about this. Any of it. The day already started all wrong, and this will just ruin the entire evening. Can we just go and get it over with?"

In response, Silas merely picked her up, cradling her in his arms, and then ducked into the backseat of the car. Once he was settled, with her still on his lap, he put a pillow beneath the knee she'd injured and urged her to relax, saying that they were only a few minutes from Drake's apartment.

Evangeline sighed. *Welcome to Drake's world* should read more like *Welcome to Drake's insane world where nothing makes sense.*

Because there was nothing normal about being sprawled on the lap of a man who obviously inspired fear in others while being rushed to a private clinic, owned by Drake, an enormously wealthy and extremely secretive, mysterious man who now, according to him—and, well, acknowledged by her—owned her.

Crazy. It was the only word to describe her previously boring, uneventful, predictably dull existence.

Things like this just didn't happen to ordinary girls from small towns like the one she grew up in. Only it *was* happening, and it was all too real for her comfort level.

21

To Dr. McInnis's credit, he seemed to pick up on Evangeline's distress and agitation, though her constant muttering of this not being necessary probably clued him in more than anything.

He gave her a reassuring smile and told her he would have her in and out in no time at all and not to worry. But when he'd said she really needed a few sutures because the cut was quite deep and she risked infection if it was left open to bacteria, germs and God only knew what else, her anxiety soared.

It was Silas who calmed her down and said matter-of-factly that she was holding up the process. That if she were to simply relax and allow the doctor to do what he felt was necessary—and he was the doctor, after all—she could have already been finished and back to Drake's apartment.

She reached for his hand, more for her comfort than anything else, but she offered a grateful squeeze, wondering why she seemed to be the only one to see past this man's rigid exterior to the kind and gentle man underneath the outward facade. It was one likely perfected out of necessity. She sensed that about all of Drake's men. That perhaps none of them had come from the best backgrounds and that they'd all likely scratched and clawed their way to success, earning every bit of the money and respect they commanded. They were certainly an odd group, ranging from the polish of Drake and the smooth words he always seemed to possess to the more crudely built and street-smart men like Zander and well, Justice. Just in a different way. Silas was a mysterious combination of Drake's polish and expensive manner of dress but with the edge Zander and some of the others possessed. But the one trait they all had in common was their don't-give-a-fuck-what-others-think attitude.

She had no doubt that while Silas had been nothing but patient and kind to her, he wasn't that way with many other people. She'd seen the hint of coldness in his eyes. And pain. Though she doubted he realized she'd picked up on it and would not be pleased to know she had.

But she was a people watcher. For girls like her, watching was as close to the lifestyles of others as she got, and she enjoyed a certain vicariousness of experiencing their worlds through watching them. As a result, she often saw far more than the average person looking on. She studied people, watched when they were unaware of being observed. It was at these times that most people allowed what they hid on a regular basis to slip and be more readily revealed.

It was presumptuous of her to think she knew anything about Silas or his past or his *raisons d'etre*. But she sensed an inner torment that went as far back as his childhood, and weren't most people shaped by their childhood? Their family or lack thereof, defenses learned early and the ability to shut others out and erect shields in order to survive.

She considered herself to be the person she was because of her upbringing, her parents' unconditional love and support and their constant guidance. Their convictions that they'd passed on to Evangeline. Her parents were good people. The best. She was one of the lucky ones, unlike Silas and, she imagined, the majority of Drake's men, if not Drake himself.

He was an aloof man who hid a passionate fire inside him. He felt strongly about what he considered his own personal code. She didn't need a primer to know that. One only had to look at the man to figure out his past had more than likely shaped the man he'd become today. A man she was hopelessly attracted to and helpless to resist, even when her mind, or rather sanity, questioned her motives and her decisions and quite frequently demanded to know if she'd lost her ever-loving mind to have plunged so recklessly, without forethought or careful consideration, into such an extreme relationship with a man she barely knew.

And yet, even as she knew she had a long way to go before she would even scratch the surface of this complicated, mysterious man, she felt an eagerness and yes, a sense of challenge, to peel back layer after layer until she reached the heart of him. Only then would she fully understand what made Drake the unyielding, uncompromising and very dominant alpha male he was. None of which she considered bad traits. Not when they expressed themselves in such delicious ways.

Well, except she'd pissed him off and blatantly disobeyed him this morning and he hadn't sounded pleased with her at all. She sucked in her bottom lip, nibbling nervously as she considered the consequences of her actions and what Drake's response would be when he arrived home.

While her cooking might distract the best of them, she doubted Drake would be deterred if he planned to address the issue of her disobedience, something he'd said he wouldn't tolerate under any circumstances. And looking back, she knew that he was right and she'd been acting like a petulant, tantrum-throwing child out to prove a point by sulkily making the choice she had. She knew the rules. Knew them by heart. And Drake had been correct. All she had to do was pick up the phone and call him, tell him her wishes, and he more than likely would have been fine with it.

Remembering something he'd written in his note just made her feel even guiltier. He'd told her to stay in and rest and to have his man take her shopping list out to get what she needed. His exact words had been, *I was hard on my angel last night.*

She sighed. He'd merely been taking care of her and it had been sweet. And she'd been a complete bitch, taking it the wrong way and bristling over the ridiculous fact that she couldn't even run to the market without a major security operation being launched.

She owed Drake an apology. A sincere one and not something designed to tell him what she thought he wanted to hear in order to placate him.

"Evangeline?"

Silas's worried tone cut into her silent reverie.

"Are you hurting? He's numbed the area, so you shouldn't feel anything when he sets the sutures, but if you do, you are to let us know immediately."

The doctor looked up from where he was preparing to stitch her knee up, concern in his eyes. "I can give you a shot for pain. I plan to give you a shot of antibiotics and give you an ointment to apply three times a day. I don't think an oral antibiotic is warranted in this case; however, if you notice any redness, tenderness or swelling in the area and especially if you feel unwell and are running even a slight temperature, I want you back here immediately so we can put you on antibiotics."

She offered a reassuring smile. "I'm fine. Truly. I don't feel anything at all. I don't need pain medication. I'm sure some ibuprofen will more than suffice if it hurts later. I was too busy thinking of all the mistakes I've made today to even register any discomfort in my knee. It kind of sucks when you realize you've been a sulky child, finding any ridiculous reason to be pissy."

She said the last with a sigh and her lips turned down into a frown.

Silas's frown was more of a scowl, surprising her, because for the first time there was none of the gentleness she'd come to associate him with.

"Admittedly my acquaintance with you has been short, and we've not spent much time together, something I hope will be remedied when Drake loosens the leash he currently has you on." Brief amusement replaced the scowl in his eyes, letting her know he was teasing her with the last of his words. "But the very last thing I would ever attribute to you is sulkiness or childishness. You are exceedingly honest and sincere, two qualities that have fallen by the wayside in society, unfortunately. Furthermore, you are completely unaware of the many good qualities you possess and seem baffled when someone pays you a compliment, as you are doing right now as I speak, judging by the look in your eyes."

She flushed because she was precisely that.

"No one has ever given me compliments until recently," she murmured.

"Then you clearly don't associate with the right people, and I'm willing to bet either the people you are exposed to are envious or, if they are men, they want very much to get a hell of a lot closer to you and you likely have no clue of that either, which angers them and is a blow to their fragile male ego."

"Okay, you have to stop," she said, becoming more uncomfortable by the minute.

But he didn't. He reached out with one finger and lifted her chin so she was forced to look at him and no longer avoid his gaze.

"What you are, Evangeline, is special. And if you ever disparage yourself in my hearing again, I'll turn you over my knee myself and spank that perfect ass until you promise me to forget all the negative words you have in your vocabulary when they come to describing yourself. Are we understood?"

Holy fuck! Oh shit. Now she was once more using words that would mortify her mother and cause her to wonder where she'd gone wrong in

Evangeline's upbringing since she'd been taught that no true lady ever used such vulgar language.

Her eyes were wide as she stared at Silas, no longer needing his hand to force her compliance. She saw the dominance glittering in his eyes as clearly as she saw it in Drake's. How had she missed it before now? *Gentle and kind, my ass.* Silas, Drake and, well, all of Drake's men, were dominant, almost surly, alpha males, but in the space of those few words Silas had so smoothly dropped on her, she saw a man who was likely far more dominant than the others. Perhaps even Drake, and that was incomprehensible to her.

She could now see the scary side that the others evidently saw and experienced on a daily basis, and here she was naïvely forming her assumptions based on two brief meetings when he'd acted the consummate gentleman.

She swallowed hard because she didn't think Silas was bluffing. There was no hint of amusement in his eyes. Only somber truth. And utter seriousness. And then, since her brain was fried, and she was to the point of babbling, she issued a ridiculous response.

"D-Drake would never let you!" she said in a shocked whisper. And to her further mortification, she realized the doctor was still there, stitching up her now-forgotten knee, and he'd been privy to the entire exchange between them.

His lips were quirked in amusement even as he never took his eyes from his job, and his hands were as steady as she'd ever seen.

Silas sent her a slight grin, only one corner of his mouth twitching to indicate what he thought of her naïve statement.

"Don't be so sure of what Drake will and won't allow, Evangeline. To do so will only lead to inevitable misunderstanding. I'm sure Drake has been very exacting in his requirements of you, the foremost being obedience. I'd say that covers a lot of uncharted territory, wouldn't you?"

Evangeline wanted to shriek. How the hell did Drake's men, *this* man, know so much about what Drake had or hadn't told her? Or were his women—and his standards and expectations—so often rotated in and out that his needs and demands were common knowledge among his men?

Hell, did they run, own or belong to some kind of BDSM club? Did they all have memberships in some place where there were handbooks and rules for this kind of stuff and did they all adhere to the same "code"?

She wanted to pull her hair out and then cover her face and wish herself a million miles away, because this was becoming more disconcerting by the minute.

"You wouldn't hurt me," she said in near desperation.

Silas's eyes softened. "No, Evangeline. I would never hurt you. Discipline doesn't have to equal pain. Unless that's your thing." He shrugged. "People are into what pleases them. It's not for me to judge. But if you're asking if I will follow through with my threat? The answer is yes. I don't make idle threats. Ever. So yes, I will turn you over my knee and spank that ass if you ever talk shit about yourself in my hearing. If you don't want that to happen, the simple thing to do is not to say stupid shit, yeah? You got me?"

"I got you," she choked out, because if he was anything like Drake, and it appeared he was, then he too would want the words and not shaking or nodding her head as an answer.

"You done?" Silas asked the doctor sharply.

The doctor looked to have already finished but was clearly immersed in Silas's exchange with Evangeline, because he was simply holding a bandage over Evangeline's knee while watching the two in fascination.

"Uh, yeah, sure. Just let me tape this over her knee."

Then he looked only at Evangeline.

"Keep it covered for tonight. You can take the dressing off in the morning, but keep the area clean and apply the ointment as I instructed, and again, if you experience any of the problems or symptoms I listed, you are to come back to me immediately."

Evangeline nodded, still discomfited by the much-too-public airing of far-too-personal information. Did everyone who worked for Drake know every sordid detail of their relationship? Or were they merely guessing based on his past relationships?

It hit a raw nerve to think that her relationship, or whatever this was between her and Drake, was following some guideline or schedule he performed by rote, regardless of who his current woman was.

Would any woman do for him? Did Evangeline's face blur among the many who'd come before her? Did she stand out? She supposed she was lucky that he at least remembered her name and hadn't called her by another woman's name. She'd likely stab him with a kitchen knife if that ever happened.

Silas helped her from the exam table and then herded her from the clinic and into the elevator that would take them to the top floor. He inserted his own key card, further proof that Drake's men were obviously trusted—and had full access to even his personal domains.

When they walked into the apartment, she saw that the groceries had been placed on the counter and when she would have hurried over to sort through them, Silas blocked her and instead pushed her into the living room and then promptly sat her on the couch, reaching for a pillow to prop beneath her leg.

"You stay put," Silas ordered. "I know for a fact Drake said he would be late arriving, and I also know he'll call to let you know when he's on his way home. Therefore, until the time you receive that call, you are to relax and not further aggravate your injury. Drake will understand if dinner is a little late, given the circumstances."

Evangeline bit her lip, refusing to remind Silas that Drake had no clue about her injury. Unless she'd already been ratted out by one of his men. A distinct possibility.

But when Drake did finally call, she realized that no, he didn't know, and furthermore, he was still not happy about this morning's transgression.

22

The phone rang, rousing Evangeline from the couch. Damn it! How could she have fallen asleep? She'd planned that as soon as Silas made his departure, she was going to get a start on dinner, regardless of his assertion that she was to rest until Drake called.

She scrambled for the phone, at least glad Silas had put it within reach. She nearly groaned when she swung her legs over the end of the couch so she could get up and head for the kitchen as she talked to Drake.

"Hello?" she asked breathlessly.

"I'll be home in twenty minutes," he said shortly.

"O-okay," she said, gripping the phone tighter.

Even as she talked, she was digging into the bags and searching for the right skillets and warming the grill on the professional-grade stove.

"Dinner will hold for a few minutes, I take it," he said.

"Yes, of course," she said hastily. "I can have it ready whenever you're ready to eat."

"Good. Then what I want you to do is go into the living room and undress. When I arrive I want you standing at the end of the couch, your belly leaned against the arm, legs slightly apart. And then when I tell you, you are to lean forward and put your hands down on the couch so that you are bent over the arm."

She hesitated, a puzzled look creasing her forehead. "Okay," she said quietly.

"Your punishment, Angel," he said, evidently picking up on her confusion. "Don't think I've forgotten about this morning."

She nearly dropped the phone but managed to get a grip before it smashed onto the floor.

"Be sure you're ready and that you've heeded my every instruction or I won't be pleased," he said in a silky voice.

"I won't disappoint you, Drake," she said in a low tone.

He hesitated this time and then he said, "I know, Angel. That I know."

And then he hung up, leaving her to stare at the phone.

She closed her eyes, refusing to focus on the fact that he was going to punish her. She had to get a start on dinner so he wouldn't think she hadn't already done so. This whole day had been nothing but an epic clusterfuck.

She thought briefly about heeding Silas's advice and telling Drake of all that had occurred the minute Drake came through the door, but then she frowned. What a coward she was being. At the very first opportunity she was trying to get out of trouble, when it was her own damn fault.

No, she'd get dinner well on its way to being prepared, and then she'd go into the living room and do as Drake had told her. She wouldn't wimp out the very first time their relationship was tested, or at least the first time she disobeyed him. Somehow she thought that would disappoint him far more than the fact that she'd disobeyed him.

With five minutes to spare, she had everything prepared and on the stove, the sizzling sounds of food cooking and the inviting aroma filling the air. All that was left were the steaks, and she wouldn't put those on until they were ready to eat.

Knowing she now had less than five minutes until Drake arrived, she fled to the living room, ignoring the twinges of pain in her knee. If she hadn't spent all afternoon napping on the couch and had been moving around, her knee wouldn't even hurt. But after so many hours of inactivity, of course it was going to protest the sudden movements.

She hastily undressed and then carefully folded her clothing and put it on the coffee table. She didn't want it to appear as though she'd rushed through the process, even if that was precisely what she'd done.

She slid her shoes underneath the coffee table and then laid her bra and panties on top of her torn jeans and shirt.

When she was naked, she walked to the end of the couch and leaned into it, running her hands over the leather arm, and then leaned forward, testing how comfortable she would be when he asked her to bend over.

Okay, that wasn't so bad.

She straightened and dutifully took her position exactly as he'd described and then closed her eyes, knowing the next few minutes until he arrived would seem like an eternity.

Drake waited impatiently for the elevator doors to open and immediately stepped off, not even taking the time to hang his coat over the coatrack. He slipped it off on his way to the living room and tossed it aside.

His breath caught in his throat when he saw Evangeline standing just as he'd instructed her at the end of the couch, her bare skin glowing in the low light. Only a lamp was on in the far corner, lending an intimate air to the room.

He walked up behind her, unable to resist such beautiful temptation. He brushed her hair over one shoulder and pressed his lips to the curve of her neck. She shivered beneath his touch and tiny chill bumps danced across her skin.

"So responsive," he murmured. "So fucking beautiful."

He heard her soft sigh, as beautiful as she was.

"Stay right where you are," he commanded.

Then he left the room to get the crop from the bedroom. This would be her first experience with anything other than his hand and the few smacks he'd administered to her ass, and therefore he wouldn't graduate to something harsher. Not until he was certain she was ready and with him all the way.

When he returned, she was still standing there, as still as a statue, her pale skin glowing in unearthly light. She was a goddess and she was all his.

He trailed the end of the crop down her spine, eliciting another shiver from her. He continued his gentle exploration, letting her become accustomed to the feel of the leather before he marked her gorgeous ass.

He moved to the side of her so he could see her face, her expression.

"I'm going to administer six lashes," he said in an even voice. "Just to remind you in the future that you are not to disobey me. But fair warning, Angel, if it happens again, I won't be as merciful."

She shifted her weight, an almost imperceptible movement, but he was tuned in to her completely and missed nothing. He was about to administer the first blow, still to the side of her, because he wanted to watch her reaction. The moment when the initial pain faded into pleasure. He wanted to watch her eyes go hazy at the pleasure he gave her.

But a sudden flash of pain and obvious distress briefly chased through her eyes before it was gone, leaving him to wonder if he'd imagined it. But no. He'd clearly seen it. He frowned because he hadn't done more than stroke her skin with the flogger.

He let his hand fall to his side as he continued to stare piercingly at her.

"What's wrong?" he demanded. "Evangeline, look at me."

Slowly she turned her head so that she faced him fully and he was no longer just seeing her profile. Her eyes glittered with unshed tears and it gutted him.

"Nothing is wrong, Drake. I won't disobey you again," she said quietly. "I'm sorry. I was wrong. I was being a petulant little child and I was a bitch. You didn't deserve that from me."

And then her weight shifted again, and he saw that she moved most of her weight to one leg instead of having both feet planted solidly on the floor. She winced, pain once more flashing in her eyes before she visibly got herself under control and turned to face ahead. She leaned forward to plant her hands on the couch as he'd instructed her earlier, but all Drake could see, remember, was the pain in her eyes. Pain that he had in no way caused.

His gaze dropped down her body, searching for any discernible source of discomfort. Then his eyes narrowed when he saw what the couch had effectively hidden from his view. A bandage on her knee.

He went immediately to his knees, turning her to the side so she faced him, and he could now plainly see the dressing over her knee.

"What the fuck?" he murmured, purposely pitching his voice low so that his emphatic words held no bite or anger directed at *her*.

He stood rapidly and then picked her up, cradling her against his chest, and then walked around to the front of the couch and carefully laid her down. Then he gently lifted her legs, wanting to cause her no further pain, and draped them across his lap so he could get a closer look at her knee.

"What happened?" he demanded.

She sighed. "It's nothing, Drake. I promise. It was stupid of me and I was clumsy. Zander and I went out to buy groceries and then he insisted I needed a pair of sunglasses and so he stopped in a boutique and bought two pairs of hideously expensive sunglasses."

She shuddered and closed her eyes, and he realized she was more upset over the cost of the sunglasses than she was over the injury to her knee.

"When we walked out, I tripped. I'm not even sure what exactly happened except one minute I was standing and the next I was facedown on the sidewalk and Zander was freaking out. He wanted to call you immediately, but I begged him not to. So he called Justice to come get us. Only Justice *and* Silas arrived, and then Silas insisted he bring me to your doctor."

Drake's eyes narrowed as he absorbed her account. "And why didn't you think it important to call me?"

"You were busy," she whispered, distress radiating from her voice. "Your note said you would be busy and that you would be wrapped up in important meetings all day and that you'd be late for dinner. It was nothing worth disturbing you over. Your doctor stitched it up in just a few minutes and gave me medicine to numb the wound."

"He had to *stitch* you?" he asked behind tightly clenched teeth.

Her eyes grew larger with fear and nervousness, but he was too determined to get to the bottom of this whole mess before allaying her fears that he was angry with her. Jesus. He should have been the one with her. The whole goddamn time.

"Only a few," she said defensively. "I don't know why he even bothered. I've suffered far worse before, and slapping a bandage over it worked just fine."

"That may have been okay before," he said, trying to get a grip on his emotions. "Before you belonged to me, that is. But it is not okay *now*. You belong to me now, and I will always ensure you are cared for above all others. Your comfort and safety are second to none other. You should not have had to go to the clinic with only a strange man to comfort you. I should have been there to hold you and to carry you up to our apartment after and ensure your absolute comfort. *That's* my job, Angel."

He pinned her with an intense stare. "Now tell me. What's *your* job?"

She looked confused and her brow creased in obvious puzzlement. "I don't understand what you're asking," she said helplessly. "I'm not being deliberately obtuse, Drake. I'm just confused by your question."

"My job is to always take care of you. To provide for you. To ensure your safety when I cannot be near and most especially to ensure that you are comfortable above all else. You only have one job, my angel. Obey."

Evangeline stared in wonder at Drake as a myriad of conflicting emotions assailed her over his matter-of-fact stating of the facts—the truth—as he saw them. She felt slight irritation. But mostly she felt profound relief. As though a great burden had shifted and had been lifted from her shoulders.

Could it really be as easy as he made it appear? That this man, this beautiful, dominant man would cherish her, pamper her, spoil her, protect her, take care of her and in return, all she had to do was to obey? It was almost more than she could fathom. Like she was in a never-ending fantasy and if she opened her eyes it would all be gone in the blink of an eye, and so she held tightly to the dream, squeezing her eyes tighter shut to keep reality at bay.

Then he leaned down and very carefully peeled away the bandage, and after a moment's inspection, he reverently pressed his lips to the wound. She was astonished that in one moment he was all raw power, bristling alpha male about to discipline his submissive, and in the next second he was so exquisitely loving and tender that it brought an altogether different kind of sting to her eyes.

"From now on if anything, and I mean *anything*, should happen to you, I want to know about it immediately. I don't care how insignificant you think it is. I expect to know about it the minute it happens. Understand?"

She swallowed and then somehow managed to verbalize her consent around the knot in her throat.

Then to her further shock, he gently slid her body further over his lap until he cradled her against his chest. He pressed his lips firmly to her brow and then stood, lifting her higher into his arms. He carried her into the kitchen and then eased her down on the island with the rest of the kitchen surrounding her.

"Tonight, I cook for my injured princess," he said, a gleam in his eyes.

Appalled, she immediately launched her protest. "In no way do a few stitches keep me from cooking dinner. Besides, everything is nearly done except for the steaks, and they'll only need a few minutes to grill on each side."

He tweaked her nose affectionately and then followed it by kissing her long and leisurely on the lips.

"Then I won't have much left to do, will I? You will sit right where you are and direct me from on high. You tell me what to do and how, and I'll have supper served in no time."

Evangeline watched in fascination as he tended to the meal, pausing from time to time to ask her if he was doing it right. And as she was watching him and as she replayed the events prior when he'd forgotten all about her punishment and had instead instantly made certain she was all right and taken care of, she had an epiphany of sorts.

Drake *enjoyed* taking care of her. In fact, he seemed to delight in it. It—*she*—mattered to him, and he took what he called his "job" very seriously. She wondered if he had never had anyone who truly cared about him and if that was why he seemed so determined to give her something that maybe he himself had lacked.

It only made her all the more determined not only to accept him unconditionally but also to do everything in her power to take care of and protect *him*. Maybe no one in his past had ever ensured that he was happy and cared for, but she'd be damned if she was going to be like those people. Drake would know without a doubt that there was at least one person who cared deeply enough about him to always ensure his happiness and comfort. And if she could do all those things by simply pleasing him and following his rules, then she would do so with no hesitation, no more questioning herself.

"Drake," she said hesitantly.

He turned as if sensing the seriousness in her tone.

"I *am* sorry," she said softly. "For today. Earlier. I was a bitch and as I said, you didn't deserve that from me. I'm ashamed of the way I acted, and I did so without thought and that hurt you. I feel *terrible* about it. Can you forgive me? I will try very hard never to give you any cause to be unhappy with me again. I want to please you. It's important to me. More important than you even know."

His expression relaxed and he walked over after flipping the steaks and wrapped his arms around her.

"You are *not* a bitch, Angel. Far from it. And I think we should both just agree to forget all about today and move on. But baby, I want a promise from you. You are to never let me punish you or even put you in a situation where you are hurting or feel any discomfort. You should have told me the minute your accident happened, and if not then, you most assuredly should have told me before I put a crop to your ass. Thank God I figured it out before I doled out your punishment, because I would have never forgiven myself for causing you unnecessary pain."

There was genuine self-derision in his tone and remorse. Her heart softened to the point of melting because he seemed so horrified that he could have caused her further pain.

"And I can't tell you how much it means to me for you to so sweetly and genuinely tell me that you care. That you want to please me and that it's important to you. I've never had that," he admitted, looking immediately chagrined that he'd imparted something he considered deeply personal. But it only reinforced what she'd already figured out.

"I want you to know that pleasing you is every bit as important to me as pleasing me is important to you. I want you to be happy. I want you to shine. For me. Only, always, for me."

She relaxed and kissed him and then drew away, a teasing grin on her face.

"So no punishment for me tonight, then?" she asked lightly.

He returned to the stove and picked up one corner of a steak, holding it up for her inspection.

"Just a minute or two longer," she advised.

Then he regarded her somberly.

"No, Angel. I think it's safe to say you've already had a little too much excitement for one day. I have never considered myself a patient man, but I'm finding lately that when the reward is great, I'm willing to temper myself. Just know that now that you better understand the parameters and limits I've set for you, I won't be as forgiving in the future, and disobedience will be punished. But I will never take it too far, and I would cut off my right arm before ever intentionally hurting you."

Her body went all tingly as a mixture of disappointment and curiosity curled in her stomach. She realized in that moment that she didn't fear Drake hurting her. Physically. He was too disciplined and restrained in all things. The physical part of her fantasized about what his punishment would feel like and if she'd revel in the burn as she had the night he'd spanked her those few times with his hand. The emotional part of her couldn't bear to ever disappoint Drake again in such a way as to warrant punishment. His approval, she realized, meant a great deal.

"What if I wanted you to use the crop on me?" she asked huskily before she could temper her words. "Not in punishment. Is that something that would please you, Drake? Because I fantasize about it and I think . . ."

"What do you think, Angel?"

"That it would please me very much," she admitted.

He was taking the steaks from the grill and putting them on a platter and went completely still when her admission hit him. Then he turned the burners off the other skillets and slowly turned, fire brewing in his eyes.

"Maybe if I wasn't standing." She plunged ahead before she lost her nerve. "A man of your expertise surely has a thousand ways of flogging a woman without me having to put any weight on my knee."

"What I think," he said slowly, "is that first we should eat. And then afterward we can have this discussion. Preferably with you in my bed, tied up and powerless to do anything but accept the pleasure I give you."

She gulped. She was supposed to eat now? And actually remember what anything tasted like?

He served portions of the food onto two plates and then put them on the table. Then he returned and carefully lifted her down from the island and carried her over to the table, but instead of depositing her into her own chair, he settled down with her in his lap.

She realized that once again, he was going to feed her, but this time, there was no hesitation on her part. She'd enjoyed it the first time he had fed her by his own hand. Intimacy had cloaked them, pulling them further and further into a hazy fog of passion and arousal.

As he began to feed her—and himself—he complimented her on yet another excellent meal.

"But you cooked, not me!" Evangeline protested.

"I hardly call slapping two steaks on a grill and turning them at the minute marker you set while simply turning on the heat under the other skillets to rewarm the food you'd already prepared cooking the meal," he said dryly. "It was delicious and I appreciate the effort you underwent to make it special for me. That means a lot to me, Angel. I only regret that you hurt yourself in the process."

"A skinned knee was worth pleasing you," she whispered. "I do want to please you, Drake. It's a need within me I can't even explain to myself. You give me so much. You make me feel beautiful and wanted. I want so much to give you back even a part of what you give so selflessly to me."

He kissed her, hugging her closer to his body. "You do please me, Angel. Never doubt that. Now, what do you say we continue this conversation in the bedroom where I can properly tend to my angel and give her what she wants and needs from her man."

"I'd say that's the best idea I've heard all day," she whispered against his lips.

23

Drake carried Evangeline to the bedroom and reverently laid her down on the bed. Then he simply stood over her, his gaze raking up and down her naked body, clear appreciation in his eyes.

For once she felt no shyness or self-consciousness. She felt . . . bold. Like a seductress with a lot more experience than she actually possessed. She didn't want to be a passive participant in whatever Drake chose for tonight, but at the same time, the idea that he would make all the decisions and have all the control gave her an indescribable thrill.

He frowned when his gaze settled over her knee and he seemed to be thinking.

"How much does it hurt?" he asked. "And don't sugarcoat it. I'll do nothing that causes you further pain tonight."

"It actually feels much better now," she said truthfully. "I fell asleep on the couch because Silas wouldn't leave until I was resting on the couch, and I fully intended to get up as soon as he left so I could get a start on dinner, but I fell asleep and didn't wake up until you called. And since I was immobile for such a long time, my knee was stiff and tender for a while after I started moving around, but it's loosened up and isn't nearly as tender."

His lips tightened. "And if you had called me, I would have ensured you did precisely what Silas told you to do, only you would have been in my arms, me holding you, while you rested."

The image was so tantalizing that in that moment she wished she had allowed Zander to call Drake.

"I wish I *had* called you now," she whispered.

He leaned down and brushed a gentle kiss over her knee and then looked up so their gazes locked.

"In the future, make sure you do."

"I will," she promised.

A gleam of a different kind entered his eyes. The one of a predator, full of heat and anticipation that had her breathless and edgy with indescribable need.

"You could make me feel all better now," she said in a husky voice that was filled with invitation.

"Oh yes, my angel. I intend to do just that. But first, I'm going to crop that sweet ass so that it bears my marks when I fuck you."

She couldn't control the shudder or the soft moan that escaped her lips.

His expression became more serious. "But I will not do anything that will cause further pain to your knee."

"I know, Drake," she said, an ache in her heart. "I know you'd never hurt me. I want this. I want you. And everything you have to give me. I'll cherish it always."

His entire face softened and a warm glow burned in his dark eyes. "So sweet and generous," he murmured. "What did I ever do to deserve such an angel?"

He walked away from the bed and she felt the loss of his warmth, the touch of his gaze and the hands that had reverently caressed her body. He returned a moment later with rope and the crop and her pulse ratcheted up, her breaths puffing erratically from her lips.

"My angel is excited," he said, approval flaring in his eyes.

"Oh yes," she said. "I want it all, Drake. I want . . . you."

He turned her, mindful of her knee, and drew both of her hands behind her to rest at the small of her back, and then he carefully wound the rope around them, testing to ensure that it wasn't cutting into her skin. He left her once more only long enough to strip out of his clothing and then he returned, lifting her from where she lay on the bed.

He settled on the edge of the bed and then turned her facedown so that her belly rested over his lap and her legs dangled over the side of his leg. His hands roamed over her back, her shoulders, her ass and then lower down the length of each leg, each touch sending her up in flames.

He administered a light smack to one cheek with his hand and she immediately gasped. Then he petted the area, smoothing away the hurt as the warm burn of pleasure rapidly took over.

Then, as he'd done earlier in the living room, he stroked her back and ass with the tip of the flogger and before she could brace herself, he popped the crop down over the opposite cheek.

Fire singed over her skin, but as with the smacks with his hand, the pain disappeared, quickly replaced with the warm hum of decadent, forbidden pleasure.

"How many do you want, Angel? How many can you take?"

"As many as you want to give me," she said breathlessly. "I'm yours, Drake. Only yours. I belong to you and am yours to do with as you wish."

She could tell her response pleased him by the warmth and gentleness of his caress as he rubbed his hand over the area he'd just struck and the sound of approval he made.

"You were made for me," he said, satisfaction in his voice. "And yes, my darling angel. You do belong to me and you are mine to do with as I please."

He popped her other cheek, causing her to flinch and then moan as euphoria enveloped her like a cloud. Her knee and the events of the day faded to obscurity, forgotten, as he began to administer her spanking, each lash harder, stronger than the last.

He was careful not to overwhelm her, instead gradually working her up, from lighter to harder and as the pain increased, so did the indescribable pleasure.

"So fucking beautiful," Drake said gruffly as he rubbed his hand over her throbbing flesh. "Your ass so red with my mark, my stamp of possession. Tell me, Angel. Do you want more? Or do you want me to fuck your sweet ass? Or maybe you'd prefer I ride the pussy that also belongs to me?"

She groaned, nearly insensible, so deep into the thick fog surrounding her.

"I want it all," she whispered. "All you have, everything you can give me, Drake. Please. I need you so much."

The words had barely escaped her lips before he straddled her hips, pushing her ass upward, spreading her with his thumbs, and then plunged hard and deep into her pussy. She nearly orgasmed on the spot. She closed her eyes, squeezing hard around him, trying to hold off her release as he began riding her hard. He was almost brutal in his possession, not pausing between thrusts.

He pumped into her over and over, his hips smacking hard against her ass, all the while caressing the burning flesh of her behind that she knew bore the marks of the crop.

"Drake!" she cried desperately. "I'm too close. I'm going to come!"

He withdrew, causing her to moan at the abrupt departure of his enormous erection through her swollen and ultrasensitive flesh. The edge of pain mixed with pleasure was a heady sensation and she closed her eyes, biting into her bottom lip to stave off her release.

Then she jumped when the crop slapped over her ass, fast and furious, peppering over every inch of her aching behind.

Not pausing in the flogging, he murmured in a husky voice, "I'm going to untie your hands so you can touch yourself while I fuck your ass, but do not get up on your knees or put any weight whatsoever on your stitches. Understand?"

"Yes," she said with an edge of desperation.

The flogging stopped and he hastily untied her wrists and gently rubbed them to rid them of any residual numbness, and then he took her left hand and slipped it between her and the mattress until her fingers slid over her swollen clit.

There was a squirting sound as Drake squeezed lubricant from the tube and then his thumbs parted the cheeks of her ass. Knowing what was soon to come she began stroking herself, and not a moment too soon as he thrust into her with every bit as much force as he'd entered her pussy.

She began shaking, her fingers slipping, glancing over the sensitive nub as Drake drove her higher and higher and ever closer to ultimate release. Just when she thought she would topple over the edge, he withdrew, leaving her precariously close to orgasm, and she groaned in frustration.

He chuckled and the fire ignited over her ass as the crop descended, taking her breath away. Her chest heaved and she inhaled sharply as the pain faded, giving in to euphoria. She closed her eyes as more blows rained down on her buttocks and she entered a hazy world that blurred around her where only bliss existed.

His hands roughly parted her cheeks and he plunged inward again, but she was too languid to continue touching herself, too lethargic to register the need to do so.

"Touch yourself, babe," Drake commanded. "I want you with me and I'm about to come all over your rosy ass."

She stroked lazily, her earlier urgency dissipating. As if sensing her state of subspace, he forwent the roughness of his thrusts and instead stroked long and slow, setting a leisurely pace.

Where before her orgasm had demanded its due, this time she climbed slowly up the peak and when Drake's fingers dug more sharply into her hips and he swelled even larger inside her, she applied more pressure, determined that they go together. Always together.

Her orgasm flooded her, the sweetest, slowest spasm that encompassed her entire body, setting each nerve ending on fire. She tingled from head to toe, delicious chill bumps spreading over her skin, making her hypersensitive to his every touch.

And when he leaned down and pressed his lips to her spine and licked his way up to her nape, the world tilted around her, blurring in the most exquisite bliss she'd ever experienced in her life.

The warmth of his release flooded her, heating her from the inside out, and then he lifted his head and withdrew, and hot jets of semen covered her back, making her shiver all over again.

For a long moment he stood there between her splayed thighs, and then he gently pulled her arm from beneath her and caressed the length from wrist to shoulder. He pressed a warm kiss to her shoulder.

"I'll be right back to take care of my angel," he said in a husky voice.

And then a short time later a warm washcloth cleaned the remnants of his release from her back and then her behind. He took care with the flesh tender from the spanking and his rough and then gentle possession of her ass. When he was finished, he slowly rolled her to her back, mindful of her knee, and she gazed up into eyes that glittered with satisfaction and approval.

"My angel has had a long day and needs to rest now, and there's nothing more I want than to hold you while you sleep."

24

Evangeline woke and promptly snuggled further into the covers, the slight ache in her behind bringing back the delicious pleasure Drake had given her the night before. She had no desire to get up and emerge from the cocoon and into reality and so she lay there for a long while, savoring each moment from the night before.

It was like having the most beautiful dream, one she never wanted to awaken from. And then remembering the ritualistic note accompanied by a ridiculously expensive gift that she'd awakened to every single morning since she'd moved in with Drake, she reluctantly turned, hoping . . .

She let out a sigh when her hopes were dashed. A single wrapped box lay next to a note. Most women would think it terribly romantic, but every time Drake left her a gift, it somehow cheapened their relationship and reduced it to a business transaction. As if he were paying her for . . . sex. When the very best gift he could give her would be for her to wake up in his arms.

She cringed and then sat up, curling her legs up against her chest and wrapping her arms around them, hugging herself as she stared at the offending box.

There was little point in putting it off, since Drake would no doubt have her instructions for the day listed in his note.

First she opened the box, dreading what it would reveal. But even she wasn't prepared for the extravagance of this offering. She dropped it as if it had burned her, and she stared aghast at what had to have cost tens of thousands of dollars.

It was a sapphire and diamond choker that glittered brilliantly in the light. The stones varied in size from very large to the smaller ones that encrusted the edges. It was certainly beautiful, but she couldn't ever imagine herself wearing it.

Hadn't Drake learned anything about her at all? That expensive gifts were totally unnecessary? Had she not given him enough reassurance that *he* was all she wanted and needed? Not gifts every single morning.

With trembling hands, she opened the note and read his now-familiar scrawl.

Good morning, my angel. I hope your knee is feeling much better. I hope you like the choker I chose especially for you. It pales in comparison to your beauty and to your gorgeous blue eyes, but I think it will complement both nicely. Be sure and inform me if you leave the apartment and also remember that you are never to do so without one of my men.

It shouldn't have bothered her. She thought she'd gotten past this last night when she'd made certain realizations about Drake and his need—and delight—to take care of and protect her. But now, no longer in the fantasy of the moment, it irritated her that he felt the need to curtail her freedom so drastically. For that matter, was it really necessary, the veritable circus act it required for her to so much as leave the building?

"You chose this," she reminded herself.

She'd been made well aware of Drake's requirements and she'd willingly signed on, agreeing to those requirements and also knowing the consequences and rewards for her actions.

Oh well, it wasn't as though it was for forever, right? Only for as long as ... what? Drake got tired of her? Decided he wanted a new trained monkey?

The thought made her unhappy even as she chastised herself for wanting it both ways. To have her cake and eat it too. She had to stop overthinking matters. Live for the moment for *once* in her life. Don't think about tomorrow until it arrives. For one glorious span of time in her life, she was going to indulge in what she wanted and put her needs before others, and she refused to spend the entirety of her relationship with Drake feeling guilt for, as he'd stated in the beginning, enjoying the ride. When in her life had she ever given in to impulse? Thrown caution to the wind and plunged recklessly into anything? Oh, that was easy. Never!

There *were* things she'd like to do. Visit her girlfriends. Or simply enjoy a day out. But quite frankly what she needed most was a break from all the testosterone that was always in abundance wherever Drake was—or rather couldn't be at the moment. If she had to spend another day with one of Drake's men hovering over her, she might well scream.

Suddenly a day alone and not leaving Drake's apartment held greater appeal than it had before.

She got up and took her time showering, and then she remembered to put the ointment on her knee. It was too late for breakfast, so she was running through her lunch options in her mind.

She was tempted to order takeout, even though she had plenty of stuff to whip up something herself in no time. Takeout had always been a luxury for her, one seldom indulged in and usually only for special occasions. The more she thought about it, the more she craved some really good Chinese or Thai takeout. And why not? She had plenty of cash on her. Drake's minions weren't around to whip out a credit card.

But then should she be saving her money? She couldn't take anything for granted, and if Drake did suddenly get tired of her and dump her, she would need every penny she had to support herself until she found a job and a place to live. Because she knew one thing already. If Drake ended their relationship, there was no way she'd go back to her old apartment knowing that Drake had paid the rent for two years.

Shaking off the unpleasant direction in which her thoughts had taken her, she went into the kitchen and then took out her phone to look up nearby places that would deliver to Drake's apartment.

After a few frustrating minutes in which she realized just how unfamiliar she was with this part of the city, she nearly gave up on the idea of ordering takeout. But then an idea hit her. Surely the doorman or the concierge would be able to give her some guidance.

Happy that she wouldn't have to give up on her fantasy lunch now that it had taken root and she could think of nothing else, she finished dressing and then rode the elevator down to the lobby.

When she got off, she looked uneasily around, unsure of where she'd find the concierge. It wasn't as though the other times that she'd been rushed through the lobby she'd made it a point to check out her surroundings.

She was saved when the doorman approached her, a welcoming smile on his face.

"Miss Hawthorn, is there anything I can do for you?"

"Yes," she said gratefully. "This is going to sound stupid."

She flushed but the doorman merely smiled and gave her a kind look.

"I assure you that nothing you ask will be stupid. Now, how can I be of service?"

"Well, um, can you tell me where to find the concierge? You see, I wanted to order Chinese or maybe even Thai takeout, but I'm not very familiar with this part of the city and I have no idea who delivers here and who doesn't. Do you think the concierge would be able to help me with that?"

The doorman looked horrified. "Of course! But, Miss Hawthorn, in the future you needn't bother calling out yourself. I can give you several menus as well as the delivery service Mr. Donovan most frequently uses. With or without a menu, all you need to do is call down and let me or the concierge know of your wishes and we'll take care of it immediately and we will deliver the food to your apartment personally."

"Oh," she said slowly, realizing that in her ignorance she'd evidently committed a faux pas.

"Do you happen to know what you would like? I know of an excellent restaurant that offers both Chinese and Thai just a few blocks from here. I can arrange to have whatever you like delivered within minutes."

She rattled off an extensive order, including several appetizers and side items since she intended to sample all of it. The doorman merely nodded and then explained to Evangeline that she should go back up to the apartment and that he would bring the food up in twenty minutes or less.

"But wait. I need to know how much it cost," she protested, as she began pulling the folded twenties from her pocket.

Again the doorman looked horrified and hastily put his hand out in protest.

"I can't take your money, Miss Hawthorn. Mr. Donovan would be most displeased. I've been instructed to take care of any and all of your requests. He will take care of it, so please don't concern yourself."

Evangeline sighed. Of course. Why hadn't she anticipated this very thing? Still, not wanting to further upset the sweet doorman, she smiled and shoved the money back into her pocket.

"Thank you, sir. And please do call me Evangeline. Miss Hawthorn sounds so formal and, well, as I'm sure you can probably tell, I'm hardly the kind of girl who needs to be addressed as *Miss* anything."

The man smiled, seemingly pleased by Evangeline's overture.

"Then you must call me Edward, because *sir* is certainly not something I'm accustomed to either."

"Edward it is then," she said, broadening her smile.

"And Evangeline, please do let me know anytime I can be of service. I wouldn't want Mr. Donovan to ever think I wasn't doing my job properly, and he was quite clear in that you were to be taken care of and that you were to receive priority service."

"I certainly will, Edward. I wouldn't want Mr. Donovan to think either of us was committing some unpardonable sin," she said with a teasing grin.

Edward relaxed, a twinkle in his eyes. "You are a breath of fresh air, Miss Evangeline. I think you and I will get along quite famously."

"I would like that very much," she said sincerely. "No one can ever have too many friends."

He looked taken aback and then absurdly pleased at the notion that she would consider them friends. But then he likely catered to the extremely wealthy and was likely unused to any sort of deference or respect. Then she immediately felt guilty for making such a sweeping generalization. As if all wealthy people were rude and snobbish. Drake possessed neither of those qualities, though she did doubt he had gone so far as to learn Edward's first name, much less consider him a "friend."

"Now, go on back up so that I can see to your food," he said, making a shooing motion with his hands. "I can't have you going hungry on my watch."

So this was the life of a rich and pampered princess, she mused as she rode the elevator back up to the apartment. It was still disconcerting to her just how quickly her entire life had been upended and the extreme to which it had changed in such a short time.

She supposed other women wouldn't waste time stressing over it and count their blessings. They would likely revel in such a lifestyle and have no problem at all adjusting. However, Evangeline's pride and the fact that she didn't see what Drake obviously saw when he looked at her kept her on cautious reserve. But if she wasn't careful, she was going to come across as an ungrateful shrew, and that was the last thing she ever wanted Drake to think of her. Or anyone, for that matter. Her mother had taught her better and would be greatly disappointed in her were she to discover that Evangeline had ever acted in such a way.

As she waited for her delivery to be brought up, her cell phone rang and it was a different ringtone. Frowning, she picked it up, seeing Drake's name as the incoming caller. He must have set a different ringtone for himself since the last time he'd called her so she'd know who was calling before ever looking to see. She smiled, thinking it endearing that he'd done such a thoughtful and sweet thing.

"Hello?" she said, with eagerness she couldn't contain from flowing from her greeting.

"How is my angel today?" he asked in a gruff voice. "Not overdoing it, are you?"

"I'm fine," she said truthfully. "I barely feel it at all."

There was a short silence and then, "I'm going to be late again tonight. I'm sorry but it's unavoidable. I have a late meeting that couldn't be rescheduled. I had hoped to be home in time to take you out for dinner tonight, but I'd rather you not wait on me since I don't know what time I'll be there. If you'd still like to eat out, I'll have one of my men come pick you up and take you wherever you'd like to go, or if you prefer, you can stay in. It's your call."

There was sincere regret in his tone that told her he had intended their evening to go a lot differently, and it bolstered her spirits to know he was disappointed that he wouldn't see her as soon as he'd planned.

"I ordered takeout for lunch so I doubt I'll feel much like eating later, but if I do, I'll make something here. I think I'd rather stay in," she said quietly.

There was a distinct pause as he seemed to analyze her response.

"Is something wrong?" he asked.

"No," she said in a near whisper. "There's nothing wrong at all, Drake. Please don't worry about me when you have business matters to attend to. I'll see you when you get home."

Before allowing him to question her further, and he would have, she ended the phone call and then turned off the ringer, not wanting to get into her conflicted feelings that even she didn't fully understand, so how could she expect Drake to?

A few moments later, she received a text from Drake that she wasn't at all sure what to make of.

Silas will be by for a few minutes to deliver you a bank card and two credit cards, all of which are in your name. He will also give you a substantial amount of cash in case you have need of it. Activate all cards and I expect you to use them for anything you need. And I mean everything, Angel.

Now she wondered if the doorman had immediately called Drake to inform him of the fact that she'd tried to pay for her takeout. She winced because she didn't want or need a bank card and *two* credit cards, much less the cash Drake had said that Silas would be bringing over. But again, thoughts of her acting like an ungrateful shrew put a halt to any further lamenting. She could accept them with grace, but it didn't mean she actually had to go crazy and break the bank on an unnecessary shopping trip. She would simply use the cards or the cash when she bought groceries for the nights Drake wanted her to cook.

She wandered through the apartment, checking out the rooms she hadn't yet been into. When she walked into what appeared to be Drake's home office, she froze and immediately retreated, feeling as though she were intruding in an off-limits area.

There were four bedrooms in all, though the only one she'd even been in or seen until now was Drake's. Everywhere she went in the spacious apartment that covered the entire top floor of the building, Drake's presence was imprinted. Even the décor reflected sheer masculinity. There was no froufrou or stylish elegance. Just all male. A strong alpha presence that surrounded her and immersed herself in him even when he wasn't here.

It was comforting and it made her feel secure even in his absence. She realized this was her haven, her sanctuary. A barrier between her and the harsh, outside world.

The buzz of the intercom sounded, and she hurried over to answer.

"Miss Hawthorn, um, I mean Evangeline," Edward hastily corrected. "Your food has arrived, but another gentleman is here to see you and has offered to bring the food up with him. Is that all right?"

"Is it Silas?" she questioned.

"Yes."

"Then of course send him up and thank you again, Edward, for your patience and kindness. I appreciate it."

"Any time, Evangeline. If there is anything I can ever do for you, let me know at once."

She moved away from the intercom and then hastily went into the kitchen, not wanting to appear as though she were eagerly awaiting Silas's arrival. Had he been assigned this particular duty or had he volunteered? She sighed, because did it really *matter*?

A brief longing hit her square in the chest because ever since she'd moved in with Drake, not one morning had she awakened in his arms. Every morning she woke alone, Drake long gone with only the prerequisite gift and a note. She'd give every single gift back just to have one morning when she woke with his arms snugly around her, and when she opened her eyes the first thing she saw was him.

"Evangeline? It's Silas," he called from the foyer.

"In the kitchen," she called back.

He appeared a moment later carrying several takeout bags, an amused look on his face.

"You planning to feed an army?"

She grinned, relaxing. "I was hungry and *everything* sounded good, so I decided to order a little bit of everything and sample it all."

He set the bags down and then reached into his pocket, pulling out a wad of bills and three plastic cards.

"Drake asked me to drop these off for you."

"Yeah," she murmured, avoiding looking at the cash and cards he slid across the island.

Instead, she ignored them and began opening the bags as the tantalizing aroma rose, making her stomach growl in anticipation.

"Have you eaten yet?" she asked impulsively.

He looked perplexed. "No."

"Well, as you can see, I have more than enough food for one. Would you like to join me for lunch? Or do you have other pressing matters to tend to?"

When he remained silent, looking as though he had no idea what to say to her invitation, she mentally groaned because damn it, she was forever blurting out stuff and clearly Silas was a busy man. All Drake's men were, and she didn't want Silas to now feel obligated to eat with her for fear of hurting her feelings.

"It's okay if you have to run," she said hastily. "You certainly won't hurt my feelings. I wouldn't want you to miss something important because you were appeasing me."

"Not at all," he said in a solemn voice. "I happen to love Asian food, so if you don't mind sharing, I'd be honored to have lunch with you."

She gave him a delighted smile and then took two plates from the cabinets along with utensils and serving spoons from the drawer. They took seats on the stools at the island, and she and Silas unpacked all the containers and the bags that held the appetizers.

"Ah, a woman after my own heart," Silas said with an exaggerated sigh. "All my favorites. Teriyaki chicken skewers, crab rangoon, egg rolls and that's only for starters. I can't wait to see what entrées you ordered."

"Pork lo mein, spicy, General Tso's chicken with fried rice, Mongolian beef, kung pao beef, orange chicken and double pan-fried noodles, spicy of course. Oh, and pad see ew. As you can see, it's not strictly Chinese. There's some Thai dishes mixed in, so we get the best of both worlds."

"I'll take some of everything," Silas said.

Evangeline laughed. "So will I. It's the reason I ordered a bit of everything. When in doubt, go for it all."

"I wholeheartedly agree."

They filled their plates to the point of overflowing and then dug in with relish. Silas appeared to enjoy his every bit as much as Evangeline enjoyed hers. It was absolute heaven. It had been months since she'd splurged on her favorite takeout, and she felt decadently indulged where just weeks before she would have felt enormously guilty over such an extravagance.

"These are the best egg rolls," Evangeline said, nearly moaning with delight. "I don't think I've ever had a better one. I need to have this restaurant on speed dial. I have a feeling I'll be ordering takeout at least once a week."

"You act as though this is a luxury," Silas observed, watching her intently.

She ducked her head and flushed, embarrassment tightening her cheeks.

"My apologies," Silas said in a quiet voice. "I didn't mean to embarrass you."

She shook her head. "I'm being ridiculously sensitive. But you're right. It is—or rather was—a luxury. One that I couldn't often afford. I work, or rather worked, long hours to make as much money as possible so I could send it home to my parents, who desperately need all the financial support they can get. I kept back only what was absolutely necessary to pay rent, utilities and groceries. Eating out, even takeout, was an extravagance I simply couldn't afford. I just couldn't justify it when my parents' need is so great. So I bought off-brand groceries and cooked for the most part because not eating out meant more money I could send to my parents each week. So yes. You could say this is next to heaven and I plan to stuff myself so full that I'll likely be sick afterward, but at the moment I just don't care."

Silas's expression was thunderous and his jaw bulged as he clamped it shut. He looked as though he were exerting great effort not to let loose a torrent of obscenities, surprising since he was so well spoken and not as rough around the edges as some of Drake's other men.

After a moment, when he'd visibly regained control of his composure, the tension eased.

"If you're game, then I vote we have a weekly lunch date. I'll bring takeout, whatever you have a taste for that week, and we'll have lunch together. Sound good?"

She sent him a dazzling smile, unknowing of the effect it had on the closed-off, hardened man and the fact that something inside him softened when he thought himself incapable of experiencing such feelings. He'd been dead-on when he'd told Evangeline that she was special. In fact, she was one of a kind, and the fact that she had no clue made her all the more genuine. What might his childhood have been like if he'd had someone like Evangeline to shine light into the darkness of his unending despair?

"I'd love that," she said, her excitement not at all concealed.

"Deal, then," he said. "Just let me know a day when you're free and

Drake doesn't have plans for you and you intend to stay in for the day, and I'll come over and bring the food."

She frowned. "But you can't just drop everything on a whim and come have lunch at the drop of the hat."

"Can't I?" he asked, his tone serious. "I set my schedule and unless Drake has an urgent matter for me to attend to, everything else can be put on hold."

Whoa. The more she became acclimated to Drake's world, the more she realized that his "men," though claiming to work for Drake, seemed more like partners—brothers in a sense—than subordinates who took orders from the "boss." Clearly they set their own schedules and came and went as they pleased unless, as Silas had mentioned, Drake had an urgent matter that needed immediate attention. And she didn't want to know what constituted an "urgent matter."

"Okay, deal." Then she frowned. "Do I have your cell number in my phone? I barely know how to work the damn thing."

He reached across the island to pick up her phone. After fiddling with it mere seconds, he leaned over so she could see the screen where her contacts were displayed.

"Here's Drake's number," he said, pointing to Drake's name and the number below it.

"What are all those other numbers?" she asked, astounded by how many numbers were in her contacts.

"After Drake is Maddox." He frowned a moment and punched a series of buttons, taking it from her sight for a brief period, and then extended it out so she could view it once more. "I took the liberty of moving my number directly beneath Drake's. If for any reason you run into trouble, I want you to call me if you can't reach Drake."

She lifted an eyebrow but didn't say anything, not wanting to inadvertently offend him. And well, it was sweet that he seemed to have taken over the role of her secondary protector.

"After me, there's Maddox, Justice, Thane, Jax, Hartley, Hatcher, Zander and Jonas. I notice your parents aren't in your contacts and neither are your girlfriends, so you should probably enter those. I can do it for you if you give me names and numbers."

Evangeline wrinkled her brow. "Who is Jonas? I don't think I've met him."

Silas smiled. "You will. No doubt there. Drake will make sure that you're well acquainted with all the men assigned to your protection."

"Does Zander really have to be in my contacts?" she asked, not even trying to keep the irritation from her voice.

Silas surprised her by covering her hand with his and giving it a light squeeze. "Zander isn't the asshole he can appear to be. Granted, you two didn't get off on the right foot, but he's a good man, and he'd go to the wall for any of us and now you. There is no way he would ever allow anyone to harm you under his watch. He's rough around the edges and has the manners of a boar, but you won't find many men more loyal than him. He's not quite sure what to make of you yet, so you have him nervous, and that is not a feeling he likes or is well acquainted with."

"I make *him* nervous?" she asked incredulously. "He could squash me like a bug with his pinkie finger!"

Mirth shone in Silas's eyes, momentarily shocking her, because he was always so quiet and solemn. Serious. As though he rarely had reason to laugh or be amused by anything.

"None of Drake's men know quite what to make of you yet. You're nothing like they've ever encountered before, so they haven't been able to figure you out yet, which doesn't make them happy because they feel at a disadvantage. I think they are intimidated by you."

She shook her head in disbelief and then laughed at the idea of all those badass, not-to-be-fucked-with men being intimidated by *her*. It was absolutely hysterical and she couldn't stop laughing. She was wheezing by the time she gained control over her outburst.

"You think I'm pulling one over on you," Silas said, his expression serious. "But I'm telling you the absolute truth. For that matter, we're all convinced that Drake hasn't quite figured you out either, and that is pretty damn funny because he can read people as easily as reading a book. But ever since you walked into his club, he's *not* been himself at all."

Evangeline frowned at that. "I'm not sure how to take that. As in I don't know if that's a good thing or a bad thing."

Silas smiled as they continued eating, the cell phone resting on the island for the moment.

"I've known Drake a long time, Evangeline, and trust me. It's very good. *You* are good for him. The best thing that's ever happened to him."

She froze, taking in the huge impact that statement had on her. Her heart fluttered and her pulse beat erratically as happiness seeped all the way into the deepest recesses of her soul.

They ate in silence a few more moments before Silas returned his attention to her phone.

"If anything, and I mean anything should ever happen, if you run into a situation that makes you remotely uncomfortable or you are hurt, threatened or injured in any way, you are to immediately call Drake first. If you can't reach him, then you call me. I have my phone on me twenty-four-seven, so it's doubtful you won't be able to reach me. But, in the unlikely event that you don't get me, then you go down the line in order and call every single one of Drake's men until you get one of them. You do *not* want to have to answer to Drake if shit goes down and you didn't call anyone, so I want your promise, Evangeline. No matter what, no matter how small or unimportant *you* think it is, you are to pick up the phone and start calling, yeah?"

Her eyes widened, but she swallowed her mouthful of food and then replied, "Yes. I got it. And yes, I promise."

"Good. Now, do you need help putting in your other contacts?"

She wrinkled her nose. "At the risk of sounding like a ditzy stereo-typical blonde, I'm completely tech illiterate, so yes please, if you don't mind, would you enter my parents' number and then my girlfriends'? There are only five numbers to enter, so it won't take much of your time."

"I don't have anywhere to be, Evangeline, so stop apologizing with your expression and worrying that you're taking up too much of my time."

"Thanks," she said warmly. "I really like you, Silas. You've been noth-ing but sweet and kind to me. You have no idea how much it meant both times you came to my 'rescue.'"

He looked as though she'd just accused him of being an ax murderer, judging by the look on his face. He nearly choked as he stared at her in stupefaction.

"For God's sake," he muttered. "I am neither sweet or kind, and no one has ever said or thought so. I'm not a good man, Evangeline. I won't lie to you. You seem to have a misguided opinion of me. You are far too trusting. It's a good way to get yourself hurt or killed." He shook his head. "No, I'm not a good man at all, but you have nothing to fear from me. I swear it on my life. Even if you weren't Drake's woman, you would have my unconditional protection, which is why I want me to be the second person you call if you can't reach Drake and you're in trouble or need help."

"And you're wrong, Silas," she said stubbornly. "I don't know what kind of bullshit you've been subjected to or who made you feel like you were somehow less, but whoever it was is a worthless piece of shit and if I ever find out who made you feel this way about yourself I'll kick their ass and then I'll have Zander finish the job since he'd probably enjoy that kind of thing."

Silas looked shocked and bewildered, a host of what could only be called "what the fuck" expressions, but then to her surprise he threw back his head and laughed. A full-throated, genuine laugh of amuse-ment, something she hadn't imagined him capable of. She stared in wonder at how his laughter, such a beautiful sound, completely trans-formed him from a quiet, polished, restrained, well-mannered man with more shadows in his eyes than true color to someone who looked years younger. The lines and grooves on his face and forehead simply disappeared and his eyes sparkled with genuine laughter. All she could do was stare in fascination, unable to look away from the breathtaking transformation occurring right in front of her.

"You are a priceless treasure, Evangeline," he said, his eyes still gleam-ing with amusement. "And I pity the fool who ever tries to mess with someone you care about. You may look like a kitten and an innocent angel, but underneath you're a ferocious lioness with deadly teeth and claws."

Still chuckling, he reached for her phone. "Give me the names and numbers of the contacts you want me to enter before you start planning assault and God only knows what else and then Drake and I will have to bail you out of jail."

She grinned, absurdly pleased with herself for being able to draw Silas out of his shell. And, well, she hadn't lied. She liked Silas. There was something about him that reminded her of Drake. And she strongly suspected that Silas had endured a very hard life dating back to his childhood, and her heart ached for the boy he'd once been. Affection, someone standing up for him, someone liking him seemed such alien concepts to him, as though he'd never experienced any of it. And that pissed her off.

She gave him her parents' names and number first and then pro-vided him with Steph's, Lana's and Nikki's cell numbers as well as the landline number in their apartment.

"That all?" Silas asked when she fell silent.

She nodded, a little self-conscious. "I don't know many people in the city, and Steph, Lana and Nikki are my only friends. I didn't exactly have much time to get out and meet people or make other friends because I worked as many hours as I could."

She wished she'd just kept her big mouth shut because the smile was gone from both Silas's eyes and his mouth. His lips tightened and he looked pissed.

But to her surprise, he didn't voice his obvious displeasure and instead reached across the island and took both her hands in his, squeezing them gently.

"Well, now you have us. All of us. Warts and all. You belong to Drake, yes, but you also now belong to us all. Drake is the closest thing to a brother I've ever had, as are the others. And because you are his woman, our loyalty, protection and friendship now extend to you as well. You have friends now, Evangeline. Don't ever think otherwise. Which is why I expect you to call on me if you have need of anything. If there is ever something I can do for you, it would upset me greatly if you didn't feel as though you could reach out to me."

"Do *not* make me cry," she said with mock ferocity. "Me crying is *not* a pretty sight. Some women have perfected the art of a tear or two and a delicate, feminine sniffle. I'm an ugly crier. My face gets all red, my eyes swell up and my nose runs like a faucet. *Trust* me, you do not want to see that."

Silas didn't respond to her attempt at lighthearted humor in kind. His expression grew somber, and sadness chased across his eyes, gone almost before she even registered it.

"I would hate for you to ever have reason to cry," he said in a pained voice. "You deserve to be happy, Evangeline. And I hope to hell Drake moves heaven and earth to make you so. Because if he doesn't, he's a damn fool."

25

It was late in the evening, and even though Drake had clearly told her he didn't know when he'd be home, she hadn't expected him to be this late. At nine, she curled up on the couch, completely nude, because she wanted to wait up for him, no matter how late he came home, and though he hadn't given her any instructions on how to be when he arrived or even that she was to wait up on him, she wanted him to come home to her. For him to know he mattered, that his needs mattered and that she wanted to please him. Wanted to see the warm approval in his eyes that she'd grown to crave so much that at times it frightened her.

She wasn't aware of what time she drifted off, only that when she sleepily opened her eyes, Drake was standing in front of the couch, his gaze burning over her naked skin.

She immediately smiled, though she was still blinking away the vestiges of sleep from her eyes, and his face softened as he leaned down to kiss her long and so very sweet.

"You didn't have to wait up on me, Angel, but I'm very glad you did."

"I would never not wait up on you, Drake," she said in a serious voice. "I wanted you to come home and for the first thing that you saw to be me, waiting for you. I'm only sorry I fell asleep."

He put a finger to her lips. "Shh, my darling. It's nearly eleven. There is no need to apologize for falling asleep. I didn't call this time because I worried I would wake you."

She pushed herself upward instead of remaining sprawled indelicately on the couch.

"How was your day? It sounded as though you were busy and you look tired, Drake. You don't get enough rest."

He smiled. "My angel worries about me and wants to take care of me. No one has ever taken care of me, or *wanted* to, for that matter."

His smile was faint, followed by a brief shadow of pain and . . . need. No matter that this man enjoyed taking care of her, it was obvious that he too needed that same care, whether or not he would ever admit to something he'd likely construe as a shortcoming in himself.

He would just have to get over it because she had no intention of taking without reciprocating in any way she could. His happiness had become important to her, and she couldn't even pinpoint when it had become so. But just as he pampered her, cherished her and lavished his loving care upon her, she would return the favor in full measure.

She frowned. "You have someone *now* who wants to and *will* take care of you in every way I can. I want to make you happy, Drake, and not just because I cede power to you and submit to you. I intend to make you feel as loved as you make me feel."

He looked shaken by her straightforward statement, as if he had never come across such a situation before and wasn't at all certain how to react. But his eyes said it all. They glowed with warm pleasure and contentment. He looked at her like she was the most precious thing in the world—*his* world.

He extended his hand to help her from the couch and pulled her up and against him so she was molded to his body. He cupped her face in his hands and kissed her lingeringly, taking his time and tasting every inch of her mouth, inside and out.

"I have something for you," he said in a husky, passion-laced voice.

The warm glow that had surrounded her, drowning her in the silent exchange between them and the look of wonder in his eyes, evaporated instantly. Dread and disappointment replaced her excitement over his coming home, and she immediately tensed.

He frowned at her reaction but didn't respond. Instead, he pulled a small box from his pocket and placed it into her hand.

"Open it," he said.

Her fingers were trembling, something he might construe as excitement or anticipation, but it was neither. She didn't *want* to open the damn box. It somehow cheapened what she considered a deep emotional bond established with the few words they'd exchanged and turned the entire evening into something else entirely.

She didn't want to see what was inside. All she wanted was *him*, for him to take her to bed so she could do exactly as she'd vowed and for once take care of him after a long day of work. Was that so hard for him to understand? Had no one ever wanted him, the man, Drake Donovan? And not what he possessed and the cavalier way he tossed trinkets her way on a daily basis?

But she dutifully opened the box and discovered a necklace to match the huge earrings he'd given her already. The very thing she'd predicted, though at the time it had been a sarcastic thought. She hadn't *really* thought he'd go that far. But she should have known better.

She gasped when she caught a full view of the diamond necklace. It was huge. Bigger than both earrings put together! It was a teardrop diamond pendant the size of his *thumb!*

Something inside her snapped and she lashed out, her disappointment too keen to hide.

"This has to stop, Drake! *Enough!* Every day you give me some outrageously expensive gift, and today this makes the *second*. I don't *want* your gifts. I want *you*. Can't you understand that? Don't you know me better than that by now?"

Tears gathered in her eyes and she was shaking with anger and disappointment.

"I don't want them," she raged. "I don't even know what to do with the first couple you bought me. What on earth am I supposed to do with the rest?"

Drake's expression turned to one of fury, but she was too angry to recognize the line she'd just crossed.

He swore violently and colorfully, turning away for a long moment, his back to her, his hands clenched into tight fists at his sides. Then he whirled back around, his eyes nearly black with rage.

"Why the hell do you have to make such a fucking big deal out of everything I give you?" he snapped. "It's not just the jewelry. You looked like you were on your way to death row when I bought you clothing. You've objected at every turn when I buy you anything, and you damn well knew the rules going in, so you can't plead ignorance. Do you even consider how that makes *me* feel? It's not just a rejection of a physical object. It's a rejection of *me* and my desire to spoil and pamper you and make you feel like the very special woman you are."

She went soft to her very soul, and she'd never felt more ashamed of herself than in this moment. Oh God, she'd never even considered that he would consider it a rejection of him when all she *wanted* was him. Not diamonds, jewels, expensive clothing, credit cards and unlimited funds. She'd made a complete and utter mess of this, all because she'd let her insecurities get the better of her and couldn't fathom why Drake had chosen *her*. He called her special, but she wasn't! Except . . . he thought she was and she didn't believe him. Which meant she'd shown him the utmost disrespect by not having faith in him. She was clearly telling him that she didn't trust him, when nothing could be further from the truth.

She went to him immediately, closing the distance between them and wrapping herself around his huge body, ignoring his rigidity and the fact that he didn't return her embrace.

"Oh, Drake, I'm so very sorry," she said, her heart breaking into jagged, painful pieces that left her utterly bereft over hurting him. "I never meant to make you feel that way. You just don't understand how hard it is for a girl like me . . ." She broke off and closed her eyes but not before Drake saw the fleeting hint of despair shining like a beacon.

Despite Drake's anger, he cupped her chin, caressing her cheek with his thumb, because something else was going on here and he'd jumped to what appeared to be very errant conclusions.

"Angel, open your eyes and look at me," he said in a firm voice.

When she finally complied, he saw the tears that threatened to fall from her glossy eyes.

"What the hell do you mean I don't understand how hard it is for a girl like you? What kind of girl are you referring to?"

She flushed and would have closed her eyes again but he gave a warning tap to her cheek with his thumb, commanding her attention.

"I've never had anything," she said in a low tone. "Except my parents' love. My friends' love. Their support. I've worked for everything *else* I've ever had, and granted it's not much, but it's mine. It was earned and I take a certain amount of pride in that. A girl like me has to work for what she gets because there aren't a lot of men out there lining up for a boring, quiet, mousy girl who doesn't need or want *things*. I just feel like you give me so much and I give you *nothing* in return."

She was becoming perilously close to those tears falling, and he could feel her distress radiating from her in waves.

"The gifts are beautiful. Very precious to me. I love each and every one of them. I'm scared to death to wear the jewelry because what if I lose it? But at the same time, every gift is a reminder of how much you give to me and how little I give you in return."

Now she was openly crying, tears sliding silently down her cheeks and colliding with his thumbs.

"All I've ever had to sustain me before was my sense of self-worth,"

293

she said in a choked, emotion-filled voice. "You can't put a price tag on self-worth. And right now, I don't feel worth much at all and I hate that feeling. It's a helpless feeling, and God, there's nothing worse than feeling—*being*—helpless. You have so much pride, Drake. Surely *you* understand what I'm trying to say."

She was coming far too close to begging for his liking. The desperation in her voice seared him to the depths of his soul.

Her impassioned outburst struck a chord deep within him. He marveled at the fact that in all the relationships or rather short acquaintances he'd entertained, never once had a woman taken issue with anything he chose to give her. In fact, there were many times the woman pouted ever so prettily that the earrings were beautiful but without a necklace to complement them the look just wasn't as breathtaking.

Never had he had a woman stand before him and speak of the one thing he was very well acquainted with. Pride. Self-worth. Of not accepting anything from anyone and earning every damn thing he possessed. And yet he'd reduced her to that by showering lavish gifts on her, as though he could buy her affection, her smile, her happiness when in fact, when he thought back on it, the brightest smiles he could remember seeing were when she saw him after a long day at work, how happy she seemed to be when he chose to stay in and allowed her to cook on the rare occasions they didn't go out. Nothing he had bought her had come close to the kind of joy and contentment he'd seen in her eyes and on her face that simply being with him seemed to give her. Was she for real? It utterly bewildered him, and for the first time in his life, he had no idea how to handle a woman. This woman. And it made him feel helpless, like a first-class fuckup.

"You're wrong when you say you have nothing to give me," he said gruffly, still grappling with revelations still swirling in his mind. "But I *do* understand, Angel. I understand only all too well."

Suddenly the distance between them was too much. Not just the physical distance but the emotional distance as well. He'd made so many mistakes with her. And even knowing she wasn't like any other woman he'd ever met, he'd still treated her the same. Lavishing expensive gifts on her instead of providing the things that really mattered to her. Even knowing the priceless treasure he possessed and that she was unique and rare, he hadn't made the effort to truly learn her.

He held out his arms, holding his breath and hoping she didn't refuse him. "Come here, Angel. I refuse to have this conversation when you look tired on your feet and all I want to do is hold you."

He exhaled a long sigh of relief when after only a slight hesitation, she walked into his arms. He wrapped them around her and for a long moment he simply held her, closing his eyes as he buried his face in her sweet-smelling hair.

Then he maneuvered her to the sofa and sat, pulling her down into his lap, once more wrapping his arms tightly around her. Her slight frame nestled perfectly against his. As if she'd been made for him and only him. Two pieces of a puzzle.

So fucking perfect. Soft, warm. So loving and generous. She was a shining light in the darkest recesses of his tarnished soul. A welcome-home gift—treasure—every time he walked through his door.

"First I want to address the issue of equality and what you can contribute to make you feel as though you give me something in return for what I give you. Though, babe, if *all* you ever gave me were you, I'd spend the rest of my life trying to catch up, because nothing and I mean nothing I give you will ever be more precious than you giving yourself to me. You can't put a price tag on something that is priceless and worth more than all the money in the world."

He felt her smile against his chest, and he caressed the length of her hair, resting his chin atop her head, marveling at the contentment he felt over such a simple act.

"You're an excellent cook and you said yourself you love cooking.

At first, I didn't like the idea of you cooking for me when I came home because as I told you that very first night, I never meant for you to be a domestic slave."

She leaned away from his chest so she could look at him, mischief in her eyes. "Just a sex slave," she teased.

He relaxed, relief surging through his veins because she was no longer tense, nor did she seem angry.

He smacked her playfully on the behind but left his palm there, cupping the soft plumpness of her ass.

"Damn right," he said with no remorse whatsoever. "But I took something away from you that I shouldn't have. I made you feel as though you contributed nothing to our relationship. You enjoyed cooking for me and you were happy that I loved your meal. Hell, I even loved those fucking cupcakes and you had every single one of my men eating out of your hand so they'd get one too. If someone had told me a month ago that the men who work for me would eagerly be lining up for a cupcake made by an angel, I would have laughed myself stupid."

She blushed but her eyes were shining in delight, the corners of her mouth tilted upward into that delectable quirky half smile that was so characteristic of her. Some might consider it a fault, but Drake found it endearing. Even now, he paused to drop his head and nibble at the corner of her mouth, running his tongue over that delicious little quirk. She shivered against him in response and his entire body tightened. So fucking responsive. He'd thought it, said it, too many times to count since she'd barged into his life, or, if he was honest, since he'd dragged her into his life.

She lit up for him. Him. Only him. Hell, she'd been around his men, his brothers, all men most bitches couldn't keep their hands off of, and yet Evangeline smiled at them, was affectionate with them all, much to their disgruntlement and bewilderment, but in no way could her actions or responses ever be construed as sensual. She wasn't a flirt. She was too damn honest, not to mention too innocent to even know how. If she liked you, she was nice to you and she let you know she liked you. It was as simple as that. And apparently she'd decided that she liked all his brothers. Men would die to have a woman go up in flames the instant they looked at her in a certain way. Or touched her, kissed her, whispered the right words. He *had* such a woman right here on his lap and in his arms. In his bed every night, offering her complete submission as sweetly as a woman ever had, and if he wasn't careful, he was going to fuck up and lose her.

He nearly shook his head. Compromise. Not a word in his vocabulary. But when it came to Evangeline, he was fast learning new words and most certainly their definition.

"I love your cooking," he said. "Best fucking meals I've eaten in my life."

And they were. He might do a lot to keep a woman like Evangeline, but he wasn't a liar. Not even to make her feel better or to appease her would he lie. She valued self-worth most of all. How hollow would that self-worth be if it was built on lies he'd told her?

Her eyes glowed with pleasure, her entire face lit up with radiance to rival the sun, her cheeks growing rosier by the second. She looked at him as if he'd just saved her from a burning building, for fuck's sake. It didn't take much to please this woman at all, and here he'd been throwing tens of thousands of dollars at her when apparently all she truly wanted was . . . *him*.

He couldn't comprehend it, but the proof was here, looking him in the eyes. She wanted Drake Donovan the man. Not the wealth, power, status or prestige of being on his arm and under his protection.

His money appalled her. The gifts he gave her horrified her. Silas had informed him that she was less than thrilled to accept the cash and credit cards he'd sent over. She'd been more excited over the fucking Chinese takeout than over a credit card with no spending limit. And he'd bet his entire fortune that she hadn't even touched the cash, much less counted it.

How did you keep a woman like his angel happy when she didn't appear to want anything?

She only wants you.

And that he could give her. If that was all it took to make her happy, to *keep* her happy and to make damn sure she never walked out on him, then he'd give her exactly what she wanted.

"Once a week, same day unless it can't be avoided, you cook for me. I'll arrange my schedule so that I'm home no later than six. And when I say unless it can't be avoided, Angel, I mean that nothing short of death will keep me from being here. Now that's all I can promise," he said in a serious voice. "You are my single most important responsibility. You gave me your trust and with that trust, you gave me yourself and you placed your faith in me that I'll keep you happy. I take my responsibilities very seriously, and therefore I'm going to continue to spoil the hell out of you. You will not lift a finger except those nights you cook for me and you will not be washing the fucking dishes afterward. That's what I pay a cleaning lady for. And what you can do for me is accept whatever I choose to give you and know that I give it not to take away your sense of self-worth or sharpen the divide between our net worths, but because it makes *me* happy. And what will make me even happier is if, as I told you the night I took you home with me for the first time, you think of creative ways of expressing your gratitude. Not be thinking of ways to pay me back and certainly not dwell on not being able to pay me back. Because that will seriously piss me the fuck off."

She surprised him by throwing her arms around his neck and hugging him tightly. She buried her face in his throat, and the soft whisper of her exhalations blew over his skin, setting fire to his every nerve ending.

"I'm sorry," she said in an emotional voice that was muffled by his throat.

He pried her away from him and glanced sharply down at her.

"For fuck's sake, what the hell are you sorry for?"

He knew his exasperation was showing, but hell, she was the single most infuriating, complex woman he'd ever known.

"I was—I've been an ungrateful bitch," she said painfully. "And self-ish. I never even considered *your* feelings. I was too wrapped up in my own insecurities and every time another gift showed up my panic increased. You're right. About all of it, and I'm so very sorry, Drake."

She lifted her hand to his jaw and caressed his cheek, the sensation like velvet, the contrast between her baby-soft skin and his much harder, life-roughened features heady and addictive. "And," she added in a husky whisper, "you can be assured I will be *very* creative in my expressions of gratitude."

He pressed a finger to her lips and sent her a look of reprimand.

"You will not speak of yourself that way. Ever. I shouldn't even be having this conversation with you considering Silas had the same exact conversation verbatim with you, and if you don't think I'll allow him to turn you over his knee and spank that pretty ass if you say that kind of fucked-up shit about yourself again, then you couldn't be more wrong."

Her eyes widened and her mouth dropped open. "He wasn't teasing me?" she squeaked.

"Does Silas strike you as the type of man to tease?" Drake asked dryly.

"Point taken," she muttered.

Then she glanced up at him, a gleam in her eyes that made him go instantly hard.

"What is that look for?" he asked suspiciously.

"Well . . . I did promise to be creative in the way I expressed my gratitude," she said solemnly, though the *too*-innocent expression on her face told him she was anything but solemn.

"Oh you did, now didn't you? Just how creative are you, Angel?"

She flashed a shy smile and peeked up at him from beneath her lashes. Then she reached up and twined her arms around his neck, having to stand on tiptoe to elevate her diminutive height.

She looked adorably shy and color rose in her cheeks. "I don't want to disappoint you, Drake. Ever. And you know I have no experience except with you."

He was inordinately pleased with her assertion that he was her only experience and that no reference at all was made to her shithead ex. He wasn't so pleased with her statement of not wanting to disappoint him, but he didn't interrupt her, because she was obviously struggling with what she wanted to say.

"What I would like is for you to teach me how to please you. Only you. You said the other night was for you, but in reality, it was all about me. Tonight . . ." She sucked in another breath. "Tonight, I want it to *truly* be all about you. I want you to have absolute control and show me how to pleasure you in *any* way you want. I want you to make me do whatever it is you want me to do to you—*for* you. And I don't want you to hold back for fear of hurting or scaring me."

She paused for a moment as she stared into his eyes as if gauging his reaction.

"I want you. Just you. Nothing else. Just you, your control, your dominance, the man you are, the man I know you to be. I'm not trying to change the rules, I swear. I don't want control tonight. I only want for you to be selfish for once and to *take* what you need from me, however you want it, need it, like it. I just wish I knew enough not to have to ask you how to give you all that I want to give you."

She finished in a whisper, a thread of regret in her voice.

He was shaken. He, a man who was unshakable. But her sincere plea cut to the very core and uncovered parts of his heart that had long ago been shut off, never to be opened or to bleed again. For anyone.

He framed her beautiful face in his hands, cradling it gently as he stared down into her eyes, losing all sense of himself.

"I'm *glad* you don't have the experience to know all there is to know about pleasing me," he said in a savage tone. "There is nothing more beautiful than a woman asking her man to guide her and teach her how to pleasure him. You make me feel like I'm the only man who's ever even entered your world, Angel. You can't imagine how that feels."

She smiled, her eyes glowing warmly. "Then you'll do it? You'll take me the way you want to take me tonight? Rough, hard, long, sweet. It doesn't matter, Drake. Because pleasing you, bringing you pleasure, gives me the same and so much more. So very much more."

Dear God, what she was doing to him in such a short time. He was in way over his fucking head and he damn well knew it. He was helpless to keep his defenses rigid and erect around her, and God help him but he didn't want to.

For the first time in his life, he wanted to let someone in. He just prayed that when that happened, and she saw the monster he truly was, that he wouldn't lose the precious gift staring at him as though he were her entire world.

He looked at her sweet smile, going over every single word—gift— she'd given him. Did she know how dark his desires ran? Did she fully understand the things that aroused him sexually? Somehow, he didn't think so. In her innocence, how could she?

He had no doubt that she was utterly sincere and here, in this moment, she would give him anything he wanted. Would do for him anything he wanted. But would she understand, or would she see his dark fantasies as a betrayal of his promise to protect her and always take care of her?

"Be very sure of what you are offering me, Angel," he said, his tone low and serious.

"I'm sure," she said with no hesitation.

"Then I want you to remember something, the most important thing of all, when I take what I want from you tonight. You gave me your trust, and you will need to not only remember that, but to believe in that trust—and in me."

She didn't look or appear frightened. There was a spark of curiosity and a delicate shiver stole over her body, as though she were imagining what he was thinking. What he wanted—would demand of her tonight.

He pulled her in closer to his body. Until nothing separated them and his arms were wrapped around her satiny, naked skin. He allowed his hands to roam down her back, cupping her buttocks and then squeezing.

"Do you trust me?" he asked, allowing her one last out. "Enough not to question anything I ask of you tonight? To follow and heed my instructions regardless of what they may be?"

She leaned her head back, determination and resolve firm in those beautiful eyes. She looped her arms loosely around his neck, but never once did she break free of his gaze.

"My gift to you is me," she said in a sweet, soul-stirring voice that was a caress all in its own. "I am yours, Drake. I know you'll never hurt me. I can't promise not to ever be afraid at any point tonight, but you need to know that my fear is not of you. Never of you. If I fear anything at all, it will be the unknown. But most of all, my greatest fear will be of letting you down."

"Then go and prepare for me," he said in a husky voice. "Take a long bath and soak for a while. There is no hurry, as it will take me a little time to make the proper arrangements for a night my angel has promised is all mine. My fantasy. My pleasure. And know, Evangeline, that you will be repaid in full measure for the gift you are offering me tonight. I too plan to come up with very creative ways of expressing my gratitude."

He trailed a finger down her silken cheek as their gazes remained locked.

"When you are finished bathing, dry yourself and your hair and then go lie down on the bed. Don't pull the covers and sheets back. I want you to lie in the middle, your hair spread across the pillows, thighs parted, hands above your head with your fingers wrapped around the slats of the headboard."

She smiled, then sighed and shook her head ruefully. "And yet again, a night that is supposed to be solely about you sounds an awful lot like I'm the one being a pampered, spoiled princess."

He regarded her solemnly. "Have no doubt, Angel. You *are* my pampered princess. But tonight, I intend only to watch, and this *is* very much for me. Just remember your promise to trust me and know that I will never allow you to come to harm, and my night will be fucking perfect."

26

As Evangeline languidly soaked in the tub, she pondered the oddity of Drake's last words to her before he'd ushered her into the bedroom and then disappeared, leaving her to heed his instructions.

They seemed in direct contradiction and try as she might, she couldn't come up with a scenario in which, as he'd said, tonight he'd only watch but had followed it with a solemn vow that he would never allow her to come to harm.

The two statements seemed incongruous. Granted, she didn't have much experience with sex, much less kinky, dominant sex or fetishes. She wasn't even sure what they were called or even the differences between a kink and a fetish or if there even was one.

Well, she wasn't going to ruin what promised to be an exciting night by overanalyzing Drake's cryptic words. She was more focused on his reaction to her impassioned statement about wanting to please him, wanting him to teach her to please him and that she wanted to give back at least a small part of all he'd given to her.

That had pleased him immensely. There was no mistaking the wonderment and surprise and yes, even delight over her sincerity. And he'd admitted what she'd already reasoned out on her own, that he had never had anyone who cared for him, who took care of him and placed his needs above their own. Had anyone ever loved him? Or at least cared deeply for him? Or were the majority of the people in his life manipulative users out to milk him for every cent they could extort?

And what of his family? He'd never spoken of them and he seemed bemused by her close relationship with her parents. In fact, she strongly suspected that he'd felt anger toward them and the fact that she'd given up so much to support them until he'd witnessed firsthand their love and concern for her. He'd even spoken to them himself and after that, she'd never seen that fleeting hint of suppressed anger when she spoke of her family.

"Oh, Drake," she whispered, her heart aching. "How lonely must it have been to live in a world where no one cared about you? How awful must it be for your worth to be measured by money and social status? Has anyone ever seen the real Drake Donovan? Has no one ever loved the real Drake Donovan?"

If it was the last thing she did, she was going to prove to him that his money didn't mean a damn to her. For that matter, she wished he had none at all because then he would never harbor any doubt as to her reasons for being with him. She would want to be with him, want desperately to submit to him and please him even if he didn't have one cent to his name.

But would he ever truly believe that? Or would some small part of him, deep down, buried under years of cynicism, always be there whispering insidiously in the back of his mind telling him she was no different from all the others?

She idly looked over at the clock on the counter by the sink and realized a full thirty minutes had passed while she contemplated the puzzle that was Drake Donovan. He'd told her to take her time, but he hadn't been specific. *She* had been specific in that this night belonged to him, and the last thing she wanted was to keep him waiting and she still had to dry her hair and position herself accordingly on the bed.

Pushing away all the senseless questions and speculation that had occupied her time in the tub, she rose, water rushing down her body. She stepped out and first wrapped a towel around her head and then took another to dry her body.

After swabbing as much moisture from her hair as she could with the towel, she sat on the vanity stool and began combing out the long tresses. She sectioned off pieces of her hair and pulled a brush down the length, following it with a blow-dryer.

She wanted to look beautiful, and her hair, when freshly washed, blow-dried and brushed out, was one of her best features. She brushed until it shone and was extremely soft, giving her a windblown look that framed her face and tumbled down her back in layers.

After giving herself one last pat-down with the towel to ensure her entire body was no longer damp, she walked back into the bedroom, relieved that Drake hadn't made his appearance yet.

She crawled on top of the mattress and with a sigh settled in the middle, her head nestled into the mound of pillows. Then she remembered his other directives.

She parted her thighs so that just a hint of the lips of her vagina were visible and then she reached upward to grasp the slats of the headboard.

Even though she was in no way bound, the feeling of being subdued, captive, a prisoner awaiting what would happen next sent delicious waves of pleasure coursing through her body. Her nipples puckered into tight, hard knots and she could feel the dampness between her legs as her clit pulsed and ached, begging for attention.

I intend only to watch.

Again his words floated through her memory, sending a fresh wave of curiosity and confusion through her veins. If he hadn't instructed her to put her hands above her head and hold on to the headboard, she would have assumed he wanted to watch as she masturbated.

And while the first time he'd instructed her to touch herself when they were going to have anal sex had made her self-conscious, she was beyond that now and was only eager to do his bidding if it pleased him to watch her pleasure herself.

She languidly turned her head when the bedroom door opened and smiled when Drake appeared in the doorway. But her smile froze when she saw he wasn't alone. Behind him walked in an extremely handsome, well-dressed man she judged to be around Drake's age.

Panic scuttled up her spine and some of what she felt must have shown on her face because Drake motioned for the man to stay back as Drake approached the bed. It was then she saw the rope Drake carried.

He sat on the edge of the bed and slid one hand leisurely down her body, his smile warm and reassuring, but his eyes glittered with need.

"Trust me," he whispered.

And at those two words and the tenderness in his expression, her trepidation dissolved in an instant.

"Oh, I trust you," she whispered, injecting all the warmth and emotion she felt into her smile.

He took one of her hands and looped the rope around her wrist, securely binding it to the slat she'd held moments earlier. Then he did the same with the other until both hands were tied, rendering her helpless to shield her nudity from the stranger standing a short distance away.

Then Drake leaned over and pressed his lips to her forehead.

"I will never hurt you, Angel, nor would I ever allow another to hurt you. My wish for tonight is to watch another man pleasure you. He is well aware of my boundaries and what I will and won't allow."

She licked her lips nervously and surprisingly, her initial fear dissipated, replaced by a warm hum of arousal. It was like tasting forbidden fruit. It felt decadently naughty for another man to pleasure her—have sex with her—at Drake's command. And then another thought took hold and guilt surged rawly through her veins.

Her worried gaze found Drake's and she stared helplessly at him, so many questions swirling in her mind. Of all the scenarios she'd

imagined, this hadn't been one of them. Drake was so forbiddingly possessive. She couldn't wrap her mind around him being willing to share
his ... possession ... with another man.

Drake's gaze softened as he stroked and caressed her breasts, cupping and palming them, thumbing her nipples to hardened peaks.

"You do not betray me, my darling angel. I won't have you thinking
it, nor will I allow you to refuse yourself to feel pleasure because I am
not the one providing it."

Her brow furrowed in genuine puzzlement, but evidently Drake
considered the matter concluded. He stood and turned, speaking in a
formal tone to the man behind him.

"Her name is Evangeline and she is mine. She is a priceless treasure
and I expect you to treat her as such. You will initiate her with gentleness and care until she is comfortable with your presence and touch.
Then and only then can you exert your will—my will—as I've outlined
to you."

Then he turned back to Evangeline. "Angel, this is Manuel, a man I
consider a friend and someone I trust. He will pleasure you, and I expect
you to heed his commands, as they are mine. Tonight, I watch as another
man pleasures and fucks what is mine."

She shivered at the coarse, descriptive language Drake used, but
then he'd likely purposely used it because he well knew her reaction
when he had used it before.

And then Drake stepped away and walked to the chair diagonal to
the bed where he would be afforded a prime view of her having sex with
another man.

She was confused, curious, conflicted and wildly excited all at the
same time. Her breaths came in rapid, short bursts and she could feel
the heat of her flushed skin.

Manuel walked to the bed as Drake had done and stood staring
down at her, raw arousal glittering brightly in his brilliant blue eyes.

"I am honored," he said huskily. "Never before have I seen such a beautiful sight than an angel spread out before me, bound to the bed, her hair scattered across the pillows like silk."

Oh, this man was good. Sheer seduction with only words.

"Touch her," Drake said. "Caress every inch of her beautiful skin."

Manuel slid one knee onto the bed and placed his palm over her belly, and she instantly jumped as a thousand tiny chill bumps erupted over her body.

"I won't hurt you," Manuel said softly.

"I know," she said just as softly. "Drake would never let you."

Manuel smiled. "Drake is a lucky bastard. Your trust in him is a gift most men can only dream of."

Her gaze skittered to Drake to see approval glistening in his eyes. He was leaned back in the chair, looking relaxed and at ease. Any worries she had about angering him over her sexual response to the man he had chosen evaporated. He looked . . . pleased. As though he had great pride in her. And if this pleased him, if this was what he wanted, then she would give it to him unreservedly.

As if sensing her thoughts, his gaze burned into hers, approval still bright in his eyes.

"Your pleasure pleases me, Angel. Never forget that. You wanted to give me whatever I wanted tonight, and what I want most is to watch while another man temporarily owns you. Whenever you are comfortable enough with Manuel, then he will take over and I will become a passive observer. But never think for a moment that this isn't something I will enjoy greatly. There is something decidedly erotic about seeing my woman tied to my bed, fucked and dominated by another man."

She moaned as Manuel's hands traveled the same path as Drake's had just moments before over her breasts. His touch was different. Were she blindfolded, she'd know the difference all the same.

"You may kiss her, lick her, use your mouth on her anywhere except her lips," Drake said to Manuel. "Her mouth is mine and mine alone and that sweetness will never be tasted by any man but me."

"I'll console myself by tasting that sweet pussy," Manuel said. "I assure you, that will be no hardship whatsoever. And those nipples," he murmured even as his head descended toward her breasts.

Her gaze found Drake's once more as she arched upward when Manuel's mouth closed around one turgid point and she sighed as he suckled gently, tonguing the tip and then administering a light nip.

To her keen disappointment, Manuel lifted his head and rose from the bed. But then she realized he was undressing and her pulse sped up. She looked at Drake instead of Manuel as he deftly removed the last of his clothing.

"Look at him, Angel," Drake commanded. "Look at the man who's going to fuck you long and hard."

She swallowed and shifted her gaze, her eyes widening at the beautiful male physique standing next to the bed. His hand curled around his burgeoning erection and he pulled back and forth, swelling and stiffening to complete hardness, until it strained upward toward his navel.

"Lift her bound hands over her head and turn her so she lies crossways on the bed, her legs over the side so you can taste—and fuck—her pussy. She likes it hard and rough, Manuel. But I expect you to take care and work her up to the point where she can accept you and is ready to fully take you."

Unfamiliar but not unpleasant hands did as Drake instructed, and Manuel positioned and then stood between her spread legs, his eyes gleaming appreciatively as he stared down at her.

He lowered himself to his knees and parted the lips of her pussy and began to softly nuzzle over the sensitive flesh. Lust surged and her hips arched. Her arms lifted, though her hands were bound, and suddenly she felt very familiar hands close around her wrists and yank them roughly back down to the mattress, holding them firmly in place.

The dual sensation of one man between her legs and Drake holding her down from the top so she couldn't move made her squirm restlessly, a moan escaping her lips. Drake's head lowered and he kissed her lips upside down.

"Let him pleasure you, Angel. While I watch him take what is mine."

Manuel licked, sucked and tormented her, taking his time devouring her pussy. The pleasure was overwhelming but her focus wasn't on Manuel. She didn't glance down at his dark head between her legs. She locked her gaze with Drake and curled her fingers around his hands, watching his reaction to this man—this stranger to her—only interested in pleasing *Drake*.

Rough hands yanked her thighs apart and Manuel's hand cupped her chin, pulling downward, his eyes glittering.

"Look at me, Evangeline."

He hadn't finished his command before he thrust hard into her. She gripped Drake's hands even harder and he freed one to stroke through her hair as he silently offered her his support.

Manuel rose over her, his body covering her, her breasts flattened against his chest as his hips undulated and rolled over hers, penetrating her deeply. But she found her gaze flitting back to Drake time and time again, absorbing the warmth and arousal in his dark eyes.

"So fucking beautiful," Manuel growled as he pounded harder into her. "Tell me, Evangeline. Just how rough do you like it?"

Even as he spoke, he thrust his hand into her hair and yanked her head upward so she was forced to look at him. He lowered his head, and for a moment she thought he would disobey Drake's directive that he was not to kiss her mouth. But he licked and nipped at her neck, her ear, and slid his lips down the curve of her neck, whispering words of praise in her ears.

"I can take anything for Drake," Evangeline said.

"I wonder if he knows how very lucky he is," Manuel mused.

"Never doubt it," Drake growled.

"Help me turn her," Manuel said to Drake. "I want that ass."

"Not until I've prepared her," Drake warned.

"I'd never hurt any woman, much less yours," Manuel said, his eyes narrowing.

Drake inclined his head. "Of course. I meant no insult. Evangeline is very precious to me and I wouldn't have her hurt in *any* way."

The two men turned her, ensuring her comfort. Drake untied her wrists and positioned her so her hand was free to touch herself. Manuel placed a pillow beneath her knees and then backed away so Drake could apply lubricant to Evangeline's opening while he himself coated the condom he wore.

Drake moved to the head of the bed, lazily reclining against the headboard so he had a firsthand view of both Evangeline and Manuel.

"You will let me know if it becomes too much," Drake said in a serious tone, his gaze boring into Evangeline.

"I won't let you down, Drake," she said huskily.

He frowned. "The only way you would let me down is by enduring pain because you think to please me. I want your promise."

"I promise," she said sincerely.

Drake lifted his gaze to Manuel, who had taken position on his knees behind Evangeline and even now caressed and stroked her bottom.

"Redden her ass before you fuck her."

"My pleasure," Manuel murmured.

Evangeline moaned softly, closing her eyes briefly in anticipation. What would another man's hand feel like smacking her behind? Her only experience with spanking had been with Drake. Would it only feel good because it was him?

She soon had her answer when Manuel's hand smacked the fleshy globe of one cheek and fire ignited, quickly fading to be replaced by the warm glow of pleasure. She opened her eyes to see Drake's gaze warm and approving.

"My angel likes the pain."

"It's only pleasure," she whispered.

Manuel alternated cheeks, never striking the same spot as he covered every inch of her behind until it ached and throbbed. She twisted restlessly, touching herself lightly, knowing not to go too far yet.

She paused when he stopped and then he placed both palms over her bottom and spread her wide, his cock bumping and nudging at her entrance. Then he stopped when the tip barely breached her opening and she began to stroke herself in earnest in anticipation of his entry.

"Fuck her hard," Drake said, repeating his earlier order. "Show her no mercy."

Oh God.

She began to tremble violently, already in danger of coming.

Manuel pushed forward just until the head of his cock fully lodged inside her and before she could take a breath, he plunged forward, lodging himself to the hilt. She cried out and bucked wildly, uncontrollably.

Manuel's hands gripped her hips to hold her still, but she fought, not against him, but against the rioting sensations that overtook her body.

"Jesus," Manuel muttered as he pushed her forward, trapping her between his body and the bed, holding her down as he pumped in and out of her ass.

He was rough, animalistic, taking her, owning her, everything Drake had asked him to do. Her hand, trapped between her body and the bed, moved frantically, chasing the orgasm that was rapidly blooming out of control.

Then to her surprise, Manuel rolled them to their sides, his cock still wedged deep inside her, and he moved her hand, replacing it with his fingers as he stroked and caressed her clit. He thrust in and out of her and Evangeline's gaze found Drake's, wanting to share this moment with him. All for him. Only for him.

Lust flared in Drake's eyes and Evangeline could see the bulge between his legs and in that moment she wished he would take her every bit as hard as Manuel was.

"Get there, Angel," Drake said harshly. "Don't make Manuel wait."

She moaned deep in her throat and threw back her head as Manuel's mouth found her neck and bit into it with enough force to leave a mark.

And then she simply let go and went flying over the edge, hurtling faster and faster until Drake wavered in and out of her focus, the world blanking around her. She was panting harshly when Manuel gently pulled out of her and then bent to brush a kiss across her forehead.

"Thank you for such a beautiful gift, Evangeline," Manuel murmured. "I'll never forget my one night with an angel."

"You can go now," Drake said.

Evangeline dimly registered Manuel's weight lifting from the bed, and she heard the rustle of him dressing and then the door softly shutting as he made his exit. She glanced toward Drake to see him get up and hastily rip his clothing off.

Then he crawled onto the bed, turned her over and was on her and inside her before she could take in a breath.

His mouth covered hers, his tongue plunging as deeply as his cock thrust into her pussy. He devoured her, consumed her, his desire and lust overwhelming.

He felt huge inside her, bigger than he'd ever felt. It was a race to completion and for the first time, he didn't take care to ensure that she was with him. But tonight was for him. She'd made that clear, and so she wrapped her arms around his broad shoulders and stroked his back softly, caressing the hard muscles as he took what he needed, gave him all that she had.

He exploded inside her within seconds and then slumped down onto her as she continued to softly stroke his back. He nuzzled against her neck, his lips exploring the delicate skin as he kissed and then nibbled.

"Mine," he growled. "So fucking beautiful and all mine."

27

Evangeline was on her side, firmly nestled underneath Drake's shoulder, one arm stretched over his bare chest and one leg draped over his. She was as limp as a wet noodle and thoroughly sated. It was so tempting to drift languidly into sleep, Drake's warm body next to hers, but she was still overwhelmed and trying to process the barrage of conflicting reactions to the way the night had played out.

And maybe she needed further reassurance, even though Drake had made it abundantly clear that he was fine with what had happened. Hell, he'd orchestrated the entire affair so it would be the height of hypocrisy for him to harbor any resentment or jealousy. But still, it wasn't as though she had any experience with the kind of lifestyle he lived in and reveled in, so how couldn't she be deeply conflicted?

"Drake?" she asked hesitantly.

He lifted the hand of the arm she lay over and ran his fingers through her hair in slow, sensual pulls.

"What's on your mind, Angel?" he asked in a tender voice.

She burrowed her face further into his chest, suddenly shy and unsure of herself.

"Did I disappoint you tonight? And are you angry that I enjoyed having sex with Manuel? That I orgasmed?"

He turned, shifting so they faced each other, and he looped his other arm around her, pulling her close to him.

"Angel, look at me," he said softly.

With reluctance and a little bit of dread, she slowly lifted her chin until she finally met his stare. To her relief, his eyes were warm. Affection shimmered in their depths.

"In no fucking way did you disappoint me. You have no idea how erotic and sexy as hell it was for me to watch another man take what is mine, what I own, and for me to command and control his pleasuring of you."

Her eyes widened in surprise because she just couldn't grasp the concept. It just seemed incongruous, with all she knew about Drake, that he would allow any man to touch her. Much less have sex with her.

"You are the most beautiful, uninhibited woman I've ever had, and you gave me something very special tonight. First and foremost, you gave me your trust unreservedly and never once showed any sign of backing out. And your primary focus was on me. Not the man fucking you. You gave me the gift of yourself. Ownership over your body to do with as I pleased and whether you realize it or not, the amount of trust involved for you to give in to anything I want is huge, and not many women would ever give a man such a precious thing."

"Wow," she whispered. "I guess I never thought of it that way."

"*You* are a gift, my angel. And everything that comes with you, everything that makes you who you are. The very *best* gift that has ever been bestowed on me."

She cocked her head to the side, studying his serious demeanor. "Why does it arouse you?" she asked with genuine curiosity. "I mean watching, observing another man take me and own me the way you do."

"First," he said in a grave tone, "I am the *only* one who owns you.

Never forget that. Manuel was here at my invitation and he was given explicit instructions about what he could or couldn't do, but there was never any doubt over my ownership. Manuel felt privileged and was honored to be allowed to have you for a brief time. What man wouldn't be? As for why it arouses me?"

He shrugged, his hand gliding down her waist to cup her ass.

"Why does anything excite someone? Some things just are. In my case, it's a huge turn-on to do whatever I wish with what I own. That your body, your pussy, your ass, your mouth, every part of your very soul belongs to me and *only* me, and therefore, that gives me the power to make decisions about how such a precious possession is handled.

"Yes, another man fucked you, but that's all he did. He fucked you. He gave you pleasure, which in turn gave me pleasure. But he doesn't own you, doesn't possess you. He doesn't have all of you and never will. All of you belongs to me and it makes me hot as hell to watch another man have power over you and bend you to my will in a manner in which I instruct him, because it pleases me to have the privilege—*honor*—to make the decision to relinquish the power I have over you, albeit temporarily."

"Is this something you will want to do often, then?" she asked quietly.

Drake's eyes narrowed as he studied her face, looking for some clue or motive behind her seemingly innocent question. But all he saw was honest curiosity.

"I think the better question is whether this is something *you* would want to happen often."

Her expression was earnest, her eyes radiating sincerity. "I only want to please you, Drake. I want to make you happy. And if giving me to another man while you watch makes you happy, then of course I'd want to do it again."

She swallowed and before he could respond, she continued on.

"I looked only at you," she whispered. "Even when he commanded me to look at him. I watched *you*, because I wanted to see *your* pleasure and *your* enjoyment. You are the one I want, Drake. Not someone else. Yes, I felt pleasure, but you know why?"

His brow furrowed as he studied her, stunned by her admission, her open honesty and the fact that she put it all out there and held nothing back. She was completely vulnerable, and he knew, he *knew* that vulnerability was one of the worst feelings in the world, and he never wanted her to feel that way with him.

"I enjoyed being with another man because I was pleasing *you*, and you enjoyed watching another man take and possess what belongs to you. *That* was my source of pleasure. I can barely recall the *physical* pleasure he gave me. It was there. I orgasmed. It felt good. I don't deny that. But *my* pleasure wasn't my focus. He didn't hurt me. I enjoyed the physical aspects. But emotionally, I was only focused on you. And because you looked at me with such warmth, pride and approval, it wouldn't have mattered *who* you chose to have sex with me. Because only you *matter* to me."

He was incapable of responding, of saying anything at all, so stunned was he by the impact her words had on him. How deeply he felt each and every one of them. He absorbed her impassioned statement, her expression, the sincerity shining brightly in her eyes, and it suddenly felt as though his heart was about to explode out his chest.

"Drake?" she whispered tentatively, her eyes swamped with worry and her lips turned down into an expression of unhappiness. "Did I do or say anything wrong? Are you angry with me?"

His heart about to beat out of his chest, he turned her roughly, spreading her thighs, and as soon as she was on her back, he thrust into her, eliciting a gasp of surprise from her. Just as soon as shock registered in her eyes, it was replaced by a hazy glaze of passion and need.

He withdrew more gently than he'd plunged into her, mindful of how tender she must be after taking on two different men in the span of a few hours, and then surged forward again, burying himself in her silken depths.

He stared fiercely down at her, even as his hips moved back and forth, setting a leisurely pace, but he ached. Down deep where he'd never felt anything, had never *allowed* anyone close enough to touch that part of him.

"No. *Fuck* no," he said forcefully. "Goddamn it, Angel. How the hell do you turn me inside out like this? You have me so twisted up inside that I can't fucking breathe. *Angry* with you? Hell no. You think you did something wrong? *Nothing* you've done is wrong. You are everything that is right and perfect and good in my world. Don't *ever* think you've said or done anything wrong. Until the day you lie to me, I will never have reason to be angry or disappointed with you."

Already close to going over the edge and losing himself in her silken femininity, he thrust fully into her and remained there, embedded to the hilt, his chest heaving with emotion and need. So much need. It was as if she'd opened an old wound, making it raw again. As if for the first time since his childhood, when he'd learned early to shut himself off to others and feel nothing, he was feeling again. It wasn't a comfortable sensation. He felt far too exposed and, goddamn it, *vulnerable*. The very thing he'd lamented her feeling just moments ago.

"I'll never lie to you, Drake," she said, her voice, even her expression extremely solemn and sincere. "I've given you my unconditional trust, and I'd like very much if you could trust me in the same way. I understand if it's too soon, if it's not something you can give me right now. But one day, I hope to gain it, because having you, having your trust, is all I will *ever* want. Not your money. Social status. Nothing but you and my hope that you'll have as much faith and trust in me as I do you."

Ice-cold fear pervaded his chest, momentarily freezing him, rendering him incapable of speech. He trusted few people in his life. Less than ten and all were his brothers. He'd never trusted any woman he'd been with much less had unconditional faith in one. Experience had taught him that the women who flocked to him had no interest in him. Only what he could provide them. But fuck it all. He had to say *something* to her. He couldn't lie there and stare at her like a fucking moron.

He could almost feel her slipping through his fingers like running water. Impossible to hold on to. Women, *especially* a woman like her, who put it all out there, baring her heart and soul made herself vulnerable, open to rejection. She, who was the most honest, sincere person he'd ever known, wouldn't stay with a man if she didn't feel as though he would ever return the very things she so unconditionally offered him.

But she seemed to understand the internal war that raged within him. She smiled sweetly, her eyes warm and full of understanding as she placed one finger over his lips.

"I don't expect you to trust me or have faith in me this instant," she said, her voice full of all the sweetness that made her the angel she was. *His* angel. "Trust and faith must be *earned* and it doesn't happen overnight. In time it will come. Or it won't. All I'm telling you is that you have both from me. No conditions. No reservations. No going back. And I hope that one day you can offer me the same unreservedly. I don't want the words just to placate me, Drake. Words are meaningless. Never give me those words unless you truly mean it. But until such time as you feel those things and *demonstrate* them, I'll be here waiting. I'm not going anywhere. Unless you decide you no longer want me."

There was a hint of sadness as she said the last, her eyes dulling before she visibly composed herself and offered him the warmth of her smile, her eyes brightening once more.

Not want her? Her entire statement was filled with enough fodder for him to be thinking and reflecting on for months, if not *years*. But not *want* her?

Okay, so maybe in his past affairs—he wouldn't call them *relationships*, because to do so would demean what he had with Evangeline now—such a statement from the woman involved would be likely—no, not even likely. It would be an *eventuality*. Inevitable. Because he never kept the same woman for more than a day, two at the most. But even given the short amount of time he'd known Evangeline, he couldn't *imagine* not wanting her. And that scared the shit out of him.

He buried his face in her hair, overwhelmed by her generous, loving nature and his acknowledgment of the selfish bastard he was.

"I don't deserve you," he said, gruffly giving voice to something he'd never before said to another woman. Something he'd never believed before now or even entertained. But he knew, whether his heart and mind were in agreement or not, that Evangeline deserved far better than he could ever give her. Even as the thought of her with another man sent fiery rage through his veins.

He closed his eyes, inhaling the scent of her hair, nuzzling lightly through the satiny tresses.

"I don't deserve to walk on the same ground as you. But God help me, I won't give you up. I *can't* give you up. You deserve a man who can offer you all the things you give to him and more. More than I can give you, Angel. You deserve far better than I can ever give you."

"Well, it's a good thing you've decided you can't give me up since I don't plan on going anywhere," she said lightly. "I'm yours, Drake. For as long as you want me, I'm yours."

He could envision the smile he was certain was on her face. The one that lit up an entire room and bathed it in sunshine. He knew without seeing her exactly what she looked like right this very moment, and it only made him feel like an even bigger bastard.

She tenderly tugged his head away so their gazes met and then cradled his face with her palms, her touch as soothing as an ocean breeze. There was such gentle understanding in her eyes that the rock-hard shell that had surrounded his heart and mind for so much of his life began to crack and splinter, and he knew he couldn't allow it to shatter and fall apart. How could one innocent woman wreak so much havoc in his well-ordered existence? A daily routine that had become an unyielding ritual, shot to hell, not to mention the conscience he had never possessed picked *now* to reveal itself? He was as merciless and as cutthroat as they came. He hadn't gotten to where he was by being soft or suffering symptoms of a conscience or by adhering to any rules save his own. And yet one tiny woman threatened the only way of life he'd ever known? The life he'd created for himself out of sheer necessity.

He knew he should cut her loose now. Do the right thing and push her away. Let her go before he ended up destroying them both. But at least the cold, ruthless man he had been for as long as he could remember hadn't disappeared—yet. And thank God for that, because as long as he remained a heartless, selfish bastard there was no way in hell he would ever let Evangeline go.

If that made him a complete asshole, then so be it. He would shield her from the reality of the world he lived in and make sure that his other life—the one she had no knowledge of—never touched her in any way.

He'd learned at a very young age that nothing is ever guaranteed and promises are rarely—if ever—kept. But he would make himself one promise right now, a risk he'd never before taken, because broken promises to others were bad enough, but breaking a vow to himself was unthinkable.

He wouldn't hurt Evangeline, nor would he ever lie to her. She deserved that much respect and it was more than he ever offered anyone else. He would do whatever it took to protect and shield her from the truth, the reality, but he couldn't bring himself to lie to her when she demonstrated so much trust and faith in him.

Trusting others was an alien concept to him, but for her, he would try. He could learn. She'd already taught him much. That good did exist in a world that hadn't done much to prove that fact to him. She'd given him no reason to doubt her or her motives, and that alone was far more deserving than what he currently offered her. Anything that money could buy, but his angel wasn't for sale. Couldn't be bought. What she wanted most was something he wasn't sure he could give her.

He trusted his men, as much as he was capable of trusting someone, but he wasn't fool enough to think they'd never betray him. Could he ever offer Evangeline something he couldn't even give men he considered brothers? He didn't have an answer to that yet, but he could damn well try.

He eased from the velvety clasp that clutched greedily at his dick, causing them both to emit a low moan after his remaining at maximum depth with no movement for a prolonged period of time.

She felt swollen and tight around him, his cock hypersensitive as her inner walls clamped down and squeezed as though protesting his retreat.

"Am I hurting you?" he asked roughly.

"No. Yes. God, I don't know. Just don't stop."

Her voice was tight and hoarse and her hands flew to his shoulders, her nails digging deep, marking him as he'd marked her in the past. The visual of her brand on his skin catapulted him into a frenzy.

He began pumping into her, his pace frantic and yet she still urged him on. She arched, meeting every thrust. Her face was a wreath of agony and ecstasy.

"Get there, Angel," he ground out even as he felt the first violent expulsion of his semen pulsing deeply into her pussy.

She cried out, her nails sharper, digging even deeper, breaking skin, and he reveled in the sharp bite of pain.

He pushed her harder and harder, faster and faster until the sound of flesh meeting flesh was loud in his ears. She screamed his name and shattered, wrapping her arms and legs so tightly around him that he could do nothing more than wedge himself as deeply as he could go and feel each and every pulse of his release jet into her body.

He lowered himself, burrowing his arms beneath her so that he held her every bit as tightly as she held him. Then he sagged, allowing his weight to cover her like a blanket, his dick still buried in her sweetness, each small aftershock as the last of his release was pulled from him quaking over his entire body.

He rested his forehead beside her temple and shuddered as her warm breaths puffed over his nape. He'd never felt so relaxed and at ease in his life even as guilt crept over him for allowing himself this selfish luxury when she'd given him everything while he still held a part of himself— his soul—from her.

But then she turned her head ever so slightly, just enough that her lips brushed the base of his hairline and she kissed him. One small, exquisite kiss that he felt to his toes. Her body still wrapped firmly around his tightened as she hugged him closer to her, if it was even possible that there was any space left between them.

"Thank you for giving me the gift of your pleasure tonight," she whispered. "I wanted so badly to do something solely for you. To please you. To show you that you matter to me, Drake. If you ever feel as though you matter to no one, remember tonight and know that you are so very important to me."

He couldn't respond for the knot that hastily clogged his throat. All he could do was squeeze her to him, not wanting anything to come between them in this moment. Not his fears, his guilt or remorse. Because nothing could ever make him regret this day. For one wonderful night, time had stopped, and he had seen heaven for the first time in his life. He had felt peace unlike anything he'd ever experienced, and he had learned what it felt like to be surrounded by the wings of an angel.

28

There was a glow surrounding Evangeline in the weeks following the night of Drake's decadent fantasy and the ensuing emotional revelations between her and Drake that couldn't possibly be overlooked.

The only shadow that clung to Evangeline was her continued estrangement from her girlfriends. In the beginning, she'd simply been so busy with Drake and focused on meeting his demands and glorying in the discovery of something new and wonderful that she hadn't given much thought to the passage of time or how she hadn't spoken to them for a prolonged period.

But then there was also the fact that none of her girlfriends had made the effort to reach out to her either. And that realization didn't sit well with her at all. If they were her friends, wouldn't they want her to be happy? And wouldn't they want to see that she was happy? How could they know if they didn't bother to even call or text her?

The argument always circled back around to Evangeline and her own culpability, and guilt would surge hard and strong because just as her girlfriends hadn't tried to contact her, she hadn't contacted them either.

The disconnect was more keenly felt when Drake announced he had to go out of town on business overnight. Evangeline had expected that he would want her to accompany him since he'd said as much in the beginning of their relationship when he'd outlined the rules, but he'd told her he didn't want her to be bored senseless since he would be in marathon meetings and wouldn't have any time to spend with her. It would be a flying trip, leaving at noon the first day and returning early the next morning. He'd encouraged her to enjoy herself with the stipulation that one of his men accompany her anywhere she went.

She'd nervously called Lana, Nikki and Steph, thinking to catch up and bridge the gap between them, but her calls had gone unanswered and her texts had not been read. As a result, she opted to stay at Drake's apartment and not go out because her heart wasn't in it. She was afraid that she'd lost the friends she'd had since her days in small-town Mississippi.

That night she'd slept alone for the first time since she and Drake had become involved, and she discovered she didn't like it very much. She tossed and turned the entire night, latching on to the ridiculous hope that he would return earlier than expected. When the morning of his scheduled arrival dawned, she was hatching a half a dozen different ways of jumping his bones as soon as he walked through the door.

As it was, within minutes of his return home, to her chagrin, her mother picked then, of all times, to call. Evangeline had cast an apologetic look in Drake's direction, but he'd merely smiled and pulled her down into his lap as she talked to her mom—and dad—and had proceeded to distract her by nibbling on her neck and various other parts of her body until she was ready to throw the phone across the room and turn around and attack him.

He chuckled when he overheard her mother inquire about her "young man" and whether he was treating her well, and then to her surprise, he'd taken the phone from her and proceeded to converse with her parents for nearly half an hour.

She watched, pleased, as Drake spoke to them in an affectionate tone, relaxed and even smiling at intervals. Happiness tightened her chest and she snuggled into his side as he continued his conversation, assuring them that he was indeed taking very good care of their daughter but that she was taking even better care of him.

Everything about her relationship with Drake felt . . . right. No longer did she battle with the questions and fears that had plagued her earlier. The last few weeks had been nothing short of magical and she wondered if dreams really did come true. She chastised herself for being so prepared for when the other shoe dropped and it was all over.

It was time to stop being so afraid of what the future held and throw herself into the here and now and enjoy every minute of her time with Drake. Who was to say they wouldn't end up in a long-term relationship?

Drake had proved to her time and time again that she hadn't been wrong to give him her trust and faith. He had taken both gifts very seriously and had respected her offering, cherishing them—and her—as he'd promised to do.

She also no longer questioned whether she was good enough or asked herself what a man like him could possibly see in her. He was happy. She was happy. What else was important? No matter how she saw herself, Drake saw someone completely different, and he never passed up an opportunity to prove that to her.

She felt like a butterfly emerging from a cocoon after a long hibernation and the freedom from long-held and deep-seated insecurities was exhilarating.

Evangeline Hawthorn was . . . confident! She was beautiful! And worthy of Drake Donovan.

A ridiculous smile attacked her face and she was so encapsulated in the thrall of her dreamy thoughts that she hadn't even registered Drake ringing off with her parents, until his lips trailed a fiery line up her neck to nibble at her ear.

"My angel looks happy," he murmured. "I hope my return has something to do with that."

She turned and threw her arms around his neck, peppering his entire face with kisses.

"Oh, Drake, I *am* happy! I missed you terribly."

He smiled indulgently at her. "I was only gone for a day, babe."

"It was one day too long," she said crossly.

He grinned. "Your parents are nice."

The swift change in conversation made her pause and then she returned his grin, her cheeks widening until they nearly cracked.

"You like them."

"Yes," he said seriously. "They are good people."

Remembering that it was doubtful Drake had had much experience with good people, she regarded him with the same seriousness.

"They're the best kind of people," she said huskily. "I'd do anything in the world for them."

"They're very lucky then."

She reached up and lay her palm over his bristled, unshaven cheek.

"I'd do anything for you as well, Drake. I hope you never forget that."

He captured her hand and dragged it over his lips so he kissed the inside of it.

"Oh you've proved that, Angel. Over and over. I doubt I'll *ever* forget it."

He followed his statement with a slight wince and a sigh.

"Is something wrong?" she asked anxiously, her earlier euphoria dissipating as she took in Drake's grim expression.

Drake stared at Evangeline, hating what he was about to do. Deceive her. Or rather lie by omission. Make something appear as something else altogether. When he'd promised himself he'd never lie to her or hurt her. And if he didn't handle this just right, not only would he be lying to her, but he could also hurt her if she misconstrued his reasons.

Knowing that the longer he remained silent and the longer he dragged this out, the worse it would appear, and that it could explode in his face, he kissed her and allowed sincere regret to show. He pulled her down onto the couch so they were seated next to each other.

"I know tomorrow night is our night to eat in with you cooking, but I have a very important business meeting here. I'll be entertaining my associates in our home. Unfortunately it's unavoidable, and I promised you that I wouldn't miss our dinners in unless absolutely necessary. This is one of the rare times when it's absolutely necessary to meet where we can be assured quiet and privacy."

Her brow furrowed in puzzlement as she processed his vague statement, and he didn't miss the disappointment in her eyes nor her attempts to mask her reaction by quickly regaining her composure.

"I understand," she said, only the slightest tremble in her voice to reveal her emotion. "Maybe we can have a do-over later in the week."

Damn but he hated what came next. How to ensure she wasn't present during his meeting without it being obvious he didn't want her there? He'd broken one of his promises—a *vow*—he'd made to himself, something unthinkable, by lying to Evangeline. He would not, under *any* circumstances, break the other promise he'd made that she never be touched by the alternate shadowy life he led.

"I know you didn't go out last night, so I thought perhaps you'd want to go out on the town tomorrow night. You name it and I'll make it happen, Angel. Whatever you'd like to do. Quite frankly the meeting will be boring as hell, and I don't ever expect you to have to suffer strangers and awkwardness in your own home. And you damn sure as hell won't be expected to please six arrogant bastards who will all be dick-sizing one another during negotiations."

He didn't have to fake the pissed-off, inconvenienced act for Evangeline, because he was both. If so much wasn't riding on this goddamn deal, he'd tell every one of them to go fuck themselves. He never opened his personal residence to anything business related. This was his only sanctuary. And now it was Evangeline's, and it pissed him off that he had to, in a nutshell, kick his angel out of her own home for the evening and play nice with men he wouldn't ever want within a mile of his woman.

She bit into her bottom lip, hesitating, obviously immersed in thought. He wished to hell he could read her right now. Ninety-nine percent of the time, she was utterly transparent, her eyes a window to her soul, but this was the one percent of the time when he had no clue what she was thinking or feeling.

He had to hold back her name and the question that would most assuredly be in his voice if he uttered it. Because he knew he would sound uncertain, and he had to play this just right. It was simply a business meeting, and he was offering her the city on a silver platter for the night. He didn't need to sound like he had a reason to be worried about what she was thinking.

"Tomorrow night is the girls' night off," she said softly. "I'd like . . . I need to see them. We haven't spoken. Not since the night Steph came over here. I—we've—let it go on too long. I need to talk to them. I tried to call them while you were out of town. I thought we could grab something to eat, catch up. But I never heard back from them."

Drake's lips thinned slightly. Damn it. He wasn't keen on a reunion with her girlfriends. Not if there was the possibility of them filling her head with a bunch of shit. But at the same time, it offered him the perfect out. She would be happy and he would effectively keep her separate from his business.

"You should go, then," he said gently.

Her eyes widened in surprise. "You don't mind?"

He pulled her further into the crook of his arm so she was nestled firmly against him.

"It's obvious that your estrangement is making you unhappy," he said.

He stroked his palm over her cheek and then cupped her jaw, feathering his thumb over her satiny skin.

"I want you to be happy, Angel. So if seeing your girls will do that, then I'll have a man take you over tomorrow evening."

"Should I plan to stay over with them?" she asked, a little hitch in her breath.

At that he frowned. "Hell no. I'll tell Maddox to have you back by eleven and if for some reason my meeting goes longer, I'll let him know, but you *will* be back here afterward. One night away from you was enough. No way in hell I'm going to spend another without you so soon after being away this time."

She smiled at that and then gave him a mischievous grin.

"So tell me, do you have to call Maddox right this minute? Or can it wait for a little while?"

He arched one eyebrow, regarding her suspiciously. "That entirely depends on what you have up your sleeve, you little imp."

She rose up and arched over him, straddling his lap, looping her arms around his neck before sliding downward to the floor until she was kneeling between his thighs, her hands fluttering to the fly of his slacks.

"Oh, I don't know. For as long as I have time to welcome you back home properly?"

She licked her lips even as she began unzipping his pants.

His eyes glittered and became half-lidded. "Well, if that's the case, then take your time, Angel. I assure you, Maddox will wait. I, on the other hand, can't. So by all means, welcome your man home properly."

29

To Evangeline's surprise—and delight—the next morning she awoke surrounded by Drake's warm, solid body. He was wrapped around her, her head nestled on his shoulder, his arms possessively anchored around her and one leg thrown over hers. She couldn't have moved if she wanted, and it was certainly the last thing she wanted.

She let out a deep sigh of contentment, thinking she'd never been happier than in this moment.

"Good morning, Angel," he murmured against her hair.

"Good morning," she said, smiling against his shoulder.

"You're smiling."

She nodded.

"Any particular reason?"

"This is the first time I've woken up in your arms," she said in a dreamy voice. "It's . . . nice."

He rubbed his hand up and down her back and then down to cup her behind.

"I found I didn't like being away from you for even one night and I was reluctant to leave our bed so early this morning."

"I'm glad. This is the very best way to wake up."

He sighed. "Unfortunately, I can't linger, as much as I'd like to. I'd rather spend the day home, making love to you and keeping you naked until you have to get ready to go to see your girls. But there are things I have to catch up on. Even a day away leaves me with a pile of shit to sort out."

She tilted her head back and smiled up at him. "It's okay, Drake. This was enough. You've made my entire day better already, and it'll make me look forward to being back with you later tonight when you've concluded your business."

He kissed her, taking his time exploring her mouth and lips. Then he rolled away, sliding from beneath the covers.

"Ah, how you tempt me, Angel. If I don't get up now, I will indeed say fuck it and keep you in my bed all day."

She rewarded him with a radiant smile and then made a shooing motion with her hand. "Go, or you're going to be late. You can make it up to me tonight."

A delicious gleam entered his eyes as he stared down at her body, exposed when he'd pulled the covers away to get out of bed.

"Oh, I'm going to make it up to you and a whole hell of a lot more."

She shivered at the promise in his voice and watched appreciatively as he turned and walked naked to the bathroom. She lay there in his bed long after he'd kissed her good-bye and departed, not wanting to leave the warmth from his body still imprinted into the mattress.

Finally, she summoned her courage and slid her cell phone from the nightstand and brought up Lana's name. She'd start there and rotate. Eventually someone would answer. Days off usually started slow because of the late night before, so she was certain at least one, if not all three, would be home.

Taking a deep breath, she hit connect and waited to see if Lana would answer.

To her shock, Lana picked up on the second ring.

"Hello?"

Evangeline's enthusiasm waned, and she scolded herself for her paranoia rising in proportion. Lana sounded groggy and as though she'd been asleep, so she likely hadn't even seen who was calling. Oh well. Evangeline was going to make the most of an opportunity.

"Lana, hi! It's Evangeline. I've been trying to call you guys."

There was a hesitation, and a period of quiet descended.

"Vangie?"

"Yes, it's me. Did I wake you?"

Evangeline silently urged Lana not to take the out she was giving her and nearly did a fist pump when Lana said no.

"How are you?" Evangeline asked. "How is everyone? I miss you guys so much. Drake has an important meeting tonight, and I thought we could all get together since it's your night off."

"Uh, Vangie, give me a second, okay?"

Evangeline's brow creased as the line went silent, and then she heard muffled sounds, Lana obviously getting out of bed and then the sound of a door shutting. A faucet running? Had she gone into the bathroom?

Understanding dawned, and directly on its heels came dread and deep sadness. Lana didn't want Steph and Nikki to know she was talking to Evangeline. She closed her eyes, tears stinging the lids. Why did it have to be a choice between Drake and her best friends? Why couldn't they be happy for her and wish her well?

"Uh, look, Vangie. I don't want this to come across the wrong way, but Steph is pretty hurt over the way things went down. I don't think it's a good idea for us all to get together yet. Give it a few more weeks. Let her chill."

"Why can't she be happy for me?" Evangeline whispered. "Why can't all of you be happy for me?"

Lana sighed. "We want what's best for you. We're just not sure this Drake guy is what's best."

"Shouldn't that be my decision?"

Lana sighed again. "I'm just telling you like it is. You know how Steph is. She holds a grudge a long time, but eventually she'll let go of it. Just give it time."

"Would you and Nikki meet me somewhere this evening?" Evangeline asked, desperate to salvage something out of this whole fiasco.

"It's not even an issue," Lana said with a hint of impatience in her voice. "We have to work tonight. Open to close."

Evangeline frowned. "But this is y'all's day off. It's always been your day off."

"Not anymore," Lana said bitterly. "Not since you left. We're short staffed and everyone is having to take extra shifts to cover until management hires a replacement, and he's a little too happy to be pocketing that extra salary, so he's in no hurry to hire someone new."

Evangeline closed her eyes, guilt and grief vying for equal attention. Despite Lana's assertion that Steph was the one holding a grudge and she was the one "unhappy" with Evangeline, it was obvious that Lana wasn't any more eager to reconcile than the others.

"I'm sorry to have bothered you," Evangeline whispered. "I'll let you go so you can go back to sleep. You have a long shift tonight."

Before Lana could respond, Evangeline slid her finger over the button to end the call and cradled the phone to her chest, lying still, staring sightlessly up at the ceiling. The tears that had threatened during the call fell freely now, sliding from the corners of her eyes, over her temples and into her hair, dampening the pillow her head rested on.

Never in a million years would she have imagined herself to be a woman who chose a man over her best girlfriends, and yet that was exactly what she'd done. She couldn't blame her friends for being upset or feeling betrayed. One day things had been normal, and the next everything had changed.

"I don't regret it," she whispered fiercely.

Drake was worth it. And if Steph, Lana and Nikki were true friends, they would have supported her from the start. They would have wanted her to be happy instead of remaining stuck in the same mundane, going-nowhere life she'd led.

She stayed in bed, staring at the ceiling, grieving the loss of three people she loved dearly. She couldn't find it in her heart to assign blame or even resent her friends for their actions. Evangeline had acted completely out of character. Irrationally, to be honest. Things had worked out, but there were so many ways the entire situation could have gone very wrong.

If it had been one of them who'd been so impulsive, Evangeline would have reacted in the same manner. She would have fought and tried to make her friend see reason.

But love didn't have an assigned set of rules. Love was worth any sacrifice. Just as she couldn't—wouldn't—blame her friends for their feelings, never would she regret her decision to be with Drake.

She loved him.

And he cared for her too. Did he love her? She wasn't sure. But she knew she had a very important place in his life. Could he love her? Absolutely. In the beginning, she would have said that never in a million years could someone like Drake ever love someone like her, but he'd proved his words over and over. He'd proved they weren't just words meant to elicit a desired response. And it wasn't just about sex, because God knew, he could have any woman he wanted with nothing more than a look.

She'd seen the way women followed him with their gazes. Openly lustful expressions. Flirtatious. Brazen invitations. And yet when he was with her, it was as if other women simply didn't exist. His attention was always solely focused on her.

She rolled to her stomach and then forced herself to sit up. She wouldn't lie there the entire day disheartened when she'd been blessed by such a precious gift. Drake. Her life had forever changed the night she'd walked into Impulse, and looking back, she wouldn't change a single thing leading up to that night because she wouldn't have met Drake otherwise.

She sighed. So much for her plans for the evening. She supposed she needed to come up with a plan B and notify Drake, who would then notify Maddox. But try as she might, nothing appealed. She had no desire to go out without Drake or her girls.

If only Drake didn't have that damn business meeting here tonight.

She came to an abrupt halt as she started to climb out of bed, her mind running at the speed of light. She knew he was having the delivery service cater his meeting and there were six guests. She could kick the delivery service's ass any day of the week and knock Drake and his associates' socks off with a decadent meal.

The more she thought about it, the more excited she became. There was no need of him having his delivery service bring in food for his meeting when she could arrange a kick-ass dinner and play the consummate hostess for him. She wanted to make him proud of her, prove that she could fit into his world and not shame him in front of the people he associated with.

She'd go all out for the meal and prepare something worthy of a five-star restaurant, and she'd dress to the nines and even wear the expensive jewelry he'd bought for her. The jewelry she'd been so reluctant to accept. Once dinner was served and she ensured everyone's comfort and enjoyment, she would discreetly disappear so they could discuss their business matters without her underfoot.

But there was a lot she had to do and if she didn't get started now, her plans would be an epic fail.

The first order of business was to plan the menu and so after showering and changing, she sat down at the bar in the kitchen and prepared a list of all the items she'd require. Then she'd simply call Edward and have him send out for the groceries.

That task completed, she went into her closet and spent an hour pondering her wardrobe possibilities. She didn't want to be over the top or look like she was trying to impress, even if that was precisely what she wanted to do. Impress Drake. But she wanted . . . classy. Beautiful, elegant and yet simple.

Finally, she chose a blue strapless, knee-length cocktail dress that was perfect. She realized with excitement that the sapphire and diamond choker that she'd never worn would look perfect with the dress, and she could wear the diamond stud earrings Drake had bought for her. She'd finish off the look with the diamond tennis bracelet and a pair of silver heels. She'd wear her hair up to best show off the choker and earrings and allow a few tendrils to float down her neck and cheeks and use a curling iron to make loose ringlets.

Her brain came to a screeching halt when she remembered the single most important barrier to her pulling off her big surprise. Maddox. And the fact that he was supposed to be taking her to her girlfriends' apartment.

She frowned. Think, damn it. There had to be a way.

Wait. Lana had said they were all working tonight. Open to close, which meant the apartment would be empty, and she still had a key. All she had to do was arrange as much as she could in advance, then have Maddox drive her to the apartment. He'd wait in the car while she went up, and she could climb down the fire escape, hustle a few blocks over and hail a cab back to Drake's.

"You're a genius, Evangeline!" she said gleefully.

Her plan was flawless and totally doable. Maddox would never suspect that she would bail out the fire escape, and she could be back in plenty of time to dress and finish preparations before Drake arrived with his guests.

Satisfied that she'd planned for every eventuality, she laid out her wardrobe for the evening and then picked a simple outfit to wear out with Maddox. Something that wouldn't impede her climb down the fire escape from the seventh floor.

The rest of the day dragged on with Evangeline checking her watch every half hour, willing time to go faster. She breathed a sigh of relief when Edward personally brought up the groceries she'd ordered and winked at her when she anxiously told him not to breathe a word to anyone about his outing. She told him the truth, that she was planning a surprise for Drake, and he seemed delighted to be included in the plotting.

Happy to now have something to pass the time with, she put together everything she could beforehand, preparing three different appetizers and two choices of sauces to accompany the veal she would pop into the oven the minute she returned home from her girlfriends'.

She mixed the ingredients for the sides and then slipped them in the refrigerator. Satisfied that dinner was arranged and would only require half an hour cooking time at most when she arrived back, she checked her watch and then squeaked. It was already four thirty!

She dashed to the bedroom and hastily brushed out her hair, securing it into a messy bun, and then found a pair of casual slip-on shoes. After a quick once-over in the mirror—after all, she was just going to her girlfriends' apartment—she hurried back to the kitchen just to double-check and mentally go over her menu one last time to ensure she hadn't overlooked anything.

"Evangeline? You ready to go?" Maddox called from the foyer.

Adrenaline surged in her veins and she took a few seconds to steady her frayed nerves and then calmly called back, "Yeah. Let me grab my purse and I'll be right there."

She sucked in a deep breath as she collected her bag and headed to meet Maddox.

Well, here went nothing. Hopefully her plans went off without a hitch and she'd make Drake proud tonight by playing the consummate hostess.

30

Evangeline dashed into Drake's apartment building, out of breath as she frantically sought Edward out. To her relief, he was in the lobby and when he saw her, he started her way, a warm smile on his face.

"I don't have much time, Edward. I have to get to the apartment if I'm going to pull off my surprise. But I need a favor. Just as I asked you not to say a word about me sending out for groceries, when Mr. Donovan arrives, you can't say a word about me being here. If he should inquire, I left with Maddox at five and haven't returned."

Edward's eyes twinkled but his words were solemn. "Your secret is safe with me, Evangeline. I won't say a word. I swear."

She hugged him, squeezing hard, leaving him befuddled and flustered.

"Thank you," she said fervently. "Now if you'll excuse me, I don't have much time."

"Would you like me to ring up to let you know when Mr. Donovan gets on the elevator?" he inquired.

She hadn't even considered that and it was an excellent idea. "That would be perfect. I never even thought about that. Thank you so much."

"Any time. Now, be on your way so your surprise isn't ruined."

She dashed past him to the elevator and moments later burst into the apartment. She immediately went into the kitchen and popped the side dishes in the oven and used three skillets to cook the veal on the stove-top. The appetizers would take only a few minutes to warm, so she would save those for last.

After ensuring everything was taken care of, she ran for the bedroom to change and do her hair and makeup. She took meticulous care in perfecting her appearance, checking her watch every few minutes to make sure she didn't ruin dinner.

Finally satisfied with the end result, she stared into the mirror, her eyes widening in shock.

She looked . . . beautiful. Sexy even. She'd gone with a smoky, sultry look for her eyes with a sheer lip gloss that didn't detract from the dramatic effect of her eyes. Her hair was upswept into a delicate knot with loose curls floating lazily down her neck.

The choker and earrings looked magnificent, totally in keeping with the classy women Drake would be seen with. And the dress fit her perfectly, accentuating her curves. For once, she didn't lament what she considered her imperfections because tonight she looked soft and feminine.

The dress just clipped the top of her knees, and the heels made her legs look longer and more attractive.

She fastened the last piece of jewelry, the bracelet around her wrist, and lightly spritzed her favorite perfume on her neck and wrists and then took a deep breath. It wouldn't be long before Drake arrived with his company and she wanted to be there to greet them and play the gracious hostess.

She'd made sure she had a wide variety of fine wines and the most expensive liquors to accompany the divine appetizers she planned to arrange artfully on sterling silver platters. She'd go check on them now and when Edward called up to say Drake had arrived, she would put out the starters on the coffee table in the living room so the men could relax while she finished dinner and set the table.

Taking once last glance at herself in the mirror, she smiled, satisfied with her appearance and eager to see the approval in Drake's eyes when he realized she'd gone to great lengths to entertain his guests.

She was quivering with excitement as she left the bedroom and went back into the kitchen to check on the side dishes in the oven and the progress of the veal on the stovetop. She sniffed appreciatively at the delicious aromas that filled the apartment, relieved that nothing smelled overdone or burned.

She cracked open the oven to see the bubbling side dishes and then she turned the veal so both sides were evenly cooked. Then she set the sauces on to warm, stirring at intervals so they didn't scorch.

Her pulse surged, temporarily making her light-headed when the call button went off and Edward's voice came over the intercom.

"Mr. Donovan and six of his associates are on their way up."

"Thank you, Edward," she said sincerely. "I really appreciate you doing this for me."

"No thanks is necessary. I'm only doing my job, and seeing to your needs gives me great satisfaction."

She balanced the three trays bearing the expertly made appetizers—after all, she had been a waitress in a busy pub—and hurriedly set them down in the living room. Then she turned and took the few short steps toward the foyer.

Evangeline smoothed her dress and then went to stand a distance back from the elevator doors so she could issue a greeting, but most importantly see the approval and pride in Drake's eyes when he realized the effort she'd put into being an asset to him and that, as she'd promised him, she would always take care of and protect him. And . . . she wanted him to be proud of her and not to ever regret his decision to make her his.

. . .

It was years of perfecting an impenetrable persona that enabled Drake to engage in conversation ranging from the random to the obscene with the "business associates" he was entertaining in his apartment tonight as they entered the elevator in his building. And actually give the impression he gave a fuck about whatever they had to say.

He rarely entertained in his home, usually opting for one of the many suites of offices and complexes he owned, a private room in an exclusive restaurant, or, depending on the business associate he was meeting with, they simply met at Impulse and took the premiere VIP suite overlooking the dance floor since Drake never allowed anyone he didn't trust implicitly into his office at the club.

Before Evangeline, it was simply a matter of not wanting his private domain trespassed on, but now he felt as though he defiled it by bringing such filth into *Evangeline's* home.

But some matters required no room or margin for error. No chance of being overheard, misunderstood or, in this case, being seen in a public place together.

Thank God he'd had the forethought to ensure Evangeline wouldn't be present, because while Drake could school his features, mask his thoughts and allow nothing of what he was feeling to reflect in his eyes, when it came to his angel, he could no more appear indifferent than she could be anything but honest and sincere in both words and expression. And Drake's greatest strength, the reason he was invincible, was that he had no weaknesses for his enemies to exploit.

Until now.

Until Evangeline.

If it was known that Evangeline was his greatest and *only* weakness she would absolutely be used to take him down, because where before he would never negotiate—never had reason to—there was nothing he wouldn't do, wouldn't sacrifice to keep her safe.

The mere thought of his angel being hurt or *defiled* because of him sent chilling fear through every part of his soul, and he was a man who feared nothing and no one.

"Sweet pad you have, Donovan," one of the men said as they reached the top floor.

Drake gave him a lazy smile and drawled, "Only the best. Only way to live."

"Hell yeah," another chimed in.

The elevator doors opened and Drake came to an abrupt halt, shock and dread turning his veins to ice when he saw Evangeline standing at the end of the foyer, a shy, welcoming smile on her face and looking so achingly beautiful that he was momentarily robbed of speech.

Oh God. No. This wasn't happening. What the fuck? He was going to kill Maddox. This couldn't be happening. It *wasn't* happening. He had to be imagining her presence, but an appreciative whistle from behind him confirmed the very real vision of the angel standing before him. And the evil he had sworn she would never be exposed to.

"Now *that* is one sweet piece," one of the men said. "You've been holding out on us, Drake."

"I wouldn't mind having some of *that*," another said crudely as the others laughed.

"Hey, Donovan. Is she part of tonight's entertainment? Because I have to say, you certainly know how to throw one hell of a party."

Evangeline flushed, embarrassment and trepidation shadowing her eyes. Uncertainty and fear flashed over her features. But then her chin came up and she calmly composed herself and started forward, her welcoming smile once more in place.

"Good evening, gentlemen. If you'd like to go into the living room, there are appetizers and drinks. Dinner will be ready and on the table shortly."

"I hope to hell *she's* dessert," one muttered in a low voice.

Drake's heart sank, and desolation settled deep into his bones for what he knew he had to do. What he had no *choice* but to do. And he'd never hated himself more than in this moment.

Evangeline had arranged to play hostess and had gone all out. For *him*. Because she wanted so badly to please him, make him proud of her and let him know he mattered.

She was so beautiful she took his breath away. She was even wearing the jewelry he'd given her—gifts she'd been uncomfortable receiving because she never wanted him to think even for a moment that she wanted anything but him. Not the material things he offered. She was dressed impeccably as if she wanted to make him proud. Worthy of him when it was he who was in no way worthy of her.

And he was about to destroy the most precious gift he had ever been given because he had no other *choice*.

"What the hell are you doing here, bitch?" he snarled. "Do you not understand orders when they're given to you? If I wanted my latest whore to dress up and play hostess in my apartment I damn sure would have chosen one with more class and with the intelligence to heed simple instructions."

Evangeline's eyes went wide with shock and devastation. She stood as still as a statue, tears gathering in her eyes, her face flushed with humiliation.

"You can't cook for shit, so do you honestly think I'd want you to serve my business associates and embarrass me when I had already arranged delivery from one of the finest restaurants in the city?"

Tears slid down her cheeks, her eye makeup smearing in dark streaks.

"Goddamn useless woman who can't even follow simple instructions," he repeated with a snarl. "Get on your knees," he barked. "Now!" when she hesitated.

Trembling and nearly falling, she clumsily fell to her knees, wincing as they made contact with the hard Italian marble floor.

Drake strode forward, reaching for his fly, opening it and pulling out his flaccid erection.

"Suck it and you better damn well make me hard and swallow every drop of my come."

She lifted her eyes, betrayal and utter devastation dulling her eyes. He twisted his hand cruelly in her hair, yanking at the elegant knot until her hair tumbled down her neck.

"Open your goddamn mouth."

Her lips trembled, fear replacing embarrassment and mortification. Fear. The one thing he'd sworn he'd never make her feel.

He wasn't gentle. He couldn't afford to be. As soon as her lips parted, he shoved his dick all the way to the back of her throat, making her gag and choke.

"Can't even give good head," he said in disgust.

He held her head in a brutal grip and began fucking her mouth with force he'd never before used with her.

Knowing there was no way in hell he'd come because he was in no way turned on by the brutality he was subjecting her to, he said in a harsh voice, "Swallow all of it. If so much as a drop spills, I'll punish you so you won't be able to sit for a week."

"Why are you doing this?" she whispered tearfully, low enough the others couldn't hear.

"Because you blatantly disobeyed me."

Utter defeat was reflected in her body and expression as she robotically knelt there, enduring Drake's brutal treatment of her. But the never-ending stream of tears was his undoing, and he was grateful the men were behind him and couldn't see the torment on his face. Torment even Evangeline didn't register because she'd mentally checked out, numbness overtaking her entire body.

He hated himself more than he thought it possible to ever hate anyone. Even his mother and father. When he'd spent a realistic amount of time fucking her mouth to make it believable that he'd come, he instructed her to swallow and to lick every drop of come from his dick and her lips.

Then he roughly yanked her to her feet and shoved her toward the kitchen.

"Throw out whatever shit you cooked and make sure every pot, pan or utensil is cleaned and get whatever the fuck you have set out in the living room in the trash can. From now on, you stay the fuck out of my kitchen and my business. Your *only* use is in my bedroom. And just so you know, you will be severely punished when I return for disobeying a direct order, one you couldn't possibly have misunderstood."

He hesitated, hating himself more and more with every hateful, despicable word that spewed from his mouth.

"What's your job, whore? What is the only job you have?"

"O-obey," she said in a choked voice.

"One responsibility and you can't even accomplish that," he said with fake disgust.

Then he turned to the men who'd accompanied him, disgusted that they were visibly aroused by Drake's humiliation of Evangeline and the fact that he'd made her suck him off in front of them. He wanted to throw up.

"Let's go somewhere we can get a decent meal. I apologize for my stupid whore's obvious ineptitude."

He started for the elevator door and then turned back, his expression as cold and chilling as he could make it. "When I get back, this place better be spotless and I want you in my bed, naked and ready to receive your punishment. And I won't have any mercy."

Evangeline stood there in shock, staring at the closed elevator doors for several long minutes after Drake's abrupt departure. She glanced down at herself, makeup-stained tears falling onto the floor.

Beautiful? Classy? Elegant?

She had been fooling herself and Drake had perpetuated one of the biggest hoaxes in history because he'd made her feel all of those things. *Worthless. Whore. Bitch.*

The words he'd used to describe her echoed over and over in her head until rage finally roused her from the numb shock surrounding her. Even as she robotically started for the kitchen like an automaton trained to follow Drake's orders, she twisted violently, yanking the heels off her feet and hurling them through the living room at the coffee table and the trays of food she'd labored so painstakingly over.

Two bottles of the wine and two bottles of liquor, hit by the flying shoes, tumbled from the table and she heard the satisfying crack of breaking glass.

She stormed into the bedroom, yanking and tearing at her dress until she managed to free herself. With shaking hands, she removed every piece of jewelry he'd bought for her and underhanded them onto the bed.

Then she sank to the floor on her knees, clad in only her panties and bra. Raw, ugly-sounding sobs clawed their way up her throat and out of her lips, the sound of terrible grief.

You will be severely punished.

Oh hell no. To hell with Drake. To hell with every lie he'd ever fed her. For building her up only so he could be the one to tear her down.

Feeling like an old, decrepit woman, she crawled to the closet and rummaged until she found a pair of jeans and a T-shirt. Drake had thrown every bit of her old clothing out when he'd moved her in;

otherwise she wouldn't take a single thing bought by him. As it was, she packed a bag with three pairs of jeans, one casual dress that was suitable for job hunting and two pairs of shoes.

The rest she left hanging, most still with the tags attached. Then she went about systematically removing any and all of her presence from his bedroom. She went from room to room, throwing away or simply destroying any possible reminder of herself in Drake's eyes.

And then she remembered the meal she'd labored so intensively over. She hoped it had burned and left a charred mess.

After lifting the silver trays and dumping the appetizers over the couch and chair and the floor, to accompany the shattered bottles of alcohol, she went into the kitchen and dumped every single skillet and baking dish onto the floor.

"To hell with you, Drake Donovan. I gave you everything and this is what I got in return. I hope you rot in hell where you belong. At least Eddie was honest."

Tears streaming down her face, she rode the elevator down only to be met by a worried Edward who rushed over to take her elbow.

"Miss Hawthorn," he said, in his haste forgoing all familiarity as if he too were just as rid of her as Drake.

She burst into a fresh torrent of tears and tried to maneuver around him.

"Please, Evangeline. Tell me what's wrong. Mr. Donovan returned shortly after he came up and he looked furious. Are you all right?"

"I'll never be all right," she said flatly, even as tears ran freely down her face.

"Let me help you, please. Tell me what I can do."

Realizing the older man was genuinely concerned and evidently ignorant of all that had happened, or at least he hadn't been instructed to have nothing to do with her, she paused.

"I need to get away from here," she said desperately.

"Of course. Shall I call for one of Mr. Donovan's men to come for you?"

"No!" she shrieked. "I need a cab and I need you to never tell anyone, especially Drake or his men, that you saw me, that you helped me, or I'm afraid your job will be out the door just like I am."

Compassion softened his eyes even as he guided her toward the door.

"Where shall I instruct the cab to take you?" he asked gently.

Her shoulders sagged and she ran a hand through the rumpled mess of her hair, knowing the fright she must look with her makeup running, her hairdo destroyed.

"I have no place to go," she whispered, knowing she couldn't show up at her girlfriends' place. She couldn't bear the "I told you so's," and neither could she take their pity. She couldn't stomach that just hours ago she'd applauded her decision to choose Drake over her friendships with her best friends. How could she ever face them again? And even if she did feel welcome, it was the first place Drake would think to look for her. Even if he fully intended to throw her out—and she was sure that was precisely what he intended—he would likely still hunt her down if for nothing more than to exact his punishment and then tell her to her face he was finished with her. Why pass up another opportunity to humiliate her even more? Far better to do it in front of her girlfriends. Fuck that. Her mother would forgive the obscenities, given the circumstances.

But then what more could he possibly do to her than what he'd done tonight? She was without pride, shamed beyond measure and more humiliated than she'd ever been with Eddie. She would never be the same woman again. Drake had utterly destroyed her, and there was nothing left but the shattered remains of her dignity. To hell with it all. She would never trust another man as long as she lived.

Edward's mouth tightened into an angry line and then he escorted her out of the building to the street side, where he motioned for a waiting cab.

"My sister manages a hotel in Brooklyn. It's nothing fancy, mind you, but I'll call her and let her know to expect you. She'll have a place for you to stay for as long as you need until you decide where you want to go."

She looked up at Edward, his features blurring behind the sheen of tears. "I can't let you or her do that, Edward. I have no money for a hotel. At least not for more than one night. Until I find a job."

He took her hands in one of his as he opened the back of the cab and gently set her inside.

"Don't you worry about that," he reassured. "My sister will take care of your arrangements."

Then he pulled several bills from his pocket and thrust them toward the driver, giving him the address to the hotel in Brooklyn.

"Good-bye, Evangeline," Edward said in a soft voice, his eyes brimming with sympathy. "It was indeed a pleasure knowing you, and I wish you well."

As the cab pulled away, Evangeline buried her face in her hands and burst into a torrent of tears.

31

Dinner was hell for Drake. The facade he'd so arrogantly reflected on when riding up the elevator with the men meeting him for "business" at his apartment was utterly shattered, and it was only the fact that he was clinging to the tattered remnants of his iron will with his bare fingernails that kept him from bailing and telling them all to go fuck themselves.

As it was, when one of the men had chuckled, clapped Drake on the back as they'd been seated in a private room at one of the restaurants Drake frequented and said, "Good show, Drake. Can't ever forget to remind a woman of their place in the world," Drake had nearly reached over and beaten the ever-loving hell out of him.

Evangeline's place in the world? Somehow, without his even realizing it, she had *become* his world. And he couldn't imagine his world without her sweet, generous smile, her endearing determination to take care of him and for him to know he was cared about. Which was all tonight had been about, goddamn it!

He couldn't stop the sight of the devastation in her eyes from replaying over and over like a never-ending highlight reel in his head. Her tears and fear. Of *him*, goddamn it. He, who had vowed he would never give her any reason to fear him, that she would always be safe with him and he'd protect her above all else. And the idea that he'd done far worse to her than her piece of shit ex was more than he could bear.

But he couldn't react. He couldn't rush through dinner so he could hurry home and get on his knees and beg her forgiveness. Forgiveness he didn't deserve. Because then these men would know just what Evangeline meant to him and they'd use every means available to blackmail and extort whatever they could from him.

Drake was a never-ending source of frustration to his enemies and competitors because he *had* no weaknesses. They had no way of touching him, hurting him, and they feared him because he was ruthless and would take out any threat to him and his business interests. Not to mention he was surrounded by his most trusted men who would give their lives to protect Drake and they were every bit as feared as Drake himself was.

But they *would* hurt Evangeline with no second thought or compunction. They'd use her as a means to an end and not give a fuck if they destroyed her—and him—in the process. They'd relish the opportunity to take Drake and his monopoly on numerous business practices completely down.

And Drake could never live with himself if Evangeline was hurt, brutalized or killed because of him. He could *never* live without *her*. And the hell of it was he was only just admitting it, but he'd known for a long time. He just couldn't bring himself to acknowledge the truth, because it made him weak and vulnerable.

How to make her understand?

He'd just destroyed something so very precious and shit all over the unconditional trust and faith she'd so generously given him with no strings, no conditions, though God knew he'd never given her any reason to do so. He'd taken but had never given her anything that *mattered*. At least not to her. Throwing expensive trinkets her way was like tossing a pet treats when all she wanted was what he hadn't been brave enough to give her. Unfettered access to his heart. He was a fucking coward who wasn't worthy to lick her shoes.

One of the men looked over at Drake, whose outwardly cool and calm demeanor masked inner turmoil unlike anything he'd ever experienced before in his life.

"That's a sweet piece of ass you've got there, Donovan, and I sure as hell wouldn't give a fuck if she could cook or not."

The others chuckled and nodded their agreement.

"I wouldn't mind having a taste of that for a while. If you toss her, let me know, yeah? And if you don't toss her right away, give me a heads-up when you do so I can move in and take a shot at her."

Drake smiled even as he seethed inwardly. "She's very talented in other ways, if you know what I mean, which makes up for her lack in others. She amuses me for now, but I'll keep your offer in mind, and when I get tired of her and the good no longer outweighs the bad, then you're welcome to her."

Drake hated every word. It sickened him to even talk about Evangeline with such disrespect and casually discuss passing her along to another man like used goods. All that kept going through his mind was seeing his angel's eyes when he'd denounced and humiliated her in front of the others. How he'd spent so much time building her up, building her confidence after the number her ex did on her. And now, in just a few minutes' time, he'd utterly destroyed everything he'd worked to achieve and give back to her.

And what he'd done to her had been *far* worse that what that shithead had done to her. Because she *trusted* Drake. She believed in him, had faith in him unreservedly. No conditions, stipulations. She'd given him and *only* him the precious gift of herself. She'd given him what she'd never given another man and he'd shit all over it *and* her.

He wanted to puke his guts up.

He had a hell of a lot of explaining and groveling to do when he got back home. On his knees. He would do something he'd vowed never to do again. Beg. Whatever it took for Evangeline to forgive him and trust him again. Because for the rest of his life, not one day would pass that he wouldn't remember this night and the pain and humiliation, the tears streaking down her beautiful face while he ripped her apart in front of others who'd stood there watching in amusement—and approval.

"Now, if we can get down to business and dispense with something so unimportant as my latest piece of ass," Donovan said acidly.

The others dropped the joking, their expressions growing serious. The leader, the head of the Luconi family, leaned forward, his voice low.

"Are you willing to back our takeover of the Vanuccis?"

"That depends," Drake drawled.

No way in fucking hell would he ever do business with men who showed Evangeline such blatant disrespect, even if it was the height of hypocrisy since Drake had instigated it all. But he could arrange to make it appear as though one of the Luconi family fed information to the Vanuccis, which in turn would start a war between the two rival families, resulting in the removal of two pains in Drake's ass.

"Name your price, Donovan," the older Luconi said in a gravelly voice. "Your name carries enough weight on its own. If you're linked in any way to us, then the Vanuccis won't even put up a fight because the last thing they'll want to do is piss you off."

"I'll consider your proposition," Drake said, pretending to give the matter serious consideration. "I'll have one of my men contact you in a few days to discuss terms. When the Vanuccis get wind of our meeting, they'll come to me with their own offer, so you better come with your best."

The older Luconi's eyes narrowed as he stared at Drake. "Now how the hell would they know we met with you unless you told them?"

Drake laughed scornfully. "You're a fool, old man. If you think the Vanuccis don't have a man inside your organization reporting every time you so much as take a shit, then you're not as smart as I gave you credit for."

Already he was planting a seed of doubt for when he did in fact leak the information to the Vanuccis, thus instigating a bloodbath between the two crime families.

To Drake's relief, the entrées were finally delivered and he ate quickly, not even tasting what was in front of him. He made it a point not to check his watch to see how much time had elapsed because he wanted these sons of bitches gone while they appeared to be taking their sweet time.

They weren't stupid. He made it a point to never underestimate his partners or his enemies. He had no doubt they were taking their time and keeping close watch on him and his actions so they could determine just what his motives concerning Evangeline were.

And so it was Drake who suggested they go for drinks after they finished dinner, leaving it to them to be satisfied he was in no hurry or decide if he was simply willing them not to call his bluff.

Thankfully for him, once they discussed the Vanuccis in depth and the Luconis tried to strong-arm a commitment from Drake on the spot, they gave up and called it a night, each going their own way from the restaurant while Drake slipped from the back as if he'd never been there at all.

He called his driver and told him to meet him two blocks from the restaurant, then hastily jumped in, instructing him to get home as fast as he could. His driver, unruffled by the demand, promptly floored it and Drake held his hands in tight fists the entire interminable way there.

He cursed every stoplight but his driver swung deftly through the streets, running intersections that didn't have heavy cross traffic. When at last they arrived, Drake was out and running before the car had pulled to a complete stop.

He took the express elevator that only ran between his penthouse and the lobby, praying the entire way that Evangeline would even look at him, much less listen to anything he had to say.

God, let her be sweet, generous and forgiving one last time and he'd never give her reason to doubt him again.

As soon as the elevator doors opened, he bolted into the apartment yelling her name. He winced when he saw the mess in the kitchen, the contents of what appeared to be an extensive menu dumped on the floor, skillets and pots strewn across the bar, the stove and the floor along with the contents.

When he hit the living room on the way to the bedroom, his dread only increased when he saw the silver trays with appetizers scattered all over the room, liquor and wine bottles smashed and huge wet stains on his furniture and carpet.

Paying them no heed, he burst into the bedroom, prepared to beg, on his knees for her to forgive him. He had a hell of a lot of explaining to do, and that explanation would raise questions he wasn't prepared to answer without further fear of driving her away. If he hadn't done so already.

But Evangeline was nowhere to be seen. All the jewelry he'd gifted her with, including the items she'd worn tonight, were scattered on their bed, and the remnants of the dress she'd worn lay in pieces on the floor.

When he checked her closet, it was full except for a couple pair of jeans and a few casual shirts and one pair of tennis shoes. Most noticeable was that his small travel bag was missing.

He sank to his knees, his chest so tight it felt as though it were being crushed.

His worst nightmare had come to life.

She was gone.

He'd driven her away.

He'd treated her despicably.

Not since his childhood had he felt such desolation and helpless despair. But this, this was *his* doing. He'd done the unthinkable. He wasn't the victim. Evangeline was. His sweet, innocent angel whose only crime was loving him and wanting to take care of him and show him he mattered.

And he'd repaid her by taking her gift and throwing it back in her face in the most despicable way a man could hurt the woman he cared about.

He buried his face in his hands, raw agony clawing at his insides. "I fucked up, Angel. But I'm coming for you. So help me God. I know I failed you. I let you down. But goddamn it, I will *not* let you go. I'll never let you go. I'll fight for you with my last breath. I can't live without you," he whispered. "You're the only thing *good* in my life. The only sunshine I've ever experienced in a life steeped in gray.

"I can't live without you. You're my only reason for living. You have to come home, because without you, I have—I am—nothing."

Dear Readers,

When Mastered was originally contracted along with books two and three of the Enforcers series, Drake and Evangeline's story was only supposed to encompass one book while books two and three would be about Justice and Silas.

But wow! Drake and Evangeline's story was so . . . big and all-consuming, and when I got to well over one hundred thousand words, I realized I was only halfway through with their epic love story.

So after I discussed the problem with my editor, we both felt strongly that it would do the story a huge disservice to cut large chunks and take out scenes just to fit a word count that covered only half of the planned story. We decided to split their story into two parts: Mastered, which is part one, and Dominated, which is part two.

And even after I split their story into two volumes, the word count for both books will be high, and by the time I finish, the two volumes will, in fact, be the equivalent of three of my "normal"-sized books.

I hope you enjoy Drake and Evangeline's journey to happily ever after and stay on for the ride to "the end" in Dominated, coming soon in 2016.

This is new for me. I've never had this happen to me in my entire career, so I'm as surprised as any of you are, believe me! But I don't want to cheat the characters or you, the reader, by giving you a watered-down, less passionate and heartrending story just for the sake of word count. That's not fair to anyone.

Much love always. You are all very dear to my heart.

                                                                    Maya